MY BROTHER-BUT-ONE

SHADOWS OVER AFRICA

T.M. CLARK

MY BROTHER-BUT-ONE

Published by Wilde Press

Edited by Creating Ink

Cover designed by Mecha

Cataloguing-in-Publication details are available from the National Library of Australia www.librariesaustralia.nla.gov.au

ebook © Published 2023 ISBN 978-0-6459192-4-0

Paperback © Published 2023 ISBN 978-0-6459192-7-1

Hardback © Published 2023 ISBN 978-1-923129-08-5

Previously published by Mira, an imprint of Harlequin Enterprises (Australia) Pty Ltd

GENERAL FICTION

This book is written in English as used in Britain and Australia. It has not been Americanised.

ABOUT THE AUTHOR

Zimbabwean-born T.M. Clark combines her passion for storytelling, diverse cultures, and wildlife with her love for the wild in her captivating multicultural books.

Writing for both adults and children, T.M. Clark is the author of Shooting Butterflies, Tears of A Cheetah, Child of Africa, Nature of the Lion, Cry of the Firebird, and the critically acclaimed My Brother-But-One, nominated for a Queensland Literary People's Choice Award in 2014. Her children's picture books, Slowly! Slowly! (a 2018 CBCA Notable Book) and Quickly! Quickly!, are beloved by young readers and are companion pieces to Child of Africa.

When she's not writing thrilling adventure stories, T.M. Clark is dedicated to helping other writers. As the coordinator of the CYA Conference (www.cyaconference.com), she provides professional development for both new and established writers and illustrators. She also co-presents at Writers as Sea (www.WritersAtSea.com.au), guiding writers on their creative journeys.

Tina Marie loves mentoring emerging writers, indulging in chocolate biscuits, and collecting books for creating libraries in Papua New Guinea. Her new novel, Daughter of Africa, is set to release later this year, continuing her commitment to captivating stories with an African heart.

Visit T.M. Clark at tmclark.com.au and follow her on social media.

facebook.com / tmclarkauthor
instagram.com / tmclark_author
amazon.com / stores / author / B018N3D2QY
bookbub.com / authors / t-m-clark
goodreads.com / tmclark
linkedin.com / in / t-m-clark
mastodon.au / @tmclark
pinterest.com / TMClark_Author
tiktok.com / @tmclark_author
threads.net / @tmclark_author
bsky.app / profile / tmclarkauthor.bsky.social

ALSO BY T.M. CLARK

ADULT BOOKS

Shadows Over Africa series

- Child of Africa
- Cry of the Firebird
- My Brother-But-One
- Nature of the Lion
- Shooting Butterflies
- Song of the Starlings
- Tears of the Cheetah
- The Avoidable Orphan

COMING SOON

- Daughter of Africa

PICTURE BOOKS

- Slowly! Slowly!
- Quickly! Quickly!

DEDICATION

2013: To Shaun, for encouraging me to follow my dreams, for supporting me in that quest and for
drinking the champagne for me when the dream
seemed unreachable. And then finally, for drinking champagne for me when the—news was good!
You are undoubtedly the best writing partner I could have asked for. I love you too! Forever.

2023: 10 years later, and I love that you are still walking beside me. This time, as we take the steps on an independent publishing journey.
You have done so much to get me over the technical 'things' of this world. Still the best! And
I still love you, more!

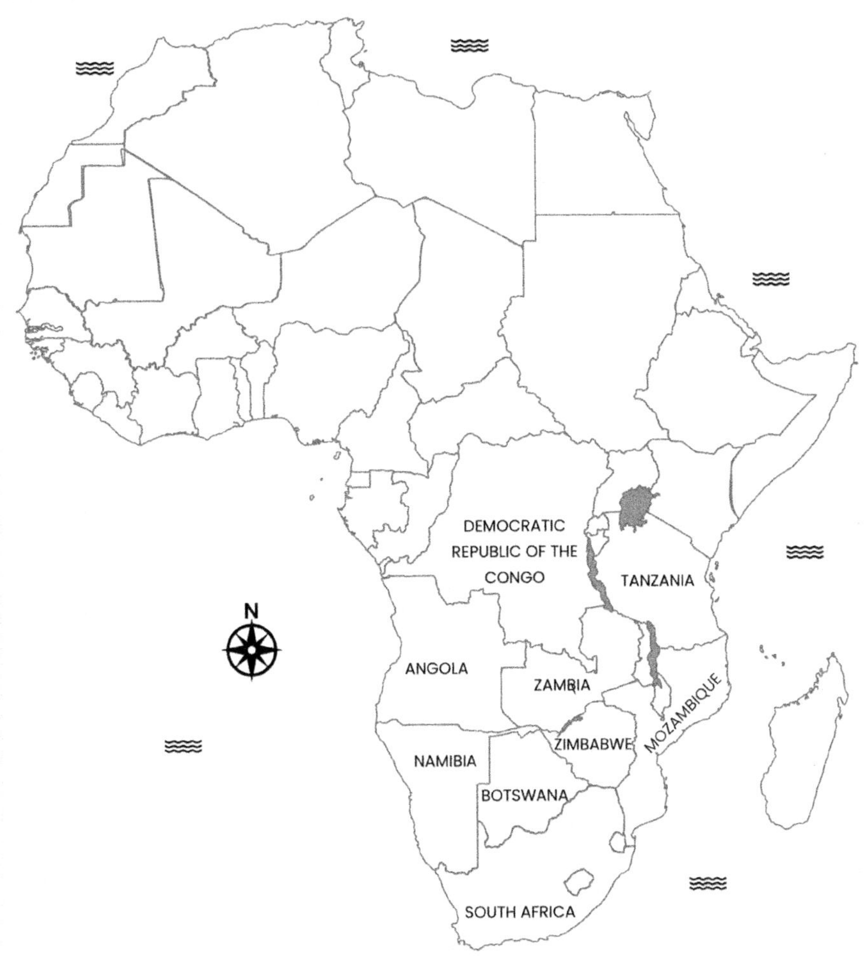
DEMOCRATIC
REPUBLIC OF THE
CONGO
TANZANIA
N
ANGOLA
ZAMBIA
MOZAMBIQUE
ZIMBABWE
NAMIBIA
BOTSWANA
SOUTH AFRICA

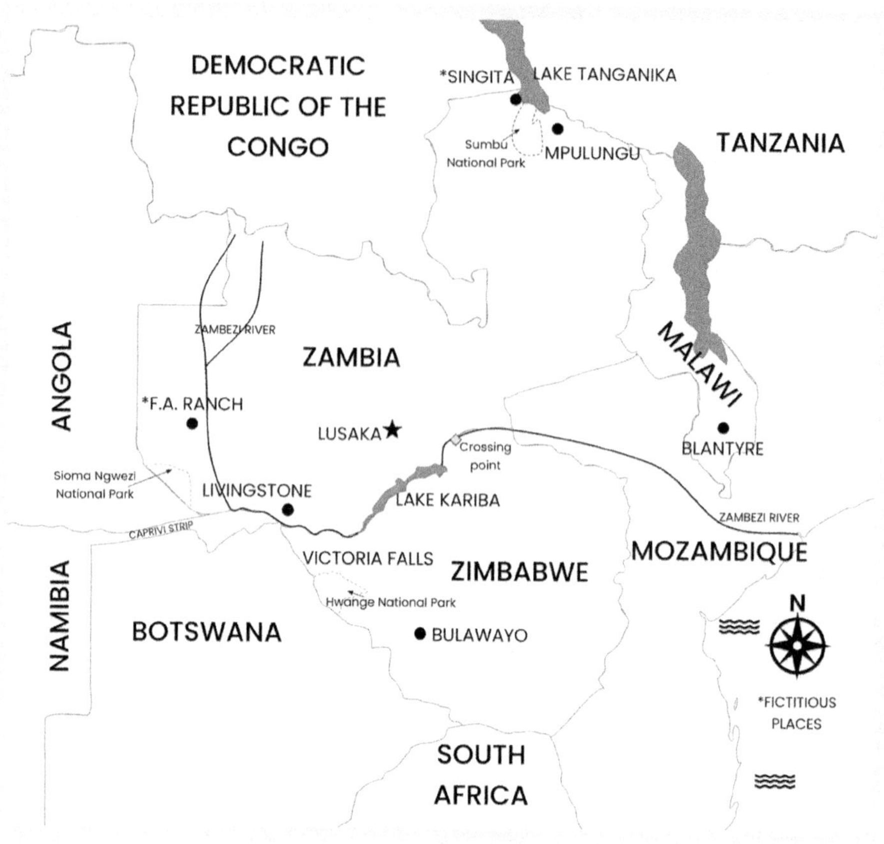
DEMOCRATIC REPUBLIC OF THE CONGO
*SINGITA
LAKE TANGANIKA
Sumbu National Park
MPULUNGU
TANZANIA
ZAMBEZI RIVER
ZAMBIA
ANGOLA
MALAWI
*F.A. RANCH
LUSAKA
Crossing point
BLANTYRE
Sioma Ngwezi National Park
LIVINGSTONE
LAKE KARIBA
ZAMBEZI RIVER
CAPRIVI STRIP
VICTORIA FALLS
ZIMBABWE
MOZAMBIQUE
NAMIBIA
Hwange National Park
N
BOTSWANA
BULAWAYO
*FICTITIOUS PLACES
SOUTH AFRICA

ZIMBABWE

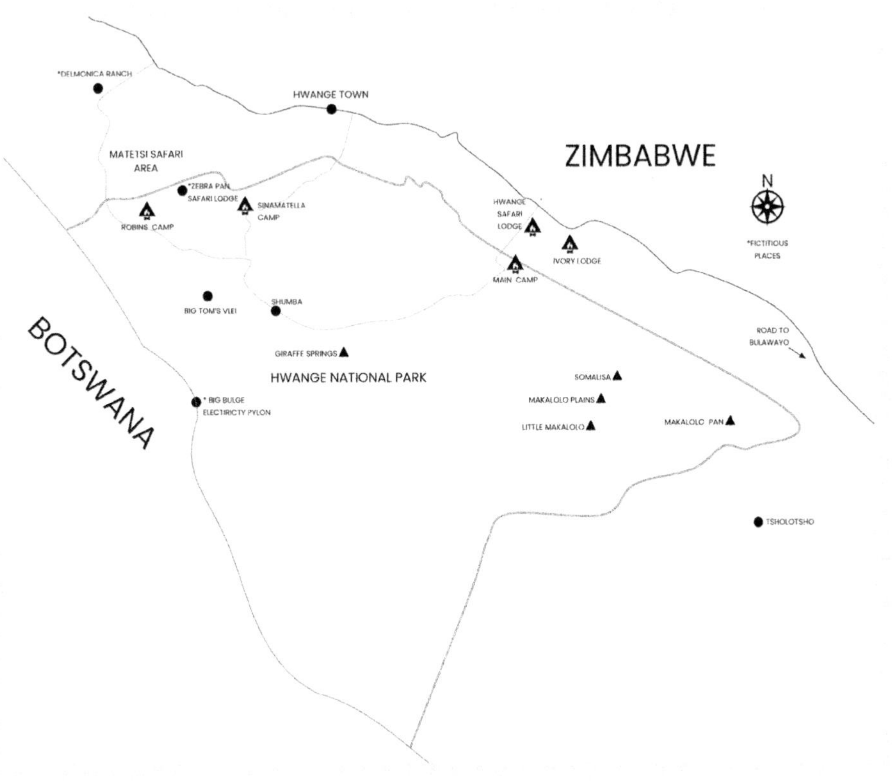
*DELMONICA RANCH
HWANGE TOWN
MATETSI SAFARI AREA
ZIMBABWE
N
*ZEBRA PAN SAFARI LODGE
SINAMATELLA CAMP
ROBINS CAMP
HWANGE SAFARI LODGE
IVORY LODGE
MAIN CAMP
*FICTITIOUS PLACES
BIG TOM'S VLEI
SHUMBA
BOTSWANA
ROAD TO BULAWAYO
GIRAFFE SPRINGS
HWANGE NATIONAL PARK
SOMALISA
* BIG BULGE ELECTIRICTY PYLON
MAKALOLO PLAINS
LITTLE MAKALOLO
MAKALOLO PAN
TSHOLOTSHO

ISIPHO RODNEY NUBE

1941

'The earth rejects your sacrifice. Like only a few children before him, this white son of yours has lived. You have offered him for three days and nights, yet he survives. The cats do not want him, nor do the scavengers. Even the sun has not taken his life. Pick up your baby, Moswena,' the sangoma instructed, 'he has earned his right to life. You must take him back to your breast, before you offend the earth and she sends drought or floods to our tribe.'

The first-time mother snatched the naked baby from the flat rock and cradled him in her arms. Immediately, the albino began to scream, his skin badly sunburned. With haste, she arranged her son in a *kaross* made of soft animal hide and secured him on her back. She rocked back and forth to quieten him. She knew children must not scream in the sangoma's presence.

The sangoma turned to her and without warning, lashed out savagely with his *knopkierie,* hitting her on the front of her body. Blood seeped from the lacerations as the sangoma rained down his personal disgust. She kept her front exposed to him, knowing that if the large knot of wood at the end of the stick hit her son, his skull would be smashed.

'He might have escaped his death today, Moswena, but life will not be kind to you now that he lives. The tribe will hate you and this child. He's a bad *tokoloshe* that brings destruction and death to all around him. The white people will never accept him as anything but a *kaffir*, so do not look to them for help. Tomorrow, you must leave this kraal forever. You are cast out for giving birth to such a child and bringing shame to our tribe.'

The tears streamed down Moswena's face, but she kept her eyes downcast. She knew better than to argue with the sangoma. He was the tribe's almighty healer, the doctor, and the link to her ancestors. Her people would never protect her from him; he was almost more powerful than their chief. When he was finished with her, she turned her back to him and trudged down the kopje, the well-worn red dirt path towards her *ikhaya* in the kraal.

He rushed past her, almost tripping her up in his haste to tell the tribe about the banishment. To instil fear into anyone who attempted to help the outcasts. Moswena straightened her back as she passed the dense thornbush fencing that signalled the perimeter of the kraal, and moved inside.

No one looked at her, their faces averted. Already she wasn't welcome. Her own mother and sisters could not come near to comfort her or help, for the banishment made her invisible even to them. To acknowledge her presence meant they would also become outcasts. This was tradition; the sangoma's whim was law.

Moswena entered her hut. She lowered herself onto the small grass mat she'd woven as a wedding present to her new husband and sat in the traditional position, legs out straight, crossed over at the ankles. A single tear ran down her left cheek. She tried not to think of the man she still loved. Her hands shaking with the pain and anger burning inside her, she took her son from her back and brought him to the front of her battered body. He lay against her, unmoving, and didn't attempt to latch onto her engorged breast. Three days without her milk being suckled had brought her great pain. Pain as she'd never experienced before—worse than any beating she'd ever received—and heat hotter than any summer she'd lived through. Her breasts felt as though red coals had been laid on them. The new beating she'd received from the sangoma had made the ache worse. Huge angry welts rose on her copper skin.

She fought the pain. Her baby's fluids were of greater importance. She squeezed her nipple and warm milk jetted out in an arc, showering his small face and running down his neck. As the pressure eased, he was able to latch on and feed. Spots of black and purple swirled and closed in around her as the pain ravaged her body. Moswena pushed it away with a deep groan in her throat, curling her fingers and toes and straightening them again.

Once her son was content and sleeping, she stood up and looked down at her legs. Her bare calves no longer bore the ribbons of gut and fur, decorations that an unmarried *tombe* wore. They were bare.

Just like her *ikhaya,* and her heart.

A husband dead in a great war with the Zulus somewhere far away, and a son no one wanted.

Banished.

Her husband had paid a large *lobola* for her just a few months ago. Twelve cattle. The whole tribe had celebrated with a party. A prize ox had been bled and then slaughtered.

Now she was a nothing. A no one.

Dead to everyone living, except her tiny son.

She smeared some root *umuthi* over her baby's skin to ease the discomfort of his sunburn. Satisfied she'd helped him as much as she could, she packed her meagre belongings: her husband's assegai, a few skin skirts and treasured beads. She gathered what little food there was and placed it carefully in her cooking gourd. She rewrapped her son in the *kaross* and tied him onto her back, with only his head poking out from the soft skins and tightened the leather below her breasts. Lastly, she rolled up her grass sleeping mat.

Balancing her life's possessions on her head, Moswena stepped out of her *ikhaya*. No one looked at her. With confidence and purpose, she walked to the fire pit in the communal area and picked up a burning stick. No one stopped her as she strode back to her hut and lit the dried thatch roof. By the time the other villagers realised she'd started a fire in the centre of their kraal she was walking away.

As she climbed the kopje where her child had recently lain open to the elements, she looked back at the large kraal she'd called home since her birth. Slowly she smiled. Other huts near hers had caught fire, and the flames were spreading. She watched as the villagers who wouldn't look at her scrambled to put out the flames. With delight she noticed that the sangoma's hut was burning. He tried to beat it out with a wet cattle skin. None of his black magic could help him now.

Adjusting the bundle of belongings on her head, she raised her voice so her son could hear.

'Come, *Isipho*, my gift. We must search for a friendlier home.'

ZOL NDHLOVU

1966

Zol heard himself breathe. He wasn't dead. He needed to shinny up a tree before the hyenas found him.

A blood-red blur and pain ended his attempt to open his eyes. His fingers hung limp, broken. He gently rubbed the palm of the opposite hand against his fingers to count them. One, two, three ... ten. At least they hadn't cut them off. He probed his face with the back of his hands. His cheekbones weren't shattered but his face was swollen and disfigured from the beating he'd taken. Hesitantly, he slid his hands around to his ears. Relief swept through him; they were still there.

Rising to a sitting position, he checked his toes. Broken, but still there. Nothing had been hacked off; he was lucky. Taking a deep breath, he used one hand to lift the other and attempted to straighten his right index finger.

He passed out.

In the darkness behind his closed eyelids, Zol regained consciousness. He sat up to take the pressure off his bruised shoulder, and after a few attempts he managed to stand. He hobbled forward, gently freewheeling his arms about, hoping to bump into a tree to seek refuge in.

He heard an animal snort nearby. Not a hyena or a leopard. It sounded more like a zebra. Zol wished he could smell through his rearranged nose, but broken and swollen shut, it was no use. He crept forward, figuring the animal would move out of his way. But he felt warm fur on his arm and the animal breathed deeply, as if its nostrils flared against him, and he heard a snort.

Leather. He felt leather. He'd stumbled into a domesticated animal.

Groping more, he felt a knee-length leather boot, and a rifle carrier ...

Stories of the Dragoons of Angola and their demon horses who would run through fire and buildings had been recounted in the training camp. They were part of the Portuguese army. Images of slaughter and chaos flashed behind his closed lids, and he dropped to his knees, praying to his ancestors, to the Christian God, Jesus, and to Allah all at once.

A deep laugh cut through the silence of the bush.

He was in trouble. Today, he was going to die.

'East is in the opposite direction, boy,' the man said. 'And it doesn't look like your ancestors were doing any watching over you either.'

Leather creaked as a weight shifted then a muffled thud signalled the man had dismounted.

'Move over, Vic,' the man said to his horse as he rummaged in a saddle-bag. The sound of enamel crockery clanging together was loud. Then the splash of liquid, a foreign noise. A cup was held against his lips. The cool liquid soothed his parched throat. Zol drank deeply.

'Slowly, boy. Slowly. Where are you heading?'

He was going to die anyway. He had nothing to hide from this man who spoke Swahili and his demon-horse, so he opened his mouth and told the truth. 'Home.'

The man gently touched around his eye. Zol flinched, both from the contact and the pain. He sucked a quick breath in through his teeth.

'Not broken, but darn close. From the blackness of your skin, you are far from your homeland. Where was home?'

Zol dropped down onto his haunches. 'Lake Tanganyika. That was before they came and took me away. I was trying to get back.'

'Lift your face to the sky.'

Water cascaded over Zol's head. The man blotted the blood from his eyes, then his cheeks. Zol opened his eyes a slit, his vision was still blurred, and the pain of a million daggers stabbed into his brain. He closed them again and hung his head in defeat, still blind to what the man looked like. His voice was deep and rich, but he spoke Swahili almost as if it was his native language, although some of the pronunciation of the clicks in his dialect were louder than needed, formed with the side of the mouth, not his tongue. But obviously a man who spoke many languages well.

'You can forget using your eyes for a while. Who left you to die?'

Zol took a deep breath, uncertain how to answer the stranger who helped him. He dreaded being kept alive for information and then slaughtered later. This was how it felt to be an animal caught in a snare. When your life is held in the palm of the hunter.

'Don't lie to me, boy. Who did this?'

'My comrades.'

'That figures. They stole your pack and shoes too?'

'They took them as punishment for deserting.'

'Thought so. Hold steady ...' The man held Zol's left hand in both of his and pulled the pinkie finger straight.

Zol saw blinding stars.

'Welcome back,' said a rich voice with a slight accent.

Zol remembered where he was.

He lifted his hand to his face. Bandages covered his eyes and his fingers were bound. Splinted straight. Reaching down, he found the same with his toes.

Dread clenched his stomach, uncertainty about his life niggled in his head. He'd heard that the men with the iron-shoed demons massacred entire villages, even ran down children with their horses. Why was a man like that helping him? He trembled as renewed fear raked through him.

A large warm hand fell on his shoulder. 'Easy, easy. Come, drink this soup. You need to get strong again.'

Zol breathed deeply. What if the man wanted him strong so that he could hunt him down again when he drained the information from inside his head? Testing his theory, Zol volunteered, 'I don't know any information. Soon you will kill me anyway.'

'That depends on you, boy.'

Zol wondered about that, but already the man had shown him compassion beyond anything he'd received outside of his village.

'Tell me about when they took you. How long ago was that?'

'Three moons ago. I am fifteen summers old.'

'Only fifteen years old. Go on.'

'The communist freedom fighters drove through our village. They made promises to my mother.'

'Guess you know now they don't keep them?' The man snorted like his horse, and the horse answered him with a snort of her own. The air was filled with a rich belly laugh. 'Yes, Your Highness. It's been just you and me for too long.'

Zol wondered about this man who was tending to him like a veterinarian would an injured animal, straightening his bones, bandaging his wounds. He communicated with his horse as if she were human. Perhaps the stories of the demon-horses had been exaggerated. Or perhaps not. But this man wasn't trying to harm him.

'They executed my cousin for refusing to join them. Right there, near the cooking fire. They put a gun to his head and shot him when he said he wanted to stay and be a fisherman. I didn't want to die.'

'Good choice.' The rim of the tin cup pressed against his lips again. 'Drink. It's cool enough not to burn you.'

Zol drank. Feeling hard biscuit touch his lips, he ate too. Swallowing was difficult.

Refilling the cup with water, the man again held the rim at his mouth. 'Where did they train you to fight?'

Zol sipped the water. It slid down his throat easily, clearing away the biscuit. 'They took me to a camp far away from my home. They taught me how to fight and shoot. They taught me how to kill people and how to move in the bush like an animal. They made the fisher boy into a man.'

The man snorted again. 'Killing people doesn't make you a man. You are just a boy with a gun.'

'They told me I was ready to fight for freedom, and gave me a full pack of rations and boots on my feet.'

The air around him swirled as the man took the empty cup and walked away, this time to refill it from a pack on his horse. A sound of a different container opened and shut. The horse stomped one leg as if irritated, or to dislodge an unwelcome bug.

'Here you go, Vic. You know I'd never forget you.' Zol heard the man patting the horse, his voice soothing. When he returned, he put the cup at Zol's lips once again. 'Drink. You need liquids. It's sweet. It'll help.'

Zol drank the sugared water.

'So tell me, how did you manage to get all the way down Africa to the Caprivi Strip?' He took the empty cup and sat on the ground, a dull thunk signalling the direction of his resting place close by.

'It took many days in a cattle truck. But as soon as the others began to disperse into the bush, I left. I was going home.'

'That's a long walk, boy. Lots of unrest between here and there, and you probably had no money.'

'Anywhere is better than with them.'

He felt the man touch his forehead, his hand cool as he lifted the bandage to gauge his temperature. 'So, do you want to run back to your village, a coward and a deserter? Or do you want revenge on these men who have caused you such harm?'

Zol knew the answer. A deep hatred for the men who had taken him from his home burned low in his belly. Joined now by a raw revulsion for the albino, the leader of the group of men who'd left him for dead in the bush. It was the albino who had broken Zol's fingers and toes, one at a time, and laughed while he crippled a fellow human. A comrade.

In reality, he couldn't just go home. Not now. They would find him again. Perhaps after another beating they might take him back to their camp for retraining. Or they might kill him on sight. But he knew deep in his gut that he wanted the men responsible for his cousin's death dead. That would be better than fresh summer mopane worms in winter. 'Revenge.'

'You make good choices. A survivor. Like me. What's your name?'

'Zol Ndhlovu.'

'Zol.' He felt his arm being clenched in a manly grip. 'A good strong name for a man about to change his life. I'm Charlie. My horse is Victoria. Don't ever cross me, or you're dead. Welcome to the Decker family.'

CHAPTER 1

1995

Scott Decker watched Kevin's plane buzz the impala grazing on the airfield's short grass. The honey-brown buck flicked up their white tails and scattered in all directions, as if a giant predator was after them. The baboons scavenging alongside the runway easily loped away on all fours. Once into the safety of the thicker bush, they turned to bare yellowed teeth at the intruder.

The Cessna straightened up, circled around once, and touched down on the grass. Bumping its way along the runway, its engine changed pitch as Kevin eased off the throttle and coasted to a stop.

Scott shook his head, smiling that Kevin had inflicted his oldest plane on yet another of the new volunteers, giving them a false picture of what were acceptable standards in Africa. Most of the international volunteers were so green on arrival that they didn't look further than the cracked windscreen and peeling paint. But the engine on the old Cessna was in tip-top condition and serviced by the same top-class aviation mechanics who serviced their fleet of charter jets.

Kevin hopped out and walked around to the passenger's side. He unbound the door from the outside and yanked it open. 'Told you my bush mechanics would work. Wire is the backbone of Africa. It holds everything together.'

Scott chuckled as he climbed out of his blue four-wheel drive *bakkie*. He watched as Kevin offered his hand, and a woman stepped down onto terra firma.

Scott walked closer. 'Hey Kevin.' His attention was focused on the blonde, her eyes as green as the new grass after a fire. A bright red t-shirt, varnished red fingernails and long shapely calves that extended from a knee-length khaki skirt to red socks that stuck out of neat ankle boots, everything about her screamed city-girl. He would bet his ranch that her toenails matched those flashy fingernails.

The aircraft hold clanked open and Kevin dropped a crate onto the runway. 'Your supplies came through. Give me a hand, Scott. A storm's been on our tail all the way. I need to tie my plane down ASAP.'

'Just a minute.' Scott was still focused on the woman in front of him. 'Where's my volunteer?'

Kevin jerked his thumb at the woman.

She slid her dark glasses up the bridge of her nose. 'Hi. I'm Ashley Twine.'

Surely there had to be a mistake, he thought. He would never have given permission for a female volunteer to join his program. Women and the African bush simply don't fit together. No way. Caught totally off guard, with a scowl on his forehead and a headache already drumming at the base of his skull, he stared at her.

She took her sunglasses off. 'Ashley Twine,' she repeated a little louder, 'reporting for duty.'

Scott's heart dropped. 'But you're female!'

He noticed her outstretched hand drop to her side and confusion cloud her eyes as she straightened her back, gaining a few centimetres in height as if preparing for an argument.

'You don't say?' One perfectly groomed eyebrow rose as she spoke and her megawatt smile sent shivers down his body. Her Australian drawl was as alluring as her smile. Given the right circumstances, he could listen to her talk forever.

But she was not what he needed this week. He ground his teeth. How had he made such a gigantic mistake?

Kevin rescued him, filling in the uncomfortable silence. 'Don't mind Scott.

Usually he's a real hit with the ladies, with those big baby blues 'n' all. Give him a chance to get used to that halo of blonde hair and he won't let you go home after your month of volunteering is up.'

Okay, perhaps not exactly rescued—Kevin had just sunk him deeper than the Chinhoyi Caves. The drought project was too important to be messed up. He'd had too many experiences of being let down by females in his life, and no way was he going to let yet another one disappoint him. Females all followed the same well-established pattern: they came; they attempted to stay; but ultimately, they hated his Africa and left.

'Kev, get back in your ramshackle tin box and fly her back to The Falls. She was supposed to be a man who can fix things. I need the water pumps in Hwange repaired fast, not a lesson on how to apply nail polish.'

'Excuse me. I *am* a mechanical engineer. I can fix anything.'

Scott looked at Ashley. She was probably around five foot eight, with legs that went on forever. He swallowed as he tried to remember everything her résumé had said about her. Her qualifications he recalled clearly, but nothing about Ashley being a female. In hindsight, he should have asked for photographs.

'I would have thought that beggars couldn't be choosers in the volunteer field, Mr Decker. You seem to have forgotten something here. I co-own a successful engineering business in Brisbane, and I've paid to come to Zimbabwe to help the animals, not be judged for my gender.'

She paused as she put her glasses on, and then pushed them up onto the top of her head as if to let the words sink into his thick head. 'In my field I've come across grumpier men than you. So, I'm going to ignore those Third World chauvinistic comments.' She flashed another smile. 'Believe me when I say, I really can repair those boreholes in Hwange National Park. You advertised for a miracle worker to restore them to their former glory. I'm your answer. So what if I'm female and I wasn't born with a little dingle-dangle between my legs?' Two eyebrows rose this time.

Scott stared at her. A dingle-dangle?

Kevin shook his head. 'Be reasonable, I couldn't head back now even if I wanted to; that storm's nearly on us. Deal with it. *Nicely.*' He deposited Ashley's designer luggage at Scott's feet, the rebuke about forgotten manners delivered in a friendly but firm manner.

Scott continued to stare at Ashley. He recognised that he was physically attracted to her, just as the elephant were attracted to the marula fruit, despite the fact the fruit were bad news. He could develop an addiction to having a woman like her around. But he could do without the wake of destruction she was sure to leave behind her when she returned to Australia.

He regretted his lack of manners and realised he'd pushed past the point of being downright rude. 'We don't usually have female volunteers. Our living quarters are set out for all-male volunteers. There are no locks on the doors. I can't put a female in digs with those guys, you'll have to move into the main homestead with me.'

He looked at her again, studying her face in detail. Eyes spitting like a desert cat, challenging him. But she was here, and the pumps needed attention. Professional reasoning won.

'Okay. For now. If you prove you can fix things, you can stay. But if you turn out to be a useless city slicker out for a cheap adventure thrill, you're back on a plane to Australia. Understood?'

'Yes, sir.' She saluted, her mouth curving into a smile as she laughed, mocking him.

He shook his head, but couldn't help the small smile that sneaked onto his lips. His Australian Princess was going to be a handful.

'Zol, this is Miss Ashley.' He introduced the black man with grey hair who had materialised at his side. 'Please get her luggage into the *bakkie*.' Scott turned back to her. 'Miss Twine. With that attitude I take it you are still a Miss?' He couldn't resist. He knew his comment would needle her, but he wanted to know if she was single. He watched her jaw clench, and regretted the way he had asked as he saw hurt flash across her face.

One week. He would give her a week, see what she could achieve, and then deal with the fallout. He would put money on her not lasting one week in the bush before scuttling back home.

'Scott Decker, I give you one week's probation to see if I want to stay and work in your project. Or I might just take that safari everyone told me I should take instead of a working holiday.'

His jaw dropped open. What? Was she psychic too? He had no comeback.

Ashley smiled at Zol. 'Nice to meet you.'

'Ma'am.' Zol nodded and returned her smile.

Kevin heaved more cargo into the *bakkie*. 'Hey, can you give me a lift to the lodge? You'll save me getting wet out here waiting for Tessa.'

Scott shouted above a low rumble of thunder somewhere not too distant in the veld. 'We can make a plan. Zol, come and help us with the lodge supplies.'

When everything was loaded into the *bakkie,* Scott opened the passenger door and motioned for Ashley to get inside. She gave him a glare to freeze hell, but complied. Kevin attempted to follow her.

She pointed to the seat. 'There's no seatbelt in the middle.'

Scott positioned himself behind the steering wheel. 'So?'

'It's not safe to travel with no belt.'

'This is Africa. Nobody cares. Move over, put your right leg over the gearshift so Kevin can get inside. Zol's going to get wet.'

Already he regretted giving in to *Ms* Ashley Twine.

Ashley turned her head to the back, where Zol sat on top of her suitcase. 'Surely he isn't going to sit out there?'

'Zol, get off Miss Ashley's fancy suitcase. Sit on the beers,' Scott shouted out the window. 'Is that better?'

'No. I meant he can't travel out there.'

'There is only room for three in the front. Where else do you expect him to sit? This is how we always travel. He's been on the back since I was just a boy. He's used to it. Anyway, it's easier for him to open the gates.' He started the engine with an unnecessary roar and cut off any further complaints.

Scott turned the *bakkie* around and headed off in the opposite direction, changing gear into second as the vehicle picked up a little speed.

The *bakkie* coasted to a stop in the driveway at Zebra Pan Lodge and Kevin climbed out. Scott shifted himself out of the vehicle and turned to watch as Ashley unwound herself from the middle seat and clambered, not too lady-like, out after him, her movements a bit stiff and slower than before. With her flight from Australia and the time zone changes, he knew she was exhausted. He'd seen her struggle to watch the road and stay awake for her first experience in Africa, and the rocking of the *bakkie* hadn't helped her. She'd almost dropped off to sleep more than once on the short trip. He closed the door quietly behind her.

Tessa walked up to them and hugged Kevin. 'Sorry, my *bakkie* broke down. Sipewe has only just got it started again.'

'Not a problem, Scott detoured here instead.' Kevin linked his hand in hers and turned to make the introductions.

'Ashley, this is my fiancée, Tessa. Ashley is Scott's newest volunteer.'

'Hi.' Ashley put out her hand.

'Hey,' Tessa said, shaking it. She looked over Ashley's shoulder at Scott standing behind her, and smiled. 'Good luck to you being the first female in his pack.'

Ashley glanced around at Scott and saw him drop his hands from what looked like a time-out gesture to Tessa. She turned back slowly. 'I guess I'm going to need it. Thanks.'

Tessa smiled.

'Come on, Sipewe,' Kevin called. 'Help Zol get the *bakkie* unpacked.' His simple instructions defused the awkward silence.

Unloading the supplies took little time and soon they were done.

'Good luck,' Kevin said to Scott as he walked towards the *bakkie*.

Scott smiled. 'Thanks, but I figure I need more than luck. I truly got off on the wrong foot with this one.'

He opened the driver's door. Ashley was already in the passenger seat, and he heard the loud click of her safety belt. He slipped behind the wheel.

Zol tapped on the roof to signal he was ready to leave.

'Cheers Kev, Tess,' Scott said, and began his journey home.

He watched Ashley's head nod.

'Put your head back on the headrest. Sleep. You can barely stay awake. I understand your tiredness, jetlag drains your last drop of energy when it finally gets hold of you. Lay down. It's a while to Delmonica, I promise to wake you if I see anything interesting, but I suspect it will just be bush and more bush.'

'I'm fine,' Ashley said, then yawned. 'I'll admit, I'm dog-tired. But what if there are elephant, or warthogs, or anything other than bush? I'll miss it.'

'You have a month to see it all.'

She looked at him. 'A week, remember?'

'Ah yes, a week. But potentially a month. Seriously, your CV looked brilliant, on paper you were exactly what our project needs. But I wasn't lying when I said I wasn't equipped for female volunteers. This is a first. It's going to be a steep learning curve for all of us.'

'That's okay.' She rotated her head to get rid of the stiffness that was setting in. 'I like a challenge. So, about the pumps? The advert for the Hwange Water Project didn't really say much about it, only that you were looking for mechanics to fix old diesel pumps, and that the work was mainly in Hwange National Park. The national park bit was what attracted me.'

'The drought has been harsh, the pumps are old and they keep breaking. The game knows where there's water, and they congregate around those areas. In order to graze the park at a manageable regeneration rate, we usually switch off a few pumps and the animals move on to the next section, giving the vegetation time to recover. We rotate the pumps regularly.' He glanced at her, and although she was listening, she was looking eagerly through the windscreen, watching. He smiled.

'But many pumps are now beyond local help. The Parks Board no longer has the funds to sink into them, and the pumps are being discarded and not replaced. The game is impacting on the drought-ravaged vegetation. We are getting parts of the national park that look more like TTLs.'

'TTLs?'

'Tribal trust lands. Areas the African population were given to live during the Independence years, and where they over-grazed the vegetation and caused deserts.'

'So, how did you get involved in a project inside the park if your ranch is outside the national park area?' she asked.

'My ranch is the first privately owned land backing onto both the hunting concessions and Hwange National Park. Concessions are land leased by the government to a group for a purpose, and that land then brings income into the park. So when they shoot anything, a cut of the price goes to the national park to help with the conservation of the species.'

'You shoot animals on your ranch?'

'Sometimes. We shoot for rations, but we don't trophy hunt on Delmonica. We have fenced the land and brought in more game. Our main farming activity is still stud Brahmans, and training game guards against poaching.'

'So, you need the pumps fixed to give water to the animals in the park, so they can be shot?'

'No; I wish it was so simple. The biggest problem is the poachers. When you have an overabundance of game in one place, the poachers are ruthless in their pursuit of those animals. They become easy pickings. That's the reason I got involved in the Hwange project: from the anti-poaching side. Zol and I began the volunteer program to restore the pumps. We believe that by fixing one problem, other problems will solve themselves. If the game redistributes, the poachers will have to work harder to find it, thereby helping us with our poaching problem.' He looked at her to see if she was still paying attention, and saw she was watching him, not the surroundings.

'The system was simple until now. We built two rondavels for the men to sleep in, and put in an adjoining shower block between them. We have a maximum of four volunteers at any time, who pay their keep to stay at the ranch. But the labour and expertise that they bring for a month are free, so the project can afford to fix the pumps with the donations it receives. Simple, until your arrival. You will have your own room and en suite in the main house.'

'Well, thank you for not putting me in a shared room with a male volunteer. I do appreciate my own room and bathroom.'

Scott remained silent.

Ashley took a breath, beginning another conversation. 'Your advert said Zimbabwe is still in drought conditions, but I could only find newspaper articles referring to your worst drought as being in 1991 and 1992?'

'Been reading up about us? Good. The worst of it was then, and we had a small reprieve with rain in 1993. But last year, the drought was back with a vengeance. We had less than our fifty-year average in rainfall again, with just on 500mm. Our average is supposed to be closer to the 750mm mark.'

'That's not a lot of rain.'

'No, but we are being hopeful, with a few showers this year already, that maybe this year the drought will break. But until it does, the pumps need to be fixed, and animals need to be watered. We have seen so many animals die because of the broken pumps.'

'That's sad,' she said. 'It seemed like a simple enough request of a volunteer.'

'Mm,' Scott said. 'Simple is not always solvable.'

'That is so true.'

He watched her turn to study the road ahead, and she appeared lost in her own thoughts. He switched his attention back to the road and the long drive home to Delmonica, the first and only love of his life.

Bordering on the northwest of the Hwange National Park, his ranch was his life partner. Even after all this time, and everything that had happened during his thirty-six years, his land had been the one constant. When his mother had decided she hated the isolation of the bush, and took away his little sister, Alex, the ranch had been a salvation to a young boy who found himself left alone with his dad, Charlie. Its wide spaces, wild animals and hard work kept his mind busy.

He remembered the day Charlie remarried, and then the day his stepmother Sarah left, taking his stepbrother Dale away too. But when Sarah died, in his grief, Dale had come home, losing himself for days in the solace of the African bush. He knew Dale hated going away to attend university in Cape Town, as Delmonica had claimed his heart too. But unlike the women, he would be back. Dale would come home, looking to the land to settle.

There was no getting away from this chunk of dirt.

Alex was lost to Delmonica. She was lost to Africa, now living in England. And despite his attempts to stay in contact with her, he had failed. Another female gone from his life.

But Dale was more like him: Africa pulsated in their bloodstream.

Just like it had in their dad's. When Charlie had been shot during the war, Zol had brought him home to die. Home to Delmonica.

The seat creaked as Ashley shifted her body, seeking out a more comfortable position. His attention was ripped from the past and focused on her. She fiddled with the seatbelt across her creamy neck. Damn, his life for the next month would be a living hell.

Now that the surprise had passed, and he knew her a little, her stubbornness left him in no doubt she would rise to his challenge, and, given her glowing résumé, he should be happy she was here to help. But he had bigger problems. Thanks to the sell-out by the British and their Lancaster House agreement, Zimbabwe's land was being redistributed under the guise of equality between blacks and whites. The idea was that a willing black buyer and a willing white seller applied for economic help from Great Britain, and the land ownership was transferred to the new black owner when the money was approved. Scott had been approached to be bought out and had refused to sell his birthright. Putting half of Delmonica into Zol's name now looked like it had been the best way to dodge that bullet.

But there was trouble brewing. The white commercial farmers' union was shouting warnings that the government was not happy with the small number of sales, and there were rumours that it wanted to begin an accelerated land reform to transfer land quickly into the hands of the majority black population. He needed to concentrate his efforts on keeping Delmonica in his possession and all his people safe.

He didn't need a female complicating his life.

They never survived the isolation of the bush and there was no way in hell he would ever give up his ranch. Not even for someone like Miss Glamorous Painted Nails.

CHAPTER 2

Ashley stretched out in the large bed and burrowed into the pillow under her head. Slowly she became aware of her surroundings, the unnatural silence, broken by calls of what sounded a little like kookaburras but definitely weren't. A dog barked nearby. Cattle bellowed somewhere close by.

She sat up in the bed. It was Saturday ... no ...

Zimbabwe.

She was in Africa.

She smiled. At last, after years of dreaming about it, she was really visiting. So what if she had chosen a working holiday instead of a traditional safari? This way she would see more of the local culture, get closer to the animals, and touch the real Africa—not the postcard option most people got as they flew in and out.

Bed?

How the hell did she get into bed? She looked down. Thank God she still had her clothes on. But her boots were off. Memories of yesterday flooded her, and she relaxed a little, remembering what a gentleman Scott had been on the drive to Delmonica and once they reached the ranch house. She remembered him showing her to her room, and leaving her there. But she had no memory of removing her boots.

Exhaustion was a lethal taskmaster.

A week. She'd given Scott Decker a week to improve his attitude, but she had also boxed herself into proving she was good at what she did. When he wasn't playing the chauvinist, he was actually nice. She crinkled her nose. *Nice* ... so were bananas, but they gave her acid.

She swung her feet to the floor and felt her toes sink into the luxuriously soft carpet. She looked down at the zebra print woollen rug spread out over the highly polished wooden floor.

'Neat,' she said aloud as she twirled 360 degrees. The antique canopied bed surrounded by white gauze curtains dominated the room. There was a rocking chair, also in zebra print, and a stand-alone wardrobe. The full-length mirror on its door reflected the white bed with black pillows and a zebra throw. Other than where she'd pulled back the covers on the one side to get out of the bed, the linen still looked pristine, as if ironed in place.

Michael wouldn't have noticed the neat hospital corners that someone had taken the time to fold on the bed. But she did. Thinking on him, Michael hadn't noticed much at all. Perhaps she'd settled for less than she should have with him. Perhaps the attention he'd shown her at first had been flattering, and it had been with relief that she'd taken him home to her parents' house for Sunday lunches. At last, her sisters had stopped trying to hook her up with countless blind dates, especially her twin Peta, as she had been the worst offender.

'But you are not here, Michael,' she muttered. 'And your opinions don't matter.'

Michael's face flashed before her eyes, and suddenly she understood.

She hadn't loved him.

She'd simply fitted him in around her career. Sure, he was fun to be with, witty and handsome, but she hadn't felt that intense physical attraction to him. He hadn't made her body tingle simply thinking of him. She'd never experienced a breathless moment when he touched her—ever. In reality, she'd never experienced that feeling with anyone. Even so, Michael had become her handbag, convenient to take places on her arm. A human accessory.

Ashley balked, astonished at the realisation that Michael could have been so attached to her life and yet had never truly been part of it, and for the first morning in a long time, her breakup with him felt right. At thirty-years-old, she was in Africa to regroup, to get away from those memories. Away from the mundane grind that had become her life.

Taking a break from real life. Having a holiday.

The idea of fulfilling her dream African safari had been hers, but the volunteering program had been the travel agent's. And when she'd seen the challenge about fixing the old pumps, she'd jumped at the chance. To keep busy and achieve something worthwhile on holiday was exactly what she needed, and what she wanted to do.

She found the en suite and had a quick shower, noticing that the white and black decor continued in the bathroom. Dressed in denim shorts and a blue top, she crossed to the bedroom window, pulled back the heavy black curtain and gasped.

A warthog and her baby grazed on the manicured lawn not twenty metres from her window. The baby ran by its mother and pushed its nose into the ground where she foraged, its little tail straight and high in the air like an aerial. Ashley grabbed her camera from her bag, then she opened the door to the covered veranda and stepped outside.

The red cement was cool under her feet. To the left was a garden, but to the right, the view was the same as from her room, only in panorama. The steps down to the lawn were even and easily navigated, and she crouched down and adjusted her telescopic lens and took a few shots.

Scott's voice came from behind her: 'You can go much closer if you want. She's used to human activity, the boys have to physically herd her out at night to close the gates.'

For a moment she'd forgotten about Scott being in the same house, and her awkward arrival the day before. 'Good morning,' she said, putting on her sweetest voice. Her mother had always said that you could catch more bees with honey.

'Coffee?' he asked, holding out a cup.

'No, thank you. I don't drink coffee. I would kill for a hot chocolate or milo if you have either of those, though.'

'One hot chocolate coming up.' He disappeared around the right side of the veranda.

Ashley studied the ranch house. It was beautiful. The first two metres were a pink-hued stone. Above that was whitewashed brick, with the wide veranda running around three-quarters of its front, topped by red gutters and a corrugated iron roof. The house stood proudly at the base of a small hill and was surrounded by tall trees. Some she recognised, like the big blue gums, but others she didn't know. Birds screeched in the trees and she strained her eyes to catch a glimpse of them.

Scott came back followed by a neatly dressed black woman carrying a tray. On it sat a single mug.

'Lisa, this is Miss Ashley. Ashley, meet Lisa.'

Ashley watched as Lisa put down the tray on the table of the garden setting on the veranda.

'Nice to meet you, Lisa,' she said, and held out her hand.

Lisa took her hand in both of hers and did a small bobbing curtsey. 'Miss Ashley,' she said, smiling broadly.

'Lisa is our cook. If you need anything from the kitchen, just give her a shout,' Scott said.

Lisa picked up the empty tray and walked away.

'Thank you,' Ashley called out to her departing back. She placed her camera on the table and sat down in the chair Scott held out for her.

Scott sat opposite her, and waited until she'd taken a few sips of her hot chocolate. 'There is a Land Rover in the garage. It's old, but it will be used for the project. I need you to get it going again.'

'You're giving me a vehicle to fix?' She looked at him, a bit puzzled.

'It's what the project needs right now, so yes.'

She held her mug in both hands and sipped. Remembering their conversation yesterday, she asked, 'How long do I have to work miracles on this vehicle and get it going?'

'A week. Prove to me you are a competent engineer. If you can get it done faster, all the better. The quicker you have it going, the sooner you can use the vehicle as yours to go into the reserve and fix the pumps.'

Ashley took a moment to consider. She would give Scott her week, and fix the darn vehicle. It might be good to stick it to him, and bring him down a notch or two. Besides, if it didn't work out, she could organise an impromptu safari and then fly home. After all, her business partner thought she was crazy volunteering in the middle of Africa and working more than she would at home, when what she really needed was a five-star luxury holiday.

'Okay in principle, but I would like to see how derelict this vehicle is before I say yes.'

'Come,' Scott said standing up, 'let me give you the tour of Delmonica.'

• • •

While Scott chauffeured her around his ranch, he explained the workings. Ashley was suitably impressed by the diverse nature of the ranch. It intrigued her. Mostly the ranch appeared modern, with brick buildings, new cattle fences and equipment. The homestead itself was enclosed with a tall electric fence, with large gates that had stood open when they passed through, but clearly were closed at night as fresh scrape marks showed in the dirt where someone hadn't lifted a stay-stake high enough and it had gouged into the ground on opening, but she soon realised that the whole ranch was surrounded by its own huge electric fence too. This one was more sturdy, with double fencing about a metre apart. The ranch was obviously of the best quality, but then they came to some traditional-looking mud huts, with red dirt that was swept so clean there wasn't a twig out of place. A fence of grey bushes surrounded them.

'What's this?' Ashley asked.

'James's kraal. He's been with my family since my grandfather's days. He built this kraal years ago and lived here with his wife Patricia and their family. The children have moved into modern buildings, so now it's just the two of them here. They are old. I put them on a pension, but James still joins in with the farm work. Says he will die if he stops working.'

Ashley studied the painted huts, so traditional and beautiful with their cone-shaped, thatched roofs and potbelly walls. Something so old-world, yet still residing on a modern ranch. Her mind touched on Kevin's plane yesterday. Another old-world beauty. But she hadn't been fooled by the battered exterior. She'd glimpsed the pristine engine, with not a speck of oil showing. They kept things here, maintained them. Didn't throw them out.

She was deeply touched that Scott had let the old people remain on his ranch and continue to potter around, allowing them to feel useful. Times had progressed around them, and yet he let them keep their ancestral home of mud and thatch and hadn't forced them into more modern living quarters she'd seen were part of the ranch layout. The whole concept was in contrast to the opinion she'd built of Scott so far. It showed that he cared, and that didn't marry with the image he had portrayed to her yesterday.

Either he was good at hiding who he really was, or he was truly a prat.

She had yet to make up her mind.

Perhaps, like the African continent, he was simply a tad hostile and intimidating to those who didn't know where to find the warm pulse that beat like a drum beneath the surface.

'We are driving home,' he said, 'in the general direction of the ranch house, but there is something I want to show you first. If we are lucky, the elephant herd will be at the waterhole.'

'Even if they aren't, just coming out and seeing your crops, your cattle grazing and the bush is amazing. It's so different from the Australian countryside.'

'Here you go,' Scott said.

They'd driven into paradise, to a cliff that overlooked a waterhole surrounded by thick bush and tall trees. Below them, spread out in panoramic view, was a huge herd of at least a hundred elephant with their babies, all covered in mud. They were milling around the waterhole, some submerged, others pretending they were taking a shower and squirting water around. Still more were drinking, their long trunks tucked up into their mouths.

The scene was breathtaking. Ashley's heart almost stopped at the beauty before her. She put her hand on her chest to ensure it was still beating.

Low rumblings sounded from the herd, then a melodic loud trumpeting as two beasts mock-charged each other, frolicking.

The sounds of Africa surrounded her.

Some of the elephant had finished in the water and started their slow plod away, back into the bushes.

Ashley looked on in awe.

Never in her life had she experienced anything like this. If she stepped out of the vehicle and climbed down the cliff, she would be able to touch one. Not that she would. The animals were huge. She looked at the moving, picture-perfect postcard in front of her and smiled. This is what she'd wanted to experience all her life. She could see perfect blue sky, the elephant in the water, taste the dust that coated her tongue, and smell the churning mud and water where they swam. Nature at its finest in the African bush.

'Wow. Look at them,' she said. 'There are so many.' She wished she'd brought her camera, but at the same time knowing that she wouldn't need a photo to remind her of this moment.

'These elephant are not on my land; they are in the national park. This cliff marks the boundary, and they don't often climb it. The waterhole is fed by a pump, so they have fresh water daily. The herds gather together in larger numbers as the pumps fail. But their impact on the environment is alarming at present. I believe that if we can get more pumps further away working again, the large congregations will stop. As the water source distributes, so should the elephant, and the ecosystem will once more be balanced. I admit, I brought you here as a bribe. I need that Landy fixed to help these guys.'

'I already told you I could fix it, but I love the bribe idea,' Ashley said.

She lapsed into silence as they drove back to the ranch house, mulling over how passionate Scott became when he spoke of the elephant and their water. Once she'd had passion like that for her work. Before her ex, Michael. Before she'd needed to get away from it all. Before she felt burnt-out and restless.

Thursday's school was out for break time. Ashley watched the neatly dressed children of all ages as they rushed around the playground, some played soccer, kicking the ball into wooden homemade goalposts. Other sat on benches in the shade under the acacia and jacaranda trees, talking to their friends. Most greeted her with a little wave or said 'hello' as she passed. The boys wore simple white shirts and grey pants, and the girls had on black pinafores over their shirts. There was no logo on the clothing: nothing to identify these children as belonging to this farm school.

She smiled. At least she wasn't late. The night before, when she'd spoken to Gertrude, the resident schoolteacher, about the visit, she'd worried that she might not get the timing right and disturb the classroom schedule. She was determined to complete a few of the ideas that she'd landed with during her week's probation at the ranch. And on her agenda was a school visit to the local farm school. Scott had given her the time off from her project, and now that she was at the school, she felt nervous. She had zero experience with children.

She stepped inside the classroom. Gertrude sat at her desk, her head bowed as she marked books.

Ashley inhaled deeply. 'Hi,' she said. 'I've brought those school supplies that we spoke about last night, and I have my favourite children's book with me.' She lifted the heavy bag off her shoulder and waved it in the air: *a peace offering before the lamb goes to slaughter ...*

'Come on in. I've prepped them that they are getting a visitor today and they are so excited. We haven't had an Australian volunteer at the ranch before, nor a woman. Actually, no other volunteer has ever wanted to come and talk to us about their country and learn about ours. This is a unique idea. Thank you so much for thinking of it.'

'Thanks. I had read about the rise of tooth decay from sweets distributed by foreigners to the local children in Africa, so I followed the article's suggestion and brought school supplies instead.'

'Thank you,' Gertrude said as she came and took the bag from Ashley and put it on a trestle table set up next to her desk. She looked at Ashley. 'It's almost the end of break so when the bell rings, I'll settle the children and introduce you. Then you can talk about Australia, your life, and you can give these out. The children will look after them if they are seen as a present from you.'

'You know I've never done anything like this—'

'They will be putty in your hands. I threatened them with homework if they didn't behave,' she said, and laughed.

The bell clanged and immediately Ashley could hear kids close by, lining up outside the classroom. After a moment, Gertrude opened the door and an organised hush fell over them. They came into the room, smallest to largest, in single file and stood behind their desks.

'You may be seated,' Gertrude began. 'Today we have Miss Ashley from Brisbane in Australia, to talk to us. She will also read you her favourite bedtime story from when she was a little girl. Let us show Miss Ashley a warm welcome.'

'Good morning Miss Ashley,' they said in perfect unison in clear English.

Ashley took a quick gulp of air as they clapped for her, and a girl at the front with beaded hair smiled broadly.

The next hour flew past as she told them about Australia as a country, of her growing up in the city, and how in university when she was studying engineering, she'd wanted to move out of the city to get away from the noise. But her office was in the city, and she hadn't managed to move away just yet.

Sometime during her talk, she noticed that Scott had slipped into the back of the classroom.

She opened up her book, *Possum Magic,* and began to read. The children sat mesmerised, listening as she animated each character in turn. The gasps of surprise and '*my wena!*' in the part when the little possum became visible again made her smile.

'The end,' she said, and closed the book. The children clapped loudly, and an excited buzz filled the room.

'Now, I'm leaving this book with Miss Gertrude, so she can read it to you again. And for being so nice to me and listening to the story, I have brought you a few little things,' she said as she opened her bag. 'Everyone can take one pen, one pencil, a small notepad and a koala. Thank you for being so good.'

The children filed past and were careful to only take what they were allowed to. There was order, until the same girl from the front of the class ran to Ashley and hugged her. Then all the other kids joined in and Gertrude had to step in and say, 'Okay, that's lovely, showing emotions, but you need to hug Miss Ashley one by one.'

Ashley smiled as she got hugs from the children, and when they were finished, she promised to bring another book and visit them again. She noticed that Scott had left as silently as he'd come in.

On Friday, Ashley again lay under the oldest Land Rover she'd ever seen. She guessed it was a 1960s model and had been a welcome challenge to resurrect, but her mood was anything but welcoming. Cooped up all week, except for her visit to the local farm school, she was feeling claustrophobic, and the easiest target was the owner of the old pink Landy.

She was no longer angry when she thought about the gender mix-up, if anything more amused about it as the days had passed. It wasn't her fault Scott hadn't specified that his volunteer preference was for a male.

'He's a genuine chauvinist,' she said aloud. Talking to the old four-wheel drive had become a habit during the last few days. She knew before she volunteered that a diesel mechanic would fix a water pump, not a mechanical engineer, and was prepared for being over-qualified for the job, but not for Scott's attitude, nor for his cold shoulder all week.

She exhaled. 'Sure, and he threw in the macho "prove yourself" bit that I just couldn't turn my back on ...' She tightened the bolt with a flick of her wrist. 'But I went for the bait, and in the end he did ask nicely, and those elephant were just amazing ...'

After another adjustment, she pushed the sleeper out from underneath the Landy, stood up and tried the ignition. 'Come on, Lucinda, old girl. Start for me.' The pink four-wheel drive fired once and caught. 'Yes!' She punched the air.

'I see you can actually fix things.'

She jumped. How long had Scott been watching her?

Listening to her?

'I'm not in the habit of lying.'

'Good. Is the Landy ready to go?'

'Lucinda will take me to Cairo and back if I need her to,' Ashley said, with a smile bigger than a Cheshire cat's spreading across her face.

'Cairo will have to wait. Zol took my *bakkie* today, so if your Landy's going, we can start work in the reserve.'

'As long as we're gentle with her gear changes, the rebuilt gearbox is a bit delicate. Even I couldn't repair some of the damage done to it.' She collected a selection of tools, threw them into a toolbox and snapped it shut. 'Just in case.'

Scott took the box from her before she'd lifted it a centimetre.

'I can do it.' Her voice was sharp.

'I know. But allow me. I was brought up to be a gentleman. Don't ask me to be less of a man because your upbringing was more liberated and different from mine.'

She looked at him. She'd never before considered the feminist movement from the other side. Admittedly, Scott was the stereotypical alpha male, used to being in total control. Standing over six feet tall, his black hair was finely peppered with grey, which made him look distinguished. His tan was natural, not out of a spray can. A week ago, she'd have believed him to be antisocial, but now she knew better.

She nodded. 'Thank you.'

Scott put a cooler box in the back of the Landy.

'Lisa's packed lunch,' he said in explanation to her raised eyebrows, 'and we need the water in this heat.' He loaded spare jerry cans of petrol and strapped them in, ensuring they didn't rattle.

'We going on a long trip I should know about?' Ashley asked.

Scott laughed. 'No, we make it a habit to always carry extra provisions, in case we need to go further afield. Once this Landy is in the pool of vehicles, the petrol in the cans will be used once a month, and replaced by the garage staff. The last thing you ever want is to run out of fuel, it's a long walk home.'

'Makes sense,' she said as she kicked out the brick from behind the rear wheel and went to get into the driver's seat. But Scott was there already.

'Habit. I know where I'm going,' he said, 'so it's probably easier if I drive.'

His logic was sound. 'Okay,' she said, and walked around and hopped into the passenger seat. There were no doors or roof on Lucinda, but the windscreen was in good repair.

She smiled. It was heavenly to be getting out into the reserve after nearly a week confined in the hot, sticky workshop.

He started Lucinda and backed out of the garage, then slipped her into first without grating the gears. 'I'm really glad you got her fixed so fast.'

'No worries,' Ashley said. There hadn't been any open animosity between the two of them during the last few days, just cool cats passing in the night.

'I'm really grateful that you proved to all of us that you are a competent engineer.'

Ashley looked at him. Was he attempting to apologise?

'You said the project really needed this Landy as the other vehicle. I volunteered for the project. A pump, an engine, it was just the size that differed.' She made a scale measuring gesture with her hands.

He smiled.

'And you know what a ridiculous concept having to prove myself was, right?'

'I know. But what I'm trying to say is thank you,' he said.

'Accepted,' Ashley said. She pulled her sunglasses over her eyes, ready to get her first glimpse of the national park since the day she'd seen the elephant.

Scott sneaked a glance at her as he drove. She sported a look of total contentment on her face. He identified with that feeling.

For the past week, he had stayed in close proximity of his home and its outbuildings, and he'd gone to great lengths to hide this fact from Ashley. He'd continued to supervise the other volunteers on their trips into the Hwange National Park, the repairs of the various pumps, his anti-poaching units and general ranch work—all the while remaining within shouting distance of her, because he didn't trust her safety to anyone else.

Another white commercial farm had been seized by the government; its ownership taken over without compensation. Some Zimbabwean minister now sat in its dining room, on the chairs owned by another family for generations. The staff had been beaten up and thrown off the ranch—removed from their homes. But the saddest thing was the funeral for the white family killed in the takeover process, set for Monday. The attacks on the farms were sporadic but becoming more frequent since Britain had stopped their financial support for Zimbabwe's land reform program, claiming mismanagement and corruption. But nothing was being reported internationally, and it was beginning to look that if the Zimbabwe government wanted a ranch, it could simply take it.

His country was sliding back into turmoil, and there was nothing he could do to stop it.

Foremost in his thoughts was a growing doubt in his ability to keep his whole family safe, from the kids in his farm school to James in his old kraal. Scott considered every person on his ranch his family, and he couldn't bear to see them hurt. A dissident war, like the one in the 1980s, he could handle. He could protect his people and property against a war like that by employing more guards, buying more weapons and putting up higher fences. But a corrupt government—no person could fight that and win.

The transition from white colonial rule to the black regime was not going as smoothly as it should. At least for now, having Zol as his business partner in Delmonica should keep the politicians' eyes off their land. Black empowerment was a priority on their agenda, and that game both he and Zol could play.

In reality, Delmonica was as much his home as Zol's. It had been since the moment Charlie had brought Zol home as a teenager. But the stress of wars and violence, had turned his hair prematurely white, and everyone joked about him being *Keghla* already, despite the fact he was only thirteen years older than Scott. But until recently, the land had all been in Scott's name. He hoped they had done enough to secure their future in Zimbabwe.

And now there was his first female volunteer to worry about. Ashley Twine was an enigma. He was responsible for her in an extremely male-dominated society: her protector. In just a few days she'd proved there was more to her than her blonde hair and a bank balance big enough to pay for an adventure in Africa.

Instead of creating chaos and friction between the volunteers, as he'd expected, she'd befriended the men.

Through humour and her gentle influence, she had them doing extra things that he would never have expected a volunteer to do, like writing home and getting stationery and school supplies posted over. Her ability to interact with everyone surprised him, like when he'd sat in the back of the classroom thinking she might need help with the children. But she hadn't.

They had, in turn, been only too happy to speak to her in English, and try and teach her a few words in Ndebele. She had laughed with them at her Australian accent on the words, but never at their English if they got something wrong.

Scott was surprised to find he'd felt envious when the children hugged her. He'd spent many hours with the children showing them interesting farming items, and how to track in the bush, teaching them the differences between animal footprints, but they'd always kept a respectful distance from the Boss.

Within one week it seemed as if Ashley had always been at Delmonica. Her natural ability to put everyone around her at ease was an unexpected quality he admired.

CHAPTER 3

They came to their first wire concertina gate. Scott watched Ashley in the rear-vision mirror as she attempted to close it. 'Need any help?'

'Is there a knack to these things?'

Scott got out of the Land Rover. 'Let me show you. You are standing wrong. Here ...' He moved his foot on the inside of hers and pushed her feet further apart. Then he adjusted her shoulders and leaned with her, his front against her back. He took the top out of the gate's secured wire with one hand and dug the bottom of the fence pole into the twisted loop at the foot of the gate, securing it with his foot. He then pushed Ashley's whole upper body forward, putting her shoulder into the concertina gatepost and forcing his arms around the stable post, effectively anchoring the gate. He pulled the top of the gate pole vertical.

'Now, slip the top wire loop onto the gate,' he instructed.

She fumbled initially, but then the wire glided easily onto the wooden pole. It was closed.

'You could have simply told me.'

Her voice sounded strained, stressed perhaps. Something was wrong. He'd upset her again. Quickly he stepped back, realising that an innocent lesson had been misinterpreted. He attempted to lighten the moment.

'But that wouldn't have been any fun now, would it?'

'Fun? Being manhandled isn't fun.'

Ah, the fighting woman who had got out of the plane was back. He frowned. He knew prickly when he saw it and she was bristling like a porcupine. Something had happened to her to make her so defensive. He wondered what had caused her abrasive attitude towards being touched.

'What did I do?' he asked.

She let out a long breath, as if attempting to control her temper, then with her hands on her hips, she faced him. 'Okay. The truth. It's frustrating as hell. All week I fixed this Land Rover and didn't get to go into the park. So I now get to venture outside, see where my first water pump is, but you're still testing me ...'

'The gate wasn't a test.' He ran his hand through his hair and swallowed, as if what he was about to say was difficult for him. 'I'm thinking we might have got off to a bad start in the beginning. When you arrived, I overreacted that you were a female. I want you to know that you are welcome here at Delmonica, but I can't simply point you in the direction of the reserve and let you go. It's too dangerous. And I thought you enjoyed the challenge of getting this old girl running again?'

'I did, but—'

'Just listen for a moment.' Scott put his hands up in front of him in a stop gesture. 'I apologise. From day one, when you arrived, I have made you feel uncomfortable, but that wasn't my intention. I needed you as a volunteer. But as a woman you needed to prove you were capable of mending anything; you needed to prove you were at least equal to or above the men. This Land Rover, it needed your expertise. Not just any bush mechanic could fix it. They would have wanted to put it on the scrap pile as too much trouble. That was the only way I could create a safe place for you here. Unless you have a clear advantage over the men in Africa, it's not worth you being here.' He paused so that she understood the importance of what he was saying. Her very survival depended on her understanding.

'The men in Africa could make your life hell if they see you as weak. I saved you that strife by giving you a challenge you could rise to, and prove yourself. That's all. I should probably have explained this to you better, but things went wrong between us from the beginning, so I'm trying now.' He looked at her. She still stood with knuckles on hips.

'I don't know why you reacted so badly to me a moment ago. I would never hurt you, or any other female. I want you to know that.'

'This is your grand apology?' she asked.

'Take it or leave it, I don't admit my mistakes often,' he said.

'Fine, apology accepted,' she said, and her arms dropped to her sides. 'But while the dialogue is open, please try not to be so chauvinistic towards me again. I might not be what you expected, but I sure as hell appear to be what you need. I really want to enjoy my remaining three weeks in Africa, experience the whole "shebang", and I can't do that if you wrap me in cotton wool like a little 1950s woman.'

He opened his mouth to answer but then thought better of it. Anything he said right now would only get him into further trouble.

She stared at him for another moment, then shook her head as if dislodging something and strode around back to the passenger's side of the Landy.

Puzzled by her behaviour, Scott returned to Lucinda, clipped her into gear, dropped the clutch and spun off, leaving a large dust cloud behind them.

If only he could leave the tension radiating from her behind, too.

Ashley took a deep breath. Scott had invaded her space.

Too close. Touching her.

It was just an innocent lesson to show rather than tell her about the gate, but she'd panicked and lashed out with her fishwife's tongue. She concentrated on slowing her breath and regaining control of her racing heart.

She wasn't six years old anymore. She wasn't being forced into doing anything. She had to relax and stop punishing herself for something that hadn't been her fault. Damn ... she'd slipped back so easily into frigid, selfish mode. That's what Michael had called it when he was leaving her. She shuddered and decided not to spend one more moment thinking of his useless butt. The incident at the gate when Scott had touched her had shaken her, although she hadn't been surprised at her response. It could have been worse. Much worse.

But what was different from her normal reaction to a man being physically too close was that when he'd moved away, she immediately missed the feeling of him touching her.

The concept of wanting or needing that physical intimacy was foreign to her.

That's what had made her panic.

She could still smell his masculine scent. Her body betrayed her as goosebumps rippled along her neck and down her arms where their bodies had touched for a brief moment. The reaction scared the hell out of her. Her body normally felt nothing. Gave no attraction signs. It had never woken up to the sexual revolution it should have as a teenager. Instead, it had always remained as frozen as it had all those years before.

And now it had chosen the middle of the African bush to react.

She needed to apologise to Scott. It was her problem, not his. He'd simply been trying to help her.

'I'm sorry. I overreacted at the gate. I just don't do body contact. It's a long story,' she said eventually.

'Fair enough,' he said, and she saw a deep frown on his face.

Wondering why he was frowning, she returned her attention to the African bush and settled back to enjoy her first self-indulgent holiday since leaving university.

They drove through the large gate and into the reserve. Ashley watched the bush intently, straining to see the elusive African wildlife. Since the spectacularly huge group of elephant, she'd seen nothing special again. Sure, she'd studied the homestead, the inside of the workshop, the warthog family that foraged on the lawn, and a few antelope in the distance of the cleared area in front of the farm compound.

'The game in this area will return once there is ample water,' Scott said. 'At present the pan is a salt flat. The borehole has been broken for a long time. When you get it going, the elephant will be the first to come back, and the other species will follow.'

'Good. I know you said the game moved away, but I didn't expect there to be nothing, no birds, no small animals. I haven't seen anything.'

'You won't here. There is no water to support them.'

She cleared her throat. 'Please don't take this the wrong way but when I was talking to the other volunteers, well, Alan, the oldest one from the UK, he said that they all have a local guide who works with them in the reserve. I've been here a week, but I haven't met mine yet.'

'You won't get a local guide.'

'So who'll guide me through the reserve? I learn fast, but there are lots of tracks, and this bush is kind of huge and there's no signage. I would hate to get lost out here.'

'You have me. I know this bush, what grows where, which plants are poisonous, which snake to back away from and which to stand up to. I'm not only a professional hunter and farmer, but a man born to the land. And I can't vouch for your safety with anyone else.' He paused. 'You aren't one of us. The workers owe you no loyalty. Women have to earn their own respect, and you only have a three weeks. I could trust Zol to watch over you, but I need him elsewhere at the moment. There's a serious poaching ring infiltrating the reserve. Zol's unique skills are needed there. It's impossible to spare him. I wasn't exaggerating the effect of having a female on board when I wanted you to return to Australia.'

'It wasn't my intention to interfere with your program. In Australia, I'm not treated like this. I'm an equal to any male, not a pampered pet.'

He smiled at her expression. 'I know. But here, you're an exotic creature. I'd be irresponsible if I didn't point it out to you. Trouble in Australia might mean a little slap on the wrist from your polite police force. But, believe me, in Zimbabwe there are worse things than death. You need to be wary not only of the wildlife, but the people, too. They're volatile.'

He glanced at her. 'We've been fighting various wars my whole life, but right now, we fight the poachers. Those people who come to steal and kill our wildlife damage our tourism. Many men, black, white and coloured, have died in this reserve fighting these organised crime rings.' He kept quiet about the land reappropriation situation. Unlike poaching that he could try to control, a kamikaze government was totally beyond his power.

He was quiet for a while and could feel Ashley staring at him. He knew his face was serious. This *was* serious. He had to get her to understand the magnitude of her situation. 'Have I scared you?'

'A little. But not so much that I want to get on a plane and fly away. Perhaps it has made me more determined to stay and fix these pumps.'

'Good. Does that mean you are staying for your next three weeks?'

'I'd like to.'

'Great, because here's your first pump, inside that shed,' he said as they pulled up to a clearing next to a small corrugated iron structure.

'Shed' was an overstatement. The shack consisted of four locally grown, untreated wooden poles, crudely cut and cemented into the ground. The corrugated iron was fastened to those poles with ever-present wire.

Wire really did seem to hold Africa together, Ashley mused.

The roof was an assortment of poles with one iron sheet, and the door swung on wire hinges. Inside sat a huge, silent Lister pump.

'Oh my, I think I saw a pump like this once before in my life, at an Australian historical village in the outback somewhere.' She laughed as she bent to see what damage had been done to it.

'I know this is one of the older ones in the park, but they usually just keep going and going, with hardly any maintenance. They are great pumps. Those bastard poachers broke this one last year. If we can get it going, we can entice the animals back and reduce the game concentration at pump eight. That should allow the grass there to rejuvenate before the over-grazing herds create a desert. Who knows? Perhaps this one will hold out till the rains come and this drought breaks.'

Ashley was so aware of Scott in the small tin shack. She knew he watched her continually. It wasn't as if he was a knight in shining armour rescuing her from anything sinister like a fire-breathing dragon, but his little gestures, like carrying her toolbox, were nice.

Nice. What an insipid word to describe this man, she thought. Genteel, old-fashioned, colonial, perhaps fitted him better.

During the week she'd been observing him, usually from a distance, but watching him whenever possible. She'd learned from talking to the other volunteers and employees around the farm that he was considered a fair but firm person to work for, and that apparently he had a heart as large as Africa itself.

Everyone loved Scott. He took a personal interest in his ranch hands' lives, helped handle crises when they happened, and was fiercely protective of all his staff. The anti-poaching units he had set up lead either by Zol or another head, had six men in each group and seemed devoted to their cause as she had seen firsthand during the week. They would do anything for Scott, even small incidental tasks when asked. The farming and domestic workers were all considered his family.

Until his apology earlier, she hadn't seen that part of his character applied to her. But after the apology, it was as if a dam inside him had broken, and he'd explained so much to her. Included her in his world.

She stole a glance.

He passed her the water bottle in response.

'Thanks.' Her hands kept working on the pump as her brain continued to spin, going through everything she'd learned in the last week.

She'd watched him with the children at the school, the easy rapport he had with them, his gentleness with the younger ones and friendship with the teenagers. Scott treated each child with respect, no matter which gender. And she'd seen him in his solitude, late at night, staring out from his veranda into the blackness of the bush, and had wondered what he was thinking. She'd noticed how he watched her, almost hawk-like, and was finally beginning to understand this streak in him: the protector. The provider.

There was mystery around Scott. She wanted to get to know him better. If only she had more time. Four weeks had seemed like a lifetime when she first landed, but already one had almost passed.

Now the remaining three didn't seem long enough.

On Saturday night, Ashley stopped at the entrance to the boma at Zebra Pan Lodge to let her eyes adjust to the dappled light. It was hard to believe she'd been in Africa a full week and a day. She felt Scott next to her, but he didn't make the mistake of touching her, not even to guide her towards the table where the other volunteers were congregated. She headed in their direction, confident she looked good in her faded denim skirt. Her favourite R.M. Williams baby pink shirt hung loosely over a matching denim and velvet ribbon decorated singlet.

She'd slipped out of her work boots and into a pair of low sling-back sandals. Arranging her hair had been easy. She'd washed, dried and left it loose. A soft dusting of translucent powder was all that was necessary in the heat, and a smudge of gloss on her lips.

Alan attempted a wolf-whistle as she arrived at the table. '*Hello Nurse*. She can look like more than a grease monkey.'

His pathetic attempt at whistling made her laugh. 'I'm sure your lovely wife would want to hear you say that.' An easy bantering between them had become the norm since he'd let slip one night that he'd won on the betting tables with the other volunteers that she would get Lucinda working.

'I'm married, not dead. I can look, but I know better than to touch. It's not worth the price. I'd lose my life. My lovely Michelle would destroy me. That's what happens when you marry a lawyer.'

Ashley knew he was dead serious. That was one of the reasons she'd found the over-protective Scott sometimes left her in Alan's company, rather than the other two single volunteers. Alan genuinely loved and respected his wife. He was certainly not looking for anything 'on the side' during his trip into Africa.

She raised her hand to her heart, in mock horror. 'Oh, the woes of married life.'

Scott held her chair out for her. She sat down to eat dinner, laughing, as he sat next to her, but not intruding in her personal space.

Ashley glanced sideways at Scott as she ate. He appeared so much older in his crisp white shirt and denim pants. She felt a smile grace her face as she thought of him. After yesterday, she knew they had reached a truce and that he wasn't going to send her home. She let herself relax more around him, inviting him into her world. Talking more. She looked around the boma.

The dining area was set up inside what appeared to be a six-foot game fence, the wire covered by thick dried reeds, enclosing the area but keeping it open to the stars above. The large circle had a space in the middle, like a stage or dance floor, with the food served buffet-style on one side. The staff moved easily between tables; not crammed too close together like they often were in restaurants in Brisbane.

The tables were covered with the lodge's signature zebra fabric, and the silverware gleamed in the light cast from the hurricane lamps on the tables. Ashley watched as black smoke escaped from one and a waiter immediately turned down the wick in the lamp.

Sneaking another look at Scott, she smiled when she saw that his lips were slightly skewed, as if he was deep in thought. Right now, it softened his chiselled face.

Had she ever noticed little idiosyncrasies about Michael? She couldn't remember any. She was beginning to doubt that the time put in with Michael had been worthwhile.

But Scott, he was interesting, intelligent and kind, although not a pushover. He was too full of male pride for that, but she was learning fast that this appeared to be a genetic trait in white colonial males. Once you got beneath the alpha male crap, they were worth knowing.

A drum began beating in the direction of the dance area and was joined by a second. She turned her chair slightly to view the show better, and crossed her right leg over her left. Someone threw more wood onto the fire in the centre of the eating area, and it flashed orange and gold as the fire leaped up to consume the new dry wood. A lone figure ambled into the area, his face hidden behind a mask.

'He's a sangoma. A witchdoctor,' Scott whispered, his warm breath close to her ear.

The dancer walked like an old man. He started chanting, and suddenly his body was as graceful as a cat as it whirled around the fire. The drums grew louder. He held a stick over his head and whacked it down violently onto the ground. Dust rose up around him, the strength of the strike defying the old man image. A line of bare breasted women shuffled into the dance arena, shaking gourds and playing African kalimbas, their thumbs making the magical music. Their legs were adorned with rattles made from strung together bottle tops and crushed Coke cans.

Mesmerised, Ashley was entranced by their traditional clothing—each uniquely different but all part of the same tribal gathering. Next came the men, robed in skins of leopard or lion, and carrying assegais and animal skin shields of varying heights. They beat their feet on the ground to the music made by the kalimbas, drums, and the women, with their shakers and whistles. The men, too, had rattles wrapped around their ankles, and each beat of their feet made dust puffs in the sand.

Scott watched Ashley. From the moment she'd stepped off the plane, he'd appreciated that she was lovely, but tonight, dressed for the dinner, she was stunning. Any male would appreciate her looks. But he had just got to know her a little, and she was so spontaneous. So alluringly female. He hadn't lied to her; she was an exotic bird in the harsh African bushveld. She looked like a model from the Victoria's Secret catalogue come to life.

Only better.

His gaze ran down her crossed leg, and stopped at her foot as it unconsciously beat to the rhythm of the drums. In the firelight, he confirmed that her toenails were painted the same fire engine red as her fingernails, and the addition of a delicate gold toe ring of elephant interlocking, tail to trunk, was a surprise as it reflected the dancing fire.

He wanted to get to know her better, find out what made her cringe from body contact, talk more about her engineering business in Australia, and how she dealt with the male-dominated mining community she often worked in. He was interested in her mind, but recognised there was more to the attraction than that. She constantly surprised him.

He didn't remember ever having this reaction to a woman. Not even when he'd been a testosterone-driven adolescent. During the past week, he'd thought he'd got to know her a little, but there was still so much he wanted to learn. She fascinated him. But he'd had too many experiences of being let down by females in the past. His mother sat at the very top of that list. No way was he letting another enter his organised life. They all followed the same well-established pattern around him: ultimately, they left.

Ashley turned to look at him, her emotions open on her face, revealing her enjoyment in the simple performance. He couldn't help but be drawn to her.

He knew he was sunk.

But as anything other than a volunteer, she was off limits to him.

He could look, and appreciate, and in three long weeks' time, he would watch her depart as she climbed into Kevin's plane and flew home to Australia.

Whistles screeched and the incessant drumming thundered. Ashley turned away from Scott, back to the bright stars in the sky, the fire and traditional dancers gyrating around it. The old witchdoctor performed a few more suggestive moves with his agile body, and then threw his stick in the fire. The dancing was finished—he hobbled out after the women.

Ashley put her hand to her lips. 'Oh—'

'I've seen that a million times, and yet that dance never gets old,' Scott murmured in her ear. She moved slightly, allowing herself to lean closer into him. Relaxed.

'A million?' she asked.

'Scott,' Zol's urgent voice shattered their private bubble.

'What is it?'

'Poachers. They've hit the elephant herd moving near the southern fence.'

'We're coming,' Scott answered.

CHAPTER 4

Rodney sighed deeply. He looked at his sun-spotted white hands covered with blood. Almost absentmindedly, he picked it off his thumbnail as it dried from its sticky texture to a crumbly substance. He no longer needed to participate in the hunt. He could sit in his *ikhaya,* an old retired man, and watch his small herd of cattle. But he loved it, craved it. Nothing felt as good as the blood sport, except perhaps unwilling women.

'Hey, *kaffir,* did you finished the clean-up? You sure there were no *doppies* left?' *Meneer* Lawrence asked him from where he sat atop the bloodied tarpaulin covering their latest successful project for transportation.

Rodney grinned. '*Ja Baas,* I counted thems. Three hundred and fifty shells, and one hundred and fifty boollets levt in da ammo *bakkie*. Five hundred in total.'

'Good. Don't want to leave evidence lying around.' *Meneer* Lawrence coughed, the sound hoarse and deep in his throat, and spat over the side of the truck. He wiped his mouth with the back of his hand. '*Jissis* Rodney, pass me something to drink, won't you?'

Rodney gave over his own water bottle from his hip, all the time sneering at the significance of the evidence they had left lying around: over seventy dead elephant with their tusks chopped out. Even the hyenas couldn't disperse that much evidence in one night.

What a night. All the killing of the elephant, the chopping to remove the tusks, and, when they got back to their temporary camp, the woman he'd stolen from the chief's village.

He licked his lips thinking of her body and what he was going to do to it, his dick already itching to be released from his rough camo pants. But he knew he must wait until the work here was done or risk yet another beating by *Meneer* Lawrence. Waiting was good; it increased the pressure in his dick, made him want the *fook* more.

Just as waiting to get his revenge on the men who had killed his mother had given him a purpose to continue living so long ago, when he was just a boy.

'Isipho.' Moswena's voice interrupted his catty practice, the slingshot held tight in his hand as he prepared to let loose another small pebble. 'We need fresh meat. You need to check the snares.'

At twelve summers old, he stood nearly as tall as his mother. They had been living almost alone for six of those. During that time, he'd learnt extra survival skills from the men who came and went by their small kraal. These men never stayed long, but while they were there, Isipho learnt well. He could set snares for small animals in the bush. He could throw his assegai with his right hand perfectly.

'Always the right hand, that is how you protect the women,' the Ndebele warrior had taught him. His rich deep voice still echoed in Rodney's head, patient but stern as he taught the albino boy how to protect his mother in preparation for after he'd left.

From the pot-bellied bushman who refused to sleep in the *ikhaya*, he'd learnt to smell water, harvest honey, and track any animal through the bush. But, most importantly, the strange wrinkled yellow man had taught him to be invisible. And this, as an albino, unaccepted in both the black African and white society, was his most valuable tool. The *tokoloshe*, or *sope*, as others referred to him, could disappear; simply vanish into the bush. Like a ghost, he could leave no tracks.

Unseen and unheard.

'I'm going,' he replied obediently, gathering his assegai up and walking away. Despite his young age, he'd learnt early that his mother was a useless hunter. If he wanted to eat meat, he had to kill it. She was good with roots and berries and could grow crops, but she couldn't hunt. She'd never learned how in the kraal she grew up in.

'You're the man in our house, my son. Hunting is your job,' she'd told him when he was old enough to understand. It had taken a few years for him to fully comprehend the importance of her words, but when he did, he'd learnt to become the man she needed him to be.

He waved goodbye to her as he dipped onto the little path that led down the steep cliff of craggy rock they lived on and was soon in the valley below. He knew where the first animal would be trapped and ambled directly to the large tree by the bush with the sour berries. Rabbits always visited there.

'Good, good.' He spoke to the rabbit that had its head in the snare made of *riempies*. He put his hand to its neck to check for any sign of life. It opened its eyes and feebly kicked out. He smiled, removed the soft leather rope and wrung its neck with his bare hands. The sound of crushing of bones were sweet music to his ears. He reset his trap, slung the dead rabbit over his back and turned homeward. They had enough meat for dinner. Tomorrow, he would hunt again. Tomorrow, he would kill again.

Before he got to the base of the cliff, he heard it. Gunfire.

Unrest was simmering below the surface of all the tribal communities. Uprising against the colonial domination. Each party who passed through their kraal would update them on the news, making sure they knew what was happening.

It was usual for local tribes to fight against each other; it had always been the way. The Zulus fought the Xhosa. The Ndebele fought the Shona. But now the wars were between the races.

White versus black.

Black versus white.

White South Africans had voted for apartheid, and many black people had been forced to flee into the bush, heading north, away from the injustices.

Just recently he knew that despite opposition from the Nyasaland African Congress and white liberal activists, Britain had combined Nyasaland with the Federation of Northern and Southern Rhodesia. The people were unhappy and armed militia were moving through the bush between all the countries.

Angolan separatists had founded the Party of the United Struggle for

Africans, to help fight for independence from Portugal, and the South West Africans were fighting against the injustice of being governed by the South African government. They could see the white settlers getting rich from the diamonds and the beef industry, while the black population were treated as second-class citizens. They feared the practice of apartheid being introduced as law, and they were getting ready to fight it. Colonisation had gone on long enough.

But the message in the hushed undertone that filtered down Africa from the slaughter in Kenya, done by the Mau Maus in their successful rising against the Europeans there, that Africa could belong to the black people again. They needed to take back their continent and save their tribal way of life. Save their cultures.

People passed their kraal more often now, but this was the first time the guns had sounded so close. Sometimes they could be heard in the distant forests, and across the savannah, but not here. Never near his home in the middle of the bush.

He ran.

Isipho felt the rabbit as it thumped against his back, its head dangling down. He breathed hard, jumping from rock to rock as he crossed the small dry river. Some months the water came down in a flood and scoured out the shrubs and trees in the ravine, but today he was grateful for the dryness. He could move faster.

He could feel the blood in his heart as it pumped furiously. Reaching the bank on the other side, he increased his speed as another burst of automatic gunfire split the air. Although it echoed off the cliff and along the gorge, he knew it definitely came from the direction of his home.

Controlling his breathing so as to minimise noise, he crept as silently as a leopard up the last part of the path. Carefully he placed the rabbit just off the track and stuck his head up over the cliff wall, listening all the while.

Nothing. Only his heart thumping a fast rhythm in his chest.

Isipho knew that something was wrong. He couldn't hear any sounds from the small herd of cattle and goats. They relied on those animals. The milk from the goats and the blood from the cows were not only important to their survival, but in one week's time they planned to drive the young bull to the outskirts of the town two days walk away, and sell it for money to buy beans, samp and sugar, necessary provisions to get them through the coming winter months. Peeking over the ledge, he looked at the horizon in time to see the herd being driven away by men dressed in forest clothes. He hadn't seen anyone like them before, but the old Ndebele warrior had explained the khaki material used for bush fighting to him in detail from his time as a labourer with the Rhodesians in the Second World War.

Panic slammed into his chest. Why were the fighters here, at their kraal? The silence around him screamed. Not even a bird called out. It was as if every animal held its breath and waited to exhale.

Finally, he could no longer hear the distant soft whistles used by the men herding the cattle. He peered over the ledge but he could not see them, even their dust had settled back to the ground on the track leading out of their valley.

Remaining low to the ground, he stepped up from the cliff and silently made his way to the entrance of their kraal. He trod softly through the opening in the thorn barrier, ensuring he made no noise, and didn't disturb the sand as he looked for his mother.

He found her lying naked on the ground in front of the cooking hut. Blood had seeped from her body into the dirt, and the puddle was growing in size.

Dropping to his knees, he reached over and turned her gently. Vacant eyes stared up at him. A lump formed in his throat, and a weight inside his chest pushed against his heart. He couldn't breathe. There was no oxygen in the air and he gulped in erratic mouthfuls, swallowing them painfully. If he could cry he would have, but he had learned early in his life never to show tears. Tears were a luxury for weaker females, not real men.

'*Sohn, standplatz weg von diesem toten informanten.*' A voice from behind shouted in a thick German accent. Son, come away from that dead informant.

Who was the man talking about, surely not his mother? Informant on who? Still holding his mother to him, Isipho turned his face towards the voice.

'*Magtag*. An albino,' the man cursed. 'Why are you here?'

'My home, sir,' Isipho told him, remembering to put his respect in at the end of his sentence. He understood the German perfectly, another gift learned from the various men who had passed through his home. He could speak a little of many languages, but he'd learnt to understand each to avoid the beatings some of them thought he needed.

'Your home? There was no child mentioned in the reconnaissance report.' The German pointed his rifle at Isipho's face.

The black barrel looked really long to Isipho as he focused hard on the metal sight at the end, hoping to never see a flash come out of the dark hole underneath.

'Boss, don't kill a *sope*, beware the *tokoloshe*,' shouted a black soldier as he ran towards the German. His accent was of Shona descent from Rhodesia.

The German lowered his rifle.

Isipho let out the breath he was holding. A rivulet of sweat ran down his forehead into his mouth. He didn't taste the salt, just the fear.

'He says this is his home,' the German said in distaste.

'Perhaps he can be useful. He'll know what happens here, who visits, and perhaps where they go when they leave. Maybe he can identify some of the terrorists,' the soldier said. 'The mother was useless and told us nothing. The only thing I got from her was a good pomp.'

Isipho felt bile rise in his throat. His anger bubbled inside as he burned to avenge his mother by running his assegai through the pig of a man.

'Come on,' the German said. 'He won't survive here alone. If he knows what's good for him, he'll soon talk. Bring him with us. He can work on my farm. He's just a kid, probably didn't even understand that this hut was used for terrorist meetings.'

Isipho realised he needed to plead ignorance. He kept quiet unless questioned, and answered only a few of their questions about the men who visited their home. He averted his eyes to the ground and didn't answer most. The men they asked after were his mother's friends, and most had shown him kindness where many others hadn't.

'What's your name, boy?' asked the German.

'Isipho, sir.'

'*Isipho*? As in gift? I just bet you were no gift to your tribe,' the German said. 'That's why the Zulu bitch had you stashed all the way out here north of the Caprivi Strip. From today your name will be Rodney, understand?'

'Rod-ney, yes sir.'

The German and the khaki-clad soldiers marched him away from his home. They didn't care about him at all. They were his enemies. They hadn't even let him bury his mother, who had been left to the vultures, the jackals and the cowardly hyenas.

Rodney took one last look back over his shoulder. One day he would have his revenge on them all.

It took many years, but eventually Rodney settled into life *'op die plaas'*. On the farm he'd learnt that he no longer lived in Angola, but was in South West Africa. Across the border was South Africa, his birthplace. His mother had spent hours telling him his history when they were alone together, making sure he understood the dangers of being a *sope*, especially in South Africa, the country from which his mother had fled when the savage sangoma and the village had tried to kill him at birth.

At the German's farm he was given weekly rations, samp, beans and sugar. He was also given an old *ikhaya* of his own in the compound, but he had to mix the mud and cow dung to fix the holes in the walls and resurface the floor. This was usually women's work, but because he and his mother had made many *ikhaya*s together, he was a good home builder. The other Bantu workers tolerated him only because the Boss had brought him to the ranch. No one spoke to him. He was alone.

His job was easy, tending the dairy herd. Each day he got up before the sun rose and brought the cattle into the dairy. Once milking was over, he took them to the bush to feed, and watched over the herd to ensure no harm came to the fat cows. In the afternoon, he brought them home and after milking was finished, settled them into the holding pens for the night. Each day it was the same pattern. Seven days a week.

Four years passed as he silently plotted his revenge on the Boss for the murder of his mother. Rodney was now sixteen summers.

There were three white daughters of the Boss who came home to the *plaas* for their school holidays. They had blonde hair, big blue eyes, and had eventually grown big boobies while they were away at boarding school. Each holiday he watched them as they ordered the servants around, demanding everything be done for them.

Their daddy smiled at them all the time, giving them expensive thoroughbred horses to ride, extending his brick house so that each daughter had her own bedroom. But they had no manners or decency towards the staff of the ranch, and referred to everyone as 'Boy'. The girls never lifted a hand to help anyone. Instead, they would sit in the dairy and do nothing.

These young ladies of the manor were the ticket to revenge for his mother.

Already he could *fook* well. The Bantu women might not talk to him during the daylight hours, but at night they slipped into his *ikhaya* to have his white cock stuck into them. They always came back for more. The harder and rougher he learned to be, the more often they visited. And they paid for their visits.

His white skin, grey eyes and yellow hair had become the Boss's eldest daughter's fascination for the holidays. Every day she was in the dairy, watching. Silently appraising him. Soon she began visiting him in the veld on her horse. She'd ride out to him as he tended the cattle and silently observe him. Sometimes she shared her packed lunch with him, but did not utter a single word. Until the day he came across her lying naked in the sun, masturbating.

She'd been swimming in the dam with her horse and was drying off, her head on her saddle and her milk white body spread out on the horse blanket. He stood mesmerised. He'd never seen a naked white woman before, let alone one who was obviously enjoying the sensation of her own fingers. He watched as her hand explored below the blonde curls and her other plucked repeatedly at her rose-coloured nipples.

He lost his breath at the sight. Fire burned deep in his belly, and his dick stirred against his rough shorts. For a while he simply watched as she pleasured herself. Licking his lips, he dared not move in case she noticed him. Pain rippled over his abdomen and legs as the muscles shook, in an effort not to mimic her pelvic thrusting. In his dazed state he made a mistake.

He stepped on a stick.

She opened her blue eyes, turned her head and looked directly at him.

He stood frozen as if he was a kudu in his Boss's hunting spotlight.

Slowly a smile curved on her lips, her straight white teeth showing. 'You want me, don't you, *kaffir*?' She sucked her lip into her mouth and nibbled on it as she raised an eyebrow. 'Is it true? Does the albino give a good one?' She waited as if to make sure he understood her. 'Our maid says you have the longest and fattest shlong she's ever seen. I won't tell Daddy. Let me see.' She placed the tip of her finger in her mouth and sucked on it, then slowly withdrew it from her mouth and walked her fingers down her breasts, to the hair at the apex of her legs.

He attempted to focus on her face, but the nest of hair drew his attention and he looked as her forefinger slipped back inside her. She arched her back like a cat, thrusting her sweet tits to the sunshine.

'South West Africa is still so colonial in its thinking. Next year when I've finished school, I'll be nineteen years old and I shall be going to university in America. The journalists there are writing about sexual freedom, and I want to experience it. But I can't wait until then. I want it now. Do you understand what I want?'

He stared at her. He couldn't believe she was talking to him at all, and that she wanted his dick. If he took her, he was a dead *kaffir*. She was his Boss's daughter. He inhaled a deep breath. The clean smell of the bush held the musty odour of her sex.

'I give it good,' Rodney said eventually, not sure whether he'd spoken English or German.

'You'd better. Or I'll tell Daddy you raped me,' she said. 'No kissing. I don't want your pink lips anywhere near mine. Understand?'

'Yes, Missus,' he said as he slid his khaki shorts down to his knees, his cock already ramrod straight. If there was one thing that Rodney knew on this farm, it was his place in the pecking order. He'd serve the Missus.

'Magtag, look at you. Mm, you are big,' she said as she licked her lips. 'Come here,' she commanded and lay flat on her back, her legs spread apart and her feet planted firmly on the ground.

He lay on top of her and pushed straight in. She was already wet from her masturbation session and he slid inside without too much friction. But she was tight, and he pushed harder, breaking her barrier.

She gave a whimper and tensed up, but he ignored it as he held his face away from hers, strongly with both arms supporting his weight and *fook*ed her hard. Slamming into her over and over, he watched her face as she squirmed in delight and listened to her, *yes, yes, oh yes, like that, do-me, do-me* cries.

Her round tits jiggled like thick whipped cream and she arched her back, meeting him thrust for thrust. Rodney stilled and watched her, her eyes closed and breathing erratic. He said, 'On your knees. It's better.'

Pulling out, he helped her turn over on the horse blanket. He covered her from behind with his body, and using her to support his weight, he palmed her tits at last, just as he banged into her from behind. Her white butt against his groin area, her little mewing sounds became too loud in the bush.

'Quiet.' He lifted himself off her back and slapped her backside. A red stain of his handprint showed where he'd hit her. He liked the way it looked.

'Don't ...' She started to object but Rodney spoke over her.

'You want good, rough is good.' He continued to grind into her.

Finally, she climaxed. He could feel her pulsating around him, and she shivered as if a ripple had passed over her body. He withdrew quickly, then moved to the front of her as she was still down on all fours, and pushed his dick in her mouth.

'Suck,' he commanded. Willingly, she complied. With his hand over hers, he showed her how he liked to be caressed and cupped, and then he taught her to swallow his essence.

By day, he *fook*ed the Boss's daughter for free, and at night it was usually her fat nanny that crept into his bed first, wanting his cock. He accepted her payment for his services every Friday when their wages were paid. He watched his nest egg growing steadily in the small tin hidden behind a loose mud brick in his *ikhaya*. One day he would catch a train back to Angola. One day he would return home and bury his mother, give her a passing over ceremony and set her spirit free from this world to journey onto the next. But he would need money for supplies. His biggest fear was that it would take so long he wouldn't remember the way home.

He met the farmer's daughter in secret in the bush every day for five weeks. Always she was waiting for him. Wanting him.

Revenge was sweet when left to stew. Albinos were not supposed to *fook* white women. And doing the Boss's daughter was just a warm-up in his plan for revenge.

One Monday, she wasn't there. He'd seen her in the dairy in the morning, but she didn't arrive at their normal spot. At first, he thought perhaps she'd returned to school, but there was still one week left of the holidays. She would come to meet him. She must just be late.

He waited for her all day. Eventually, he returned to the dairy with the cattle in the afternoon.

She was there. Sitting in the dairy, next to her father. She ignored him completely, except for opening her legs when he entered the room so he could see up her dress, to the blonde hair that covered her womanhood. Then she closed them again.

The next day, she was waiting for him in their normal rendezvous place.

She teased him mercilessly. 'Did you miss me, *kaffir*? Did you miss what we do? You want me still, don't you?' She laughed at him, climbed back on her horse and rode away.

She tormented him the whole week, sometimes allowing him to *fook* her, but mostly not. He began to hate her with a vengeance, for she'd found his weakness. Sex and blood.

He liked to do her during her monthlies. He loved the smell and the feel and the look of himself coming out all bloodied. He'd had her once like this already, and this week was to be her next bleed. Soon she'd leave the ranch, her holiday completed. He only had two days until she returned to boarding school. He was running out of time.

Rodney could take no more of her torment. He decided it was time to complete his revenge. He counted the money stacked in his tin. There was enough for a train ticket back to Angola. He sat on his sleeping mat and sharpened his knife. Tomorrow he would carry his possessions with him.

It was time.

She was waiting for him under the tree, eager as ever, acting as if she'd never ignored him. 'I want something different today,' she said, dropping her jodhpurs on the ground and kicking them aside. She lifted her cotton top up and over her head, her little pink nipples already like pebbles in excitement, waiting for him.

'I want it harder. Rougher. My nanny says you are better when you are rough. Do me like you do her.' So he did.

He was as rough as he was with any of the black women in the compound. He scratched her tits, and bit her shoulder. She whimpered and he could hear her breath deepen. It excited him more. He pulled her blonde hair back and while he thrust his hips hard into hers, causing her white skin to burn with friction against the horse blanket, he smacked her face with the flat of his hand. She jerked her head up in surprise and her nose made contact with his fist. Red blood squirted out her nostrils. She began screaming and trying to buck him off, tossing each way, but he grew harder still, delighting in their union as they remained joined at the hip like dogs.

'No screaming, this good and rough,' he said as he pulled her head back to face him with both his hands.

'No, stop. I don't like it. Stop!' Panicked, she dug her nails into the backs of his hands as she tried to drag them away from the iron grip he had on her head.

He bent forward and licked the blood from her top lip.

'No, no kissing,' she stammered.

He licked her again and pumped into her, excited by her fresh blood and knowing this would be the last time he'd ever have sex with her.

She threw her head from side to side, shouting, 'Get off me! Get off me!'

He pinned her down with his body as she fought him, bucking, attempting to get away. Her face reddened as he slapped his open hand across her cheek when she bit his shoulder, elated in the feel of her nails gouging flesh from his back and down his arms.

No longer the willing woman.

He trailed his tongue down from her forehead over her nose and lapped again at the blood splatter. The salty iron flavour fuelled his lust. Once again, he rocked his hips into hers.

Slowly she stopped fighting, and stopped shouting.

'No, no ...' was all she murmured now.

He bit her nipples until they bled, all the time grinding into her, loving the feel of her around him, and tasting her blood.

'No, no ...' she repeated in a whisper. Her ragged breathing disclosing exactly how close to the end of her strength she was.

Rodney almost lost his seed; the feeling was so overwhelming. He was taking her, and even though she didn't want this at first, he was totally in control of her. He pulled her with his teeth on her throat.

The pain drew her upwards once more.

'Stop! No stop!'

He slammed into her again, and she gasped loudly.

'I *fook* you,' he shouted as he slapped her face.

She screamed. 'I hate you! I hate you!'

'Harder, harder. You wanted just like your nanny. Now *fook* me,' he said, and he licked her breast.

She begged. 'Stop, please. Please stop.'

'No.' He continued to pump into her.

But she looked away from him.

'No! Look at me!' he shouted, jerking out from her and pulling on her chin to bring her attention back to his face as he sat down on her chest, his dick proudly in front of her mouth but just out of her teeth's way, in case she decided she still wanted to fight him. He came onto her face.

Only then did he stop.

Completed.

She lay still on the ground, her face full of his seed, and didn't wipe it away. Fat tears ran from the corners of her eyes. 'You raped me,' she said quietly. 'I'm going to tell my daddy.'

'No, you wanted it like your nanny. You got good *fook*.' He reached over, and grasped his knife from his pack. Then he cut her from ear to ear. Her eyes went wide as she stared at him, and her hands came up to clutch her throat. Not a sound bubbled out of her mouth.

Rodney wiped his knife on her nest of blonde hair, still wet with her recent sexual adventure. He stood up, put his clothes and pack on, and walked away as silently as a leopard.

Fook for fook.

Blood for blood.

His mother for the farmer's first daughter. He was even with her father.

He vanished into the bundu, intent on travelling to Angola. Yes, Rodney knew how to *wag-'n-bietjie*, to bide his time.

'Rodney!' *Meneer* Lawrence's voice interrupted his thoughts, wrenching him back to the present. The metallic smell of fresh blood, the heavy strap of the bullet bucket digging into his shoulder and the uncomfortable hardness of the elephant tusks he sat on.

'Open the fucking gate, you useless *kaffir*!'

Rodney jumped off the back of the truck, and rushed to the boundary gate they had made in the fence in preparation for the attack.

He closed the gate after the truck had passed through and by the time he reached the vehicle, *Meneer* Lawrence had the tailgate down. Rodney reached into the front section of his bullet bag and retrieved the soft cloths. He stuffed them into the hinge part of the *bakkie* to absorb the uncongealed blood that could splatter onto the road and leave a trail on the tarmac, giving away their progress and where they would exit later. They had already lined the sides of the truck but they had found from experience that the blood pooled at the back and so they always put extra cloths there to soak it up.

Rodney closed the tailgate and *Meneer* Lawrence made his way to the front. Rodney clambered back onto the tarpaulin at the back. He heard the gear change as the truck switched from the local thick soft *goosie* sand onto the tarmac and smiled. Part one of their plan was working and next would be part two. Crossing back into the national park to hide where the national park anti-poaching units would least expect them to be, by re-entering the park off the tar road and heading as far into the thick bush as they could.

His smiled widened. His tracking skills and reputation as a poaching legend were just as good these days as when he and *Meneer* Lawrence had first worked together in the jungles of Rwanda. When Rodney discovered that a clever white man could accept an albino as a partner, as his tracker, and as his colleague.

As an albino, he knew he would never get far alone, but with *Meneer* Lawrence and *Meneer* Joubert he had followed the African proverb: 'If you want to go fast, go alone. If you want to go far, go together.'

Together they had many secrets.

Together they had shared much and were rich.

Together they had success.

CHAPTER 5

Ashley retched again. Acid burned her throat and nose as Scott held her hair up, away from her face. He patted her back, the consoling rhythm not soothing her distressed constitution. The tears she attempted to choke back lodged in her throat. She'd never witnessed such utter destruction and mutilation. The only part taken from them were their tusks, chopped out and stolen in the black night.

Dead elephant lay everywhere, the huge grey-maroon shapes scattered in a clearing. Little identical shapes lay in the inner circle of the larger animals.

Scott smoothed her hair. 'They protect their young to the death.'

'It's barbaric. Why? Who?'

'Money. Although there's an international ban on ivory trade, the black market's booming. There's a huge demand for it, especially in the East. The money from one tusk will feed a family in the surrounding park area for a few years.'

'So many, all dead.'

'This particular poaching ring are professionals. They've planned this for months, manipulating the elephant into this area. Even before they brought in their ground crews and the helicopters that cornered the jumbo. At least their hunters have shot everything.'

'But the babies? They were only babies,' Ashley said with a huge sniff.

'In a warped way, they're being kind to the youngsters. This way they won't remember.'

Nearby, a sadistic laugh sent a chill up Ashley's spine. She shivered.

'Hyena.' Scott quickly filled in the source of the sound for her. 'You can hear them waiting on the outskirts of this slaughter. On the positive side, the scavengers in the reserve will have plenty of food tonight.'

Ashley looked at him blankly. How could he find any positives in this situation?

Zol shouted, 'Scott, we've got tracks!'

'On my way,' Scott replied, walking towards Zol's voice.

The men looked at the spoor. Tyre marks cut deep into the dry African sand where heavily laden trucks had driven away from the grim crime scene. Scott and Zol, their heads low over their torches, pointed to the dirt below.

Ashley heard other muffled voices rumbling in the night, and she turned and shone her powerful torch towards the sound. Men materialised out of the shadows and walked towards her. The front man smiled and his teeth flashed white in the torchlight as he lifted his hand up to shield his eyes.

Her mouth opened but no sound came out. Her feet wouldn't move. She was frozen at the sight of the armed men. All wore camouflage clothing and toted an assortment of guns.

'Ahhggg,' she managed eventually, but it came out more like a church mouse whisper than a scream as fear gripped her throat.

Scott looked up. 'Vusi, you're here. Good. Zol has the spoor. Get going. They have about five hours on us. Follow their tracks.'

'They're friendly?' Ashley squeaked.

'If you are not a poacher. They are part of my anti-poaching unit. Each man carries authority from the President: shoot to kill any suspected poacher.'

'Okay,' Ashley said.

'Keep in radio contact. I'll be at Delmonica.' He put a hand on Zol's shoulder. 'Take special care, my brother. These ones are ruthless. Again they have picked up every spent shell. It's as if they knew they had the time to clean up after themselves before we'd react.'

Zol nodded and joined the team. As if by magic, the seven men disappeared into the dark night. Ashley couldn't even hear their footsteps as they walked away. She turned her attention back to the carnage in front of her and watched some men put a chain around the front of an elephant and winch it up onto the back of a large flatbed truck. 'What are they doing?'

'Those are the Parks Board workers. They'll utilise as much as possible from the carcasses, making biltong to sell to the tourists and supply meat to the local restaurants and lodges. They'll cure the hides and sell those. Mostly, they'll try to minimise waste from this catastrophe. The high-valued ivory might be gone, but the elephant body's still valuable, if they can get it into cold storage quick enough. The park will get a small injection of capital from tonight. But what they have lost is greater.' He stroked her cheek. 'Let's go home. There's nothing more we can do here.'

They left the workers performing their grim task of loading carcasses onto their trucks, and drove back to Delmonica in silence, using the main bitumen road through the reserve. Ashley sat still, shell-shocked. Scott had insisted she take the middle seat as she'd done on her first journey with him, her legs around the gear lever. He kept his hand in contact with her as much as he dared, his palm absentmindedly brushing her leg. She wondered if it was to reassure himself that he wasn't alone, or to reassure her he was there.

She didn't mind the contact this time. She needed it to believe that there was still some good left in the world.

They saw no herds of buffalo, no elephant and no antelope on the deserted roads. It was as if the reserve itself was mourning the loss of the giant monarchs of the savannah.

'Sunday is the day of rest, so tell me again why I have to learn how to shoot this thing?' Ashley asked Scott, as she looked down at the weapon in her hands.

'Remember last night, the elephant?'

'Hang on. The poachers are after the animals. You kept saying "don't bother things and they won't bother you". I won't go after a poacher, I promise.'

He smiled. 'You still need this crash course in weapons use. You will be in the park, and they are in the park. Look in the mirror, you'll be a spoil of war if they catch you.'

Ashley stared at Scott; she hadn't given that angle any thought. He had hinted once before and his words came back to her now: *there are worse things than death if you get into trouble in Africa.*

She shivered. She'd always taken her safety as a given in Australia. Here in Africa, it wasn't the case. It was a hard continent. A place where there were more grey areas than black and white in the eyes of the law. She needed more than four weeks to understand it. Africa and Australia were oceans apart in so many of the everyday customs and the shooting range highlighted this fact. Not that she frequented shooting ranges as an everyday occurrence in her life, but even she knew the range was rough.

She turned back towards the target. Another difference between their countries—in Australia, because of occupational health and safety regulations, she'd have worn earmuffs to protect her hearing. Here, Scott had laughed when she'd asked where they were.

The boards he'd set up as targets, already shot to smithereens, bore a rough cardboard body outline. The range was in the back garden, away from the house and workers' compound, but still not fenced. The small hillock, or *mannetjie,* as he called it, at the back wasn't that big, just a mound of dirt pushed together by a front-end loader, to do its job of absorbing stray bullets that missed the targets. Scott had informed her he didn't want any of his cattle shot, and that was the only reason why he'd bothered to construct the bank at all.

Standing square on with her feet slightly apart, her right hand loosely caressing the gun and her left supporting underneath, she slipped off the safety catch again. Slowly, gently, she squeezed the trigger. *Bang!*

She heard a dull thunk as the bullet sank into the soil behind the target. 'Ouch!'

Scott looked at her and frowned. 'What?'

'My arms are aching. I must've fired this gun more than a hundred times in the last two hours. Every time it goes off, it yanks my arms from their sockets and manages to jump at least forty centimetres into the air.'

'You're getting better. You compensated for it this time. You hit the target, at last.' A huge grin spread across his face.

'Whoop-de-do.'

'If it's life or death, you had better hit your target,' he told her firmly.

'Okay, I give up. You win. I'll go home,' she said, but she knew it was just lip-sync, she had no intention of leaving.

'No longer a viable option, I really would prefer it if you stayed here,' he said seriously. 'I need your skills in the pump project.'

A small smile passed over Ashley's lips. She was amazed at the progression and change in their relationship in such a short time. It would be interesting to see where it went. She was still leaving in three weeks, but she'd never done casual before. This was new territory.

But with Scott, she *might* be willing to explore that possibility. After all, it was Scott who, once they got home last night, had kissed her nose as if she was an innocent schoolgirl and sent her to her room.

'Enough for now, you still need to be able to fix those pumps,' he said, removing the .38 revolver from her hand. He checked the safety was on before slipping it into its holster on his hip next to the 9mm he'd been using. 'Besides, it's lunchtime. My stomach thinks my throat's been cut.'

'That's a gross expression.'

'Gross or not, it's true. Come on, let's go eat.' He took her hand as they headed back to the ranch house.

On the veranda, Alan sat at the table, his head in his hands, nursing a hangover from the night before. 'Did you have to do that today? Every shot vibrated through my head.'

'Have another beer. It's the best treatment.' Scott passed him a Lion lager.

Alan held up his hands. 'Thanks, but no. I couldn't.'

'Where are the others? Any sign of them?' Scott asked. After rushing out on his volunteers at Zebra Pan Lodge last night, he assumed they had all returned to the ranch in their various modes of transport.

'William went off with the hunters he met at the dinner last night, and David hasn't got out of bed yet. He was still snoring when I came out.'

Ashley looked at Alan. 'You don't look good.'

'I think I'm going to throw up, I'm getting too old to party,' Alan managed, as he got to his feet and ran for the men's room.

'Want one?' Scott asked as he bent into the bar fridge again and this time withdrew two cold lagers.

'No thanks. I'll stick to my soft drinks.'

'You don't drink at all?' He returned the lager and grabbed a diet soda in its place.

'Sure I do. Chocolate milk, soft drinks, juices. Just avoid alcohol.' She accepted her drink. 'Thanks.'

'Why?'

'I've seen too many people make huge mistakes under the influence. Do stupid things and have to live with the consequences.' Ashley laughed at the comical expression on his face. 'I don't have an alcoholic parent stashed in the cupboard or anything.'

'So then it's personal?'

'No and yes. Bronwyn, my business partner, was badly hurt in an avoidable car accident. It put me off drinking. I still drive Bronwyn on girls' nights out. She drinks, I drive. She never blamed me for the accident, but I do blame myself.'

'Perhaps you were both at fault and neither should be pointing the blame at anyone else. But not drinking, that's not a bad thing.'

'Truly? That's your honest opinion?'

Scott laughed. 'No. I think you're weird, but then you're an Australian, so it's expected.'

She chucked a pillow at him from the couch.

His mobile CB burst to life with Zol's voice. 'Scott, come in. Over.'

'Scott here. Come in, Zol,' he replied as he ran for the main unit in his study, where he could hear with less static interference.

Ashley sat down to lunch without him. Her stomach growled as she smelled the aroma of the lovely meal Lisa had laid out for them. Homemade bread with butter on the side, sliced ham and other cold meat selections, some of which Ashley couldn't give a name to. Bougainvillea flowers decorated the platters where, in a restaurant in Brisbane, lettuce leaves or herbs would have been used in abundance. But there was no frivolous waste of food here in Africa. She made a mental note to tell Lisa that she'd done well and was up with the best of the best chefs in the city.

Scott came back onto the veranda as she ate. He quickly threw together a dagwood-style sandwich and surprised her by kissing her half on the cheek and half on the lips, haphazard and distracted.

'I'll be home later tonight. Don't go anywhere. Zol wants me to check out something for him, and I can't take you with me. Please stay near Alan.'

Within a few minutes, he was in his *bakkie* and driving out the main gate. She watched from the veranda as the dust column behind his vehicle settled back to earth, her fingers touching her lips. Even when her lunch was completed, she sat staring at the road he'd travelled down, lost in thought. He had kissed her almost as if it were a habit on leaving. *Shocked her* ... a little. But it had been interesting—soft, too fast ... familiar.

Finally, she looked away, pushed her chair back and strolled out to the swimming pool where she pulled out a large cushion from the cupboard, and placed it on the lounger in the sun. She opened the fantasy novel she'd picked up at the airport in Brisbane, but her mind wasn't on the words. She was thinking about a sexy farmer who was full of surprises.

She was attracted to him. *Her African man.* He was tough, but gentle, an anomaly within the male world she'd known. Anyone would have thought she was in love.

No, that can't be right. I can't be falling in love with Scott.

It was simply that she was beginning to care deeply for him.

But she'd only known him such a short time.

And exactly where was it written that you needed years to get to know someone?

Her mind fluttered to another time, another country, when she'd thought she knew what love was. She'd known Michael for three years before they'd become intimately involved, and just look where that had got her. A week was fast, but then, when you were trying to cram a lifetime into four weeks, seven days could seem like an eternity.

Alan joined her at the pool. 'I'll never drink again, I swear it.'

'Sure you will. You feel like hell today but tomorrow when the others toss you a cold one, you'll drink it. Men always do.' She smiled to help sweeten her words.

'I know I need to put you in your place, but I don't have the energy. So all I can say is, "Yes, dear".'

'Yes, dear? What is that supposed to mean?'

'When I say it to Michelle, she simply smiles. I was hoping it'd work for you too.'

She laughed. How wonderful Alan and Michelle's relationship must be.

Alan put his head down and soon she could hear his soft snore.

The clean crisp smell of Africa filled her. A go-away bird jumped from one mango tree to the next, chattering as it went, then lifted off as a flock of queleas descended into the trees and onto the lawn. Within moments, the fat black and white kitchen cat raced into part of the flock that had settled on the lawn. They all took flight, noisily rushing upwards, like a giant whale into the sky, and flew off in a westward direction. Ashley couldn't help smiling at the cat as it sat, indignant, looking at the departing birds.

Midmorning on Monday, Scott sat in the passenger seat of Lucinda, his sunnies pushed high on his nose, his fingers drumming a non-tune on the butt of the hunting rifle he'd placed barrel downwards on the seat between himself and Ashley. He knew he was scowling, but wasn't in the frame of mind to ease the tension radiating from his forehead.

Last night he'd been called over to Tessa's lodge. He'd met with two rangers whose reserve in Kenya had suffered a similar attack just two weeks previously, and they were hot on the trail of the poachers. The information they had relayed was extremely valuable, and worth losing sleep over.

Kenya and Zimbabwe had now officially joined forces, and were pooling resources. The government officials would handle the necessary paperwork later. Right now, the people on the ground needed to cooperate to enable them to catch the mastermind behind the organised poaching ring.

It seemed the poachers had disappeared across the southern border and into Botswana. Zol had lost their spoor once out of the reserve, where they crossed onto the main bitumen road and the blood splatters had just stopped.

They had reached a dead-end tracking them.

Zol and his anti-poaching unit were zigzagging back and forward in the bush, hoping to find something more. A clue of any type to identify them. If one was there, his unit would find it.

Many of the men in the anti-poaching squad had once been part of some military organisation somewhere in Africa. All were well trained. Some were local, while others were from as far away as the Congo and Ethiopia. Each had been hand-picked by Scott and Zol. They could disappear into the bush for months at a time, and they could find anything or anyone when they were asked to.

He thought back to a 'problem' client Tessa had experienced at her lodge five years before. All the hunting guides had a standard unwritten rule with the ranchers and local hunters: no matter what bribe a guest hunter offered to deny any blood show, whether it was a graze, a single drop, or a full bleed from a wounded creature, the ranchers and hunters would better it by ten grand. As a consequence, not many bribes from clients were accepted. The hunting guides kept their jobs, and were richer for revealing the truth, and the hunting association slowly built their shared lists of blacklisted, dishonest hunters.

Tessa's South African hunter's name had already been on the blacklist, but it had been during Tessa's drug using days, before she'd met Kevin and cleaned up, and she had missed it. This particular hunter had given various safari companies trouble. He would wound an animal and then wouldn't follow it. In Tessa's case, he'd wounded a lion, not fatally, but there was a blood show. Tessa had stood her ground well in the showdown with him. He'd become aggressive and one of her game guards had stepped between the client and her, fearing for her safety.

The guard had been right. The hunter had punched him. The guard pulled his 9mm on the client and cocked it, which was when Tessa's chef, Yellow, had radioed Scott for help.

Zol had been the first to respond, and he'd resolved the situation Africa-style. He'd force-marched the hunter out of Tessa's lodge and into the bush to look for the wounded animal. Amazing what a man did when a razor-sharp hunting knife was held to his throat ...

For three days, they tracked the wounded lion. Zol remained at the hunter's side, but the other members of the unit, illusive and silent, hadn't been visible, although their presence was felt. Twice the hunter had tried to escape, but each time an anti-poaching unit guard had returned him to Zol.

After the first escape attempt, Zol had taken the man's shoes and made him walk barefoot. On the next attempt, he'd taken his trousers. When they caught up with the lion, its wounds had started to fester in the hot African sun. Zol had used his knife to cut the hunter on his arm, deep, and left the wound open with no bandage. Flies swarmed on the fresh wound.

Soon the hunter was begging for forgiveness. He confessed to all the times he'd lied to the ranchers in the area. Zol had signalled to Kwiella, one of the others in his elite group. Within half an hour, they had put the lion put out of its misery, and the hunter in a *bakkie*, heading for the local police station and jail. That particular hunter had never bothered the area again.

Zol and his unit were a formidable force. They would catch up with the poachers soon, and then justice would be done. Scott smiled.

. . .

'Penny for your thoughts.' Ashley's voice interrupted his silence.

'They're dark, and not worth sharing,' he said, still gazing out but not seeing anything from the passenger seat of Lucinda.

'Oh, come on, Scott,' Ashley said as she changed gears, and drove over a particularly high pile of elephant dung.

'I was thinking about what Zol and the unit will do to the poachers when they catch up with them.'

'What can they do?'

'Nothing pretty.' The harshness in his voice caught her attention.

'Scott! Come on, let me in ... I'm trying here.'

'It's not intentional,' he said. 'I'm trying to keep you innocent to all the harsh reality that's Africa. We live by a different code here, one probably not accepted in your First World country, but it works just fine for us. Well, up to a point. Sometimes in Africa, the punishment is fitting for the crime, but international law would call it something else. Cruel, barbaric, maybe torture even.' He paused. 'Here, we shoot to kill poachers on sight. We don't ask them why they are in our national parks. I'm sure you and your countrymen would find this morally unacceptable, but to us, it's a good solution to our problems. A dead poacher doesn't return; one less for us to worry about.'

'After seeing what they did to those poor elephant, I can understand that sentiment now. But before I got here, I wouldn't have,' Ashley said. 'So, what'll they do?'

'Who?'

'Don't play these games ... I'll win. Zol and his unit, smarty-pants.'

He wished he could smile at her sassy comments, the attempt to lighten his mood, but he couldn't. 'No punches pulled. If they can get to the poachers, they'll teach them a hard lesson. And afterwards, if they are alive, hand them over to the police. Black-on-black justice is harsher than anything you can imagine. But these poachers, they are different from the many others we have come across so far. More sophisticated. They might have local help, but the technology they are using is state of the art. We know they have hit Hwange Reserve before—two years ago, in fact. Then they moved up north, to Kenya. We must have got close for them to have relocated their operation, but they've come back. The pressure is on us now to catch them.

'My unit's not unique in this area, many of the other ranchers who border onto the reserve, and those who hold national park concession lands, have similar anti-poaching units. The reserve itself has a few of its own units. They are a necessity here.' He stole a glimpse at her. She appeared to be listening intently.

'But Zol and his unit are the elite of all the guards. Each would put his life on the line for an animal. They are like Marines. This is a passion to these men, not just a job. It pays better than most farm labourers' wages, and even better than a city job in a factory, even better than the gold mines of South Africa. Better than their military careers before. Probably the highest paid anti-poaching unit, with good reason. They're paid bonuses on results.'

'Zol, too? He's more than just a member of the anti-poaching unit though, isn't he?'

'Zol co-owns Delmonica with me. To cut a long story short, politics happened. He either became my partner on paper or I lost my ranch. Zol is family. Has always been treated like family. I signed over half the farm to him. His stake in the unit is bigger than any other's.'

She seemed to take in all that Scott was saying. 'What if your units fabricate the evidence?'

'Possible, but not probable. The people here have a great pride. It goes back to the roots of the Ndebele nation and the tribal system, ruled by kings like Mzilikazi. Hwange was his royal hunting area, and pride and honour are still important. And for those foreign to this land, like from the Congo, the Ndebele people would never allow them to get away with that. It would reflect badly on them. They would visit a sangoma and magic *muti* would appear to sort out the problem.'

'Muti?'

'Medicine.'

'And how can medicine sort out the problem?'

'The Ndebele people are extremely superstitious of the traditional healer or witchdoctor.'

'As in black magic or voodoo?'

'A little like that, yes.'

'Remind me never to tick-off one of your anti-poaching men, okay?'

'I'll try to remember.' They came up to the gate. 'Turn here.'

'But we went through a different gate last week—'

'It's an alternate route. You come out at the same pan. I thought we might check out the state of this road. It may get a little claustrophobic with the *wag-'n-bietjie* bushes scratching Lucinda, but we should get through.'

'Wag-a-what?'

'*Wag-'n-bietjie*. It means wait-a-little. That's their common name. They have black hooked thorns, which grab you and tell you to *wait a moment*.'

'You're kidding?'

'No. Scout's honour.' He nodded and gave a small three-finger salute.

Two hours later, they arrived at the next pump site. The road was passable, and the bushes had indeed grabbed hold of her clothing. But it had been worth it. Ashley had seen the most stunning herd of buffalo. The cattle of the veld, as Scott called them. She'd sat mesmerised as they trudged around Lucinda, snorting and stamping their feet. A few bellowed, but most of the herd ignored their presence. Flies buzzed around their ears, ignoring the roughness of the buffalos' tongues as they licked their shiny black noses.

'We're deep inside the northwest side of the game reserve, and they're not afraid of us here. Most high-density tourist action is in the east, near Hwange and main camp. Don't be fooled by their docile nature. After the hippos, buffalo are the most unpredictable and bad-tempered animals.'

'The hippos?'

'Sure, they're responsible for more deaths in Africa than any other wild animal, other than the mosquitoes.' Ashley watched the buffalos, the way they tossed their heads to the side, and she smelt their unique stench. She basked in the glory of nature for a while until Scott tapped her arm.

'Ease out of the herd. They're getting restless.'

So she'd inched Lucinda forward, and, once clear of the buffalo, followed Scott's directions of which track to take and which game trail to not turn into.

CHAPTER 6

An hour later, relaxed at the pump site, Scott sat back on his haunches against a wooden pole in the shack. 'There is a hunting story told around the campfires in this area, about a hunter who wounded a buffalo. Apparently, his weapon jammed. The buffalo charged him, but he took off his shirt and threw it as a decoy, and he managed to run, leaving the buffalo pummelling his shirt into the dust. He climbed the nearest tree, but it wasn't high enough. The small vee in the bottom had him standing just above the buffalo's vicious horns.'

Ashley reached for a wrench and he put it into her hand. 'Thanks,' she said, and carried on working on the pump.

'The buffalo was furious when he discovered the hunter wasn't in the shirt. He knocked the tree repeatedly, trying to dislodge the man, who clung desperately to its branches. Eventually, the buffalo lay down beneath the tree. The hunter, tired of standing in the tree, sat down, his legs dangling either side of the trunk. In his tired state, he made the worst mistake of his life. He fell asleep.

'By the time his tracker returned with help the next morning, the hunter was dead. The buffalo had trapped one of his legs against the tree and licked the fabric off his trousers. Eventually he licked through all the layers of the man's skin too, and the blood had literally drained from the hunter's body.'

Scott sat quietly looking at her. 'There are other stories about those docile-looking creatures. The buffalo is one of the legendary big five for good reason, and a formidable foe.'

'Is that true?'

'Legend has it that's how the story goes, and I believe it, although no one actually knows who the man was or how long ago it happened.'

'So it could be rubbish?'

'There must be some truth in it. The cantankerous buffalo is notorious for such episodes.'

The pump went back together, its parts fitting as snug as a jigsaw puzzle. Soon she had the outer case reassembled and was tightening the grounding nuts into the cement square on which the old Lister pump sat. Scott checked the level of diesel in the 44-gallon drum next to the pump.

'Nearly three-quarters full.'

'Let's try her out.' Ashley grabbed hold of the crank handle hanging from a wire hook on the corrugated wall behind the pump, fitted it to the engine, flicked the switch, bent her knees and cranked.

Harder. Faster. Faster. Her arm felt as if it would be ripped out its socket. Then the crank flew off and the engine fired. Putt ... putt ... putt, putt, putt—the sweet sound of success. Once she was sure the pump was running to her satisfaction, she ducked outside and listened to the sound of water cascading into the tank in the clearing.

'It's working,' she shouted.

'Yep. I noticed. Did you doubt it would?'

'No. But it's a sweet sound,' she said as she smiled at him.

She walked over to Lucinda and sank down to the dusty ground, her back against the wheel, resting in the shade. Scott opened the cooler box and handed her a bottle of water.

'Listen. You can hear the tank is beginning to fill. Soon it'll spill out into the cement trough and into the pan. Then the game will return to this area. The elephant can smell the water from miles away.'

'If there are any still alive,' she said.

'Plenty. Do you know, in Zimbabwe we still need to cull our elephant population? There are too many, so we do organised culls, pretty much along the same lines as the poachers you saw the other night. We utilise the meat, the hides—everything. It's a cruel reality, but it's that or they will destroy everything and then starve to death, and drag many species down with them.' He took a swig of his water. 'We have rooms back at the Parks Board headquarters that are filled to the roof with ivory, and if we could get the ban lifted on trade, the money generated from that alone could help the park tremendously.'

'That's nearly as barbaric as the poachers.'

'Yes and no. We at least utilise all the animal, and don't waste anything like they do. All they take are the tusks.'

'Justify it any way you like, it's cruel in my eyes.'

'We limit their numbers, and balance the ecosystem in the park. It's a fine line we walk when a two-tonne animal can destroy the whole park for all species, or we can somehow control them.'

He walked over to the tank, sitting on stilts high above the ground behind the tin shed and climbed a few steps up the wooden ladder. He knocked on the bottom of the tank up from the valve tap and smiled to himself.

'Ashley, we've got a problem here,' he called to her.

She rushed over.

'What? Where?' She stood directly in front of him as he opened the valve and watched the icy-cold water cascade over her head and down over her entire body.

Silence followed.

Scott realised Ashley was in shock. He laughed. Ashley with nothing to say was a one-off event, he was sure.

'You bastard!'

'Hey, at least I waited till it was full enough so you got clear water, not rusted junk off the bottom of the tank.'

'Oh, thank you so much, your royal highness,' she said, but she was smiling, and continued to stand in the shower of water. 'At least it's cooled me down. It's wonderful. And it doesn't smell like sulphur, like the borehole water I've come across in Australia.'

'Nope. Pure water in this region. Comes out clear too, no sediment in it.'

He couldn't take his eyes off her. Her clothes were totally saturated, her hair plastered to her head, the baby pink t-shirt she wore clung to her like a second skin. A willowy tree nymph in denim shorts, laughing as she frolicked in the water that continued to spurt out of the tank, splashing onto the dry, cracked earth. Ashley jumped in the puddle the water had formed, splashing the muddy water towards Scott. He watched as she moved towards him, her t-shirt bulging with water, dripping out the bottom of the improvised bucket she'd formed with it. This was a side of Ashley that was new to him. He liked her this way: carefree. Challenging.

'Don't you dare,' he said, holding out his hand to stop her. He switched off the valve and climbed down off the ladder.

She raised an eyebrow as she quickly closed the distance between them. The water hit him smack in the stomach, and snaked down inside his shorts. Her body clung to his as she rubbed her wetness into him. She had initiated a closeness to him that they had not managed before. She had crossed over some barrier in herself, and he wasn't even sure she realised it. She wasn't flinching away. Even the icy water couldn't cool his arousal.

She stilled.

His arms clamped around her and his head descended to meet her lips in a passionate kiss.

He ran his hands down her back and drew her closer. He felt her arms caress his neck, and her fingers run through his hair, subtly bringing him closer to her. Her scent washed over him and he groaned deeply, somewhere in his chest. A primeval mating call.

He felt the answering one from her.

He lifted the hem of her t-shirt, seeking access. She moved her lithe body, accommodating him, and her shirt flew up over her head. His hands roamed freely, brushed over her breasts.

'You okay, Ashley?'

'Yeah.'

She ran her hands down his chest, feeling every muscle ripple in response to her touch, as she lowered her hands and then pushed them under his shirt, and was rewarded as she heard his quick intake of breath.

Breaking the kiss, she unbuttoned his work shirt slowly, trailing kisses down his chest as she moved lower, towards his abdomen. The first button on his khaki shorts snapped undone. Then the second.

'I've gone to heaven,' he murmured.

'Not yet.'

'You're an angel come to tempt me to death.'

He eyed her up, and framed her face with his hands.

Flecks of fire shone in his ocean blue eyes.

'You sure you're okay?' he asked.

She smiled. 'Yes.'

He kissed her again, his lips warm and soft.

'Scott, come in.' Zol's voice shattered the quietness of the bush from the new CB radio fitted in Lucinda.

'Dammit!'

'You really need to get that,' Ashley said against his lips as she kissed him.

'I know.' Scott rolled his eyes and exhaled deeply. He backed away, shaking his head, attempting to clear the haze so he could respond to the call. He walked over to Lucinda and reached in to grab the handset.

'Scott here. Come in, Zol.'

'We picked up tracks. They doubled back into the reserve and are heading towards the Gwabazabuya River.'

'Have you located their camp?'

'Negative. I'm sure they're there. Sipho followed them in. Sunday's in the same area.'

'Good. What do you need?'

'Where are you?'

'About one hour south of Big Tom's *Vlei*.'

'Rendezvous at the main fence in four hours at the tip of the big bulge, near the electricity pylon.'

'I'll be there.'

Zol hesitated then asked, 'Is Miss Ashley with you?'

Scott looked at Ashley as she finished shimmying into her wet t-shirt. She smiled.

'Positive.'

'Detour via home.'

Ashley frowned and shook her head.

'That'll waste time. I won't make the rendezvous.'

'Drop her off at Big Tom's *Vlei*.'

Again, Ashley shook her head. She wanted to stay with Scott to help, not be cooped up in the farmhouse again.

Scott winked at Ashley, her wet t-shirt did nothing to hide her dark nipples underneath. 'Negative.'

'Is she armed?'

'Affirmative.' Scott glanced at his .303 wedged into Lucinda's seat. Ashley's .38 sat snugly with his 9mm in the glove compartment where he'd put them that morning.

'See you at the rendezvous point. I'm checking out something south of Makalolo. Out.'

'Take care. Over and out.'

'Shit. Duty calls.' Doing up his shirt, he walked around Lucinda and opened the glove compartment and removed their handguns. 'Put this on, and keep it on. Here is more ammo. The belt already has spare bullets in it. Your gun has six rounds. The holster will be a little big, but you should get used to it.'

He helped her strap it on, with the .38 sitting just below her right hip, resting on her rump. Then he did the same with his own 9mm holster.

'Hop in,' he said, motioning to the passenger's side. Almost mechanically, he retrieved his .303 from the crack in the front seat and loaded a round before he slipped the safety into place; the icy sound of metal sliding on metal was foreign in the bush. He put the rifle between them, the barrel facing down into the floor.

'Dammit,' he cursed. 'When we put in the radio, we should have fitted Lucinda with a gun carrier too.'

'Scott, what's going on? What are we driving into?'

'I don't know. But if Zol wants a rendezvous, it means he's found something incriminating. Something he can't speak about on the radio. He said he was near Makalolo, but he wants us near the big bulge. I think he's trying to throw someone off his scent. He's probably nearer the poachers than he wants them to know.'

'Are we in danger?'

He picked up her hat from where it sat on the seat, and positioned it on her head. 'We're always in danger. Every time we go anywhere in the reserve, I watch for signs of poaching, and as you and I travel together, I guess then, yes, that puts you in a certain amount of danger, too. But this rendezvous is different ... I should take you back to Delmonica or drop you off at one of the safari lodges on the way.'

He put his own hat back on.

'Good thing I paid holiday insurance,' Ashley joked dryly. 'I don't want to go home. I'm going with you.'

Scott smiled at her. He reached for her leg and gave it a squeeze before running his hand up her thigh in an intimate but reassuring gesture, which was made difficult to achieve with the rifle between them.

'You know I'll protect you.' He looked at her, his blue eyes meeting hers in open honesty.

'But who is there to protect you?'

'Perhaps there's a God somewhere up there who thinks I'm doing an okay job protecting the animals. Perhaps he'll intervene, should I need him.'

'Scott. Be serious.'

'I am. Now stop worrying. We have a few hours' travel before we meet up with Zol and the unit. Good thing you put those extra jerry cans of petrol in this morning. We'll need them later.'

'Long enough for me to dry out my socks?' she asked as she slipped off her boots and wrung out her baby pink socks.

'Definitely.'

They cut cross-country and soon bounced onto a small dirt track. The *middle mannetjie* was so high that Lucinda ploughed it flat as they drove over. Dust flew everywhere, and when they hit the occasional clump of elephant dung, the stench made Ashley want to retch. She pulled her rapidly drying t-shirt up over her nose.

Scott appeared unaffected and continued to focus on the road. Suddenly he turned Lucinda sharply and the bush track joined a smoother, graded road. In the Park Board's attempt to keep the game in and the poachers out, the boundary fence stood eight feet tall. The drive along the fence line was a thousand times better than the one in the bush, but the heat blanketed down on Ashley and Scott. While in the bush, pockets of trees had given welcome shade, but in the open there was nothing. The road was utilised as a firebreak so, while small shrubs grew sparingly, clinging to life in the hot soil, all the bigger trees had been cleared long ago.

'What's on the other side of the fence here?' she asked.

'Botswana.'

'Is it national park too?'

'No. A hunting concession. The delta catchment is further north. If we keep on this road, we'll reach our rendezvous within an hour.' He pointed out a tree on the Zimbabwe side of the reserve. 'See that huge sausage tree?'

'Yes, strange name for a tree.'

'Notice the huge brown fruits hanging down?'

She looked at him, then replied in a sarcastic tone, 'You'd have to be blind not to notice them, Scott. They must be at least three feet long.'

'That tree has legends attached to it, but the reason I pointed it out is that the locals are harvesting them commercially now.' He smiled at her. 'They are used as a potential cure for some types of skin cancer associated with aging and prolonged exposure to the sun. And the cream, which was once thought to be a sangoma's *muti*, is now gaining international recognition.'

'Amazing.'

'Usually, all the trees are harvested of their pods, even here in the reserve. It's a lucrative business, and the children from the Tosholotsho homeland brave the game guards to gather them. There must be a reason why this tree has not been touched this season.'

'After the buffalo story, I'm almost afraid to ask, but I'll bite. What legend does the tree have?'

Scott laughed. He sneaked a look at her. 'A young woman would sit under it and pray for breasts like the sausages on the tree. She asked for these so that, when she was in the fields gathering wood, she could toss her breast over her shoulder for the baby strapped to her back, and she wouldn't have to stop working.'

'You're kidding?'

'No, honest.' But he was grinning.

'Well, don't expect me to sit under any tree. I'm quite happy with mine as they are, thank you very much.'

'Me too,' Scott agreed mischievously, gazing at them.

'The road, Scott. Watch the road,' Ashley yelled as they hit the soft sand on the side and began a slow skid.

'Picky picky,' he mumbled, correcting the Landy. But he kept his focus on the road after that.

Looking for wildlife, Ashley gazed into the bush. Scott's trained eyes invariably spotted something first and he would point it out to her. A kudu here, a small steenbok there; a majestic sable slipping silently into the shadows of a huge tree, its scimitar-like horns a fascination to Ashley; a zebra proudly wearing its distinctive stripes in the dry, yellowed grassland of a *vlei;* and the silent wildebeest who accompanied them everywhere.

'There, see the wildebeest? He can smell well. The zebra sees well, so they stick together, each in turn warning the other of impending danger. They coexist,' Scott explained.

She knew she was being pulled deeper and deeper into the heart of Africa, but she couldn't stop herself. She couldn't stop imagining what a life in Africa would be like, and she couldn't imagine Scott living anywhere else but under the copper sun in Africa.

Oh my god! Am I thinking long-term here? When did that sneak up on me? And how the hell did my mind make the jump from kisses and cuddles to staying in Africa?

She didn't notice that Scott had slowed and they'd come to a stop.

Scott manoeuvred Lucinda into the shade of a huge camel thorn tree and began to unpack yet another one of Lisa's magnificent meals.

'We are here, it's almost three o'clock, but we might as well eat lunch while we wait. Zol and the others should materialise soon,' Scott said as he unrolled the grass mat for them to sit on.

'And if they don't?'

'Zol always keeps his word. He once said to a young boy, "I promise to keep your daddy safe. I'd rather die than return without him." Months passed. My father and Zol were fighting the war against communism, and then one day our dogs went ballistic. Zol stood at the security gate, my father tied onto his horse. Both were wounded and covered in blood, but Zol smiled, and reminded me that he'd kept his promise. He had brought my father home.'

Ashley's heart broke for the young boy witnessing such brutality. She frowned. 'Oh, Scott ...'

'My father lived to fight and die another day. Zol brought him home again that time, too. Zol keeps his word. He taught me that it's the single most important thing a man possesses. His word. If you speak crap, you deliver crap. If you promise, you must deliver.'

Smiling, Ashley lay down on the picnic mat next to Lucinda.

Time passed Africa-style, with no one keeping an eye on the clock. Scott continued to chat about the legends of the area, of the native tales he'd grown up with. Hand in hand, they watched the sun set, the giant red fireball shimmering as it sank beyond the African sky. The crickets chirped, and an owl hooted somewhere nearby.

Scot sat up. 'About time,' he muttered.

'Where?' Ashley asked as she too shifted her position on the mat.

Zol materialised out of the black night. Along with Vusi, Sunday, Sipho, James, Mistake and Kwiella who suddenly appeared from the outline of the scrub, as if they were mirages that chose to take shape.

'Good to see you, Zol.' Scott embraced and clapped the older man on the back. The others gathered around and shook his hand, nodding in greeting to Ashley as one by one they lowered themselves onto the dirt on the outside of the picnic mat to sit baboon-like, on their haunches in a circle, talking Ndebele. Ashley invited them to sit on the mat but Zol refused, and the others followed his lead.

'Miss Ashley, it's not our way,' was all the explanation that Zol gave Ashley.

But they did share what food was available, and drank bottles of water and Coke during the debriefing.

'The poachers are camped here.' Sipho indicated a place on the map spread between them. 'They have a large stash of ivory, rhino horn and many animal skins. There are forty or fifty people in the camp, including two black women and one white woman. She might be coloured. No children. I could recognise one man, a head of a tribe from the Tosholotsho homeland.'

'That explains the lack of movement through this area to harvest the sausage trees,' Scott said. 'Estimated time to their camp?'

Sipho scratched his head. 'Maybe one hour on the road, but they will see us coming. Forty minutes if we go bundu-bashing and if we are lucky to find an easy way for the *bakkie*.'

'We are too close here. Anyone else you recognise?' Scott asked, looking around the men.

'I see Boss Lawrence from Nyamandhlovu drive away, with Boss Joubert, the butcher from Bulawayo,' reported Mistake, in broken heavily accented English.

'You sure?'

'Yes, Boss,' Mistake said.

Scott got a small notepad out from under the seat in Lucinda. 'Okay, we have at least three local helpers. Anyone else distinguishable?'

'The big man who drives the truck. He has a scar down his cheek, dark black from North Africa,' Kwiella reported, 'and the old freedom fighter, the *Sope*.'

Scott looked up. 'The albino? You certain it's the same one?'

'Boss Scott, that man cut off my brother's ears and tongue. I know that man and his stink.' Kwiella spat into the dirt.

The discussion was serious so Ashley kept quiet, not wanting to interrupt the men. Instead, she sat still, trying hard to understand what was being said. Most of it was in Ndebele, but when they mixed it with English she got a smattering of information and could guess what was happening. The few words she understood made her realise there were a few people involved in the poachers' ring, and Scott and Kwiella appeared to be worried about someone.

'If it's the albino, we must move soon. He could've picked up the rendezvous from the radio and they might know we are close.' Scott glanced at Ashley.

'Boss Scott, there is also the army commander for the President's Guard. He was in the truck with Boss Joubert,' Vusi said.

'What?' Scott asked a little loudly.

'Eric Mbeki, Commander in the President's Personal Guard. He was there.'

'I heard you the first time, Vusi. I only wish I hadn't. All right, this ring is too big to take down without help. Eight men are not enough. Sipho, Kwiella, surveillance on the north and west. Mistake, Sunday, on the south and east. Vusi and James, I want you running between, checking on information. Radio silence, everyone. You know the drill. I want them watched 24/7. Zol, come with me. We'll need reinforcements. We need—' Scott was cut off as gunfire rang out.

Men who had moments before been squatting, flattened themselves against the dirt.

Scott pushed Ashley down onto the ground, making her less of a target. He held her down with his right arm, and put his left hand over her mouth. A single white streak rose into the sky above them.

'*Baleka*!' Zol commanded.

As the white flare exploded and lit the night sky above them, the anti-poaching unit jumped to their feet and sprinted into the shadows of the trees on the rim of the flare. Bursts of semi-automatic gunfire followed them.

Zol, Ashley and Scott were illuminated by the flare, exposed to anyone around them to see. Both men were shielding Ashley, putting themselves between her and the poachers. In the sudden attack they had no escape route planned. They were sitting ducks, lying in the open under the tree next to Lucinda.

Scott rolled Ashley with him under Lucinda for shelter. Zol bumped into her again on the opposite side.

'Keys?' Zol whispered.

'In the ignition.'

Zol manoeuvred down and around Scott and Ashley and onto the right side of the vehicle. Then he silently slipped up into the driver's side, in between the seat and the pedals.

A single shot rang out. It zinged over Zol's head and into the tree trunk behind him with a sickening *thunk*. Then, just as the flare began to lose its illumination, Zol started Lucinda, jammed Scott's rifle on the accelerator and jumped off, leaving the Land Rover to roll on the hard dirt and gain momentum. Scott held Ashley still, waiting as the Landy cleared off from them. Waiting for a safe distance to form between them and the vehicle.

Bullets rained into the Land Rover. She continued straight for a while, hit a bump, then turned south. More bullets followed, the metallic *ting-ting* of metal destroying metal.

But by the time the next bright flare illuminated the sky, Zol and Scott had pulled Ashley off the ground, flanked her and each holding an arm, were running in the opposite direction into the night, away from the departing Lucinda and the poachers.

To Ashley, it seemed like the gunfire never stopped, except when Zol let go his iron grip on her arm and ran a little out in front of them. 'No vehicle sounds. Good, they are also on foot.'

'Thank God!' Scott replied as he remained at her side, holding her arm.

They continued at a fast pace through the bush, ducking when they felt bush overhead and dodging the black shapes of solid trees in their path. Ashley thought they ran blindly and if it had not been for Zol so close in front of her, she'd have been lost.

Her lungs burned with the effort. Her heart pumped so fast she could hardly breathe, and a cold sweat ran down her back. Scott still dragged her forwards, through the black bush. She fell again. He half lifted her as she struggled to disentangle herself from the *wag-'n-bietjie* bushes that had snagged her hair.

'Zol, wait. We have about a thirty-minute lead. We need to camouflage Ashley.' Scott hissed loud enough for Zol to immediately stop his easy gait and turn to help.

He reached into his pack and gave a tub to Scott.

Scott opened it, put a little in his hand, then bent down and added sand. Then he poured water from Zol's bottle into his palm. He started smearing the mixture onto Ashley's face.

'What is that?' she asked, keeping her voice low. 'It smells revolting.'

'We need to dim your face. It's snuff and sand mixed together. We have no camo cream to blacken your face. For the night, so this'll have to do.'

'Not good enough. Miss Ashley still shines like an angel,' Zol said.

'Take your shirt off,' Scott said. 'No Ashley, not you. I was talking to Zol.' He smiled at her and she could see his white teeth flash in the darkness of the night.

Zol removed his shirt and passed it to Scott.

'But Zol needs his shirt,' protested Ashley.

'He's black. He'll blend. Your shirt is like a target. Put Zol's shirt on now.'

'I am!' She pulled on the damp sweaty shirt. The adrenaline rush began to wear off and shock was setting in. Her hands shook as she struggled with the small green buttons.

'Don't dare go to pieces on me. You're stronger than that. We need to cover distance or we'll be hyena fodder.'

Her chin lifted defiantly. 'I'll manage.'

She watched Scott quickly rub his own face with the snuff mixture. Roughly he pushed her hands aside and did the buttons up for her. Then he hugged her close and gave her a sound kiss on the mouth.

'Good. Zol's shirt masks your scent too. It's pretty distinctive in the bush, broadcasting that you're not native to the area.' He smiled as he said it. He was now nearly as dark as Zol. 'Ashley, you're doing well. I need you to continue to be strong to get through this.' He stepped back and looked at her critically.

Her long blonde hair was loose, her hat probably left sitting where they had eaten their late lunch. Any inexperienced tracker could follow the strands already left on the *wag-'n-bietjie* bushes. Her hair was so light, someone would see it like a halo in the bush. 'Is there any way you can keep your hair up and away?'

She immediately ran her hands through it and roughly started a French plait down her back.

'Nice. Zol, what have you got that we can tie up Ashley's hair with?'

Zol rummaged in his small pack and then all the pockets of his pants. He took his boot off and sliced a tubular piece off the top of his sock.

'Socks?' Scott asked.

'Gertrude.'

'We will talk, another time. Here Ashley, use this.' He handed her Zol's sock end and floppy jungle hat. 'Wear Zol's hat, and make sure your hair stays covered. Pull it low over your head and down at the back. That's it,' he whispered, as he fitted the hat onto her head.

Ashley's teeth began to chatter.

Scott applied more of the snuff and sand mixture to her hands and legs. He made sure her shirt was buttoned up to the top button, the sleeves rolled down and fastened. Then he took her holster out from under the shirt and rearranged it correctly on her hip. 'You need to keep this close,' he whispered, his lips gently brushing her ear.

A shiver ran down her spine.

'You see any shine, Zol?' he asked.

'No shine,' Zol said, after doing a tour around Ashley, scrutinising her. 'If we move north and a little east, we should get onto the main road through the centre of the reserve. We can shadow the road till we get to Shumba camp. There we can get help. Send help to the men. I think they might have got Mistake or James, someone definitely got hit in their direction. I heard a bullet strike flesh.'

Ashley took a deep breath. She was trying her best to control her shivers.

Scott shook his head, signalling for Zol not to say more about the men they both knew were shot. For now, he needed to keep Ashley going, not give her a reason to fall apart.

'We split here, Scott,' Zol said. 'You take Miss Ashley. I'll double back and deal with the poachers behind us.'

Ashley took another breath. The men in this country were nuts. In the middle of the pitch-black bush, with wild animals everywhere, Zol was going to double back and try to get the poachers off their track.

Zol nodded to Ashley, put his hand on Scott's shoulder and then, like the first rain on sun-parched soil, melted into the bush.

Comprehension hit Ashley. If Zol knew how to blend into the bush, so could the poachers. And they could pop out at any time without her seeing them, until it was too late. She began to hyperventilate, light spots danced in front of her eyes and she could hear blood thundering in her ears.

'Steady. We must start moving again.' Scott bent her forward and rubbed her back in circular movements.

'I'm so scared, Scott.'

'It's natural. Control the fear. Don't let it control you. Breathe.' He continued rubbing her back and, after a few minutes, she straightened and breathed deeply.

'Don't worry. Once we are on the go again, your adrenaline level will top up, and you'll be strong enough to move mountains.'

'Thanks for the vote of confidence,' she replied dryly as she began to trot again, quite certain her body wouldn't cope, but also determined not to quit.

She was going to survive to see another day.

The sky was inky black, with stars peeking out of it's velvet curtain. Ashley had no idea how long they had been running, but she guessed close on an hour and a half, maybe two hours.

'Break. I need a break,' she gasped, too tired to open her mouth fully.

Scott tugged her arm, his strong fingers gripping the fabric and propelling her along behind him. 'No, don't stop. Another few minutes. You can do this, you can ... Run. You'll find your second wind. Let it do the work. Just keep moving.'

Ashley forced her exhausted body to move again, although the response was sluggish, as if it refused the instructions given from her brain and did not want to cooperate. But slowly it moved on its own and she felt Scott relax his iron grip on her arm and release her.

'That's my girl,' he encouraged softly.

It seemed like they'd been blindly bashing through the bush forever. Scott led, and she followed as close as possible in his footsteps. Her heart pounded and her whole body burned, but she ignored it. She ran knowing that if she didn't, she'd be dead.

After a while, she noticed her body was no longer feeling as pained or stressed about the demands placed on it. Her breathing freed up in her lungs and she felt a lightness she'd never experienced before, as if she could continue at this pace all night. She continued running behind Scott.

She inhaled through her nose and out through her mouth, dodging the bushes that clawed at her face as she passed. Her mind blanked out the terror that chased them as she focused on not losing Scott in the darkness of the night bush. The moon rose, huge, yellow and luminous. Animals chatted out there somewhere, but Ashley hardly heard them, blocking out everything else and concentrating on her breathing.

'Keep to the shadows. Moon's rising. Stay closer to me,' he instructed.

She obeyed, adjusting her step closer to his moving figure, almost into his shadow now cast by the moonlight. She realigned her focus point on his back, trusting him to keep clear of danger, and blazing a path for her to blindly follow. At last, he slowed a little, and then stopped beneath a huge mopani tree. They had startled a few small antelope as they ran, but hadn't encountered anything bigger, although Ashley had heard animals crashing away from them through the bush.

Now their luck had run out.

On the other side of the tree, a huge herd of buffalo took shape. Above the rushing of blood in her ears she was aware of their restlessness, the loud stomps of their hooves like deep-sounding drums as they milled around.

CHAPTER 7

'Up! Now!' Scott's hands firmly around her waist, he picked her up and swung her into the tree. Looking around, she grabbed onto branches as he pushed her backside, and clambered up as quickly as she could.

'Need a hand?' she turned to help him but he was already in the tree.

'Climb higher,' he said in a whisper.

She clawed her way up into the branches, testing the strength of each before transferring her weight, slowly gaining height. 'So, exactly why are we in the tree?'

'Big cat. Probably lions. The buffalo are spooked and it's not from us. We were downwind from them, so there must be a predator around. I don't want us to become the prey. Move up more. Let's see if we can spot the culprit.'

Ashley climbed still higher with Scott close behind her. She came to a place where the thick branch bowed slightly towards the trunk, and chose to settle there. Scott hung his legs over the branch above her, his back to the trunk, too. She searched the *veld* for a sign of any lion or other big cat predator. Nothing. She saw only the buffalo shapes, and heard only their grunting and low bellows.

'There.' Scott pointed. 'Beyond that fallen tree. One female lioness, poised to attack.'

Ashley stared into the yellow-tinged night. Suddenly, with a twitch of her tail, the cat exposed herself. 'I see it.'

'Look to her left. Another one slinking along. And a third one, there, behind the buffalo. She looks like an older lioness.'

Ashley stared at the feline hunters. They were so beautiful. She'd never witnessed anything like this before. The adrenaline that should have made her limbs stiff and cramped after the abrupt halt continued pumping, this time with excitement.

The moon slid behind a wispy cloud, and the matriarch lioness began her charge. Her tail slammed down onto the hard earth and she launched into a sprint towards a half-grown calf.

The buffalo scattered.

The youngster was expertly cut from the herd, and the notoriously protective mother buffalo lost her fight for her baby as the first lioness sunk her claws into its fat rump. Within seconds, another lioness had pounced on the calf's shoulder. A third joined the melee, hanging from the underside of the animal's neck, her teeth sinking into the jugular vein.

The calf had no chance. Together the lionesses dragged the youngster down to the ground and the loud bellows fell silent as it lost its fight for life.

Ashley watched as the lionesses ripped into the food, obviously starving, snarling at each other in competition. Where moments before they had been a team, now each fought to claim her share.

'Here comes the male. On the left, there. Can you see him?' Scott spoke close to her ear.

'Yes.'

'Watch.'

Ashley had not needed Scott's instruction, she couldn't remove her eyes from the scene below. She was fascinated and enthralled.

'Lazy sod. He never helped with that kill,' she said.

'That's a lion for you. The women do all the work and the men take the glory.'

'Hmm ... Look, there must be at least ten lions attempting to eat that buffalo calf.'

'A big pride, and there are still a few young males hanging back, probably about fifteen in total.'

'Would they have attacked us if you didn't get us up here?'

'It's possible. Some lions have been known to become man-killers, and if we got in their way, yeah they'd kill us.'

Ashley swallowed. 'Good thing for this tree then.'

'And such a comfortable one at that. No thorns,' Scott said.

The moon, now free of cloud, illuminated the kill in a bright silver light.

'What's the time?' she asked.

'Already ten o'clock.'

'Seems like we ran forever.'

'We were on the move for close on three hours, and later we will run again. But for now, just watch those lions, they are what will keep us safe for a while.'

Within an hour, the whole carcass was stripped clean by the feasting lions, their faces and legs red with blood. With its belly filled, a lion would walk off into the darkness. The remaining lions flopped down onto the ground to sleep.

Woohop-whoop.

Ashley gasped, then put her hand over her mouth as if she would take back the involuntary sound if she could. 'What was that?'

'A spotted hyena. They've smelled the kill and have come to investigate.'

'Can we go now?'

'Not yet. The lions are full, but there are still too many in the area. After they feed, they rest, and they could kill again tonight. The hyena shouldn't attack us. They are cowards and we're bigger than them, so they don't pose much of a threat. Only if we slept on the ground, and if we gave them the chance, they might come and bite off our faces. And no, they don't climb trees. So we are safe.' He smiled at her, then reached out and ran his hand down her dirty cheek. 'Ashley, I'm not meaning to scare you, just fast-track your education to surviving in the bush. We'll need to move again tonight, but not for a few hours. If the poachers come up on us, they'll find the lions, and those cats will not be happy. You'd do well trying to get a little sleep.'

She huffed. 'Yeah, right.'

'Hang on, I'll sit with you, it will make it a little more comfortable to sleep.' Scott moved in the tree, settling into a vee behind her. Gently he moved her until her legs were either side of the branch, and she snuggled her back into his chest. When he began to massage her shoulders, she flinched away.

'I'm—' he began his apology at the same time she said, 'Sorry, it's a habit—'

She knew her reaction was unnatural, especially after the time they had spent together earlier in the day. She really liked Scott, and wanted him to understand that physical contact had become associated with a childhood incident.

'I can't believe I'm telling you this, it's just ...' She took his silence as her cue to continue. 'I was six,' she said. 'I had no concept of sexuality, or rights and wrongs. We had an older neighbour, a boy who was fourteen or so, who used to play with us. One day we were playing hide and seek with my sisters. The boy and I were hiding in a cupboard. He was more sexually aware than me, and his proposition and frontal exposure at that age, it took its toll on my own sexuality.' She looked down at her hands, wound around each other.

'It's okay,' Scott said.

She smiled weakly at him, and placed her hands on either side of the branch. 'He was in the process of attempting to manhandle me into a sexual act when I screamed, and my sister Sue, who was twelve, opened the cupboard and pandemonium broke loose. Sue saved me then, and I've been the "ice queen" since. The touch-me-not kid; the one who doesn't do the kissing thing; who didn't do the parade of teenage boyfriends. Even Michael, my ex, never touched me unless I initiated it.'

'What happened to the boy? Was he punished?'

'We never told anyone, but my sister punched him in the face so hard she made his nose bleed. I still run it through my head over and over, and I can't believe that I did nothing. That's what bothers me so much, I did *nothing*—'

'You were six years old. You couldn't do anything. Don't blame yourself. It was his problem, not yours.'

'I know that. But normally when a man comes close, I can't help the shudders that come over me.'

'I have noticed less of those over the last week. At first, when I touched you there was lots of it, but this afternoon, a big difference. You're melting, ice queen. You don't need to live in that cold castle. It wasn't your fault. Don't ever think it was. Let it go.'

'You think I haven't tried?'

'I'm sure you have, and gone to counselling.'

'No counselling. I was always the tomboy, no one expected me to have dark secrets like that. I never even told my mother, it was just Sue and I who knew, and now you.'

'Where can I find him? I'll fly to Australia and beat the crap out of him for you.'

She smiled at that. 'I have no idea what happened to that family.'

'It's over twenty years ago, it's time you let the boogieman out of the cupboard, so to speak, and freed yourself.'

'Guess it's just a habit now ...'

'Habits can be broken. I'm going to rub those tired shoulders now. You know the touching is coming, try not flinch.'

His hands rested gently back on her shoulders, and she didn't attempt to pull away at all. No adverse reaction. It was almost like she wanted his hands on her, and having shared her secret, her body was at last responding to what her brain was saying. 'Thanks for listening, and not judging me.'

He didn't answer; just continued his massage.

The night sounds all around them played a hypnotic tune and slowly Ashley relaxed. She let her head fall back and brush against his arm.

He bent forward and kissed her briefly then pulled away and ran his finger down her cheek.

'Scott?'

'I'm not sure I could handle it if I lost you.'

'Really?'

'Yes. Now sleep.'

Ashley closed her eyes, and rolled her head on her neck to relieve the tensioned muscles. She could feel the heat from Scott's body as it pressed against her. It felt good. Right. Bone tired, her mind began to drift.

What seemed only a short time later, Scott shook her awake.

'Come on, it's almost two.'

The hyena was still whooping, its call loud, a nightjar sang in the darkness, and the jackals cried to each other far away in the distance, the forlorn sound sending shivers up Ashley's spine. The moon had passed over them and was on its slow descent from the sky. Together they climbed down the tree.

Zol appeared at Scott's side.

'Four men, one good black tracker. No albino, we are lucky. They are gaining on us. They have a hunting torch and a portable battery pack to follow the spoor clearly. There were five, but one took a leak and ...' Zol looked down at the ground.

Ashley didn't understand. 'And what?'

'Miss Ashley, he won't be following us again. Ever,' explained Zol.

She gasped. 'You killed him?'

Zol said nothing.

Her legs didn't want to support her, and as they began to buckle under her, Scott caught her around her waist.

'Ashley, we need to move. Zol did what was necessary to buy us more time, slow them down. Understand, it's them or us. This isn't a game. If they catch us, they'll kill Zol and me. They'll rape you, pass you from one man to the other.'

'But the Geneva Convention—' she began.

'You are being naive. This is a Third World country, not Australia. I've tried to explain to you there are worse things than death. Being passed around like a rag doll between those men would be worse than death for you—and for me. Zol has protected us, he's done what needed to be done. We need to continue to do our part. You must get angry with the poachers, and remain angry. Use the anger to fuel your body so that you can survive,' he said as he hugged her to him. 'You up to it?'

She nodded, not sure if she was reassuring him or herself with the gesture. 'I don't have a choice really, do I?'

'No.'

'Miss Ashley—' Zol started.

She reached over and touched his arm. 'I understand, Zol. It's just that I wasn't brought up with this kind of violence. It's all new, and really scary to me. Thank you.'

He rewarded her with a bright grin, then turned his back and started moving away. 'How many lion, Scott?'

'Probably fifteen.'

Zol nodded. 'They'll kill again before dawn. That calf was not big enough.'

Ashley glanced back at the tree. The hyenas looked at them in curiosity, and she knew this moment would be forever etched in her mind: a photographic memory, set in a time frame, firmly imprinted into her brain. All she had to do was survive, to make sure she kept that memory for a long time to come.

. . .

The moon was in its final display for the night, in competition with the first colours of pre-dawn light, hinting at the beginning of a new day on the opposite side of the sky. Radiant reds, oranges and hues of blue ignited the skyline as if an artist had thrown his paint pots across a canvas, slashing colours parallel with the distant horizon.

Ashley froze in her tracks. Zol had motioned with his hand for them to stop. He sneaked forward silently and then disappeared into the thick bush. Her heart hammered in the unnatural quiet, the deep sound of the blood pumping through her veins loud in her ears. She peered towards the place that Zol suspected was the location of a waterhole.

Zol could smell water. Scott had explained that owing to the storm on the day she arrived, the water should have collected in the depression of the small saltpan they knew was nearby.

A guineafowl called out, and a *ri-peep-eep* sound echoed from Scott, his hands working over his mouth, mimicking the fowl to perfection.

Ashley looked at him, amazed. She'd learned so much about him before this escapade, but his bush skills were astonishing. He dropped his hands and said, 'Come. That was Zol. All's clear.'

Together they stepped out of the thick bush. Before them was a clearing, the radiant light mirrored on the water surface occasionally broken by an energetic water skipper, or a shadow from a dove or a weaver flying overhead. The pan was small and there was thick mud all around it, churned up by its frequent animal visitors. Zol was digging a hole in the mud.

'What's he doing?'

'Digging for clean water. The water in the pan is dirty, and we can't drink it. He'll take the clearer water from the hole, and he has water purification pills to drop in, so we'll have clean water to drink. Last thing we need is dysentery or cholera.'

'Now see, that's why I love you,' she said. 'I'd have gone and drank the water directly from the pan.' She hit his arm playfully with the back of her hand, and began walking towards Zol.

. . .

Scott looked at her. Had he heard right? Had Ashley just said she loved him, or was it a moment of facetiousness, casually thrown at him? She seemed unaware that a bolt out of the sky couldn't have shocked him more than those three little words. He wanted to crow like a rooster, but instead, he simply stored the memory close to his heart.

As if sucker punched, he realised that he cared for her.

Was it as a soulmate? He had no idea.

Had he fallen in love with her? He didn't think so.

Lust? Definitely. But love?

The concept would have sent him running for the hills before, but with Ashley, he was willing to explore it. He knew one thing for certain: her four-week stay was definitely going to be too short.

For a moment he was still, as if caught in the headlights of an oncoming vehicle, then he followed her. He couldn't—wouldn't—let her know how he felt. There was too much at stake if he got tangled with her ... his ranch—his heart.

Ashley and Zol had collected water in a small steel pot from Zol's pack, and he was tossing in the purification pills. He handed Ashley a tin mug, beautifully decorated with bright beads in a native Ndebele pattern. She dipped it into the pot then drank the cool water in a deep gulp.

'Yuck, it tastes like chemicals.'

'Rather chemicals than cholera,' Scott said as he reached them. 'Drink faster. Down it, it's easier.'

Ashley drank again. Scott watched her throat contract as she swallowed. Had it only been yesterday he'd nibbled exactly where the soft hollow of her throat met her chest?

She wiped her mouth with the back of her hand. 'It's not so bad when you chug it down fast,' she said, but pulled a face that said otherwise.

Scott indicated for Zol to have his turn next. The small pot needed filling to make a second round, but soon they had all drunk their fill. Zol produced three pieces of biltong from his pack, and they sat on the edge of the clearing, shaded by the trees, and ate breakfast. Together Zol and Scott sorted through the small pack and carefully checked the supplies.

'I didn't know I was so hungry,' Ashley said, once she'd finished her last bite of delicious biltong, the texture almost like the Australian jerky she'd grown up eating as a treat in the city.

'Unless we find an ostrich egg, wild plum bush or something else along the way, that could be all you're going to get till lunchtime,' Scott told her. 'We have another seven sticks, plenty of water purification pills, some dehydrated peas, onion pieces and some beans. We only have one water bottle, and that must remain with Zol. The pot has a lid, so if we are careful, we can carry a small supply of water with us.'

'Sure, more chemicals for the science experiment,' she joked. Her spirits were high. They had survived the night and in the daylight the bush didn't look as daunting or oppressive. In her mind, everything was going to work out just fine.

Scott and Zol knew what they were doing.

Sure, the poachers did too, but she was going to hedge her bets on Scott and Zol.

She had to—her life depended on it.

'Ashley, take off your t-shirt. If we use it to make a pack, I'll wear it under my shirt.'

Ashley turned her back on the waiting men and removed Zol's shirt, slipping it between her thighs as she tugged off her t-shirt. Putting Zol's shirt back on, she turned and handed her warm t-shirt to Scott.

His eyes met hers and she could see desire deep within them. But something else too—a tenderness as if they caressed her face. Her skin goosebumped in awareness and longing. She smiled as she realised she didn't feel the urge to run in the opposite direction.

Scott wanted to bury his face in the softness of the t-shirt and inhale her feminine scent, but instead he took out the Swiss army knife he always carried on his belt and cut the shirt. Looking at her he said, 'Thanks, I'll buy you another to replace it. We can go shopping in Sandton City in Johannesburg if we can't find one locally.'

Ashley stared at her ruined R.M. Williams t-shirt, and then watched as he modelled a makeshift pack out of it.

He stretched the small sleeve and cut it so that he could make a knot in the bottom of it forming an enclosed space. Into this, he stuck the pot, sitting it firmly inside the sleeve. He put three pieces of biltong into the bundle, then balled the pot over and over in the fabric till it was tightly bound. Finally, he adjusted it to sit securely on his waist, then he pulled his own shirt down over it. Ashley realised she'd been staring at his sixpack. She swallowed as she found herself short of breath.

Scott smiled at her. 'All ready to move? Zol is going to double back and see what our friends are up to this morning. We're heading northeast. Hopefully we'll get to Shumba today. From there I can contact Tessa and Kevin. He can fly in to collect us in his helicopter.'

'He has a helicopter too?'

'Sure. A whole aviation business. Kevin part-owns one of the biggest independent aviation businesses in Zimbabwe.'

'You're kidding? And he flies that piece of junk held together with wire?'

'The plane you came in on is his "baby", the one he began his business with. He flies her home every now and again just for an excuse to keep her. He says he can't afford to forget what he started with.'

'Now that's interesting. I thought he was just another bush pilot.'

'He is, just a successful one.' Scott contemplated admitting that he was Kevin's business partner. Ashley already knew more about him and his ranch affairs than any other volunteer ever had. Actually, more than any other person knew, other than Zol. But he didn't want her knowing more at that moment, as he still wasn't sure how much more of himself he could share. 'Pull your hat down again, you are showing too much of your face in the front.'

'I'm surprised you can see my face under the stuff you plastered all over it. It feels like my skin's cracking.'

'By tonight it will be if we don't keep it covered. A whole day in the sun with no sunscreen on your fair skin, and your face could have third-degree burns. Keep it covered with Zol's hat. It's double protection, keeping your hair from leaving a trail a mile wide for that tracker to follow, and keeping your face from burning.'

'What if we don't make it that far today?' Ashley asked.

'Then we're in trouble,' Scott said.

Zol clasped Scott's shoulder in their farewell ritual, and jogged off into the thick bush behind them. Scott turned her around by her shoulders to face in the opposite direction, gave her butt a small slap and said, 'Time to move.'

He strode away from her.

An astonished Ashley quickly caught up. He changed their pace from a fast walk to a slow trot. She ran next to Scott, not behind him. He glanced in her direction and smiled, but within seconds, he was focused on escape again.

Hours later, the sun hot and high in the sky above them, they came to a bitumen road. Ashley's legs had once again found an easy gait, but she knew Scott kept his pace down to accommodate hers. They had stopped for a small morning tea of water and shared one piece of biltong. Her stomach had long ago stopped grumbling for more. She kept running because she understood if she didn't, she'd be dead, and that was not a viable option.

'Bush, quick,' Scott hissed.

Ashley knew the drill well. She ran straight off the road and into the scrub at the side. She crouched low, but kept moving till she heard a signal from Scott. If she heard a guineafowl, she'd lie flat on the ground, arms over her head and remain there until he came and found her. If she heard a fish eagle she could stop, crouch low and wait for him to call her either by name or with a wolf-whistle. If she heard a lion she was to run for her life.

Her ears strained against the natural noises of the bush. The incessant buzzing of a fly. A fish eagle called. She stopped and crouched low, peering through the bushes to where she'd just run from, straining to see Scott. She felt the ground under her vibrate, and heard a large diesel vehicle approaching on the road. It amazed her that he could hear the motors long before she could.

The distinct sound of exhaust brakes being released as the vehicle slowed then stopped. She listened to the conversation. Scott's voice, loud in the deserted bush. 'Hi. Could you give us a lift to Shumba? My *bakkie* broke down, and I couldn't fix it. Damn radio's broken too. We could do with a lift.'

'We?' an African voice asked.

Scott let loose a wolf-whistle. Ashley straightened up, made sure her gun was concealed under Zol's shirt, and walked out of the bush with as much normality as she could manage.

A large air-conditioned luxury coach stood with its door open, the painted zebra stripes on its side displaying the logo of one of the safari industries of the area. She smiled at the driver as Scott reached down to help her up the stairs.

'Thank you, Elliott,' she said, reading his name tag.

'My pleasure, Madam,' replied Elliott, as he closed the door with an automated swish.

Ashley sank onto the velveteen seat closest to the door. Scott sat next to her, immediately putting his arm around her shoulder.

Turning slightly in his seat, Elliott said in hushed tones, 'There's a toilet on board so you can freshen up, and a minibar downstairs. Help yourselves. It's on the company.' He smiled broadly, and then spoke into the microphone headset. 'Ladies and gentlemen, as you can see, we have picked up two park rangers whose vehicle has broken down. Please make them welcome. Thank you for your patience. We'll continue on our journey through this lovely national reserve.'

A small round of applause went up and a few calls of 'welcome on board' could be heard. Ashley felt her face grow warm.

Scott shook his head as she attempted to conceal herself in the seat. He moved to stand near Elliott, drawing the crowd's curiosity away from her.

After a while, Ashley got up and made her way down the aisle and into the galley. The toilet was a welcome sight and she realised she'd only gone once since late yesterday afternoon. In her nervous state, the urge to urinate had disappeared. Once she was done and had worked out how to flush the tiny toilet, she looked into the vanity mirror.

She was a mess.

She washed her hands, face and neck as best she could, then turned up the sleeves of Zol's shirt and pocketed the hat. She looked almost human when she checked her reflection again. Outside the lavatory, she helped herself to four cold Cokes from the fridge. With the bottles tinkling against each other, she made her way back to Scott.

'Drink?'

'Silly question,' he said, and smiled at her as he took two of the drinks. He downed the first one without stopping.

Ashley dragged heavily on the bottle of the sugary drink, happy for the energy boost to her body. She smiled at Scott. Talking in a hushed tone, she asked him, 'How do you know you can trust the driver?'

'I don't, but it's a bus full of tourists. Hopefully they won't try anything with all these witnesses around.'

'And Zol?'

'He'll see my sign in the sand next to the road and know we caught a lift.' He reached for her hand. It was beginning to feel cool in the air-conditioning.

A large herd of elephant crossed the road ahead and the bus stopped. The tourists, no longer straining to catch a glimpse of the new arrivals on the bus, focused their energies on the elephant instead. Their cameras clicked and whirred as they filmed the majestic beasts ambling along, taking their own time over the bitumen and into the bush on the other side. One baby elephant up to its normal inquisitive mischief began to approach the tour bus. The driver put the vehicle into reverse and slowly backed it away. A mother or 'nanny' trumpeted at the retreating bus as if it was her victory, smacked the little elephant with her trunk and brought it back into the herd. The tourists loved the show.

Scott clutched his seat, worried for everyone. Not accustomed to being out of control of a situation, he wasn't sure if the bus driver was up to facing an enraged elephant. Elliott turned around and spoke quietly with his microphone off his head.

'Mr Decker. I recognised you right away when you flagged me down, but I had to be one hundred per cent sure I wasn't making a mistake.'

'A cautious man, Elliott. A good thing in this day and age,' Scott said.

'Zol is my comrade, so you and your madam are my friends-but-one.'

Scott looked at Elliott's face with its earnest, open expression. There was no hint of malice in it. He trusted his gut instinct. 'Thank you. Can you take us nearer Zebra Pan Lodge?' He didn't correct Elliott's assumption about Ashley being his wife.

'It's already two o'clock, we have until six thirty to get out of the reserve and back to the Hwange Safari Lodge. I should make it, if I drop you on the bitumen before the dirt road into Zebra Pan. Is that close enough?'

'Thanks. That'll be great.'

Elliott revved up the bus. The elephant had cleared and he spoke into his microphone. 'Ladies and gentleman, I've been told there were lion spotted not long ago in the Deka Safari Area. We are going to make our way towards there now. I'm in the front should you have any questions about the various animals we view.'

'He's good,' mumbled Scott into Ashley's ear. 'Did you hear our conversation?'

'A little, he knows of you and will take us nearly to Zebra Pan Lodge.'

'You got the gist. Put your head down, Zebra Pan is still two hours away. I'll wake you when we get closer.'

'Mmm,' she replied, half conscious. Her body had already decided for her that it couldn't move anymore, and rest was what she needed. She snuggled closer into Scott and drifted into a dreamless sleep.

Once again, Scott was shaking her shoulder. 'Ashley, I need you to stay on the bus.'

'Where's the bus going?'

'Hwange Safari Lodge. It's a big hotel, lots of people around.'

Elliott took his microphone off his head and whispered. 'Mr Decker.'

Scott immediately moved to sit close to Elliott and they talked in such low tones, Ashley couldn't hear them. What seemed like an age later, Scott stood up and came back to his seat.

'What?' Ashley asked.

'Elliott saw a *bakkie* behind us. It's got hunting lamps mounted on the back. He wanted to know how bad the trouble is that we've placed the tourists in. They have a radio code on the CB for emergencies, but given the magnitude of the poaching ring, he agreed with me that he doesn't want to call for help as we can't trust too many people in this.'

'Why's he helping?'

'His livelihood depends on the animals, and he detests poachers. He started in an anti-poaching unit on one of the other private farms in the Dete area. Poachers killed his family. While he was still in hunting training, he reported a blood spoor from a client. The client turned out to be a poacher who was scoping the area. They thought they could intimidate him into keeping his silence.'

'That's sad.' She glanced at Elliott, her forehead furrowed deeply.

'Unfortunately, it's common. In various stages of intimidation, sometimes the hunter or tracker's wife is beaten and raped if they find out who the informant is.'

'How barbaric!'

'We're going to stop the bus, and while Elliott makes a show of checking the tyres, we'll monitor the vehicle. It may pull over to help or there may be trouble. If they are innocently using the same road, keeping to the same speed, then they should simply pass us. Hopefully it's nothing, but if not, I'll cut across from here and get to Zebra Pan on foot. I need you to stay on the bus. If anything happens, Elliott will make sure that he remains with you when you get to Hwange Safari Lodge. Book into a room and I'll pay them later.'

'How do you know I can trust him?'

'He knows Zol will cut his throat if a hair on your head is damaged. Zol is akin to my brother, and Elliott thinks you are my wife, so you get the same protection.'

'You have some strange customs, do you know that?'

Elliot's voice interrupted them. 'Ladies and gentleman. We are stopping for a brief while. I need to check on one of the tyres on the bus. Please everyone remain in your seats. Remember this is a game reserve, and there are dangerous animals outside. Thank you for your patience.' Elliott pushed the button and with a swish the door opened and the hot air rushed into the cool, air-conditioned coach.

'Go to the loo, so if they do come on board, they won't see you,' whispered Scott. He squeezed her shoulder and then disappeared down the stairwell to exit the bus.

She did as she was told. This was no time for heroics. She trusted Scott's instincts, and responded to the tone of his voice by following his command. The only problem was when she was inside the small lavatory, she had no idea what was happening outside.

After what seemed like an eternity, the bus started up again, and continued its journey. She left the galley area and slowly peered over the stairway at the seat Scott had been in. But Scott was not there.

CHAPTER 8

Scott's body strained under the bus. He quickly looped his legs onto the front axle, his hands clung like a monkey to small ridges underneath. Within seconds, the wheels of the blue vehicle cruised past, showering the bus in dust as it veered to the right and off the bitumen road to pass. Then it stopped and began a slow reverse back to the front of the bus. A pair of dusty brown crocodile-skin boots exited onto the road. Thick hairy legs sprouted from the boots. They approached Elliott, who was making a show of checking the rear tyres.

'You gotta problem?' the man asked in a heavy Afrikaans accent.

'I thought I had a rock stuck between the tyres,' he heard Elliott say. 'But there is nothing. I knew I shouldn't have gone off the road earlier to get a better look at that snake. There's an American woman on the bus who's been wanting to look at snakes all day.'

Scott could picture Elliott shaking his head as if he didn't believe snakes were good enough to watch all day, and the woman had been wasting everyone's time.

'Look there, she is taking pictures of you and I talking now through the window. She's a writer, a journalist or something.'

Scott smiled at Elliott's ingenuity at ensuring the tree-trunk legs realised he was being monitored from the bus. Everyone knew there was no slipping anything past a journo.

Elliott said, 'Perhaps the tyre pressure is not correct, and the inside one is going flat. Do you have a pressure gauge?'

'Yous stupid or somethink? You can't check that with a normal gauge. That's a bus not a taxi, *kaffir*.'

'Perhaps I should get back to the hotel so the mechanics can check it out. Thanks for stopping.'

'*Ja*. I wanted to know if you saw anyone in the reserve today? Someone try flag you down to stop for them?'

'No.'

'I'm looking for my friends who was hunting last night outside the boarder. They didn't return to camp. I thinks they gotted lost.'

'I'll keep a look out for them. I can ask the other drivers for you on the radio?'

'*Nee*, is okay. They probably back at camp now laughing because I is looking for thems.'

'Hope so. If not, call the hotel and we can organise an official search party for them.'

'*Ja*.'

The boots walked down the length of the bus towards Scott's hiding place, then stopped and turned back towards Elliott. 'Hey, if you sees them, bell me on the local CB frequency. My name is *Meneer* Lawrence.' He walked back to his *bakkie* and drove off.

Ashley returned to her seat like a zombie. Obviously, as discussed, she was to go to Hwange Safari Lodge.

The *bakkie* must have been trouble. She felt panic rise in her throat. Telling Scott she was okay was one thing, believing it was another. She was alone in what she had so recently learned was a hostile country and the one person she'd depended heavily upon throughout the last twenty-four hours had just deserted her.

Left her alone.

On a bus in the middle of the bush.

The same bush that held the poachers who were trying to kill them.

She sat down heavily and forced herself not to look back to where Scott might be in the bushes somewhere. She had to survive this last section of the trip back to Delmonica. Scott had to survive too.

She felt the bus accelerate again. The speed limit in the reserve was sixty kilometres an hour, but at that speed the tourists would hardly see the game. Elliott was pushing hard, trying to make up time for the long detour and still get his guests out of the reserve by closing time.

'Madam Ashley?' He called to her.

'Yes.' She crossed the aisle to sit directly behind him.

'Mr Decker will move fast in the bush now. It's good you come to the lodge, safe with me.'

'Thanks.' But she didn't feel safe from being left by Scott.

An elderly woman tottered to the front of the bus, the telescopic lens attached to the camera around her neck nearly the size of a football. 'Excuse me, Elliott, but I thought I saw the game guard get out, and he didn't get back in.' She sounded distressed at the thought of leaving anyone behind.

Ashley frowned.

'That's correct, Madam,' he said. 'There is a man-made waterhole nearby where we stopped. He wanted to check it was working, and his colleague here will collect him from there later, when she has reliable transport again.'

'Oh, as long as he's all right,' the woman said, sounding happier for the knowledge.

Ashley smiled brightly at the woman, who nodded at her. 'He's ruggedly handsome, isn't he?' she said, a dreamy tone to her voice. 'Wouldn't want to lose him.'

'I won't,' Ashley answered and grinned.

Ashley looked at Elliott, who was smiling broadly. She didn't understand what he was so happy about. She was going to a safari lodge she'd never heard of, with a man she'd only just met, not a credit card on her person and the only thing that was more important in her mind was that out there in the bush, Scott was running for his life, again.

But this time he was alone.

• • •

After watching the *bakkie* speed away, Scott checked the oncoming road and, while the bus was moving slowly, dropped down onto the bitumen and remained as still as possible as the huge metal beast drove over him. He stood up and saluted to Elliot as he drove off. Scott knew he'd seen him, as the speed of the bus immediately increased. Hating watching Ashley being driven away from him, he turned into the bushes. He had to get off the road and out of sight.

Scott headed north. He could travel much faster without Ashley, and he knew that she'd hold her own. She learned fast, didn't panic, and he missed her presence already. But he had needed to put her safety first.

Two hours later, he finally began noticing familiar landmarks. He headed into Zebra Pan, and directly into Tessa's office.

Tessa was on her executive tilt-back chair, her feet crossed over each other and propped up on the desk. Kevin was perched on the corner of the desk.

'Scott, what the ...?' Tessa asked as he entered after one sharp rap on the door.

Scott closed the door behind him. Kevin looked at him and raised an eyebrow at Scott's appearance, his torn clothing, sweat stained shirt and stress ravaged face.

'Hey Tessa, Kevin. How much information do we have on those rangers from Kenya?'

'Nothing. They're staying here, waiting to hear from you about the last killing spree those poachers went on—' Tessa began.

'The ring is huge. Well connected. Top dignitaries from Zimbabwe are involved. I wonder who in the Kenyan government is also in on it. No wonder we can never catch them, they are in the *goddamned* political loop.' Scott's fists bunched up and the muscles in his forearms corded.

'When did you last eat?' Tessa asked, already picking up her phone on the desk. 'Yellow, please bring a large steak burger with chips and salad to my office. Thank you.'

'Ta, Tess,' acknowledged Scott, taking the drink that Kevin had just placed in his hand and flopping down into the visitor's chair.

Digging in the fridge for a beer, Kevin said, 'Care to start at the beginning?'

Scott filled them in on the last twenty-four hours.

'So where is Ashley now?' Tessa asked.

'Hopefully at Hwange Safari Lodge.'

Tessa shook her head. 'You idiot. You actually left her?'

'No. Elliott's with her. I told you. And the last thing those poachers would have expected me to do is to place Ashley in someone else's care—find her protection anywhere else but with me. Elliott will look after her, make sure she is safe until we can fetch her—once these poachers are rounded up. She isn't anywhere near them.' Scott pulled his hand through his hair in frustration.

'Elliott isn't you, Scott. Are you mad or just plain stupid? You should have seen how she looked at you at the dinner. It reminds me of how Kevin looks at me. I'm not even sure she knows it yet. And after everything you have gone through, she's now counting on you, and you've deserted her.' Tessa's voice rose in volume and pitch as her anger showed. Kevin put his hand on her arm to quieten her.

'Scott, I'll fly to the lodge and collect her. Lady Luck is with us—yesterday I brought home our new chopper. She handles like an eagle, smooth as. Tessa, you and Scott get hold of Themba Sazulu, the police member in charge of Hwange. I'll collect him after Ashley, and bring him here. He's an old-style, play by the rules type person, and I wouldn't think he would be involved. The chopper seats four, but he's a big man. Hopefully I'll still have enough light left to fly over Shumba. Zol should recognise the markings on the chopper; perhaps I can save him a long walk. And while I'm gone, please have a bath. You stink, buddy.'

Scott gave his armpit a sniff, and wrinkled his nose. 'Yeah, I do.'

Kevin kissed Tessa quickly and mumbled quietly, 'See you later, love.' He walked out of the office calling at the top of his voice, 'Sipewe. Come.'

Tessa glared at Scott. 'I agree with Kevin, you stink. I hope that by the time Ashley gets here, you have a really good speech for her, because if I were her, I'd be packing my bags and flying back to Australia tomorrow—'

A knock on the door interrupted Tessa's lecture. Yellow entered, grinning, and gave Scott his food.

'Thanks, Yellow,' Scott said as he took the tray from her, and watched as she left the room.

Tessa patted the desk to indicate somewhere to put the tray. 'Once you are fed, use one of the showers in the pool area. I'll send some clean clothes from the safari shop for you.'

'Thanks, Tessa. But Elliott will protect her.'

Tess shook her head. 'You have no idea about female logic, do you?'

'Obviously not, since you still think I did the wrong thing by Ashley.'

Eating fast, he'd soon devoured the burger. He dipped the last chip into the tomato sauce and popped it into his mouth.

'Exactly just how involved are you and Ashley?' Tessa asked.

'What do you mean?' Scott didn't look at Tessa, not wanting her to see his feelings. She was one of his best friends, and would read him clear as a conservation chart.

'Well, that answered that one. Now you're a rat too. Come on, arguing is getting us nowhere. Go and shower. I'll send one of the guys with your clean clothes.'

He looked at his long-time friend. She was the closest he'd come to having a second sister, and he knew she could see through him. 'Thanks, Tess. I care for Ashley. I think maybe I've fallen for her to be honest, I don't know. The shift in the status of our relationship has been complex, and it's all happened so fast. But she is so strong, and so alive, and patient. The whole time, she never complained about the conditions of running, she just did what she had to do to survive with Zol and I. I don't think I've ever met anyone quite like her. I really like her, Tess. She's different from other females. Not complicated. Just Ashley. And wanting her to survive, and stay here with me longer to explore what we have wasn't something I thought would ever happen to me.' He looked at her then, the truth shining through on his face.

Tessa smiled. 'Oh Scott, that's so sweet.' She placed her left hand over her heart, its large solitaire diamond engagement ring flashing in the sunlight.

'Yeah, well don't go blabbing to the world, would you? I'll tell her in my own time, okay?'

'Just make sure you do. I know how emotionally constipated you are. You always have been. But she doesn't know you well enough yet to "get it". Don't expect miracles from her. You are going to have to be honest with her. And I'm assuming that she feels like this about you too. Remember I'm going on how I saw her look at you at dinner before the poachers hit the elephant. And you guys have had time together since then. I'm happy for you, Scott.'

'Humph. Together but not together.'

Tessa shook her head. 'Shower, Scott.' She pointed in the general direction of the pool.

'I'm going.' He headed towards the pool area of the lodge, and a refreshing shower.

By the time he emerged from the ablution block, with his hair untidy but clean, wearing khaki pants and a t-shirt advertising 'Zebra Pan Lodge, the heart of your safari experience', he was feeling like a new man.

Tessa was sitting on a lounger, waiting for him. 'Ashley rang while you were in the shower. She was safe in a hotel room. Then Kevin radioed through that they are airborne and on their way to collect Themba. But he's worried about the light for looking for Zol.'

'Zol won't complain if it gets dark and we can't look for him. Hell, he could surprise us and be here in person before the morning. That old man's stamina is still amazing.'

'You're lucky to have him. I know how much he means to you.'

'Thanks. For everything.' He pulled her to him and hugged her, roughly rubbing his hands up and down her back.

Tessa broke the hug. 'I haven't spoken to the Kenyans yet. I wasn't sure what to say to them. I kind of hoped you might like to ...'

'Sure. What rondavel are they in? I'll go and knock on their door now.'

'Pan Bushman.'

'Thanks.'

Scott strode purposefully towards the rondavel.

A tall black game ranger, with native beading around his neck identifying him as from the Masai Mara Game Reserve in Kenya opened the screen door. 'Hello, Scott. Come in, come in. You have news?'

Scott stepped into the rondavel, hoping to begin to unravel the hierarchy of the poachers, but mostly to question the loyalties of the visiting Kenyan game rangers.

Scott paced next to the *bakkie*, waiting for the helicopter to touch down. Hunched over, he ran towards the craft while the rotor blades still turned slowly, his eyes on Ashley in the front passenger seat. He yanked open her door and noticed that already she'd flipped the earphones off her head and was attempting to exit, only to be held back by the seatbelt.

He helped her unclip the safety harness quickly and she leapt out into his waiting arms. His reward for being there to meet her was a deep, soul-seeking kiss.

He kissed her. Losing himself in the warmth of her mouth, trying to tell her without words that he'd missed her, that he was sorry to have been separated from her. Show her that he cared. He ran his hands lightly down her back, over the ethnic pattern of the dress she was wearing, and pulled her closer to him. She didn't attempt to pull away at all—she'd crossed a bridge when they were talking up that tree.

'Enough of that, you two. Come on, we need to get back to the lodge.' Kevin interrupted them with a smile. Themba Sazulu was lumbering out the rear door of the helicopter.

Zol was conspicuous by his absence. Scott questioned Kevin with a frown.

'Lost the light. I did a small flyover towards Shumba, but other than plenty of jumbos and a huge herd of buffalo, I couldn't see much. We'll leave at first light to search.'

Scott shook his head. If Zol could have, he would have revealed himself to Kevin's chopper. Searching for him would prove futile. When he could, Zol would make contact again. Until then, Scott could only pray he came to no harm and returned safely.

Scott held Ashley's hand tightly on the back seat of Sipewe's open-backed, game-viewing *bakkie*. Kevin sat as passenger in front with Sipewe.

Themba had the middle seat all to himself, spreading sufficiently to occupy two seats. He stretched his huge arms out behind him over the seat, the light blue fabric of his short-sleeved shirt straining at the seams. 'This is the life. Night-time game viewing, a helicopter ride. My children are going to be so jealous when I tell them about my day at the office.' He began laughing at his own joke.

Scott thought kids all over the world would probably be jealous of the police chief's afternoon's activities, but definitely not of the situation he was about to handle. He wondered if Ashley grasped the irony of the situation too, that it was dire and yet aspects of the day were so magical.

He sneaked a peek at her. She wasn't smiling. 'You okay?' he whispered.

'No, no I'm not.'

'I'll explain it all, I promise. Just let us get through the next hour or so, then we will be on our own and I can explain. Okay?'

'Not really. But I don't have a choice, do I?'

'Not unless you want everyone to hear.'

She shook her head.

He smiled at her and squeezed her hand in reassurance, then lifted it to his mouth and kissed the knuckles, one by one.

As they came around a bend near the waterhole, Sipewe stopped the *bakkie*. 'Look.'

At the edge of the water was a white rhino and her small calf.

'Oh my ...' Ashley said.

Scott smiled at the gestures of the cow towards her baby, and could tell they were those of a protective and nurturing mother. He put his arm around Ashley's shoulders as they watched the rhino mother gently run her square jaw reassuringly over the little one's back.

'They don't often come up this far north. It's good to see them here,' Scott said, but he wasn't looking at the rhinos anymore. He had turned to watch Ashley's expressions, and the pure excitement written on her face.

She's one amazing woman, he thought. To still find it in her heart to look at the surrounding beauty that is Africa and delight in it, despite what she'd just been through.

Together the occupants of the *bakkie* watched in silence, as the copper sun slunk away from the African sky and the water turned blood coloured. The rhino and her calf eventually ambled away from the waterhole and into the bush.

Back at Zebra Pan Lodge, Scott, Ashley and Themba made their way to the bar area which had been converted into a 'conference room'. Tessa, always the perfect hostess, had drinks ready on a tray and snacks on the coffee table, which were being enjoyed by the Kenyans. A whiteboard had been brought in. They had already pieced together what they knew of the poaching net, making the information on the board look like an organisation chart with spider's legs.

'Please to meet you.' Seli, the older of the two Kenyan game guards, pumped Themba's hand in greeting.

'Likewise. I'm hoping it will be mutually beneficial to both countries,' Themba replied as he sat heavily on an animal-print lounge chair. He waved his fat arm at the board, still keeping eye contact with Seli. 'Can you explain these links, and who these people are?' Although he smiled at the command, everyone present realised that he was taking control of the situation. This was his territory.

Seli cleared his throat. 'It's frightening that someone as high up as Eric Mbeki, the commander of the Zimbabwe President's Guard, is involved. It makes me wonder who in Kenya would be his counterpart.' He looked at the second guard.

'I agree with my colleague.' Sambo nodded as he took a seat opposite Themba. 'I do wonder too, but my main concern begins lower down the ranks. During our investigations over the years, all the rangers gave their information to our senior game guard, Elias Kitia. It was his responsibility to monitor poaching in the Masai. But there was no record of any incident at all when I took over his position one month after he disappeared. Not a single file for the last ten years findings.'

'You suspect him?' Kevin asked.

'I don't know. I must believe in the good of the man first, that is our way. Since we don't know where Elias is, and by law we are supposed to be innocent until proven guilty, perhaps ... But perhaps not. The fact is, Elias isn't here. It's now my responsibility, and we only have a few facts that we have been able to reconstruct.' He looked at Seli, as if questioning whether he should carry on exposing the skeletons within their own organisation.

Seli nodded.

Scott smiled as he saw the exchange from the elder man, silently giving permission to the younger man to speak out against an older person in their tribe. The acknowledgement of the traditional value didn't go unnoticed by the other men in the room either.

Sambo took a deep breath and blew it out through his lips. 'Elias was the head ranger for almost ten years. In that time the poaching grew worse in the park. We have lost many elephant, rhino and other animals. Once poachers even killed a whole pride of lion that a British wildlife documentary team was following. The poachers shot the couple involved during the night, along with the lions. It was very bad publicity for Kenya.'

'I remember that. So you think this is the same ring?' Themba asked, no emotion readable on his face.

'They appear to have the same tactics. They're not afraid to kill people, leaving no witnesses to talk,' Seli answered. 'I've been a ranger for nearly forty years, and I've seen a lot of things during my time. But our lion killings and your elephant cull the other night, they're the same. Helicopters brought into the reserve, silencers on their weapons, every bullet casing removed after the attack, nobody living near the parks hearing anything—it's professional. I studied the elephant photographs you gave us; each one brought down with precision to avoid breaking tusks. Like our lions, each male killed with a single shot, skinned on-site, for its head and skin. Deadly accuracy and planning. They must have night-vision scopes. These poachers know the animals and whoever set up these operations has lots of money to equip them with the latest technology with which to hunt them.'

Scott nodded. 'I agree. Of the five who were following us yesterday and today, there were two white men, one old, one young; two black men, southern African origin; and one very black man, Kenyan or Ethiopian origin. They carried Russian assault rifles—various versions of the AK47s—and Zol swore he saw an old South African R1. The origins of the guns mean nothing as everyone has access to so many weapons these days. All had telescopic scopes attached, even the semi-automatics. Some of the weapons were older, but they were all well maintained. That screams money and time, as if they are not in a hurry. It's that combination that is going to be our enemy in this ring. If we spook them, and they go underground again, there is no saying where they will pop up next, in whose territory, but it will be devastating again. We need to get them now.'

Ashley accepted another Diet Coke, which she swirled around in the can. Tapping her foot, she looked at the information on the whiteboard. It was simply notes with no logic.

'Scott, do you mind if I show you something with that information on the board?'

'Go ahead. Any help we can get is accepted,' he said.

'Great.' She smiled at him briefly and then stood and walked to the whiteboard. She swung it over and addressed everyone.

'All right, this is an FMEA: Failure, Mode, Engineering and Analysis. It's an analytical tool. Work with me here.' She drew a small square on the board.

As a group, they followed her lead and worked together as she first filled in the blank side of the board, and then flipped it over again and continued her mapping. When they were finished, all the information previously scribbled on the board was in a coherent order.

'So that's what they teach you in engineering school?' Scott asked.

She gave him the best dumb-ass look she could. 'We have gone through logically and put all the information in where we know it goes, and taken into consideration the pros and cons of each situation.' She pointed to a box. 'Do you go after them now? Yes or no? If you say yes, you follow it through here.' She motioned where to follow the lines. 'Here are the outcomes we need to achieve, and here are the risks. Now we work out how to achieve them with minimal loss of time, and minimal use of resources.'

'Amazing,' Kevin said. 'Do you know, the aeronautical engineers are always rattling on about those things, but I never took much notice of them.'

Ashley grinned at him. She understood this type of environment, the business 'find a solution' styled meeting, however out of kilter she felt with the uncharted territory of poaching. She was good at finding solutions.

'Right. The next logical step,' she pointed with her marker to the FMEA behind her, 'is to wait for Zol. Alternatively, we go after him in the helicopter tomorrow at first light. Depending on the information he has, we modify our plan of action accordingly. We already know the location of the poachers' last camp, from the unit before the ambush. The aim is obviously to go in there and ...'

Scott knew he was beaming. This was a side of Ashley he hadn't seen: the high-powered, do-it and get-it-done woman. He liked it.

'Okay, everyone.' Themba called a halt at last. 'It's late. I need to call Elmon Muleya, Zimbabwe's Army Brigadier. I know that he hates the commander with a passion and would love nothing better than to see his downfall. Perhaps, Kevin, we can fly him from Harare tomorrow? Having Elmon on a small private charter flight wouldn't bring about as much suspicion as bringing in an army helicopter.'

'Sure,' Kevin said.

Themba nodded. 'I'll phone him and tell him as little as I can, we don't know who is listening on his phone. We all need to get some sleep and there is nothing we can do until the morning.' He stood up, nodded politely to everyone, and left the room.

The Kenyans followed suit, walking, with their small paraffin lamps glowing softly in the darkness, down the path towards their rondavel.

Ashley copied the FMEA onto an A4 pad and wiped the board clean.

'You sleeping here tonight, or do you want to borrow a *bakkie* and drive home?' Tessa asked Scott.

He glanced at Ashley. She looked exhausted, with black circles under her eyes making their green colour like the pool he'd seen as a boy deep in the Chimanimani Mountains. 'If there is a spare bed going, I reckon we'll take you up on it.'

'The Elephant rondavel is free, it has two bedrooms. My *bakkie's* in the workshop, if you want it in the morning. Otherwise, breakfast's at six. See you then.'

'Thanks, guys, for everything,' Scott said. Taking a lantern, he led Ashley to the Elephant rondavel.

Kevin held Tessa's hand as they watched the departing figures. He said quietly, 'I think they'll be all right.'

'I hope so. I like her, and hope she stays around. But sometimes Scott is so dense, almost naive where females are concerned. He hides on his ranch.'

'Do you think she's only after a holiday fling?'

'No. She seems too level-headed for that. I think she's fallen for him too. She wouldn't have forgiven him so easily for separating from her otherwise.'

'Come on, Tess. I know someone else who is neglecting someone tonight ...' He kissed his fiancée. He felt her pinch his butt cheek affectionately, and he smiled at her.

Tessa rested her forehead against his. 'I guess since your business partner is sorted out now, my hot-shot flyboy, what are we standing around in the bar area for?'

He let her lead him towards her own cosy cottage, set a little way from the tourist lodges, but if truth be known, he was almost pushing her along in front of him to get her there faster.

Ashley watched Scott as he stopped to open the screen door and then the door. But then he held it ajar with his foot, blocking her entrance into the rondavel with his body.

'Hold this,' he said, passing her the lantern. As she took it, he bent slightly and lifted her up in his arms. With one arm snaked around his neck, she hung on tightly, her other hand still holding the lantern, their only source of light.

She looked into his face. Being carried like this she was level with him, eye to eye. She wanted to ask so many questions, but didn't voice them for fear of spoiling the moment. Ghosts of past relationships haunted her, when she had spoken at inappropriate times.

'Spit it out, I won't bite,' Scott joked softly, his face serious but gentle.

'I want to say things but I can't.'

'Can't or won't?'

'It's not that ... I just don't want to spoil the moment.'

'Nothing you could say would spoil this. You want to say something to me? Say it.'

She hesitated, chewing the inside of her lip. 'This is nice. I've never been carried before. I'm no lightweight. You make me feel like a princess, rather than a giant Amazon.'

'An Amazon warrior ... that has possibilities. But tonight, African princess does kind of suit you, so may I carry you in now?' he asked, softly brushing her lips with his as he stepped into the room.

He saw the flash of her smile as he carried her inside. The screen door bumped back into place with a dull thud.

Scott strode through to the master bedroom and gently placed Ashley on the king-size bed. He took the lantern from her and put it on the bedside table and followed her down, not wanting to let go of her for a second.

'I was so scared when you left me on the bus,' Ashley admitted.

'I'm sorry,' he murmured. 'It wasn't an easy choice.'

'I know.'

He tried to hug her to him, but she resisted slightly. She was staring at him, her green eyes slanted in silent question, her brow slightly creased in a frown. 'I'll always protect you, Ashley,' he said. 'Getting you out of the bush and into the civilised world was my priority. If I was on the bus, and the poachers recognised me, I would have been putting not only your life at stake but also all the tourists on the bus. Leaving you was hard. I wanted to take you in my arms and wrap you tightly, keep you safe from everything. And not just as a woman, but as my woman. I recognised what we have is more than just a moment. But if the poachers had found me on the bus, a massacre could have occurred. And I can't lose you, Ashley. Besides the damage it would cause to my volunteers program, it would break me as a man.'

She reached up and smoothed his cheek, a small smile of forgiveness and understanding ghosting across her lips.

Scott gathered her now unresistant body close to his. 'It's my job to protect what is mine. It always has been. Since the first time my dad Charlie left me in charge at Delmonica while he went off to war somewhere, I have been the protector. The last move the poachers would ever expect from me was to pass "my woman" on to someone else to look after. They would have been counting on me keeping you close, and keeping you safe. You were my biggest weakness. To put you on the bus, and leave you in Elliott's care, I increased both our chances of survival. They wouldn't be looking for us separately, only as a pair. But it was a tactical decision, one that I was torn in two making. And I'm sorry. Despite knowing what you have been through, how you react to adversities, I left you on the bus. Tessa was right, I should have believed in your strength and given you the chance to come with me. I'm sorry.'

'Me too.' She was still hurt, but his explanation made sense. And in the end, she was all right, he was okay, it was just Zol they were waiting to hear from. 'Promise you'll never do it again.'

'Forever's a long time to keep a promise, even to a princess,' he said as he nipped her ear. Already he could feel the change in her mood.

'Forever's not so long, depends on how we spend it,' she said, and pulled his mouth to hers, confident that this was what she wanted.

CHAPTER 9

Zol crept through the dense bush. He could hear the leopard cough. It was close, but there was no refuge from this exquisite predator in the trees above him. Leopards were good climbers, and would take their prey up into a tree to avoid having it snatched away by hyena or wild dogs. His ears strained to differentiate the night sounds, checking all were natural and that no man stepped close by.

Zol knew he should be getting near Zebra Pan Lodge. The moon was beginning to sink in the sky, so it was around three in the morning. The last of the poachers' group were still hot on his tracks. He'd doubled back twice in the last twelve hours to spy on them. There were only two men left: one white hunter and his tracker.

He could use a man that good in his anti-poaching unit. The tracker was from North Africa, his coal-black skin different from Zol's, whose colour was more a strong espresso coffee. Obviously the tracker was full-blooded Kenyan or Ethiopian. Although Zol was tall, this man was taller, probably from Masai descent, he thought.

Once more Zol began a wide sweep around the back of the poachers. The white man was probably in his late fifties or early sixties. His beer gut was large, and the buttons of his khaki shirt strained against the fabric. He'd lagged behind the tracker yet again. Now he smoked a cigarette, drawing it into his lungs, the tip glowing amber in the moonlit night. He tilted his fat neck and exhaled upwards into the air then sucked deeply again, as if his life depended on the substance he held in his hand. Zol could smell the sweet distinctive twang of *dagga* mixed into the hand-rolled cigarette.

Zol detested both smoking and drugs. He'd seen his people fouled by both. His mother had named him Zol after the narcotic substance. She claimed his father and she had got high the night she conceived him, and had boasted 'the Zol' had helped her fall pregnant.

His grandfather had raised the *lobola* price higher, because she'd proved she could conceive. Then, still unmarried, she'd born a son. Her father doubled her *lobola* again, he was so proud of his daughter.

But Zol's father couldn't afford to pay it. The *lobola* was too expensive for his humble cattleman's purse. So he'd left their village in Malawi, and gone into the Congo to become a freedom fighter. There he'd been paid good money to send home to pay for his wife, but died for a worthless cause before the marriage could take place. His grave in the rainforests somewhere was not even marked. His father had never returned home to his lover, his son or his homeland.

Zol put his thoughts aside. He needed to concentrate on the present, not the past.

The leopard was closer, his cough louder. The immediate surrounds had quietened down, as if waiting for the night predator to choose his victim and sacrifice it to the moon. A mosquito buzzed in Zol's ear, and he closed his hand over it silently, squishing it between his fingers and neck. He watched as the white hunter carelessly threw his cigarette stub on the ground, and extinguished it with the heel of his crocodile-skin boot. The boots were dusty and dull, but Zol knew boots like that were expensive and wore well. The trade in wild crocodile skins had diminished over the years with the legal farming of the animals.

Zol liked the idea of the crocodile being worn as shoes, the creatures being walked on by men, but so far every man he had met who wore them thought they were better than everyone else. None of them respected their fellow man, or seemed to understand that the animal that was related to the dinosaur was a coward, often stealing children from banks of the rivers, dragging them underwater and drowning them. Most of the men who wore these boots were like peacocks, strutting their exotic feathers for all to see, then fighting their own reflections in a mirror, until they died from repeatedly battering into the same inanimate object. They were all show, and had no brains in their heads.

None of the men who wore these boots had ever shown self-respect either. Zol thought that perhaps the spirit of the cowardly beast remained in the leather, and when worn by a man would cohabit his body, changing his behaviour and making him a human-crocodile hybrid: sleazy, cunning, underhanded and ruthless, with no good qualities to speak of, except perhaps money. But money alone didn't make a man happy.

Zol crouched low against an acacia tree, watching as the white man put his hand inside his shorts and scratched his genitals, then farted loudly into the night as he adjusted his semi-automatic rifle on his back. Finally, the man hitched his shorts up under his huge gut and set out in the general direction the tracker had gone. He hacked up a ball of snot from his throat as he went and spat it into the bushes, wiping his mouth on the back of his hand.

A flicker to the right of his vision alerted Zol to the presence of the tracker.

'*Baas*, he's turned direction again. I think he comes behind,' began the black tracker in heavily accented English.

'Bloody *kaffir*, he's not going to get me. This *boer* will shoot him dead. I fought in the Suid Afrikaanes army when I was younger. I knows his tricks. He is messing with your *kop*.' He coughed, doubling over with the effort. 'Uuugman,' he choked out between coughs, 'those smokes'll kill me one day.'

The tracker peered into the bush behind them, weary that his boss was making so much noise in the night. Shaking his head, he turned around once more and started retracing his steps.

'One man. We must stop him before he can inform anyone about the camp,' began the white man.

'Boss, there were three that first came this way. For the whole day we only see the tracks of one cunning man. What happened to the other two? We haven't seen any bodies.'

'Perhaps the lions got thems?' the white man asked hopefully, a crusty, sinister laugh rippling up from his belly.

'What about the others who ran into the bushes?'

'I told you last night. Boss Lawrence *kun* take care of thems.'

'This one in front is clever. He thinks like a mountain gorilla. He doesn't want to get caught,' said the tracker.

'No one ever wants to get caught. But we catch him. I'll make him pay for what he did to my *seuntjie*. For putting him down that ant bear hole. I want his fucking bloody black neck in my hands, and I'm gonna rip his fucking throat out while he begs me to let him die faster. Fucking bloody black bastard.'

The tracker continued his forward journey without commenting. They walked in silence for half an hour, Zol ghosting behind. Suddenly the tracker put his hand up in a stop signal, and the white man reacted instantly. Silently he pulled on the barrel of his weapon from behind his back, sliding it around under his arm and up into his shoulder. He slipped the safety on the rifle.

A low rumbling could be heard.

'Bloody jumbo,' muttered the white man.

The elephant herd were directly in front of the men. Zol quickly began skirting the poachers, not sure of the volatile nature of the white man. He checked to make sure he was downwind of the beasts, then slowly began to leave the poachers behind him in the night. He heard the *pop-pop-pop-pop-pop* of the semi-automatic rifle going off.

Zol fled. Sprinting to put some distance between himself and the elephant, as he was not sure what direction they would run if they stampeded. He saw a huge camelthorn tree. The base of its trunk was as wide as two men. He shimmied up the trunk and waited for the fallout.

He heard trumpeting and more shots went off, but these had the dull sound of bullets that cut flesh. The stupid white man was shooting the elephant. The tree trembled and about fifty elephant broke into the clearing. Stampeding. Running blindly. Flattening everything in their terrified path. Small duiker and impala leaped in front and then darted to the side, getting out of their way. The elephant thundered past, trumpeting their unhappiness. Waking the night.

Zol clung to the tree.

Moments later, the fragile quiet had almost been restored, and the elephant' noise died away in the distance. A lone cow hobbled into the clearing near Zol's tree, a tiny baby elephant plastering itself to her side.

The mother was mortally wounded. Liquid pumped out of her stomach area and blood frothed at her mouth, pink bubbles dripping, which indicated a lung puncture, and multiple rivers of blood ran down her forehead. The assault rifle, not powerful enough to penetrate the elephant's skull, had merely inflicted wounds that bled profusely, obscuring her vision in her left eye. One of her tusks was broken and bloodied, splintered off cruelly about halfway down.

Hot tears welled up in Zol's eyes. He watched as she passed him by, reassuring her baby with her trunk, and trying to reach the safety of the herd, before she died with dignity, among friends.

The silence that followed was louder than any normal night sounds. Zol listened. Nothing. He climbed down the tree trunk and retraced his steps carefully to see what had become of the poachers.

The white man was dead. Nobody could be twisted at that angle and still be alive. His legs were turned in the wrong direction from his hips. His huge body lay still as a grotesque monument to the elephant defending her baby. In her rage, she had impaled him many times in the chest and stomach, using such excessive force that one of her tusks had become lodged in the hard ground, the strong ivory splintering at an angle. The part left behind protruded out from between his ribs. His entrails spilled out and hung like red tinsel on a Christmas tree, decorating the bushes surrounding his body. One side of his head was squished in, causing his eyes to bulge unnaturally out of their sockets, and behind them, grey-pink matter seeped into the African soil.

Zol left the man where he lay and began seeking out the tracker. There was no sign of him in the immediate area, so he moved out and started a meticulous search, working in larger concentric circles, radiating outward.

There he found him.

The black man was wounded, but he still breathed the night air. His collarbone was broken, and the white tips of the bone jutted out like a small mountain range from his black flesh. Blood welled up around the area, and slowly trickled downwards. His right arm was smashed and his body had definitely taken a pounding. He was grey in the face.

Zol gazed at the unconscious man. If he left him, he would be hyena fodder, but to take him with him would cost Zol the rest of his strength. Having only snacked in the past forty-eight hours and used up the last of his water, he was running on empty. Zol scratched his head. The tracker was a middle-aged man, grey hair beginning at his temples, deep lines engraved into his face showing years spent in the African sun.

'You are lucky,' he said out loud to the tracker, as he made his decision to patch him up. First, he pulled the arm of the broken collarbone straight and, putting his foot on the junction of the tracker's chest and armpit area, he popped the shoulder back into place with a sharp click. The man cried out in pain even in his unconscious state. Next, Zol straightened the broken arm. The crunch of bone on bone was sickening even to him.

Zol bandaged the arm with a small splint on both sides. Using his reserves from the medikit he carried, he put field dressings on the worst of the lacerations. He used the tracker's pants to make strong straps and secured the shoulder and arm tightly, then he made a small traverse to drag the man behind him. He thought about when he was younger and strong enough to carry the man the whole way home, when his master's horse would have helped him, and he smiled.

'Boss Charlie, I'll give this man a chance, like you gave me,' he spoke up to the sky.

Zol remembered his chance meeting with Charlie, the man who had given his life a purpose. Unconsciously smiling at the tracker, the last survivor of this part of the poaching party who had ambushed them yesterday, Zol knew this was the right thing to do. He had to give this man a second chance, as Charlie had given him. A chance to turn his back on what was wrong, and do good with the rest of his life. Charlie had given him hope, and the means in which to live and turn that hope into a life.

Finally, Zol had the poacher's tracker at the base of the same tree that saved his own life. Once more he climbed up, this time hauling a dead weight with him, up into the branches. He tied the man high up in the tree, below the chattering buffalo weaver's nests amongst the evil thorns. The tracker would be safe here. The hyenas wouldn't get him. The leopard he'd heard earlier might investigate. Zebra Pan was close by, and hopefully he'd be back early in the day with reinforcements.

In this man's head was information that Zol wanted, and he intended to get it out. One way or another.

Zol sat on a pool lounge on the wooden deck near the Zebra safari lodge swimming pool. He watched as the sun splashed pink across the waterhole. The impala flicked their ears in the pre-dawn light. A fat warthog wallowed in the mud, oblivious of life around him, focused on being completely covered with thick, sticky sunscreen. The resident fish eagle cried a morning wake-up call as it soared overhead, then dived into the pink waters of the waterhole to catch a large catfish for its family's breakfast, its razor-sharp talons holding its prize as it circled round to its nest on the opposite side of the pool. Noisy chatter shattered the tranquillity as a flock of Egyptian geese flew onto the waterhole.

He loved this pre-dawn time. He hated to move away and spoil the peacefulness, but he needed to wake Scott. He'd seen his spoor at the airstrip, and he could see signs that Miss Ashley had been there too, her smaller boot prints alongside Scott's.

He hoped they had stayed the night there. Together. Scott deserved to be happy. Find his soulmate, to put the *tokoloshe* to sleep. Just as Zol had eventually found his Gertrude. He smiled, acknowledging it had taken him a long time, but he'd found her at last.

Slowly, he stretched his old body, so the ache in his back was relieved. He heard the first stirrings in the compound, of the kitchen staff waking and moving around.

Zol ambled to the kitchen.

Yellow saw him silhouetted in the doorway. Recognising him instantly, she shook her head and pointed out the door. 'Zol, if you come one step into my kitchen, I'll ... I'll ...'

He smiled and walked inside. 'Hello to you too, Yellow. I know you'll be cooking that warm bread for breakfast. I'm hungry.'

She put her hands on her hips. 'I'll feed you like everyone else, at the table. When you come in my kitchen, you steal everything. Are you okay?' she gestured to his bloodied state with her hands.

'I'm good. The blood isn't mine.' He smiled, her comment about his thieving was partly true. The last time he was in Yellow's kitchen, only about a month ago, he'd raided her pantry for stocks for his unit, and then left a note for Tessa. He knew that Scott would reimburse Tessa, and she wouldn't mind. Her camp was closer than retuning to Delmonica on foot. But he hadn't thought that Yellow would be so angry.

'I left enough food for two days, until Scott could replace your stocks, Yellow. So why are you screaming like a *tokoloshe*?'

'You took every *koeksister* I made. There were none left for the morning safari.' She pointed her finger at him. 'Every one!'

'But they were so good, and my men love your cooking. They all think you are the best cook in the area.' He noticed her face lighting up at the compliment.

'Really?'

'True.'

Yellow wiped her large black hand on her white apron. She smiled a broad grin at Zol's words. 'Okay, Zol. What are you taking this time?'

'Nothing. I'm looking for Scott.'

'He was here yesterday, and I didn't hear any vehicle leave late last night. Miss Tessa'll be awake soon as I drop her tea tray in.'

Zol nodded. He could wait.

'Come, sit. You have some coffee in my kitchen, and *koeksisters*?'

'Thanks.' Zol knew he was grinning like a young child, but he couldn't stop. He sat down in the well fitted-out modern kitchen, where a huge yellowwood table graced the corner, in stark contrast to the white melamine fittings surrounding it.

A small bunch of drooping, tufty, yellow and cream camel-thorn flowers sat in a glass. Pollen was sprinkled liberally on the table in a halo around the glass. He waited while Yellow gave him a large mug of sweet coffee, and a container of *koeksisters* and a cloth. Once he had wiped his hands clean, he dunked his first sweet pastry into his steaming coffee, watching Yellow expertly place the tea tray on her upturned hand and swish out of her kitchen.

Patiently, he waited.

On returning, Yellow began talking to Zol before she was even fully in the kitchen.

'He's in the Elephant rondavel, with Miss Ashley. Miss Tessa said to not go inside, but to knock on the door. She likes Miss Ashley. You know you are going to give Miss Ashley a fright looking like that.'

Zol's grin returned. He liked Miss Ashley too. He wondered how long it would take until Miss Ashley became Madam Ashley. Scott should keep this one. She was different. She didn't know the African ways, and she was pale, but she learned fast. Ashley was strong, not small and breakable, and she was not afraid of the bush. Best of all, she could fix things; build the ranch.

'Thank you.' He took his mug and plate to the sink.

'Can I take Scott and Miss Ashley their tray?' She eyed him suspiciously.

'I can carry a tea tray correctly,' he said, looking indignant.

'Sure, but remember what Miss Tessa said.' She handed him the morning tray, laden with coffee and tea, a few *koeksisters*, and some golden-brown muesli rusks. He could feel her eyes burning into his back, watching his every step as he walked to the Elephant rondavel.

A rap on the door three times, followed by a guineafowl call. Instantly Scott sprang up.

Ashley was still asleep. He wished he could wake her and make love to her again. Instead, he slipped out of the bed and into his pants, and left the bedroom. He yanked open the front door, beaming widely at his friend. 'Come on in, old man.'

Zol carried the tray over to the table, then he grinned back at Scott. 'How much is Miss Ashley's *lobola*?'

'You dog.' Scott laughed. 'When is your wedding, Mr I-wear-socks-that-Gertrude-gives-me?' Scott deflected the question back at Zol.

'Her father wants fifty cattle. I'm trying to get the price down. Tradition says eleven cattle, he's cheating me.'

'She's worth one hundred, you old codger. Don't insult her.'

'It's not your fat cattle that will be leaving Delmonica,' Zol pointed out.

'Right.' Scott looked Zol over, relief spreading through his body. But as he scrutinised Zol, his expression changed to one of concern.

'Blood?' He pointed at Zol's pants.

'Not mine. Come, sit. We have lots to catch up on.'

Scott sat down at the table to eat while Zol filled him in on the details of what had happened after they had parted the previous day.

Ashley began to surface. She could hear the low rumblings of male voices. She reached out her hand for Scott, but the sheet was cold next to her. She lifted her head to hear the voices more clearly. Scott's was distinct, but the other? It was low and steady, and rhythmic.

She jumped out of bed, pulled on her new kaftan and rushed out the door. 'Zol!' she shouted. 'I'm so glad to see you.' She threw her arms around his shoulders. 'I'm happy you are okay.' Then she went over to Scott and kissed him on the lips. 'Good morning to you, too.'

She let Scott pull her down to sit on his lap, and draped an arm around his neck. She turned to smile at Zol, and looked properly at him for the first time.

'Zol, you're covered in blood!' she screeched, suddenly noticing that Zol was sitting bloodied and had no shirt on. He still wore the suede boots that she now knew as *veldskoene*.

'He's fine,' Scott said. 'It belongs to someone else who is, hopefully, still alive.'

She nodded at him and smiled, relieved. 'Perhaps you would like a shower, Zol?'

'That would be great,' he replied, looking down at himself.

'The bathroom is through there.' Scott pointed to the second bedroom.

Nodding in reply, Zol left the room. Within seconds they could hear the water running in the shower.

'Tell me?' Ashley looked seriously at Scott, a frown on her forehead.

'Hopefully the tracker has survived his last few hours up in a tree. But he's injured, so we'll need to get him first thing this morning. The rest of that group are dead.'

A knock sounded at the door.

Without looking to see who was there Scott shouted, 'Come on in, it's open.'

Tessa and Kevin walked through.

'Good morning,' Scott said.

Kevin's face showed his worry. 'Hi, yourselves. Yellow told us Zol was already here ...'

The four sat around the table and discussed what Zol had told Scott.

Soon Zol came out into the lounge area, wearing a complementary fluffy white bathrobe, the Zebra Pan logo on the right breast area.

'You look better,' Ashley said.

'I feel better, too. Now, if Miss Tessa will open the tourist shop early, I can get some pants to wear to meet the Kenyans, rather than wearing this dressing gown and looking like a pampered city tourist.'

Half an hour later, the helicopter left the landing strip to collect the tracker from the tree. Themba rode shotgun to witness the carnage left by the elephant, and attempt to find the traumatised herd, check that the aunties were watching over the orphaned baby elephant, or whether the Parks Board needed to intervene to re-home the little one for its survival.

Scott and Ashley returned to Delmonica to check if any of the other members of the anti-poaching unit had materialised during the night, and to make sure the volunteers were continuing their work on their allocated pumps.

But most importantly, Scott had to ensure that the volunteers understood they were only to go into the reserve armed with an anti-poaching guard. Their own private militia. Although the men already carried firearms, Scott was not taking any chances with their safety. Not with the poachers so brazenly operating inside the reserve.

CHAPTER 10

Rodney spat on the road, the blood from his lip a sizzling crimson blob on the hot bitumen. The sunspot on his lip oozed blood freely, and it ran down the side of his chin and dripped onto his camouflage shirt.

'This is your fault, you albino ape. Your fault, you hear me?'

Another punch landed in his face. The pain shot through his body, black dots danced before his eyes and slowly his right eye swelled shut. He dropped to the hot road and covered his face, shutting out the noon sun as it cooked everything beneath it. Another blow landed on his body, the sole of the boot biting hard into his spine.

'We have lost men. Not one of the party that followed the farmer and his *kaffir* have checked in. We've had no contact with Joubert or his useless son for forty-eight hours. A woman! You attacked without my permission because you saw a woman. You and your dick you can't control. I thought we were over this years ago ... years ago. You already had that bitch only nights back, and we buried her six feet under in the veld. Now you go sniffing for more cunt, just because she was with the farmer.' *Meneer* Lawrence wiped his face with his hands, sweat clinging to his fingers.

'Shit, Rodney. This time we are in shit. You hear me? You landed us in shit. Now we have to up the whole operation before we've finished. What am I going to tell those Russian investors when they come for their money? And the Chinaman? He'll cut off our balls and eat them with chopsticks and soy sauce, bloody communist bastard.'

Rodney lay still and stayed quiet. He knew not to talk back. To say anything at this stage was useless. Get the beating over with and then give it time for the anger to settle. The bitumen burnt his legs, but it was better than getting more fists in his face.

Later, when he approached his master with his plan, the white idiot would jump at the chance to get his money back, and Rodney would get to *fook* the tall blonde woman he'd seen in the reserve with the farmer. His dick twitched at the thought, and he savoured the metallic taste of blood in his mouth in anticipation. Soon he would have her: his new obsession with Angel Hair. But first he had to get *Meneer* Lawrence to get their original team together. They had work to do, before the sun set, and an old arms cache to visit—and he needed to make it seem like *Meneer* Lawrence's idea.

But for a while, he needed to stay where he was. Not move, as he would get more of a beating. He had learned that lesson when he was younger, when to move, when to run and when to fight. He cleared the blood out of his eye, and wished it wasn't his blood being spilt today. It was always better to draw someone else's blood, not spill your own.

He thought back to his first blood show, and the introduction of power to him. Power over others. It was only after he'd accepted he had this special power that he confirmed that women were shit within the human food chain. Lower than the bush pig.

Later, he had learned to *fook* them and gain satisfaction from their screaming, along with the spilling of their blood. But he remembered the day he learned about the glory of blood.

He'd been about five summers old, a small herd boy in a village out in the savannah. The goats had wandered far from his new home. He'd followed them diligently, as he'd been told, keeping them safe. But a Ndebele warrior had sneaked up on them, and killed one with his assegai. Isipho had hidden in the grass, afraid of the stranger. He watched while the man made a small fire and cooked some of the tender innards. Then he slung the remains of the carcass over his shoulder, kicked out the fire and walked away, goat blood dripping down his back. Isipho had watched him leave. Only then did he sneak out of the grass.

He was very afraid. If he told the villagers that a Ndebele warrior stole the goat, they would laugh at him. Ndebele warriors did not roam so far north anymore, nor so far west. They would say he was lying, and he wouldn't be allowed to watch the goats. He would be forced into doing women's work again. But if he left the goats and followed the warrior, a lion could attack and kill the remaining goats, and it would be his fault, as he should be watching them. Making up his mind, he quickly gathered the goats together and herded them back to the village.

The chief's third wife's shrill voice hurt his ears. 'Stupid boy, it's too early to bring the goats back.'

He ignored her. He penned the goats in their boma, and went to his mother's newly thatched *ikhaya*. He took his dead father's assegai from next to her sleeping mat, and the sharp knife from near the cooking pot. As he popped his head out their hut, the third wife of the chief grabbed his ear and began tugging him back to the goat boma.

'Where is the brown goat, boy? Where is my goat? You were supposed to keep the goats out until the sun is going to sleep. This is too early. Why have you brought them back, you lazy boy?' she screeched at him, pulling his ear towards the ground, hurting him, forcing his body to bend down.

He tried to escape her grasp, but couldn't. He attempted to answer, but she cut him off with a hard slap across the face. His ear rang inside where her big hand had hit him.

'Don't lie to me, boy. Where's my goat?' she asked again.

Isipho snapped. He was sick of being bullied by everyone. At every kraal they had joined, someone had beaten him, or pulled his ears, or pushed him into the dirt for being a bad luck omen—an albino who wouldn't die when given to the earth in sacrifice. He and his mother had only been in this new kraal for one moon. Already this woman had hurt him too many times.

With all his strength he pulled his ear from her grip and twisted away from her. Then he rounded on her, his assegai and knife pointing directly at her, his body crouched in an attack position. 'Leave me alone,' he yelled, as he slashed at her with the assegai, its sharp point cutting deep into her fat belly.

She began to scream.

Isipho had never heard such a noise in his life. He dropped the knife to pull at the assegai shaft with both hands to get it out of her. Eventually, silently, it slid out, but bright red blood flowed over her fat fingers where she held her stomach and dripped onto the dry sand. Isipho stared at it. She continued her hysterical screaming, but was now doubled over and holding her belly.

Women came running from everywhere. His mother rushed towards him. 'What happened? What have you done?'

The fat third wife of the chief continued to scream.

'She hurt me again, and was stopping me going to get the Ndebele warrior who killed the brown goat,' he said.

'He has killed me,' the wife wailed. 'He's a *tokoloshe* and should leave this kraal.'

'He's only a small boy.' His mother defended him. 'You should have listened to what he wanted to tell you before you hurt him,' she spat, angry that once again her child was being unfairly targeted by superstitious ninnies. 'A Ndebele warrior is near. We are not safe. If there is one, there will be others,' she highlighted the danger to the women.

'Nonsense, they don't raid this far anymore,' the first wife argued.

'How does he know it's a Ndebele?' asked one old woman with no front teeth, her mouth caved in to a black cavern.

'We lived near a Ndebele kraal for a while. My son would know one if he saw a warrior again,' answered Moswena. 'If my son says they have come, then I believe him.'

A silence fell between the women. Even the screaming stopped, as the women realised their danger. Ndebele men were renowned for their strength on the battlefield, and their vicious raping and slaughter of women in enemy territory afterwards.

'I must go and follow the Ndebele and get the goat back,' Isipho said.

'No. No, you stay here in the kraal. Our warriors will track this Ndebele and make him pay for killing our goat,' instructed the chief's first wife. She turned to walk away and go to tell the chief, still sitting in his *ikhaya*. He hadn't even risen to see what all the commotion was about.

The third wife looked at Isipho. 'You're a dead boy, you hear?' She hobbled away, clutching her wound.

Isipho ignored the chief's wife's advice, instead wiping the blood from the blade on the assegai, fascinated that already it was drying black and thick where once it was red and liquid. He dipped his finger in and tasted it. The salty, metallic taste made his heart beat faster. Quickly he finished cleaning the blade, then began his journey to find the Ndebele warrior before any other woman in the camp decided to tell him what to do.

The spoor was easy to follow, as the blood from the goat made a red line in the dirt. It was as if he was simply following a piece of red *rimpie*. But he knew that come nightfall, if he hadn't caught the warrior, he might never catch up to him.

The tracks changed direction and stopped. From the ground, Isipho saw that the warrior had been joined by many other men. There was a dark patch of blood spilled on the ground where they had cut up the goat and shared the fresh meat between them. They had even taken the skin with them to dry and use for other things.

'The goat is gone, my son,' his mother said softly, from behind him.

'I couldn't stop this happening, Mother. Will we have to move again?'

'Yes. When we return, they will start their nonsense about you bringing bad luck to their homes, and we'll move on.'

'Will we ever find a home where we are not chased away?' he asked, the tears running freely down his face.

'Perhaps we should make our own this time. We can return, collect our belongings, then go further north. We'll find a safe place.'

Already he'd had more homes than he could count on his fingers and toes. He looked down at the spoor again and kicked sand onto it, then noticed something alarming. 'Mother, look!' he cried as he followed the spoor around in a large arc. 'They have turned direction. They are heading towards the kraal.'

Moswena followed the direction of the tracks with her eyes, then as she looked up, she saw thick black smoke filling the sky. They knew, without doubt, that their kraal had been razed. Scared to return too early and become victims themselves, they hid in the bushes until it was almost dark. Only then did Isipho and his mother creep towards their recent home.

Burnt out with just a few patches of thatch still smouldering, the kraal was lost. Everyone was dead.

'Come, Isipho. Collect anything you can find that will be useful to us, and we'll leave this place. These people brought this on themselves for not listening to you. The men here didn't even get to lift an assegai, see how they are dead running towards their *ikhayas*. They never listened to your warning at all. See the fat wife, she can't hurt you anymore and even in death she's ugly. Look, the second wife, also dead. There's no reason left here for us to try to fit in. We can take the goats that are still alive and leave.'

Rodney smiled. All those years ago, his first taste of blood had been good. The white-*kaffir*-boy had learned his first lesson in life that day: to fight for himself.

He wouldn't let his recent mistake undermine him. Once *Meneer* Lawrence calmed down, he would listen to Rodney's plan, and they would take care of everything.

Just as they had been doing for the last fifteen years.

CHAPTER 11

Just before lunchtime, Scott walked into the Elephant rondavel. Zol stood over the sleeping tracker in the second bedroom. 'You look like you're guarding him. What's up?'

'The Kenyans wanted to rip him apart. Meet their ex-head ranger, Elias Kitia. Only a little persuasion from my hunting knife and a healthy tirade from a flustered, sweaty-faced Themba threatening jail here in Zimbabwe for murder, made them back off.'

'So I missed all the action?'

'It was not impressive. They are rangers, not fighters. Once they had calmed a bit, they began to map out who they last remembered him being with, and all his acquaintances that they knew of.'

'Good thinking. Did Kev fly the doctor in?'

Zol nodded. 'He said that Elias will live. He needs to go to hospital for his shoulder and arm to be set properly, but he can't give him an anaesthetic until his chest heals a bit unless we take him into a hospital larger than his little clinic in Hwange. But if we do take him anywhere, others will have access to him. They could finish him off before we can get the information we need. The doctor gave him morphine for now.'

Scott studied the man on the bed. The elephant had done a good number on him and an even better number on the stupid Mr Joubert. The Kenyans were lucky; they could still challenge Elias as to why he crossed to the other side of the law. As for the butcher, who knew his reasons? 'Was anyone sent after the wounded cow?'

'She was dead when we flew over her this morning. The elephant were already in mourning around her, the herd were touching her with their trunks, saying their last goodbye. I was glad we couldn't hear the rumblings of their sorrow over the noise in the chopper. She was not that far from where we collected the tracker.'

'And Joubert?'

'Themba and Kevin took photographs and packed up what was left of his body. The jackals had had a go at him—lucky it wasn't the hyenas. Kevin flew him to the morgue, guess someone will want to bury him properly one day.'

'The others?'

'Probably hyena fodder. Except Joubert's son. He was down an ant bear hole, but Joubert found him and put him up high in a tree. We'll need to collect him today, if the other poachers have not already found and retrieved him,' Zol replied solemnly. 'Tell me, Themba mentioned that Elmon Muleya, the Army Brigadier, was flying in to the lodge as soon after lunch as possible. Apparently, his troops are already on stand-by?'

Scott nodded. 'Looks like we might be ready to take down the ring by dawn.'

'That's if they haven't already moved out. An operation like that's very mobile. We got too close, and they will attempt to disappear.' Zol made a *poof* sound.

'Yes, but hopefully, while they're running, they won't carry out another mass slaughter.'

'There is that side to it,' Zol said. 'What about our unit? Any word?'

Tessa walked into the rondavel looking flustered. Scott hadn't seen her look so stressed for many years. 'Tess, what's up?'

'There are at least fifty armed men sitting by the pool and under the shade of the decking. They're arriving mostly in units of four. How is it that news travels so fast in the bush? I heard no drums. The last to arrive are Ken Norval's men from Matetsi Private Game Reserve near Victoria Falls. There are ten of them, and their *bakkies* are prepped for all-out war. Ken spared nothing in their fit out, and instructed them to report to you, Scott. I knew Matetsi was doing well with their river safaris, but their guards just proved it.' She took a breath. 'Guess it helps to have the biggest private game reserve in Zimbabwe on our side, and so well equipped.'

'That's good news. The more manpower we have, the better. But you're right, somehow the news is out there, and if they're hearing it, the poachers have too.'

'I've got twenty international tourists who flew in this morning. They're out there taking pictures of the anti-poaching units and posing with them, like it was a movie set.' She took a quick breath. 'I've briefed them that there was an active ring of poachers in the reserve, and we were gathering information to try and locate them. They simply don't comprehend the gravity of the situation. Most of them asked to be involved in whatever way they could including going in with hunting rifles, like a hunting safari—only, after poachers. What century do they think Africa is still in, hunting men for sport? Sometimes I wonder what they take us for. It's a goddamn adventure in their eyes, not a war.'

Scott smiled at Tessa. Zol laughed out loud.

'It's really not funny,' she said, 'but I can just imagine all the tourists when they go home. They will all get book deals when they sell their stories of being caught up in a real-life poaching drama. But this is our life, this is real. They can fly out in a day or so, and take their photographs and memories, but we live this day in, day out. If we don't stop the poachers soon there will be no more of the big five for them to photograph.'

'Come here.' Scott reached out and dragged Tessa to him. He held her for a while and stroked her back. 'Tess, everything is going to be fine. The reality is that those book deals, they won't happen. There's no way any of us are taking tourists with us on an operation. They will be sitting in your lodge sipping their daiquiris and their Red Bull and vodka mixes, while we go get the poachers. That's our job. Unless any of them are special ops, which is unlikely, they would be more hindrance than help to us. But you can keep them safe here and out of our way once we get moving. Don't worry about your tourists, just entertain them like you always do.'

She stepped back. 'Thanks, Scott. I needed that. But they still make me mad! People don't hunt people for sport, the last of that type of behaviour was the poor bushman in the 1800s. Really!' She walked out the room.

. . .

Scott sat opposite Zol in the Elephant rondavel, their lunch spread out before them. Despite the large number of tourists coming in that day, Tessa had managed to rearrange her camp to accommodate everyone, without having to clear them out.

'At last,' said Scott. 'Everyone is at lunch, we have a little peace and quiet. I wanted to show you this.' Out of his pocket, he took the A4 paper on which Ashley had copied her FMEA the night before. 'This is the plan. It depended on what information you brought with you, but now we need to go back down to the Gwabazabuya region and find the others. They are witnesses to who's involved in the ring, and we're going to need them to testify in court. Besides, I don't want to lose them.'

Zol nodded. He admired this quality in Scott. Compassion. Unlike his father, Scott had never officially fought in any war, and he had a softer side. Zol had noticed it when he was younger, but he didn't mind it. Not so Charlie, who thought it a weakness in his son. Instead, after Charlie died when Scott was fourteen, Zol had tried to make sure Scott understood that life was precious.

Scott had the ability to kill a person, and would do so if it was necessary. But Zol felt that he and Charlie had spilled enough blood, and Scott should never have to.

'Ashley was sleeping soundly at Delmonica when I left, but she might have woken up by now. She said she'd man the CB radio, just in case our men broke silence, and I explained about the click system we had set up. Gertrude said she would help her. I brought our mobile units anyway. She'll ring me on my cell phone if she hears anything, to keep off the open airwaves. The signal isn't too good on it but it's workable. The poachers are probably listening to the party line, so we can keep off that one too.'

'Where are the other volunteers?'

'I told William and David to work on the ranch, not to go into the reserve. They have two guards each with them. I asked Alan and Jabulani to stay at the homestead. I didn't want Ashley, Gertrude and the other ladies alone there.'

'Jabu was a good choice to pull from the anti-poaching unit and station with them. Good, we can almost relax.'

Scott walked through to the main bedroom he and Ashley had used the night before to use the bathroom, and as he completed his ablutions, he noticed Ashley's laundry packet from Hwange Safari Lodge sitting on the floor. He lifted it up. It was heavy. He broke out in a cold sweat. 'Shit. Shit. Shit. Shit. I'm an idiot.'

Inside was Ashley's .38, complete with her holster and all her ammo. He'd naturally assumed she'd re-arm herself in the morning. His heart sank to his stomach.

Zol jogged through the door. 'What?'

Scott held up her holster. 'She left this.'

'Is Alan armed?' Zol asked, shaking his head.

'He's got a 9mm, but we both know he isn't the best shot in the world. But Jabu is with him, they should be fine.'

'Still no harm in praying that she won't need it then, is there?' Zol said.

Scott picked up his cell phone and dialled Ashley's cell numbers from a folded piece of paper. The long wait as it clicked through all the different international exchanges killed him.

'Hello, Ashley speaking.'

Relief spread through Scott at just hearing her voice. 'Checking in on my sleepyhead.'

Static could be heard on the line.

'She's awake, having some strong coffee and something called *melktert*, courtesy of Lisa.'

He couldn't help smiling. 'Leave some for me. Don't eat it all.'

'You might need to fight Alan for a slice, he's consumed most of it already. It's really nice, like a custard tart, only better.'

'Leave me one piece at least for tonight.' Then he asked seriously, 'No news yet?'

'Nothing.'

'Keep listening. You left your weapon in the bathroom ...'

'Oh no! I forgot. Sorry, guess that was not my brightest moment. I was kind of distracted with everything else that had gone on.'

'Hey, don't worry about it, I'm sure you won't need it anyway.'

Zol shook his head and walked out of the room.

Scott knew a frown cut deep into his own forehead. 'Zol thinks I should be harder on you for forgetting.'

'He's probably right. How about you come back here and we can make up a punishment to fit the crime?' Her voice was seductive but challenging at the same time.

'Don't tempt me.'

She giggled, the sound melodious on the plastic phone. 'Well just think on what we can do to make up for it when you get home.'

The sassy woman was full of cheek as always.

'I need to go. See you soon. Bye.'

'Bye.'

Scott pushed the end button on his cell phone. He was feeling a little easier with Ashley's decision to regroup and man the CB. He walked to the master bed and lay down, staring at the ceiling while he waited for the afternoon's meeting with the army brass.

He felt as relaxed as a coiled spring.

With the arrival of Elmon Muleya, the core party of the anti-poaching unit began work in earnest. Themba sat with Kevin, Tessa, Seli and Sambo, Zol and Scott, with a still-sleeping Elias Kitia in the bed in the second bedroom. A surprise addition was Elliott, who had arrived just after lunch. He had his kitbag all packed, was armed with both assault and hunting weapons, and declared he now worked for Miss Ashley. In greeting, Zol clamped him in the old comrade's grasp, and together they had sat talking, off in one corner, until the meeting began.

The Kenyans had mapped out all the acquaintances they knew Elias had. The comprehensive list included a few ministers of state and other government officials who, in his high position, Elias would probably have come into contact with. They handed out copies of the list to everyone.

On the whiteboard, Tessa was filling in names of the dead and where their bodies were last located. Elmon had brought a huge topographical map of Hwange and its surrounding areas. Its laminate finish already had black rings to mark the spots where Mr Joubert and the other bodies had been found. Zol had put bright purple marks where they would find bodies lying in the bush. There was a rough cartoon-like car, indicating Lucinda's position, and Zol had put two question marks with little tents, showing two possible base sites for the poachers. Elmon had marked in red an area west of the game reserve but inside the Tosholotsho homeland, where his army troops were massing.

Elliott sat silently, watching and listening. Looking at the map, and the activity planned, the poachers would be snared soon enough.

Gertrude strode onto the veranda after lunch, where Ashley and Alan were both on recliners in the shade. 'There's a fire on the ranch. Tobias, the tractor driver, is going to investigate the smoke. Ashley, please can you call Scott and let him know, the workers are loading wet sacks and the drums filled with water.'

Ashley dialled Scott, and at last she heard a ring. Almost immediately he answered. 'Scott, Gertrude said there's a fire, and Tobias is going to see where it is.'

'Might just be a grassfire, it's been really hot, but it might be poachers. Make sure the farm workers go in the tractor and trailer, and that they take Jabulani with them. I'm sure that Gertrude would already have them loading the trailer.'

'She does, and yes they do. I'll make sure Jabulani comes too. I'll call you when we get to the fire and tell you more when we know.'

'No, Ashley. Stay put. It's not safe.'

'But it's a fire. It could burn the pumps if it gets near them.'

'And it could be the poachers, so you need to stay there. You've already had to run for your life once on this volunteering trip. I can't get back to the ranch right now to make sure it doesn't happen again. Let my workers fight the fire, they're trained for it.'

'But I can help.'

'No, you could cause more trouble simply by being there. Don't go.'

'You can't tell me what to do just because we have something going—'

'I'm instructing you as your boss. Don't go, Ashley.'

Silence followed as Ashley bit back more argument and realisation of Scott's source of authority sank in.

'Fine,' she said at last, hating that she had to listen to him.

'Call me when the workers get home so that I can speak to Tobias and get the details.'

'No problem. Bye.' Ashley ended the call and glared at the phone as if it was a cobra. She strode to the garage area. 'Scott said Jabulani needs to go with the workers.'

Without a sound, Jabulani nimbly launched himself onto the back of the trailer. Gertrude waved Tobias on, and the tractor rattled away slowly, heading towards the smoke. Ashley stood for a time watching until it disappeared behind the trees.

Two hours later, the tractor rattled back up towards the house. Ashley and Alan hurried to the garage area. Gertrude stood waiting, her face unreadable as the tractor came to a stop. One of the workers clambered down and began refilling the water containers. Jabulani pulled a balaclava off his face and sat on the side of the trailer, his rifle at the ready, pointed outwards. He was still poised for action even within the home fence, should it be necessary.

'Did you get it all out?' Gertrude asked.

'I thought so, but we were on the way home when we saw the new outbreak. It's bigger than the first one, more flames,' Tobias said.

'Do you think someone is lighting fires inside the reserve?'

'I don't know. But I needed to get more water, more men and more sacks. We need a second vehicle out there.' Tobias frowned. 'We had it under control, but now it's bad again. The fire is getting into the trees. It's burnt from the reserve into the top part of Delmonica. We have set a burn line, but it's come around again. It's coming towards the ranch.'

Gertrude nodded her head as Tobias uncoupled the trailer, then took the tractor towards the farm workers' compound.

'Seems we have a big fire on our hands,' she said as she ran her hand over her hair.

'At least he said it's just a fire, and it's on Delmonica, so that means no poachers,' Ashley said.

'Tobias will bring more men and take more water with them. They'll fight it.' Gertrude turned to walk to the kitchen.

Twenty minutes later, Alan saw Ashley climb onto the back of the trailer as Tobias started the tractor to leave. 'What are you doing, Ashley?'

'I can't sit around and do nothing. I'm quite capable of helping fight a bushfire.'

'I've volunteered here before. Scott expects to be listened to. He won't be happy if you leave the house.'

'He might be a mad at first, but when he sees we got the fire under control faster because there were more hands to help, he'll be fine.'

'No, he won't. He'll put you on the next plane home. Don't cross him. I've seen him send volunteers home for disobeying him.'

Gertrude heard the conversation and signalled Tobias to stay put. She stormed over to where Alan stood, shouting up at Ashley.

'Ashley, get off the trailer. Women don't fight bushfires.'

'Oh good. Now we are adding gender inequality to this argument,' Ashley said as she sat down heavily on the side of the trailer.

Gertrude rolled her eyes. 'No. I had the workers load the *bakkie* too. I thought at least we could run the water up and down the fire line, even if we don't fight it. It'll be a little faster than the tractors. Tobias asked for our help, they need another vehicle, and we don't have another driver.'

Ashley grinned. Taking Gertrude's outstretched hand, she jumped down from the trailer.

'No way in hell are you two leaving me behind,' Alan said as he joined them. 'And we take Jabulani with us in the *bakkie*, so that we still have protection and I can argue with Scott that we did listen to him, in a way ...'

Ashley concentrated on the dirt track ahead as Scott's *bakkie* bounced over another bump in the road. The tractors in front of them lumbered along like hippos out of water, ungainly as they bumped over the rough terrain. She watched their slow progress along the fire line. Alan, next to her in the passenger seat, had tied a rag that Gertrude had handed him securely over his nose and mouth, matching the one she wore.

They could smell smoke as they arrived at a gate. It lay thickly across the bush, coating everything with a grey tinge. Ashley slowed and Jabulani jumped off the back. 'Thanks, Jabu,' she called out as she passed him.

He nodded, closed the gate behind the *bakkie* and stood still. He put his hand up in a stop sign, and Ashley braked and stopped completely as he beckoned her to come close. 'Come, look, see.'

They climbed out of the parked *bakkie*. Alan lifted his hand to help Gertrude out of the back as she nimbly jumped down. She'd insisted on sitting on the back with Jabulani and the other workers. Ashley had just smiled and shrugged her shoulders. She'd been in no mood to argue about the dangers of not wearing a seatbelt.

Together they went over to stand next to Jabulani, who pointed at the ground.

'I'm looking, Jabu ... but at what?' Ashley asked.

'See the tracks? Those are from a large vehicle. Two tyres on each side. We never bring the cattle truck this way. Boss Scott says he doesn't want his truck getting stuck in the sand here.'

'Someone else has come this way?' Ashley asked.

'Yes. But this is our gate, so no one else should come here.' Jabulani pointed at the sign attached to the gate, an unnerving warning to those who entered uninvited. Like the sign at the front entrance to the ranch, it stated clearly: 'Trespassers will be shot.'

A chill cascaded down Ashley's spine.

'Maybe the poachers.' Jabulani crouched down and ran his finger along the ridge of the track. 'The truck is heavy, has lots in it. See here, it pushes the sand up.'

'I'm going to radio Scott,' Ashley said, walking to the *bakkie*. She reached in and pushed the talk button.

'Scott, come in.'

Silence.

'Scott, this is Ashley, come in please.' Silence.

Gertrude, now standing by the *bakkie*, looked around at the countryside. 'We must be in a dead spot where the signal can't get through.'

Ashley called again. 'Scott. Scott. This is Ashley, come in.' A static noise followed but no answering call. She pulled her cell phone out her pocket. 'No signal.' She tossed it onto the seat.

'Come on, we're wasting time. We can tell him when we get home, after we get that fire contained,' said Gertrude. 'Let's go. Jabu, keep a sharp eye out, if the poachers are here.'

'I won't let anything happen to you Gertrude, or Miss Ashley and Mr Alan. Scott and Zol would kill me if I did.'

'Thank you,' Gertrude said. 'Come on, let's get moving.'

'I'll keep trying,' said Ashley. 'Jabulani,' she called out loudly, as she watched him following the tracks a little way along the road. 'Get in, we need to go.'

They returned to the *bakkie* and drove on towards the smoke, following the tractors as they took a right-hand fork in the road.

'This is the road we took to the first pump I repaired,' Ashley told Alan as they bounced over the *middle mannetjie* and headed for the smaller track.

Soon the tractors stopped at the pump site. Ashley pulled up behind them and surveyed their surroundings. She climbed out of the *bakkie* and left her door open as she stared at where her pump shed had been. Black charred earth with rubble and a few buckled sheets of corrugated iron in a pile was all that remained. Everything was destroyed: the tin shack, the diesel drum and the old Lister pump were all gone. Burned by people as despicable and cowardly as the hyena. She stared at the devastation.

'How could they do this?' Anger burned deeply in her belly and acid crept up her throat.

Jabulani scratched his head. He looked confused by her question.

Gertrude was silent, shaking her head, her mouth covered with a rag. The last of the black smoke from the diesel drum was beaten down by the workers with their wet hessian sacks, then they began walking westwards, following the line of the fire blazing in the grass. Now that the engine and the fuel were no longer burning, the fire had changed back to the normal hues of a bushfire, orange with white smoke.

Ashley took a breath behind her makeshift mask. 'Why?'

'To stop you repairing it. They want the animals somewhere else in the reserve,' Gertrude said. 'Let's get on the radio again.'

Slowly, Ashley walked to Scott's *bakkie*. Even in her distress, she noticed that Gertrude, walking next to her, was silent; her step like a desert cat, making no sound and leaving hardly any footprints in the sand.

Jabulani climbed onto the back. He held out a hand, and Gertrude grabbed his wrist and swung up onto the *bakkie*. She said, 'I've told the workers we'll move the *bakkie* along the fire's edge, leaving the water drums at intervals, and find out how far it goes. If we can get in front of it, the four of us can fight it from the other side, that way we should put it out faster. It seems to be slow burning, and as there's no wind, it hopefully won't get away from us again. At least it doesn't seem to be in the trees any longer.'

Turning to Alan, Ashley said, 'Come on. There's not much more we can do here.' She climbed in, slammed the door and fastened her seatbelt.

Alan got into the passenger seat, wiping his forehead on his dirty sleeve, sweating profusely from the intense heat in the small clearing. He left the rag over his mouth and nose, the smoke still permeating through.

'You couldn't have done anything to stop this happening, even if we had been here earlier,' he said as she started the ignition.

'I'm finished trying to analyse life here. It's all too hard.' She looked briefly at him, then back at the dirt track.

'There are four fixed pumps in this area. Your number one is gone. When the fire is out, we should check the others close to here. Perhaps they're still okay and the animals will have some water.'

Ashley tried both her cell and the CB again, with no luck.

'Damn technology,' she grumbled at her phone, as she looked again at a no signal screen. They drove through the bush, along the fire's edge. Every kilometre or so they stopped and dropped a water drum off, then continued on trying to get in front of the smouldering blaze. The tractors crawled behind them, the workers looking like a road gang as the wet sacks swung freely from their hands. Up and down, up and down, accustomed to fighting fires, beating the flames out.

Emotionally drained, Ashley stared out the windscreen. An alien feeling invaded her heart, one of pure hatred towards the poachers for the mistreatment of the majestic wildlife around them. What had started out as an adventure holiday had turned into a nightmare.

Although no longer blazing, the creeping fire had spread from the reserve onto Delmonica. They would need to cross back through another gate and onto the ranch to get in front of it. She stopped and waited as Jabulani jumped off the back of the *bakkie* and opened the gate. She let out the clutch and crept forward.

Hell exploded around them.

There was an almighty roar and the *bakkie* shook under her, lifting in the front, then it rolled sidewards into a tree, before slowly rocking back onto its wheels.

Deafened, she looked around her silent world. She was securely held within her seatbelt and the airbag had deployed, so she couldn't see the dials behind the steering wheel. Alan's mask had been pulled off his face and blood trickled out the corner of his mouth. Slowly, he collapsed forward, his body offering no resistance or showing any sign of consciousness as his face struck the dashboard.

Turning her head, she looked for Gertrude, but saw nothing.

She tried to focus on the gate to see Jabulani, but her vision clouded. As she stared into the white haze, she saw an unknown white man mouthing words at her, through where the window of her door should have been. But she couldn't understand or hear him. His lips continued to move as the white haze contracted around her vision.

Darkness zeroed in on her, and she slumped into a black abyss.

CHAPTER 12

The anti-poaching parties gathered at Zebra Pan Lodge. Organised and sombre, they all sat waiting for instructions. But every man was on his feet when they heard the sound of a distant explosion, followed by the hollow popping of automatic gunfire.

'Landmine,' Zol said.

'Russian,' Elmon concurred.

Themba nodded his agreement, identifying the distinct sound from years of war.

Scott flew off his chair and outside to the CB radio in Tessa's *bakkie*. 'Ashley, Ashley, come in.' Silence.

Zol was by his side. 'Gertrude, Gertrude, come in.' Nothing.

The CB crackled into life. 'It's Lisa, Boss.'

'Is Ashley there?'

'No, Miss Ashley, Master Alan, Gertrude and Jabulani went to help with the fire.'

Scott turned to Zol, his face wearing a worried expression. Zol punched the side of Tessa's *bakkie*. The metal crumpled under the force.

Scott brought the CB mouthpiece back to his face and pushed the talk button. 'Did you hear that explosion?'

'Yes.'

'Did you feel it?'

'Yes.'

'Damn,' Scott swore.

'That means it was closer to Delmonica than Zebra Pan. I'll get some of the other units to come with us.' Zol turned and marched down to the pool area.

Scott continued on the CB to Lisa. 'Anyone checked in?'

'No.'

'Listen, Lisa. Bring the staff inside the security gates and lock them. Until I know what's going on, I want everyone safe.'

'Yes, Boss. Over and out.'

Scott could imagine Lisa rushing outside to *Shaya Insimbi,* the huge old plough disk that hung in the tree. The staff knew that if it was rung, everyone had to come up to the main house area. The practice had always been in place when Scott was growing up during the war years, and it had never been forgotten. Even now, when the country was supposedly at peace, the signal remained in place to call the staff together should the need arise: for fire danger, rogue elephant sightings, or just the simple get-together for Christmas *boksie,* the handing out of buckets filled with goods and food for Christmas. The *insimbi* would ring, and his people would gather.

Tessa and Kevin joined him at the *bakkie,* Sipewe not far behind. Kevin asked, 'Have you and Zol decided on an explosion area?'

Scott nodded. 'Closer to Delmonica. Lisa felt tremors, we didn't.'

'What happened to my *bakkie*?' Tessa asked, pointing at the new dent in the door.

'Zol happened. Don't worry, we'll have it fixed. Something's very wrong. Ashley, Gertrude and Alan left with Jabulani earlier to help put out a bushfire, but they're not back yet and haven't been in contact with us or home base.'

'Elmon and Themba said it's better we handle this ourselves, until we know what we're facing. It might simply be an old arms cache going off, and if they get involved too soon the poachers will know they are here.'

'Good thinking on their part,' Scott said. 'How's the fuel in the chopper, Kev?'

'Full. I'll head out towards the reserve. See what I can see. Probably two, two and a half hours of light left at most. When you are mobile, call me on channel 23.'

'Got you. Take care.' Scott shook Kevin's hand and Sipewe climbed into the driver's seat of Tessa's *bakkie*, to drive Kevin to the airstrip.

Scott walked away to check on Zol. He had never seen Zol lose it before now, but then he had never seen Zol in love either. Now both their women were missing. It was up to them to locate Gertrude and Ashley. He quickened his pace, hearing Zol's voice calmly speaking loudly in Ndebele.

The units of men were already assembled. The relaxed atmosphere had disappeared, and in its place was an elite militia, ready for war, willing to die for the cause they believed in. They sat silently, listening to Zol's instructions.

'Elliott, I want you and three others with us in one *bakkie*. In the second, I need another six guards.' He nodded to Scott, acknowledging his arrival. 'Lastly, two groups of six men, ready to mobilise now and willing to go in on foot as scouts when we find the blast area. Everyone got radios?'

'*Yebo*,' came the united answer from the units.

'Channel 23,' Scott instructed.

A flurry of activity ensued as the anti-poaching units changed frequencies on their assorted radios.

Scott continued. 'Those remaining behind, stay alert. Don't go anywhere until we send instructions through Miss Tessa. Once we establish what caused the blast, we'll continue with the original plan.'

Zol and Scott led the volunteer units out to the *bakkies* parked near the sheds. Everyone climbed on board their allocated vehicle. They left Tessa, a grim expression on her face, standing stiffly in the lodge's shed area.

Scott noticed she didn't wave goodbye as they drove off.

Half an hour later, the units sat silent in the *bakkies*. Under Scott's and Zol's instructions, no one radioed their base stations to say they were on the move. Twenty-one highly trained anti-poaching guards focused on one objective: finding the missing vehicle.

They travelled towards Delmonica; the only sounds were the hum of their vehicles as they travelled in convoy, scanning the bush, looking for signs that something had passed by and Kevin's chopper overhead.

Kevin's voice broke the silence in the *bakkie*. 'Scott? Kev.'

'Kev, Scott. Go!'

'The fence is down, looks like a single burnt-out vehicle, *bakkie* of some sort, at the top gate from the reserve into Delmonica.'

'Any movement?'

'Negative. A bateleur eagle circling in the sky above me could mean something is down there.'

'Negative movement?' Scott double checked.

'Affirmative. Widening my area of search now. Out.'

Zol's face looked grey.

Scott signalled and the two vehicles behind halted. Six men departed, merging into the bush. A little while later they paused again, and six more men disappeared into the bush. The three four-wheel drives continued, Scott and Zol in the first *bakkie*, with six men remaining: three of Norval's team, Dennis, driving with Mazwi and Majola in the next, and Elliott driving alone, in the last.

The burnt-out *bakkie* came into view. They all stopped their vehicles. Zol and Scott climbed out and slowly walked towards the carnage. Alan was beside the vehicle. He'd been shot with a single round, in the temple, and didn't look like he'd even had time to put up a fight.

There were many tracks around the vehicle. Looking at the ground the whole time, Elliott and Dennis skirted the area in a huge circle. Mazwi and Majola stayed at the vehicles, waiting for instructions on which direction to pursue. Zol put his hand up and called to them to pick up tracks outside the clearing, and they disappeared into the bush.

Elliott and Dennis found Jabulani. He lay face down, and despite the bullet wounds ripped through his body, Elliott could see Jabulani had been crawling towards the *bakkie*, until, execution-style, someone had shot him, too, in the side of the head. Jabulani's hunting knife was still in his hand. Even injured, he'd continued to try to protect his charges.

'I have Jabu,' Elliott called.

Zol and Scott came over to where they stood, staring down at the congealed blood on Jabulani's head, already buzzing with flies and midges. Zol turned him over, and Elliott handed him two plaster strips and a bandage from his first-aid kit.

Zol taped Jabulani's eyes closed and put a bandage around his head to keep his mouth shut. He crossed his arms in front of him and, using what was left of the bandage, tied them in place. Then he and Elliott carried him to the back of the *bakkie* and laid him flat.

'Sleep in peace, my friend. I will avenge you,' Zol swore to his fallen comrade.

Scott placed a hand on his shoulder and squeezed. He could feel Zol's shoulder shaking with the rage he knew burned inside the older man.

They did the same with Alan's body, dressing it for burial and then loading it next to Jabulani in the *bakkie*.

Scott said, 'Dennis, drive back to Zebra Pan. Take Alan and Jabulani, and ask Miss Tessa to get Kevin to take them to the doctor from Hwange. Keep your radio on. When you get back, inform Miss Tessa personally of what we found. I don't want it on air. The poachers will be monitoring us. Tell Miss Tessa two bodies were dragged from this place. At the moment only the men are dead. There is blood, but we'll let her know more later. Tell her to carry on with the original plan. We are going after the others.'

Dennis nodded and climbed into the *bakkie*. He backed it away and then turned around, driving slowly to show respect for the dead bodies in his care.

'Zol, let's go,' Scott said, climbing into the first *bakkie*. Zol sat on the bonnet, slightly to the passenger's side so as not to obstruct too much of Scott's view and wedged his feet on the bull bar. Elliott slipped into the driver's seat of the second vehicle with Mazwi and Majola, and together the two trucks followed the tracks made by the kidnappers' transport.

After a while, they came across a place in the bush where a second vehicle had met the first. But then they separated again, with the truck heading in one direction and the lighter vehicle going in another.

'Elliott, go south, with Mazwi and Majola. Follow those tracks,' Scott said. 'Good luck.'

Zol and Scott watched as Mazwi took over driving from Elliot, who climbed onto the bonnet much as Zol had done, and they drove off, Majola standing on the back holding onto the roll bar.

'Drive,' Zol said, and they began to follow the tracks they had allocated themselves, heading west towards the Botswana border. Night was slowly creeping over the horizon, the lazy sun slinking into the bush just when Scott and Zol needed her light. Zol cursed in the dappled shadows of the trees, and continued to bounce gently along on the *bakkie*'s bonnet. He soon turned and held up his hand.

'I know,' Scott acknowledged. 'We've lost the light. Foot time.' The two friends instinctively tuned in to each other's thoughts over their years together, the old *keghla* and the boss's son, now a grown man.

Scott radioed Tessa. 'Tessa, come in.'

'Tessa here.'

'Don't hold dinner for us, we're still busy.'

'Sure. I got your message. Good luck. Over and out.' The radio went silent.

'Kevin's a lucky man,' Zol said.

'We're just as lucky. Now let's go and find our women,' Scott said hoarsely, the dull ache in his throat growing when he thought of the time it was taking to save the women and of what the kidnappers could be doing to them. He thought of Ashley with her blonde hair, fair skin and lips he had been kissing just that morning. He shut his eyes as he attempted to block out the image in his head of what was going to happen or could be happening to her. Ashley bound in chains, tortured, raped, gang raped and passed around a campfire on the bare ground ...

Zol interrupted his dark thoughts. 'Don't think it, Scott.'

'It's hard not to.'

'We'll get to them. We don't have a choice.'

Blurry shapes draped in clouded rainbows swam across Ashley's vision, as her head bobbed back into a sleeping position on a hard ground. Her eyelids were heavy as they continued to shield her eyes. Pain set in as consciousness invaded, and she became aware of her aching body. Her hands were tied tightly behind her back. Pulling at them desperately to free herself, she felt the rope bite into her wrists. She stopped struggling and tried to think clearly. She wriggled gently and felt her feet touch a solid object. Her sore eyes opened to slits and the darkness rushed away. A tree trunk. She was tied up under a tree. And if she moved her arms, her feet would move too. Her hands were bound tightly and then secured to her trapped feet!

She was hogtied.

Animals got hogtied, not humans. What type of people did this to a human? Salty tears burned her eyes.

She checked her immediate surroundings, but couldn't see Alan, Gertrude or Jabulani. The darkness of night pressed into her eyes. She focused on the moving shapes in front of her, and her vision slowly cleared enough that she could see two white men, one with a huge dark beard and dressed in jungle clothes, arguing with the other over something that lay at their feet. Gertrude.

The larger man was speaking in a foreign language and gesturing towards her. The smaller man picked up Gertrude and slung her over his shoulder, much like one would carry a sack of potatoes or a large packet of potting soil, and walked towards Ashley.

Her vision was clearing under her puffy eyelids and she blinked rapidly. He was an albino. So it must be the poachers' ring that had captured them, as she didn't think it likely there was more than one albino in the area.

He carelessly dumped the unconscious Gertrude half on top of her with a thud. Ashley screamed in pain, as her body absorbed the weight of the impact.

'So, layde, yous is awake now?' The albino spoke with a slight slur, and she noticed that only one side of his face moved as he leered at her. The other side was deadpan, expressionless.

He leant over her and roughly ran a calloused hand down the vee of her shirt. She struggled to get out of his reach, but even as she shrank away from him, he pinched her nipple. She winced and renewed her effort to free her hands. 'Leave me alone! Get your hands off me!'

'So yous is Scott Decker's woomens now?'

She stared at him, not sure if she should answer truthfully. Was she Scott's woman? They had spent a night together. Or should she lie and deny that she knew him at all? She hesitated to answer.

He ran his sun spotted hand over her hair and roughly pulled the band out of the back. He spread her loosened hair out with his fingers and, bringing a strand to his nose, inhaled the fragrance. She attempted to pull it from his grip by tugging her head quickly.

'Yous not so sures if yous are or not? Yous can't answer?' he asked her, taking another breath of her hair. 'But the bush telegraph says yous are his. Now I haf his woomens, what is I gonna to do wif yous?' He shoved Gertrude off her and pushed her out of the way, then moved his hands under Ashley's breasts and scrunched them in his foul palms. Quickly his hands descended on the outside of her shorts, over her stomach, and down to her groin. He took a huge hunting knife from its sheath at his hip, and cut the rope that bound her feet.

Ashley couldn't move. Her body felt like a dead weight and now that her feet were loose, the blood was rushing into them. The pins and needles sensation made her feel sick it was so bad.

'Kant *fook* wif legs closed,' he said, and sheathing the knife again, he pinned her legs with his body weight as he sat on them.

He began to unbutton his fly.

Ashley realised now what Scott had told her earlier, about her safety. She had been arrogant, strong-willed and selfish. She had ignored everything he'd said and done her own thing anyway. And now she was facing the consequences. Bile rose in her throat.

There are things worse than death in Africa ...

There was no one here to save her, no one coming to her rescue. She was going to be raped. But this was not the cupboard, and she was not a helpless child anymore.

She heard him close to her ear. 'So yous not going to speak to the albino?' His yellow teeth showed in a grimace. His spit spattered her face as the garlic smell of his breath made her gag. 'Is okay. Woomens who talk and not *fook* is no fun.'

Adrenaline kicked into her numb body, and she began twisting, bucking and kicking to try to topple him off. Fighting for more than her life now, with every ounce of strength she possessed, she pushed at him. He toppled off. He stood up and came back towards her, more determined.

'Iz better to heve a woomens who scream.' He ripped at her blouse and the top button popped off. He fumbled in the process of trying to get it to part more.

'Get away from me!' she screamed. She lashed out at him with her feet and landed a good kick, causing him to fall again.

The dark-bearded white man walked over and let loose a sentence in the foreign language he spoke. He smacked the albino over the top of the head with the flat of his hand and kicked at the unconscious Gertrude. '*Moenie fok nie*!' he shouted. And although Ashley didn't understand all the words, she realised he'd saved her from certain rape.

The albino had one more feel of her breast.

'Woomens so sofftt, *Meneer*, so good,' he said. Moving as fast as a striking cobra, he pulled out his knife again and slashed at her chest. Searing pain shot through her from above her left breast—real pain that her mind acknowledged.

He'd cut her deeply. Crimson blood oozed out and soaked into her shirt.

'I said *no*. Not yet,' the white man ground out savagely in English. This time, his fist flew into the albino's chest with a dull *thud*, the force toppling the albino over Gertrude. The white man grabbed the front of the albino's shirt and pulled him off her and Gertrude, before roughly pushing him aside, away from them.

Ashley heard his words, *not yet*, and knew she was far from safe. She thanked God for her conscious state. But her troubles had just begun. Her body ached from the explosion, but with the removal of the ropes from her legs, she could feel them responding. Her toes moved, her legs moved, her hands had a little more feeling. Although they were still bound, the tight pressure that had been there before was now gone. Her chest burned as if someone had stuck a branding iron in the fire and placed it on her breast.

She sat up. The white man returned to her and bent down to her level. In a heavily accented voice he said, 'I is watching you. Your Scott is so busy trying to save the animals, he won't be able to save you too. Scott and the army, they will learn not to fuck with me. They will learn this reserve is mine. The animals are mine. I decide what lives and what dies.'

'You'll rot in hell for what you've done. You're the animal who should be shot.' Her chest heaved with her outburst.

'Oh, the little Australian bitch has a temper.' He laughed a guttural sound deep within his throat. 'Ugh, shame ... and the Australian government is so weak. Typical First World country, they think that saving one citizen is worth it. They will pay your ransom eventually.' He hacked up phlegm and spat it near Gertrude's head. Then he looked at the albino.

'Don't spoil the booty, Rodney. We need them well. Once we have these pretty fillies on tape in Lusaka, then you can think about what you can do with them. Until then, hands off.'

'*Jissis, Meneer*. You always lets me have the woomens, but after the vidio camera is tooken pitchers I gonna *fook* thems?'

'After, yes. Not now.'

The albino smiled, a manic grimace that reminded Ashley of the Joker from Batman. Only this was real, not a cartoon. And there was no superhero in black spandex and driving a black turbocharged car coming to save her.

He walked away with the white man, leaving them alone. She looked around for Alan and Jabulani, but still couldn't see them. Her chest hurt. She heard a mosquito buzzing around and was grateful the night was cooler and the flies were not as active as during the day. Remembering one of Scott's stories about flies and maggots, she blew down on her chest, trying to help her skin crust over faster.

'Gertrude?' she called quietly.

Only silence, heavy and quiet.

She wriggled over to Gertrude, trying not to attract the attention of the albino she knew stalked somewhere nearby in the camp. 'Gertrude.' She nudged her.

Gertrude didn't stir.

Ashley slumped down onto her side next to her. Her hands ached, still bound tightly behind her back. Taking large gulps of air, she tried not to panic as she nudged Gertrude again, a little harder this time.

Still nothing.

She concentrated on her surroundings. First, she focused on the camp, counting the people present, starting with the white man with the bushy beard, Rodney the albino. There was a big truck sitting off to the side, its back covered with a tarpaulin of sorts, and a net with pieces of rags on it. A small fire burned in the ring of stones at the centre of the camp, and a large black man cooked something in the three-legged cast-iron pot sitting in the coals of the fire. He appeared to hobble around as if walking hurt him. Two other black men dressed in camouflage clothing sat on stools near the fire, cleaning their weapons. One looked like a lanky teenager still waiting to grow into his clothes. Five people in all, that she could see.

She listened to the sounds of the bush, to a cricket greeting the night and the incessant sound of mosquitoes buzzing everywhere. She didn't know if she was still in the reserve or out if it. The moon was rising over the trees, silver and bright.

'Scott, help me,' she whispered desperately into the heavens above her, holding on to his image in her mind as the focal point of her existence. This whole kidnapping was her fault. If she hadn't been so strong-willed and stupid in insisting that she went out to fight the fire, they wouldn't have been caught in the ambush and everyone would be safe at Delmonica's ranch house.

Everyone being hurt was her fault. And the worst realisation was that even if she did get out of this alive, Alan had been right. Scott would put her on a plane back to Australia and she wouldn't get to spend more time with him. And that was all she wanted other than her life right now: time with Scott. To hold him and not feel the shivers that had always been there before. In just two weeks, Scott had crashed through every barrier she had put in place over the years to protect her heart. For the first time in her life, she wanted a man's touch, craved both Scott's touch and his company. She had ruined the trust before she got to talk to him about the new feelings that were emerging from her cold heart.

The cook hit a spoon on a tin plate, and the poachers gravitated to him for their meal. Once everyone was served, he brought her a tin plate of food and an enamel mug much like the one Zol carried, only this was missing the beautiful beadwork. Just plain, as if no one cared enough to bother decorating it. But it was filled with steaming black coffee.

'Thank you,' she said. He didn't smile back at her, and on closer inspection, Ashley realised that he couldn't. He had no lips. Just scar tissue, grotesquely covering his skin where lips should have been. As she studied him, she noticed that he had no ears either, just a small stump on the left side of his head and a smooth scar on the right. A sick feeling grew in her stomach.

Who had mutilated this man and why?

He stepped behind her and loosened the rope from around her hands, and as she massaged her wrists, he motioned for her to eat. She looked down at her food. There was a thick wedge of bread, surrounded by a stew of some sort with onions, vegetables and meat, swimming in gravy that had begun to congeal around the rim of the tin plate. She sipped at the coffee, and he again gestured to the food. Slowly, she dragged the plate in front of her, realising that she needed to eat to keep up her strength so she could get away. She began to eat, forcing each mouthful down with extreme effort, despite the surprisingly tasty flavour of the stew.

He stood in front of her, watching her as a hawk would a mouse, while he held her ropes in his big hands. It was then that she noticed the tips of his fingers were also missing. The silent cook slowly squatted down while she ate, rocking rhythmically back and forth on his haunches.

'This is nice. You're a good cook. Thank you,' she complimented him, as she gave him the empty plate, mopped clean with the bread. She finished the sweet coffee and returned the mug too. He passed her a tea towel pulled from his apron, and motioned to her chest. She placed it inside her shirt, tying it to cover the cut with the clean cloth and make a pressure bandage of sorts to help stop the slow seeping of blood, protecting it from the flies.

He put the dish and mug on the dirt and rebound her hands behind her back.

'Please no, please,' she begged. 'Please don't bind me again, please.'

But he ignored her pleas and used a little harder force to hold onto her hands and tie them together behind her back. After testing that they were tight enough, he picked up the crockery and returned to the fire without a backwards glance.

The food sat heavy in her stomach, threatening to return. Violated and stripped of the rights that she had taken for granted, she fought the tears that swelled in her eyes. Blinked them away, clearing her vision. She had to find a way to get herself and Gertrude out of this mess. She'd already survived a night in the bush on the run with Scott and Zol, now all she needed to do was think more like them, like a local, not like a fish out of water.

Ashley sat near Gertrude, watching the camp. The glow from the fire illuminated the poachers, sitting drinking beer after their supper. After what seemed like a long time, Gertrude stirred slightly and attempted to stretch. 'Gertrude,' she whispered loudly. 'Wake up.'

Gertrude grunted and then attempted to roll over.

'No, don't move. If I can get close enough to you, perhaps I can untie your hands.' Ashley slowly shuffled on her behind over the dirt, and turned her back on the fire to try to undo Gertrude's bonds. They were tight, and despite feeling one of her nails tearing painfully on the rough rope, she could not grip it sufficiently to untie Gertrude.

'Oh, my head hurts. Where are we?'

'The poachers have us in a camp. I can't see Alan or Jabulani.' Ashley knew she was talking too fast, but she couldn't help it. Better to babble and be alive than silent and dead, she thought.

Gertrude tried to sit up. Ashley watched her grit her teeth and move through the pain. She shuffled on her bottom. 'How many people in the camp?'

'Five that I could see earlier.'

'I'll try to untie you. Quick, before they notice we're moving around.'

Ashley sat with her back to Gertrude and, as Gertrude worked on her restraints, a shouting match broke out around the fire.

'*Jissis* Rodney, I said *nee*. No more marks on the women, until after the video. We are taking a big enough chance already, doing this kidnapping behind the investors' backs. If they find out ...'

'Just one little *fook*. I promises I not use my knife and cut any thems.'

'No. Don't go near them. Vakani, take this 9mm. You sleep, guarding the prisoners tonight. If Rodney goes near those women, shoot him. Understood? But only if he goes near them.' The voice had a hard warning in it.

The cook tucked the gun into the band of his pants, at the small of his back, where his apron ties crisscrossed before returning to the front. His face was unreadable.

'That should keep you away, Rodney. You know he despises you and won't hesitate to shoot you. Give Vakani half a chance and you will be eating lead. Understand?'

Rodney nodded.

'Yeah right ... you had better. Vakani, what have we got for pudding?'

The cook hobbled away to the rear of the truck.

'Not the albino?' Gertrude said.

'Don't I know it? He was getting close to raping me when that white man stopped him,' Ashley said, her voice shaking.

'He's an animal. We have to get out of here. He cuts everything. During the war of Independence, when they were captured, he cut off Kwiella's brother's ears, his lips and his tongue, then he made Kwiella eat them.'

Ashley dry retched. She turned her torso towards Gertrude so she could see the blood-soaked tea towel.

'Oh, my ...' Gertrude focused on untying Ashley's ropes again.

Ashley wiggled her fingers. 'The cook. He has no tongue or ears or lips.'

'Kwiella never mentioned if his brother survived. You'd think he would have died.'

'Poor guy. But he's one of them?'

The last knot on Ashley's ropes came undone. 'Got it. You're free.'

Relief flooded through her. It was just one little part of getting away, and yet having no ropes on her, she felt free. She rubbed her wrists and turned around to get started on Gertrude's ropes again. This time, she could see what she was doing, but still could not get them undone.

'Let me try the feet first. Maybe that will let some slack on the hands.'

Gertrude adjusted her weight to give Ashley access to the knots.

'One down, one lot to go!' Ashley whispered as she pulled the rope off Gertrude's feet a few minutes later.

Gertrude rotated her ankles in circles. Ashley knew she was silently enduring the pain of the blood rushing back into her feet, grateful for any sensation in them, rather than none. No longer having the tension of the rope pulling on her wrist knots, Ashley quickly released Gertrude's hands. 'There you go.'

The men at the fire dispersed. Vakani, with the 9mm sitting snugly inside his apron band, stoked the fire high with new fuel and inspected around the fireplace, making sure there were no scraps lying around to lure hyena into the camp. The white man and the two black men disappeared into their tents, just out of the ring of light. Rodney sat near the fire. Eventually Vakani walked towards the women, carrying a small three-legged stool.

Gertrude lay down again, as if still unconscious, making sure her feet were tucked away behind her and not immediately visible. Ashley pulled her ropes back onto her hands, in case he checked on her, and lay down. She could hardly breathe. Her heart beat so fast in her chest, she wondered if it would burst. The rush of blood in her ears was loud, smothering all other sounds of the bush around them.

He sat down a little way from them, in the warmth of the fire but close enough that they couldn't whisper freely anymore. He took the handgun out, stroked it almost lovingly, and then cocked it.

The metallic sound sent shivers down Ashley's spine. She saw Gertrude flinch.

Vakani lay down on the ground and tipped the stool on its side. Using the sagging canvas for a headrest, he crossed his arms, and the gun, silhouetted by the fire, poked above his broad waist. There he stayed, not moving. Obviously asleep, but on guard.

Rodney slunk towards him. Immediately Vakani raised his arm and pointed the gun directly at the albino's chest. The small click of the safety being taken off was magnified in the quietness of the night.

Rodney backed away, a sneer on his deformed face. He walked to the tent set furthest away from the women, and the harsh ripping sound of a zip closing behind him was like a door being slammed.

Vakani settled the gun back in its position at his waistband.

Through his tent flap, Rodney watched Vakani. Hatred like hot tar bubbled in his chest. He knew a matching one echoed in Vakani's fat belly. But having to watch Vakani sleep so close to the women, and Rodney himself not allowed to touch them. Not thrusting his knife into Vakani's belly and gutting him like a woman after he'd *fook*ed her had been a mistake that had come back to haunt him, even now, twenty years later.

Rodney had still been a freedom fighter the day he sliced up Vakani, and the boss-boy at the Dando's dairy farm. Together they had tried to stop the freedom fighters from cutting all the hamstrings of the dairy herd by alerting the farmer to Rodney's presence in the area. Rodney's signature calling card during this time was naturally associated with his love of knives. He always ensured that the farmers knew which 'terrorist' had passed through, spared their lives and those of their families, but not always their incomes and livestock.

Rodney's first big mistake was in only mutilating Vakani and humiliating his young sibling, Kwiella. He should have killed them both. His second was in thinking that years later the mute man wouldn't have the courage to come after him with a burning log and smash in half his face, crushing his cheekbone and eye socket. The damage to his facial nerves meant that half his face was useless. Their tolerance of each other sat on a razor's edge, and it was only *Meneer* Lawrence who kept the mutual contempt spilling over into more bloodshed.

Vakani was already working for *Meneer*s Lawrence and Joubert in the poaching industry when Rodney joined their operation, so he couldn't get rid of him then. Anyway, good cooks were hard to find and, in the intervening years, Vakani had somehow learned to cook well enough to be called a chef. *Meneer* Lawrence kept both of them on a tight leash, making sure neither finished what was started so many years previously.

Both had their strengths and usefulness to the team.

Both men lived with their mutilations.

His penis throbbed with wanting the woman, with hair as light as sunlight and softer than feathers. She'd smelled like softness, her hair so similar to the German's daughter all those years ago ... He needed more blood and a good *fook*. His body shook with want. He was angry with *Meneer* Lawrence. For so many years, he had given him loyal service, and this is how he was repaid, by not getting to *fook* the women until after they had crossed over into Zambia.

He would show him soon. He always did ...

CHAPTER 13

Scott and Zol jogged.

An owl hooted in the distance, a sable broke cover and crashed through the bush. They could hear elephant somewhere off to their right, their low rumblings telegraphed in the quiet night. They pressed on, following the vehicle's tracks.

The forlorn cry of a jackal and the grunt of a warthog nearby, safely settled in its burrow were heard. Years of bush training ensured that they missed nothing, checking each broken plant, every subtle track mark, turning off the main track when the signs indicated, the moon both illuminating and shadowing their task. Eventually, as the moonlight dimmed and the first of the million stars that light up the night theatre began to disperse, they smelled the sign they needed.

Wood smoke.

They followed the scent, and soon they could make out the rough silhouette of a bush camp. One large truck, with its back towards the fire, obviously held the supplies. The fire was in the centre of the camp, with four tents pitched close by. Everyone appeared asleep, including one guard, his head resting on an overturned three-legged stool. He had to be guarding the hostages, but Scott couldn't catch sight of them yet.

Zol and Scott quietly backed away and then skirted around the camp.

Only then did they see what they were searching for: Ashley's outline in the dim light. Scott's body hair rippled and stood rigid. Then he saw Gertrude sitting next to her. They were too close to the guard to simply slip away ... damn.

Zol tapped him on the shoulder and signalled for him to follow. As stealthy as a leopard, Scott crept after Zol, away from the woman who he now knew he loved with all his being. He also knew that if Ashley or Gertrude had been dead, Zol and he would have cut each throat of the poaching party involved without flinching. Until this moment, he had never truly comprehended the term that you would die for someone's love. He was willing to die for Ashley to live.

Once away from the camp, they debated an idea. They couldn't see any perimeter guards and were discussing how to snatch the women, when Scott's radio clicked twice. They clicked back, but drew their weapons just in case. Out of the bush materialised Sifiye, Dumisai, Banga and Miracle, four of the men from Norval's patrol they had dropped off earlier.

'Boss Scott, we saw nothing where we were, but we could smell the smoke from the camp and were scouting the area when we saw you two.'

'We must be getting out of practice,' Scott said to Zol.

'They saw us.' Zol grinned and shook their hands in greeting.

They all hunched around in a small circle as Zol explained their plan, and how, as there were now six of them, it would be much easier. Soon Banga and Dumisai moved away, and Zol left with Sifiye. Scott and Miracle slunk back towards the camp, skirting the women and coming up behind the tents.

Silently, they set a trap at each entrance, with a rope pulled tight, just past waist-height, at the two tents that faced the same direction. At the third and fourth tents, both modern flexi-pole, they crisscrossed ropes between the two, so that when one person came out the ropes would tighten on the other tent and pull it over. Then they quietly drifted back towards the women to wait for the pre-dawn attack.

A lion roared.

Gertrude sat upright. Ashley watched her as she turned around. Gertrude tried to sign to her, but Ashley had no clue what she wanted her to do. Gertrude held both hands palms out towards her, to sign wait. Sit and wait.

That one Ashley understood.

A nightjar sang out into the darkness, followed immediately by a lion's roar. Soon there was an answering roar in the distance, less guttural, but an *immediate* answer. Gertrude smiled, understanding help was on its way. Even though she suspected it was Zol, she still stared at the fire, which had burned down slowly, the coals glowed red. But she was too far away from it to check if embers dropped from the logs, a trick he'd shown her about how to judge the distance of a lion from your camp. She couldn't make a decision on the lions, or if they were lions at all.

She thought not.

Within moments, a crashing sound came from the left. A lone buffalo rushed into the camp, his large black body silhouetted against the fire. Sounds of the rest of the herd thundered suddenly, following their leader, running for their lives into the night, obviously away from the lions.

Kicking at the loose ropes that didn't hold her, Gertrude screamed, 'Run! Ashley, run!'

The mass of moving bodies cast shadows into the far side of the camp. In front of Gertrude, Ashley took off, sprinting into the bushes behind the camp, the ropes from her hands dropping as she gained momentum and moved her arms to get up speed.

Mayhem erupted in the camp behind them and shots shattered the night.

Gertrude didn't look back. She knew that if she tripped, she'd be trampled. She ran blindly into the bush, following Ashley. Their chance to escape had arrived, and together they had embraced it, heedless of the dangerous buffalo herd behind them. Catching up to Ashley, Gertrude saw a large acacia tree in front of them. She thumped her on the back to ensure she got her attention and shouted, 'There, up the tree.'

Gertrude folded her hands into a lift, and Ashley scrambled up the trunk. She reached down for Gertrude and hoisted her up into the branches, the thunder of the buffalo stampede close by.

'Climb,' Gertrude said as she scrambled up into the safety of the sturdy limbs, ignoring the huge thorns on the tree in her relief to be out of immediate danger.

CHAPTER 14

They heard a lion roar. Another roar followed.

Scott lifted his forehead above the fallen tree that had been used for firewood by the poachers to check on the women. They had vanished.

'Oh my God, where is she?' he said out loud, momentarily panicking at losing track of Ashley.

Miracle tugged at Scott's shoulder and he turned to follow. The buffalo crashed into the camp, spurred on by Banga and Dumisai making noise behind them. The beasts stampeded, funnelled into a pathway made by the thick undergrowth they had dragged into place around the camp during the night. Not trampling the poachers' tents, but passing through with enough mayhem to create the chaos needed for the men to capture the poachers.

The one flaw in their plan had been the exposure of the women. They had assumed they would remain near the tree, safely out of harm's way.

Scott ran through the bush. He could make out Ashley ahead of him, her blonde hair shining like a beacon even in the reduced light, with Gertrude close behind her.

The buffalo sounded closer. He forced his legs to move faster.

They followed the women as they ran towards a large acacia tree, its heavy canopy black in the early light. The crashing of the buffalo grew louder.

Scott swung up into the acacia tree he saw the women had sheltered in.

'Scott!' Ashley screamed, and started working her way down the branches towards him. He was stretching out his arm to help Miracle. Miracle barely managed to get his legs up and into the tree as the buffalo thundered past.

The beasts disappeared into the thick bush.

'Are you okay?' Scott asked Ashley.

She nodded. 'Yes. Gertrude and I are, but we couldn't find Alan or Jabu.'

'Alan and Jabu are both dead,' Scott said as he hugged her close. 'Gertrude, are you sure you're okay?'

'I'm well, Scott,' Gertrude said. 'What took you and Zol so long?'

'Detours ... Did we get here in time? Did they hurt you?' he asked.

'Ashley is cut, and they beat me a little—' She didn't get any more words out as the high-pitched screaming of a man in serious pain interrupted her.

'Stay here,' Scott ordered Ashley and Gertrude. The two men dropped neatly out of the tree and ran back towards the poachers' camp, weapons drawn and ready.

The campfire had been bolstered with wood, casting a bright circle of light that illuminated the entire camp. A gunshot sounded, muffled, but the sick hollow sound of a bullet ripping into flesh was clearly audible. Scott instinctively hit the ground then looked towards the tents. Miracle was a split second behind him.

Scott could make out a man lying face down where the chest-high ropes had been placed. Another rolled over and over on the ground, screaming in pain. The third tent was sealed off and rolled in a ball. The occupant was swearing profusely in Afrikaans as he fought to find the opening.

Behind the fourth tent, a black man stood with a 9mm held in both hands. He shot into the tent again and again. Zol and Sifiye broke through the bushes behind the tents, Sifiye rugby-tackling the man. The gun deflected away to the left, as if the shooter could not grip it firmly enough. The three of them fell on top of the tent's occupant.

The shooter was large. He struggled like a wild man, and it took a while for Zol and Sifiye to pin him down, speaking to him in Ndebele all the time.

'Stop fighting. Remain still.'

Scott checked on the first downed man, who was still alive, a strong pulse beating in his neck. Miracle had brought the screaming man under control, with a swift knock of the butt of his rifle to his temple.

Blood was gushing from where a large hunting knife stuck out of the man's chest. In the gloom of the night his eyes shone white with horror. Miracle grabbed the bone handle of the knife and pulled it out. It made a sickening, sucking sound, then came free. The poacher was lucky he had already passed out. Miracle applied a field dressing to the wound. The bleeding slowed to a seep now that the knife no longer held the vein open.

Banga and Dumisai ran into the poachers' camp.

A moment's silence surrounded the men, but was abruptly broken by loud swearing and the sound of nylon being cut roughly. Banga went over to the collapsed tent and, as *Meneer* Lawrence disentangled himself from what was once his sanctuary, he cocked his rifle and poked the barrel into the poacher's chest. The big Afrikaner's hands travelled slowly up to the top of his head, to the surrender position.

'Body count?' Scott asked.

'The Afrikaner, silent fighter, one kid by the ropes, knife victim, and the sucker shot in the tent.' Zol quickly supplied the statistics.

'That's five. All we saw accounted for. Banga and Dumisai, make sure each one is tied up securely. Sifiye, Zol and I will search the camp to ensure there are no surprise occupants.'

'Ek is *Meneer* Lawrence, not the Afrikaner, jou dom *kaffir*,' shouted the white man.

'*Ja Oom, ek verstaan*,' Zol answered in perfect Afrikaans, his insult at calling the Afrikaner his uncle very clear in the tone of his voice. He understood and spoke it perfectly. Men of the Grey Scouts had been totally bilingual and everyone spoke at least the basic three languages. English, Afrikaans, and kitchen-*kaffir*, a dialect of all African languages mixed together, and understood by all. His days in the mounted horse regiment of the Rhodesia army with Charlie had been a memorable time in his life. Adventurous and profitable. They had broken all the rules together, but they had at last fought for a cause they both believed in, and were not just paid for.

Dragging his mind back to the present, Zol ensured that he had tied *Meneer* Lawrence and the gun-wielding cook safely to a tree.

'Scott, the women?'

'Fine, I was with them for a second, up a darn thorn tree.' Scott removed a field dressing from his first-aid kit. The knife victim was bleeding through the one Miracle had put on him moments before.

'Thank that God of yours, will you?' Zol said, tears sparkling in his eyes.

'*Ubani gamalaku*?' Scott asked the wounded black man.

'Jafari. I'm the truck driver. Please don't kill my son, Abdulla, he's only a boy,' Jafari pleaded. Scott tossed Miracle the field dressing and moved on.

Zol opened the fourth tent to check the body inside. 'You!' he hollered, and grabbed his hunting knife from his belt with lightning speed.

'No Zol, don't!' Scott shouted.

Zol held the albino dangling in his grip, a knife to his throat. The albino stared blankly at Zol, emotionless.

'Zol, there are too many witnesses,' Scott said quietly. He put a hand on Zol's shoulder. 'Another place, another time, my brother.'

Zol dropped Rodney and he crumpled into a pathetic pile. But as he began to realise he wasn't going to have his throat cut, he began cursing loudly.

'*Fook*ing Vakani, *ek sal jou moer, jy is een dood kaffir*. Next time I gets yous fore shoor, man,' he shouted at the cook.

'You're not getting to kill anyone for a long time,' Zol said to him as he looped a thin nylon rope around the albino's hands and feet and tightened it.

Amazingly, the bullet spray Vakani had pumped into the tent with the albino inside, had inflicted flesh wounds only, and nothing vital had been hit. Bandages and dressings were put on his five bullet wounds by Miracle.

'All clear,' Zol shouted when each man had reported back to say they couldn't find any other occupants in the camp, his foot firmly on the hogtied albino.

'Sifiye, Banga and Dumisai, set up a perimeter check,' Zol instructed, then he wolf-whistled into the night.

Minutes passed before Gertrude and Ashley ran in to the camp. Scott and Zol hugged their women, savouring the moment.

'Should I radio Miss Tessa?' Miracle asked.

'No, I'll do it,' Scott replied, beaming over Ashley's head. He pulled his radio from his belt. 'Tessa, come in.' Nothing.

'Tessa, come in.'

'Kevin here. Scott?'

'Hey, nice to hear you.'

'Did you bring the birds home?'

'In the bag.'

'Copy that.'

'Stage two?' Scott asked cryptically.

'Proceeding as planned.'

'ETA, two hours.'

'See you.'

'Yeah. Over and out.'

'It's going down now,' he told the group of men standing near him. He held Ashley's hand tightly and looked at her.

Zol began directing the men. 'Miracle, help us get those bodies loaded into their truck. The prisoners can also be tied together inside the back. Time to get moving.'

'Dumisai *boya,*' he called into the night, leaving just two men circling the perimeter.

'Leave everything except the fire. Kill that. We'll come back in the daylight for photographic evidence to put these bastards away for life,' Scott instructed.

'Come, we need to help,' he said gently as he led Ashley to the fire, where Gertrude was shovelling sand into the flames. Ashley grabbed another spade and began throwing sand at the fire with vigour.

While the men loaded the prisoners, Zol and Scott combed the camp, making sure they were leaving nothing that would help put the poachers and kidnappers behind bars that could 'disappear' into the bush. One of the items they found was a video camera. Scott didn't switch it on to view anything. The police could do that once they had the whole group of poachers in prison.

Zol started the three-tonne poachers' truck. Banga and Dumisai sat in the back of the truck, watching Rodney, Jafari, Abdulla, Boss Lawrence and Vakani. Miracle and Sifiye kept their guns trained on the prisoners who rested upon a stack of ivory, the blood on the tusks had darkened to black but still reeked of freshness.

They began the drive to Zebra Pan, and to the rest of the waiting anti-poaching units.

Bouncing along on the road, Ashley became more and more conscious of Scott sitting next to her crammed together in the front of the truck. The danger over, now all she wanted to do was go home. Strangely, Delmonica meant home.

Scott smiled and tightened his arm around her. Ashley's stomach tightened.

She realised that not only did she want the man next to her, she wanted to be with him, where he was. In a simple single-storey, sprawling farmhouse where the wisteria crept over a pergola at the back and the fragrance filled your senses. A home where a grapevine wound its way around the side, and the small mossies came to eat the sweet fruit. And the swimming pool, instead of being sparkling blue with chemicals, was a dirty brown because it was really a reservoir for holding water for the cattle. Where the garden beckoned with roses, hibiscus, and cactus plants full of ripe prickly pears.

Scott was African and could never leave.

Home was where Scott was, not Brisbane, Australia.

She thought about her inner-city apartment, with its stark, modernist decor and panoramic views of the city and the river. The sterile-looking stainless steel kitchen she'd never bothered to use. She knew she didn't want to return to it. She thought of her family: her parents and her sisters. Being one of six wasn't an easy job, but right now she would give anything to see them and let them know she was okay. Not that they were aware that she had been in such danger. She fought a rising sob in her throat.

She felt the warm body of the man beside her, holding her hand so tightly she thought the blood would stop flowing to her fingers. She looked up at him and saw that he watched her. In the early morning light, she reached up to him as he bent towards her, and she met him at least halfway for a kiss so gentle on her lips it was almost a whisper.

'Thank you,' he said quietly.

'For what?'

'Staying alive.'

'My pleasure,' Ashley said, smiling. 'And thank you.'

'For what?'

'For coming to get me.'

Scott smiled.

Zol brought the truck to a stop. In front of them was one of Norval's *bakkies*, Elliott sitting on the bonnet, with Mazwi and Majola in the back.

'I heard you had a successful hunting expedition without me,' Elliott called out. 'Not fair, Zol.'

Zol grinned. He put his head out the window. 'Couldn't have done it without help from my comrades. You want to let Scott and Ashley ride with you? Would be more comfortable than in here.'

'Sure, then you get more time alone with Gertrude. Remember, Gertrude, if he ever decides he doesn't want you, you can knock at my door.' Elliott smiled mischievously.

As Scott and Ashley climbed into the lighter and faster *bakkie*, the radios came alive.

'Scott, come in.'

Scott reached for the CB. 'Scott here. Come in Kev.'

'Nothing here. It's been cleaned. Completely.'

'That's too bad. We got a fist full of five.'

'You serious?'

'Affirmative. ETA, thirty minutes, at this speed.'

'Direction?'

'Head northeast along the track. You'll find us.'

'I'll buzz you, keep you company the rest of the way. I have both big wigs with me.' Scott smiled at their luck. Themba Sazulu and Elmon Muleya would be hailed as heroes for hauling in the poachers. Scott would hopefully manage to keep his and Zol's names out of the picture.

'Over and out,' he said, and couldn't contain the smile that spread over his face.

But the smile didn't last long. After a short conversation about the happenings at the morning's raid on the poachers' camp, Elliott looked at Scott.

'But you're still missing four of your scouts from the original ambush. Eight people at the ambush. You, Miss Ashley and Zol got back. Only one man, Sunday, found dead. You still have four men missing. Vusi, Sipho, Mistake and Kwiella are not accounted for. Where are these men from your unit?'

'I don't know,' Scott said honestly. He had a sinking feeling that he might have won this round of the battle, but at what cost?

Ashley stood next to Scott as they watched the saga unfold. Kevin had flown Elmon and Themba out to the poachers' vehicle and Themba had taken over the driving of the large truck, Zol and Gertrude happily surrendering their places to the dignitaries. Ashley and Scott climbed back into Elliott's *bakkie* and they drove into Zebra Pan Lodge, the two smaller anti-poaching vehicles flanking the poachers' truck, the helicopter flying low overhead.

After a staged photo opportunity for the few members of the international press who had begun arriving in their own transport, the poachers were whisked away in a small squadron of police and army helicopters, heroically flying in to remove them from the Zebra Pan airstrip. The strip was the busiest it had ever been, but for Ashley the removal of Alan and Jabulani's bodies was the saddest and most heart-rending moment.

She watched in silence as all the anti-poaching guards assembled and carefully carried the bodies from the room where they had been examined by the doctor at Zebra Pan, pronounced dead, and sealed inside black body bags. The guards passed each fallen man overhead in turn, all the way to the *bakkie,* where more guards gave them a military-style escort as they were driven slowly down to the helicopter waiting at the airstrip. The men walked beside the vehicle, until finally, one last time, they laid them in the helicopter. Once Kevin had flown off to the morgue at Hwange, they saluted with gunfire, firing up into the sky. Ashley wept at the sight of the genuine comradeship these men shared.

When they returned to the lodge, the doctor stitched up her chest and gave her a tetanus booster in one arm and a strong painkiller in the other.

'There you go. Now Scott can have you back to himself and perhaps put you to bed,' he suggested in a fatherly tone. He smiled at the response on her face, as first she raised an eyebrow then rolled her eyes at him.

'No, that's not what I meant. Not that ...' he spluttered. 'The stitches are not dissolvable, but the wound would be better if it didn't get wet,' he warned. 'I'll see you in ten days, in my clinic, to remove them. Tell Scott I want to check on the wound at the same time for excessive scarring, so he must not play home doctor, even if he wants to.'

Smiling she said, 'Thank you, for everything, Doctor.' She walked out of the makeshift clinic in Tessa's office.

Scott was waiting for her outside the door, slouched against the wall. He immediately straightened and asked, 'Will you be all right? Did he give you the okay?'

'Yep.' She smiled sleepily, feeling the injection take effect as the pain eased.

'Come, you need breakfast. Yellow and her kitchen staff have cooked up a fantastic spread.' He took her hand in his and guided her to the deck area of the pool, where the festivities had already started. The anti-poaching units were celebrating in their own traditional way with dancing and singing.

Scott helped Ashley with her plate of breakfast, and they sat down at a table and watched the men perform their 'gumboot dance'. They banged their feet rhythmically on the floor and then lifted up their boots and slapped loudly on the side, making a unique hollow sound depending on where they struck the thick rubber. They chanted their tenor chorus in unison as they leapt in the air, danced and waved their weapons around, the assegais of the modern African warrior. The men were united in their struggle against the poachers.

Ashley watched the assorted tourists celebrate alongside the anti-poaching units, learning the traditional dances and the more modern style of *toi-toiing*. There was no holding them back from celebrating the victory, even if they were new to the cause.

'Scott, I'm so tired, please take me to bed,' she eventually asked him, not able to stay and celebrate any longer.

'Any time, babe, any time.' He stood and offered her his hand, which she accepted. He helped her out of the chair as an old-fashioned colonial gentleman would, then swung her up into his arms and cradled her against his body.

She laughed softly as he stumbled on the step leaving the pool area and was asleep before they reached the rondavel.

Back on the pool deck, Gertrude sat silently next to Zol, holding his hand and watching the celebrations. Old traditions dictated that they didn't show affection in public, but for now, Zol had ditched his traditional values. He was with the woman he loved, she was alive and well, and they were together. A battle-scarred man couldn't ask for more in life.

'Come, time to sleep,' he told her, as he looked at her exhausted face.

She rose, and together they began to amble along the pathway to the Elephant rondavel.

'We survived, Zol.'

'I'll always find you, no matter what. You know that, don't you?' he asked her.

'I count on that more than anything in life. That you are there for me, always.'

'Your father can have his cattle for your *lobola*. You are worth one hundred times more.' He squeezed her hand. 'But don't tell him I said that or he'll up the price again and I won't be able to afford the wedding.'

Gertrude smiled.

A sweet smell penetrated Ashley's sleep. It dragged her from her troubled dream and into awareness of the world around her. She listened to Scott moving around the room, his steady, heavy tread a welcome distraction from the horror she relived in her foggy mind. Slowly, she opened her eyes. On the pillow next to her was a single gardenia flower. She reached out and ran the back of her fingers over the pale creamy petals.

'Hey, sleepyhead. You're awake at last,' Scott said. He crossed to the bed and sat next to her. 'How do you feel?'

'Alive.' She moved. 'Uughh, I ache all over!'

'Come, I've run a bath for you. I thought you might like to soak in the spa for a while.' He smiled at her and then brushed his lips against hers. 'How's your chest?'

'Feeling tight, but not burning, thank goodness.' She put her hand up to the area, now covered in a waterproof Band-Aid. 'I'm going to have a lovely scar to remember him by.'

'We can have it seen to by plastic surgeons in Johannesburg or Cape Town. They should be able to fix it, make it look better.'

'Why are the specialists so far away?'

'Most medical professionals left during the war, then after independence in 1981. We had a good twenty years where people started returning, then the land grab started and 'the *Régime*' began to get greedy. Those few who had stayed packed up, too. Only the old and stubborn remain.' He laughed. 'I guess I'm in that category: stubborn. Have you noticed everywhere in Third World countries, it's always the average family who suffer most for their government's bad decisions? Our doctors and specialists deserted in droves, but the powers-that-be can afford to fly south for care, so they don't give a shit. It's the everyday worker, the domestic cleaner, ranch hand, industrial man who can't escape, and they are the ones who pay dearly. Often with their lives.'

'Come here,' she said as she sat up and reached for him. 'It's too early in the morning for the weight of the country to be on your shoulders.'

He kissed her and said, 'Out. Bath time for both of us.'

Laughing, she entered the bathroom adjacent to the huge master bedroom of the suite. 'Oh my! Look at what you've done!' she exclaimed. 'This is so ... Oh Scott.'

She was in awe. He'd managed to scrounge together at least fifty candles, and had every one lit and surrounding the huge bathtub beneath the window that overlooked the waterhole area. Although the sun was shining in the sky, the interior of the rondavel was naturally dim under the thatched roof. The warm yellow wash from the candles created a romantic aura about the room, and the smell of gardenia hung thickly in the air.

'I hope you like gardenias because everything in the pamper pack supplied has that smell,' Scott said light-heartedly.

'And the one on my pillow just appeared magically?' She raised one eyebrow at him.

'No, I picked that one out of the small arrangement on the dining room table especially for you.'

Ashley started to laugh. It bubbled up louder and louder, and she found she couldn't stop. Her laughter became hysterical tears. Scott walked to her and hugged her gently, mindful of her injuries. He stroked her back and rained down tiny kisses on the top of her head and onto her cheeks.

'Come on Ashley, honey, don't ...' he tried to soothe her.

Suddenly, amidst her tears, she became angry. It burned from her stomach upwards, and she cursed loudly. 'Why? That's what I want to know. I don't understand, Scott. Why the fuck did they do this? Why did they attack us? You weren't even there, so it isn't like the last time when you were their target. Why did they choose to hurt me and Gertrude, and poor Alan and Jabulani? We did nothing to them,' she shouted into Scott's chest. 'Nothing! It's not fair.'

'Revenge. They were going to ransom you back to us. To make it worse, the albino, Rodney, and Zol have clashed before. It's a long story. It goes back to before Zol was horse boy and companion for my father during one of his wars he fought in. Here, let's get in the bath and I can tell you the whole sorry tale.'

She wondered how bad this association between Zol and the albino was, that he was prepared to rape her and carve her up. Or was it perhaps that he was simply deranged?

Scott helped Ashley into the bath. She looked pale. Large blue-black tinges remained under her eyes, and she had lost the sparkle of confidence and energy that she exuded when she arrived from Australia. He hated Africa for a moment, that it had taken her vibrancy away so fast.

He watched from the side as she surfaced after sinking beneath the hot water to wet her hair. Steam rose up around her, and the fragrant bath water swirled with her movement.

'Probably a bit late to ask but what about your stitches, can they get wet?'

'Not supposed to but since the doc put on a waterproof Band-Aid, they should be fine. He gave me spares. They're in the pocket of my jeans in the bedroom.'

Scott climbed into the bath with his water nymph, who moved over to make room then wrapped her legs around him once he'd sat down. 'Now that's a nice welcome.'

'You're going to smell like gardenias all day. What will Zol say?'

'Nothing. He'll probably smell like one too,' he said, but he was laughing.

Ashley joined in with his laughter, and this time she didn't dissolve into tears.

'Turn around so I can wash your back,' Scott said as he lathered the soap on the washer.

Ashley turned around, and as he washed her back, he gave her a massage at the same time. He watched as she twisted her head back and forwards, and rolled it around. He could see her eyes were closed. At last, she began to relax.

'I like to see you like this,' he commented, his mouth close to her ear, nibbling her lobe softly. 'I need to tell you something,' he said. 'I thought I wouldn't get a chance to tell you, but I wanted you to know. I love you. I really love you.'

Ashley turned around and looked into his eyes. 'You'd better, Scott

Decker. I have *never* been so scared in my life as in the last few weeks I have been in Africa.' She promptly burst into tears.

Scott dragged her closer to him and hugged her, letting her cry. He held her, savouring her scent, feeling her warm body against his, and knowing that what he said was true. They could hash out later that she had been in her predicament because she had disobeyed him and ventured outside the security fence, putting everyone in danger. But then, that was the Ashley he loved: the strong-willed, independent, don't-get-in-my-way-no-matter-what woman with a will of iron who had stepped off the plane and captivated him ever since.

But he knew that at that moment in his life, the relief of having her safe and knowing she was mostly unharmed was immense.

He also knew that if she had been harmed in any sexual way, he wouldn't have stopped Zol from killing the albino; he would have joined in and slit the man's throat with his own hunting knife. As it was, he had a burning desire to do just that for hurting her at all.

'That's nice.' She sighed softly against him as he stilled a hand he didn't know was drawing circles on her back. He could feel her take a deep breath. 'Thank you for coming to rescue me. I want you to know that I think I have definitely fallen in love with you, too. I wanted to tell you and I didn't think I would get a chance either. I'm so glad you came to get me, so that I could tell you. I love you, Scott Decker.'

His heart thumped loudly in his chest and he crushed her to him.

'Good. I'd hate to think that all my energy spent on rescuing you was going to waste.'

She giggled, the sound like tinkling bells to his ears. It could have been irritating, like a teenager's giggle, but on her it was sexy as hell.

'Are you going to be all right, after our intense beginning?' he asked seriously.

'Yeah, I reckon so. It's all new, but I can cope with you.' She pulled away from him, straddled her legs around his waist and placed her hands on his shoulders.

He stared directly into her green eyes and glimpsed a depth to them he hadn't noticed before. A softness. A new light. As she bent forward and kissed him, he knew she had meant every word.

CHAPTER 15

To Ashley, three weeks in Africa seemed like a lifetime.

Michelle had arrived from the UK, and they were all attending Alan's funeral service on the veranda of Delmonica's ranch house. The preacher, who was from Bulawayo, had requested a quiet minute during the service.

'Friends, let us take a moment to listen to the sounds of Africa that Alan loved so well. He felt he could return here, year after year and give his time freely. These sounds will now comfort Michelle in her knowledge that he is not suffering, but is free of all worldly pain ...' He bowed his head.

Ashley saw Michelle stare blankly out at the bush. She thought her tolerant to have the funeral here and not in England. But Michelle had been adamant that this was something she and Alan had discussed, and she had always promised she'd do this if the unthinkable happened.

'"Should anything happen to me while in deep dark Africa, don't fly my remains back to this cold country, love. Just bury me there in the sunshine, where the air doesn't smell of exhaust fumes,"' Michelle had quoted Alan.

'Ashley, I need to keep this promise I made to him, you must understand,' she'd said between sniffs. 'Alan loved Africa, he would have lived here quite happily, but I couldn't, so instead he only visited.'

Ashley thought of her own reactions to Michelle. At first, she'd been taken aback by her. Indeed, she was as lovely to look at as Alan had bragged, and her photograph in his wallet portrayed, but there was more to her than looks. Michelle was genuine in her grief for her best friend and husband. The death of her other half had left the fiery lawyer devastated and in deep mourning. And she showed compassion for Jabulani's death, too.

'Michelle, what happened to Alan is ... I can't find the words. You need time to heal for a while once this is all over. Take as much time as you need here, I know that Scott won't mind,' Ashley offered warmly. 'Stay. See for yourself that the poachers are jailed for their crimes, and know firsthand that they will be punished.'

'Now that's a great idea,' Michelle returned. 'If it's all right with Scott, I think I'll take you up on that. See how long the case takes to come to court. Otherwise, I can always fly back for the proceedings.'

'It's a deal then, you'll stay for a while.'

A fish eagle called loudly in the sky, screeching to his mate somewhere in her nest. The haunting sound brought Ashley back to the funeral proceedings.

'God the Father, God the Son and God the Holy Spirit, be with you always. Amen.' The preacher had completed the service.

Jabulani's and Sunday's funeral was the day after Alan's, and couldn't have been more different: a traditional Ndebele burial with a modern twist. The dead men were wrapped in cowhide and were placed facing south in the small cemetery on Delmonica. Jabulani's only son, Griffin, a small proud boy of five, threw an assegai into the grave. Since Sunday had no family nearby and no sons, Zol threw his own assegai for him. Then the black preacher from the Zionist church, dressed in his distinctive white robe and carrying a prophetic staff, held a small but decidedly loud sermon for the men.

When he'd finished, the anti-poaching guards from the neighbouring ranches and concessions performed a twenty-one gun salute. Only then did Jabulani's widow throw one solitary handful of soil onto his body, and Zol performed the same ritual for Sunday.

Jabulani's widow was wailing and crying and placing her hands on her head. The other women were doing the same.

'Oh my God, look at them. They're all devastated,' Ashley said to Scott, the worry in her voice clear.

'That's how they show their respect to Jabulani and Sunday.'

Ashley nodded. She knew she was still on a steep learning curve as to how things worked in Africa. 'So the funeral is over then?'

'For you, yes. For me and Zol, no. I have to attend Jabulani's house and sacrifice an ox.'

'You'll do what?'

'Sshhh ... Not me myself, with Jabulani's family. They'll kill the ox we gave them and eat the meat with no salt. Once all the meat is eaten, the bones will be burned and the sangoma will make *muti* with them. Everyone there is given some and then we go to a river and bathe. But since there is no river nearby, and there are sometimes crocodiles in the dam, they have modernised that part of their tradition and everyone now takes showers.'

'You sound like you're describing something from the pioneer days?'

'Don't mock it. You have only been here three weeks. There is so much you still need to know. I'm sorry that you have to learn about this particular tradition so soon, but it's far from over.'

'I'm interested. Not meaning to mock, honest. So what else happens?'

'Traditionally, neither Jabulani's nor Sunday's body would be buried today. But since they know both men died unnatural deaths, we have already consulted the sangoma. We have permission for Jabulani's son and brother to bury him at sunset, and Zol has permission to bury Sunday, too.

'To help their spirit cross over, they will have a ceremony in three months' time. The tools used today to dig the graves will all be washed in ceremonial beer brewed especially for the occasion. They believe that Jabulani's and Sunday's spirits will cling to this life and not pass over into the ancestral heaven unless they do these traditional ceremonies.'

'Who am I to judge them? But there is a priest at this funeral?'

'And a sangoma. Look to the left of the priest. See the man with the traditional skins around his neck, the headwear with the feathers? He's their link to their ancestors, their spiritual healer.'

'But that's what the priest's for, surely?'

'It's a strange mix. They each accept the other and as long as there is harmony within their "flock" they are all happy.'

'So in three months' time Jabulani and Sunday are allowed to cross over?' she asked, trying to understand the customs of that part of Africa.

'No, hopefully they both cross over before that. But in a year's time, we will kill another ox and brew more beer, but only with grain grown after their deaths and from other people's fields. That party is supposed to call their spirit back. People dance and sing and the widow is allowed to remarry if she wants to, her mourning time is over. Then Jabulani's spirit is truly gone; there is nothing to hold him here any longer. Sunday has nothing holding him, but we will follow the same traditions for him.'

'One question. What's in the *muti* that the sangoma gives you?'

'Don't ask. But I can tell you, he and I have had stern words on the spread of HIV and hepatitis. He no longer spits into anyone's drink, nor bleeds himself or any other living thing into the *muti*. We are lucky in the region, our sangoma attended university in Harare before he got his calling, so there is an educated man under that persona.'

Ashley laughed. 'I'll never understand how modern times and tradition meld together in Africa.'

'Sure you will. You simply need longer than a four-week vacation to learn it.'

'Vacation? Some vacation,' Ashley said seriously. Her heart suddenly feeling sadder than it had even been with attending the three funerals so close to each other. But it was Scott's words that kept rattling inside her head as she stood next to him.

Was he telling her she was welcome to stay and explore that opportunity?

She knew one thing for certain: she loved Scott.

Scott said he loved her.

Her body loved Scott too, and had stopped its shudders at any touching. And they touched. Often. She blushed just thinking about what they would do in the bedroom that night.

But in her mind, she also knew her time in Africa was running out. She needed to make the important decision that Scott had just hinted at. Did she stay in Zimbabwe and see where this relationship was going? Or did she return home, and see if it was a flash-in-the-pan holiday fling?

If she returned to Australia, she could always fly back to Scott, back to Delmonica. Tears pricked her eyes at the thought of leaving. The ranch and its people had got inside her heart, and she didn't want to leave it. It was as if once the sand from the African earth had touched her skin, it had burrowed like a putzi fly under her skin.

She shivered thinking about the prospect of a maggot under her skin—the horrid lump that formed, and having to dig the maggot out of yourself, if you were unlucky enough to get one.

She felt Scott pull her closer as they stood together, and she snuggled into him, inhaling his scent.

Home. Scott smelled like home.

There was no denying that Scott and his beloved country, its people and their wildlife were now in her bloodstream, and she knew that some days would be like maggots, but most days, if she had Scott in her life, it would be like butterflies—bright, beautiful and awesome.

Even as she debated, she already knew her answer.

She wanted to stay.

She wanted Scott, forever.

Scott could never relocate to Australia. If they were to have a life together, and she thought they could, then she would need to move to Zimbabwe.

She smiled.

It wasn't hard to move somewhere that held her heart. But she needed to make sure that Scott felt the same way.

That this was the forever kind of love, not the 'until your plane leaves' kind.

The problem was that she didn't have any idea about how to get him to ask her to stay. She might be a liberated Australian female, and been brought up as a feminist, but there was no way that she was going to ask Scott if she could stay. He needed to make that offer to her. He had to believe that she would stay with him, not abandon him like his mother had. In no fairy-tale she knew did the princess ride up to the prince and ask to shack up with him in his kingdom. She masked her giggle as a cough.

'Scott,' she whispered.

'Mmm,' he answered, bending his ear closer to her as the preacher droned on.

'How much longer do you think it would take me?' she asked.

'A lifetime.'

'Is that all? I could do that,' she said. 'I'd certainly give it my all.'

Scott turned her into him and pulled her close. 'I would so love being with you every second as you learn.'

Three days later, Scott covered Ashley's eyes as he led her out the door of the bedroom they were sharing in his ranch house, and down the stairs towards the shed. 'Don't try and peek, Ashley. That's not playing fair.' When they were inside the shed, he lifted his hands off and said, 'Surprise.'

Ashley stared at the shiny new dark green four-wheel drive double cab. It had a huge gold and red ribbon tied around it. 'It's to replace Lucinda. She was past further resurrection, so I bought you a new one. Look, it has an automatic gearbox, because you said you preferred not having to worry about changing gear. And it has five seats, so you can entice passengers to sit inside with you instead of on the back. Zol even said he would sit in the back seat if you asked him to.'

The hooter in the *bakkie* sounded loudly, and she jumped at the noise. She turned and stared at the cab. Inside, its front paws on the steering wheel, was a little black and white ball of fur. A puppy, wearing a matching gold and red ribbon around its neck. Almost trancelike, Ashley moved towards the vehicle. 'Oh my, Scott, a puppy. You bought a puppy, too.'

'Well, she'll be a dog one day. Right now, she's a puppy and should probably get out of there before she soils your new upholstery.' Laughing, he opened the door, and the bundle of fluff cascaded into Ashley's arms, licking her face, and nipping at her hair.

Ashley noticed the small giftbox hanging from the puppy's ribbon. She looked at Scott. 'And this?'

'It's for you,' he said quietly. 'Here, let me hold the pup.' He gently took it from her so she could untie the box. She ripped the gold paper off and inside was a square box. Ashley held her breath as she slowly opened it. A brilliant square-cut pink diamond, set in a cluster of square white diamonds on a rose gold band, twinkled up at her.

'Marry me, Ashley. Stay with me.'

'Oh, Scott. This is ...' She hugged him. The puppy, squished in-between, licked them both furiously.

Scott broke away laughing and put the fur ball down. He gathered Ashley to him again and kissed her possessively. When they eventually pulled apart, he asked, 'I know three weeks is quick, Ashley. I know people are going to think we are mad, that this is a relationship that will burn out just as fast as it started, but I don't see that. I see us together when we are old. Sitting on the veranda, you with white hair and me with no hair, and our grandkids running about. But us, still holding hands. I have never wanted that with anyone else. I want you in my life permanently. Please, Ashley. I'm asking you to stay in Africa, marry me, share my life with me and let me share yours?'

'Yes! Yes, it's a yes!' she shouted at him, then hugged him again and covered his face with kisses.

The puppy began gnawing on his trouser bottoms, so Scott broke the kiss and scooped it up. 'And what are you going to name your dog?'

'Renegade,' she said without hesitation.

'Why?'

'Because that's what I feel like right now. I feel like a renegade Aussie. Since I arrived just a few weeks ago, everything has been surreal. I have gone against every fibre of my beliefs about life here. I love it here, but I don't understand it. It is as if the dirt calls to me. And here, with you, I finally feel free. I feel that I can care for someone other than myself.' She looked at him, into his blue eyes, and knew that she hadn't made a mistake. This was where she wanted to be. With Scott. In Africa.

Always.

'I love you,' he said barely above a whisper.

'I know,' she replied with a smile. 'But it's nice to hear you say it again. Are you sure marriage is what you want?'

'With you, yes. I'll settle for nothing less.'

He picked her up in his arms, the puppy still nipping at his *veldskoene*, and walked back towards the house. 'Don't ever think of leaving, Ashley. I can't live without you now,' he said, and she sighed contentedly into his shoulder as he kicked the bedroom door closed behind them, locking the puppy out.

CHAPTER 16

2000

Five years of hell in the Zimbabwe prison, but finally Rodney was out.

Amnesty 2000. A new millennium. A new start.

An overflowing, overcrowded jail system emptied out. Cleaned out, to start again. He'd been set free with a pair of shoes on his feet, trousers and a shirt. He'd had nothing on him when he was arrested, so there was nothing to claim on his release. To the jailer, he was nobody.

But a short visit to *Meneer* Lawrence's house, and he had money, more than he needed, to travel back to Angola. To go home and regroup.

Meneer Lawrence had found God while in prison, and he had no plans to re-join any of his poaching partners. Rodney's special services weren't needed anymore.

Meneer Lawrence said he was cured of the blood lust. His God had shown him a different path.

Rodney had passed his use-by date. Their business partnership was ended.

Rodney sat cross-legged on the cracked floor in the dilapidated hut, the rain pounding on the collapsed thatch roof and running down the wall in rivulets. He shivered as the wetness seeped through his meagre clothing and pressed into his skin and bones. The window, its glass broken years before, rattled in the wind. The gusts of wind shook what was left of the old *ikhaya*.

He looked out through where the door should have been, and could visualise his mother walking towards him with her stack of firewood on her head. He could hear her chanting, haunting him, as she walked alongside him, looking for this place, their last home together. He'd buried what remained of her when he visited his home so long ago, now he'd come home again, to heal.

Lightning flashed brightly outside. He heard the sizzle as the bolt struck something nearby. But he didn't care. He was free. He had fresh air, he could feel the breeze and the rain, and he was alone at last.

Although the hut was ruined, he didn't want to pitch the tent he carried. He wanted to feel the elements and know that he was still alive. Still able to feel. Because after the Zimbabwean jail, he'd wondered if he'd ever make it to the hut again.

The trial had been easy—he'd already known the penalty for poaching was death before he killed his first animal in Zimbabwe. But the money had been good, and the blood had been even better. However, no one had told him that while death was easy, life imprisonment was hell. Until he began his years in captivity, he hadn't comprehended that life in prison would be so hard.

The closeness of the other inmates constantly around him.

The lack of food.

The bloodlust that at first, he'd attempted to curb, but in the end had saved his life after he established his place in the pecking order within the grey walls with the razor wire on the top, where the bell ruled your life and the guards took pleasure in ensuring your life was misery.

In his mind, he could still see the walls of his shared cell. Covered in black and white newspaper tear outs, stuck on the wall with tape, smuggled in and bought in blood kills. All about the trial, and pictures of the blonde bitch.

He swiped his hand over his top pocket and although there was no responding crinkle as the paper was wet from the storm, he knew her picture was still there. Carried with him to ensure he never forgot who was responsible for putting him in jail.

Meneer Lawrence had reminded him of it almost every day.

If he hadn't attacked the farmer and the blonde bitch the first day, they would never have been found.

He had paid for that mistake every day for five years.

Now he was free, and he could almost taste his revenge on her.

She looked so much like his first blonde schoolgirl in South West Africa all those years ago. His first rape and slaughter. He felt a stirring inside that he hadn't felt for the last hard years.

He knew he would have Ashley Decker soon. He could almost feel how she would scream when he *fook*ed her, only this time he would keep her tied up, make her know how it felt to be a dog held against your will. Captive. And each time he *fook*ed her, he would tell her how much he thought about his revenge and what he would ultimately do to her.

Cut her up, piece by piece.

Soon he would take his revenge on the blonde bitch who'd been responsible for locking him in hell. But for today, he would rest.

He would sleep.

The cold rain dripped on his face and he savoured the feeling.

CHAPTER 17

'Madam, you can't do that, you are having a baby soon,' Elliott scolded Ashley as she tried to move a pump from the back of her four-wheel drive. 'No, let me do that,' he insisted, as he pushed her hands away politely.

'I'm pregnant, not useless, Elliott ... Please, between you and Scott you would swear women who are having children should be in a glass room, protected from everything.'

'Yes, Madam.' Elliott lowered one end of the pump and then the other onto the trolley.

Ashley looked at her friend. He was now officially 'Madam Ashley's spanner boy'. Unofficially, he'd become her own private militia. Elliott went everywhere with her, like an armed shadow. With good reason. They lived in a new Zimbabwe, the years of peace and prosperity they had experienced since independence had ended. Now they were in an economic meltdown, mostly from the government spending billions getting involved in the Democratic Republic of Congo's civil war, protecting diamond mines whose wealth never returned to Zimbabwe. Combined with yet another drought, the 'bread basket' of Africa was hungry. The people were rising up, rioting and forcibly taking over white commercial farmers' lands en masse. The poaching in the reserve had worsened, too. It was as if the levels of poaching had regressed five years, back to when she had first arrived in Zimbabwe, before she was blissfully happy with her married life to Scott.

She too was constantly armed, although they had no wish to engage poachers alone. The memories of the last poaching ring they had destroyed were still too vivid in both her and Elliott's memories. They were full of sadness too, the losses too great a void to fill in a few short years.

It had taken what was left of Zol's unit two months to get back in contact with them at Delmonica, but when they did, Vusi, Sipho, Mistake and Kwiella had been hailed as heroes, and ultimately decorated by their government for the extra information they had brought with them as a result of following the poachers through the bush. The amount of information they had collected, documented and been able to prove was formidable.

Later, as the events leading up to and including the abduction were revealed, Jabulani and Sunday had been given medals posthumously by the Zimbabwean government, for sacrificing their lives for the conservation of indigenous animals.

Collectively, Zol's unit had helped bring down one of the largest, most internationally networked rings ever known. The evidence they had presented in court was both sickening and bizarre, and when the stories had first surfaced of women's bodies, mutilated for sexual sport and then buried in the bush in between poaching 'hits', the international media had publicised the gruesome evidence. The very public trial had effectively destroyed organised poaching for a short time.

No stone was left unturned, from the implicated Kenyan and Zimbabwean politicians to the Russian and Chinese diplomats who were deported but were not able to be prosecuted because of diplomatic immunity, to the American and Dutch businessmen who had helped finance the operation. The President's Guard had been rocked, and it now had a new leader: Themba. The guards had brought in photographic evidence of each incident after the ambush and the list of names on the prosecution list had grown as the local ground crews had been rounded up.

Michelle and her partners in her London law firm had worked pro bono with the Zimbabwe lawyers to bring her husband's killers to justice. In the process, they had closed down a substantial poaching ring. Eventually, sentence was passed. On a list of charges that including abduction, attempted rape and first-degree murder, Rodney and *Meneer* Lawrence were jailed for life.

'Ashley, come in.' The CB barked at her, breaking her dark thoughts.

She walked around to the cab. 'Ashley here.'

'What're you up to, love?' Scott asked.

'Elliott is offloading the pump as we speak. There are signs of activity in this section, a big truck, but not one of ours. We'll fasten this one down and head on home.'

'How old is the spoor?'

'About three days.'

'Do they lead in and out?'

'Hang on, I'll ask Elliott.'

Ashley put her head back outside the cab, 'Hey, Elliott. Scott wants to know if the tracks lead in and out?'

'Just in, Madam,' he grunted, as he pushed the trolley up to the tin shed.

'Just in.'

'Shit. Ashley, get out of there, immediately. Leave the pump and come home.'

'No. Elliott said the tracks are old. You're panicking for nothing. I was just having this same argument with Elliott. I'm pregnant, not handicapped. We'll be finished within an hour.'

'I'd rather you came home, but I know how stubborn you are. That's one of the things I married you for—your tenacity.' She could almost hear him laughing.

'Thanks. I love you, too. I'll check in when we leave here. Over and out.' She smiled into the CB mouthpiece, her body warming at the thought of her husband waiting for her at home.

She patted her belly, rounded and large in front of her. Who would have thought that this pregnancy could have evoked such strong feelings in all the males on the ranch? Scott and Zol treated her as if she was spun glass. And Elliott, he wouldn't let her do anything. She was happy that they cared, but it was a bit much all at once.

Ashley tossed the CB mouthpiece back into her now battered green four-wheel drive and arched her back. Man oh man, did she have a backache.

Elliott was already in the shed. Ashley followed him in, wrench in hand, to refit the nuts on the replacement Lister motor's mounting block. Thank God for overseas sponsorship, she thought, as this was the second time she was replacing this particular pump, and each time with a later model. One positive thing that had come about after the sensationalism of the poaching ring those years before was the foreign investment into the park.

The poachers had burnt the first pump five years ago, and after the trial, the volunteers had been able to replace it. But last month, someone had poured sugar into the motor and it had seized up beyond repair.

Elliott already had the pump lined up and looked at her as she walked in.

'I take it you need this?' She handed him the wrench with no further argument.

'Thank you, Madam.' He tightened the bolts.

'You know, Elliott, you could almost do this part yourself now.'

'Yes, Madam, but I still need you to do the fixing.' He grinned at her cheekily.

'Perhaps, next time one breaks, Junior here will already be in the world and you'll need to bring the pump home for me to fix and then you can reseat it. Tighten that coupling more,' she instructed.

They worked well together. Ashley smiled as she thought of how Elliott had installed himself in her life. Now she couldn't imagine a day without having him around. Elliott had stayed with Scott and Ashley after the abduction. He'd stood near Tessa's *bakkie* the next day, complete with his rucksack. Scott had nodded to him. He'd climbed on the back, driven home with them, and never left the ranch.

Zol had allocated him a house in the compound, and there he'd remained. He was a bona fide employee of Delmonica ranch. After that, when Ashley resumed her duties fixing pumps, Elliott had simply been around, waiting to go with her wherever she went. Elliott and Renegade, her constant companions.

Elliott had chosen to work with Ashley. Eventually Scott had left her in Elliott's care more and more. But it was only after their wedding that Elliott became her full-time assistant. Scott went about performing his own ranch duties, managing his Brahman stud, and Ashley took over the running of the volunteer program. Elliott helped her constantly, and they'd reached the stage where she thought she could leave him to manage the volunteers completely. She broached the subject as he finished tightening the bolts.

'Elliott, what if you were to take over supervising the volunteers?'

'No, Madam.'

'Why not?'

'Because I'm your assistant. I go where you go. I do most things you ask me to, but my job is to protect you. That's what I told Zol I would do, always protect Madam Ashley.'

'Protect me. From what, Elliott?' she asked, her curiosity pricked.

'Danger. There is new danger coming.' He looked away from her, something she'd noticed both he and Zol did when they didn't want to enlighten her further.

'Does Scott know?'

'Yes. But he says not to worry you with your baby, just to keep close and protect you, always.'

Ashley smiled at him. 'Oh Elliott, when am I ever going to teach you men on this ranch that I can look after myself? Haven't I earned a little respect after all these years?'

'Yes. But it's not like normal now. You are the best shot Madam, and you aren't scared of the Egyptian cobra, or the boomslang, and you shoot the rabies leopard when it came to attack the children in Gertrude's school. But Madam Ashley, can you kill a man?'

She stared at him. What was he talking about?

'What man, Elliott?'

'The last amnesty. When they let all the prisoners go because the jails were too full. Rodney the albino and *Meneer* Lawrence, they came out too. But Boss Scott told me not to tell you before the baby is born. I think now he is going to fire me.'

'No, he won't. I won't let him. Are you sure he's out?' She could feel her skin going clammy at the thought of the disgusting albino and his leash holder who permitted him to behave like an animal. Memories she thought hidden deep within her surfaced, and she ran out the shed and vomited, her stomach heaving again and again.

Elliott brought her water from the back of the *bakkie*. 'I'll drive home,' he said quietly.

'No, I'll be okay. It's shock, that's all. Finish the pump. I'll put my head down for a moment and I'm sure I'll be right.' She dragged her cement feet to the *bakkie* and climbed into the cab. Renegade hopped nimbly inside and sat in the back, but when Ashley turned on the motor and ran the air-conditioner on high, blowing the cooler air into her face, the dog seemed to realise she needed more than company and nudged her shoulder.

Stroking Renegade with her left hand, Ashley reached up and pulled the rear-view mirror down with her right. She peered into the small silver square and baulked at the sight she saw reflected back at her, her ghastly pale colour and eyes like a bushbaby, huge in her face. The thought of the albino being out of jail unnerved her badly. She patted her belly as if to reassure herself her baby was still safe in there, untouched by the horrors of the world outside. Then she ran her finger along her breastbone where the ridge of scar tissue reminded her of what she'd overcome. Renegade whined, wanting Ashley's attention focused back on her.

Ashley smiled at her dog and petted her. She was stronger than this. She had survived. He had not raped her. She had reacted when he'd tried and he hadn't managed to harm her physically, other than to cut her chest. This was a smaller scar to bear than the cupboard incident, that mental scar was with her still, despite thinking through it logically. She still hated that she had done nothing to stop the boy so many years ago. Rodney had not won; she would never give in to him.

Her mind returned to the courtroom five years earlier. She'd faced him at his sentencing, and recalled his leering snigger over his shoulder as he was being led away in chains and the disgusting things he said he would do to her someday. Now he was free.

But that didn't mean he was in her vicinity.

She took her 9mm out of the leather holster on her hip. Unclipping the magazine, she made sure it was full before she returned it with a reassuring metallic click. Ashley placed it back in the holster, but didn't do up the small press-stud on the leather strap at the top. Elliott had asked her if she could kill a man: it was a question she didn't want to have to ever answer.

The diesel pump started, its rhythmic pulsations breaking the quiet of the bush. A white egret that had been drinking from the water trough started in fright and took to the air.

Elliott put the wrench back in the toolbox and closed the box on the back of the *bakkie*. He walked around to the passenger's side, removed his rifle from his shoulder and got into the front seat. He placed the rifle barrel downwards, between his legs. 'Nice and cool inside here, Madam. You okay now?'

'Fine. I got a shock. I never thought he would be out, that's all.'

Elliott didn't attempt to touch Renegade, but did acknowledge that she was already in the *bakkie* with Madam Ashley where she was supposed to be. 'He'll never get to you. I won't let him, Scott won't let him, and Zol would kill him this time if he came near you or Gertrude again. Rodney knows that.'

Ashley smiled weakly, tears brimming in her eyes. She wiped at them.

'Darn hormones ... Thanks, Elliot. I'll hold you to that promise.' She put the *bakkie* into drive and turned it in the direction of the ranch. She reached for the CB.

'Scott, come in.'

'Scott here, over.'

He answered immediately. Ashley could picture him sitting at his desk, catching up on the paperwork in the office. She smiled at the thought.

'We're on our way home.'

'Great. No problems getting the pump in?'

'No, Elliott did a fine job as always. Hey, honey, you sound worried ... anything I should know?' She plied him gently for information.

'Nothing at present. It'll wait till you get home. See you in an hour. Love you.'

'Yeah, me too. Out.'

'He didn't tell you,' commented Elliott.

'No, not yet, but he will by the end of the day, and you'll be off the hook. Don't worry.' She smiled across the seat at him, then stopped to let a kudu cross the road, its massive twisted horns regally placed on its head and its huge ears twitching, listening.

Ashley crossed her arms over the steering wheel and looked at the animal. 'He's beautiful, isn't he? I never tire of seeing the game.'

'Yes,' was all Elliott said as they watched the large male walk into the thick bush and disappear from sight, his striped sides blending perfectly with the bush.

On arriving home, Ashley watched Elliott walk to the volunteers' quarters to check up on the new arrivals that week: Ken from the States, Eric and Bernard from Germany, and young Deon, only nineteen, an engineering student from South Africa. There was never a doubt that Delmonica would keep the volunteer program running. Droughts came and went, but the pump program would always continue. It was necessary for the ecological survival of the national park. In 1996, the rains had come, but then last year yet another drought began. Now their main job was to maintain the pumps and keep the concentrations of game spread evenly throughout the park. The bush was recovering slowly from the beating it had sustained and life was distributed evenly around the park once more.

But its very existence was still threatened by poaching of all kinds, from the humble wire snare to the high-tech operators. Hwange was a smorgasbord for the bottom feeders of the world.

Ashley waved at Elliott as he turned to see if she'd gone into the house yet, as if he was waiting for trouble from Scott for spilling the beans. She smiled. Her revenge on her husband would have a double-edged sword that they both enjoyed, but she was still mad at him.

She lumbered up the steps and into the study. Renegade threw her black and white body down by the door, and settled her head into her paws. Scott saw her coming and pushed his chair out from the desk. She straddled his lap, facing him, her belly between them.

'Hi,' she said, already seeking the comfort of his touch.

'Hi yourself. I'll never get used to us being apart. We should be joined at the hip wherever we go.' His arms came around her and drew her closer to him.

'Mmm ... and that would achieve sooo much ...' She nibbled at his bottom lip.

'Yes, but it might be fun.' He kissed the tip of her nose.

'So ...' She dotted kisses over his face. 'What did you want to tell me?'

Scott spread his warm fingers over her breasts. They were fuller, growing with her figure. 'Nothing, my sexy wife who smells like diesel and grease. Oh, heaven,' he said as he looked at her sitting on his lap, dressed in her blue work overalls. His body responded to her closeness.

'Later ... Let's talk about it later ...' he said breathlessly, as he stood up, lifting her with him, with her legs wrapped around his waist.

'Bedroom?' he asked, nipping softly at her mouth.

'No. Here.'

'Lisa could come in any minute—'

'She won't. If we close the door, even Renegade will leave us in peace.'

With her still attached, he crossed the floor and closed the door to the study, giving them a small sanctuary away from the world. He sat down again in his office chair, Ashley wrapped around him.

He sniffed at her neck. 'You feeling all right? You've been sick today.'

'Earlier, but I'm fine now. Do I need a mint?' she asked.

'No, it's on your clothes. Let me help you get them off.' He undid the front zip the whole way down, kissing the skin he'd exposed, then slipped her overalls off her shoulders. He kissed those gently too.

Ashley murmured and dropped her head back. Then she drew his tongue into her mouth in a searing kiss, making sure he understood she needed more than a tease session. Right now, she needed to know that he was there for her one hundred and ten per cent. Her hands gripped the back of his head, massaging his scalp. Tugging at his shirt, she ran her nails down his chest.

'Ash,' he whispered into her hair as he broke open the clip on her bra and her breasts spilled out. 'Whoops.' He threw the broken clip on the polished floor. 'I'll buy you another one.'

'I needed a new one anyway, that one was getting too small.' She laughed as she bit into his neck and pushed forwards slightly. The chair tilted backwards.

He ran his hands over her back and pushed her overalls down over her backside, as she allowed him room to manoeuvre the clothing out of the way. The office chair toppled over completely, depositing them on the floor as it skidded backwards and hit the wall.

'Oh, my hat ... look what we did!' She laughed. 'Idiot man.'

'Married to an idiot woman with a big belly,' he said, and kissed her.

They lay joined together after bounding over the edge of reality into their own private utopia.

Scott stroked her back. 'I love you, Mrs Ashley Decker.'

'I know, Mr Scott Decker. I love you too.'

'What ...? Did you feel that?' he asked. 'She moved. I felt our baby move. She moved against my stomach.' Total illumination lit his face, and she pulled him to her and kissed him.

'I felt it. I can't help but feel Junior in there play soccer in my stomach.'

He slipped his hands between them and onto Ashley's bump, and could feel their child moving around inside her, doing summersaults.

'Did I tell you how beautiful you are, mum-to-be?'

'Yes, but a girl never gets tired of hearing it.' She laughed at him as his hands began making erotic circles around her belly, totally distracted from the baby who had decided to settle back to sleep again.

'Ugh, acid,' she said as she moved away from him and sat up on the cool polished cement floor beside him. She looked at him. His hand was still threaded through one of hers, her other one massaging her chest trying to keep the acid down.

'You know, don't you?' he said. 'That's what this seduction was all about. You wanted to have total control the first time we were together after he attempted to rape you, and now you have done it again. The same urgency, the same control issue. You know Rodney's out.'

She nodded her head.

'He won't get to you, Ashley. You can't let him have any power over you ...' He squeezed her hand.

'I know, but it was still a shock finding out he was let out in the amnesty.'

'That's Africa for you. I did warn you that justice here was different from the system that you knew and understood.' He cradled her to his chest. He hooked one leg over hers, bringing her whole body closer again.

Pain speared into Ashley's back. 'Owie! I need to move, my back ...'

Scott quickly lifted Ashley up into a sitting position, and helped her stand up. 'How long have you been getting back pain?'

'It started this morning when I was driving.' She rubbed at her lower back with both hands.

'I think we should have it checked out by your doctor. You know he said that back pain can be a bad sign in older pregnant women.'

'Don't you rub me nearly being thirty-five into this ...' began Ashley, slightly defensive about her birthday fast approaching. 'Besides, you know how he fusses over every pregnancy in his practice. He's worse than a broody hen.'

Smiling at her and knowing it was simply the hormones talking in his wife's sweet body, Scott remained silent. That way she'd have nothing to fight with him about. All the fathers in the neighbourhood had imparted that piece of information onto him really fast when he'd told everyone he and Ashley were expecting. In fact, even Zol, who now had four small children, had told him not to argue with a pregnant wife.

'You always lose to the hormones,' he'd said.

At the time Scott had laughed—but not now.

He was worried about this new development. So far, the pregnancy had been a breeze, when they had finally got pregnant. But she was only five months along and shouldn't be having back pain yet. The video they'd ordered on the subject had been very informative, and the midwife who had put it together had had a calming effect on them when they'd watched it. They had even practised the Lamaze breathing exercises together in the evening, as they were hoping for a natural birth.

He picked up his shirt and pulled it over her head. 'You go get showered, and I'll call the doctor in Hwange and see if he can see you tomorrow.' Scott gave her a small push towards the door.

'Sure. Anything to please "the Master" in my life,' she joked at him, giving him a lingering kiss in parting.

Outside the door, Renegade lifted herself up and padded softly after Ashley.

'Your shadow's found you,' Scott called out to her, and she smiled, already reaching down and patting the dog on her head.

Scott had barely put his cut-offs back on and settled down to call the doctor when he heard Ashley scream out his name. He couldn't get out the door fast enough, automatically grabbing his rifle from the rack on the wall as he ran towards her.

'Scott! Oh no, oh noooooooo. Scoottttt, Sccccoooootttttt!'

Her agony slashed into his soul. Something was very wrong. She was in their bathroom, her hands bloody. Her legs covered in it, and a pool of dark red gathering at her feet.

'I'm haemorrhaging. Scott, help me. Help our baby.' All reasoning was gone from her voice, and only pure panic remained.

'Shit. Shit. Shit.' He swore as he folded up a towel and placed it between her legs. He had read up about this and watched the baby birthing videos, but nothing had prepared him for the reality of seeing Ashley in trouble. His stomach clenched and every muscle in his body strained for action—to stop the blood, to make Ashley all right.

He held her shoulders. 'Ashley, honey, you have to calm down. Ashley, look at me, look at me.' He tried to break inside her panic attack.

She looked into his face, the tears spilling freely down her own.

He kissed her softly. 'It'll be all right. We need to stop the bleeding and then I can phone Kevin and the doctor.'

'Boss Scott, Madam Ashley, do you need help?' Lisa's timid voice sounded from outside the bedroom door, where she was knocking softly.

'Lisa, get in here!' called Scott. He lifted Ashley up and carried her through to the bedroom and deposited her gently on the bed. Lisa had opened the bedroom door fully and was already waiting for instructions.

'Lisa, Ashley's in trouble. See if you can get the doctor on the phone, then see if we need to get hold of Kevin. We need the chopper. We are going to have to get her to hospital.'

'Yes, Boss,' Lisa said as she scrambled out of the room.

Scott elevated Ashley's feet with all the pillows on the bed. He grabbed another towel from the cupboard in the bathroom and wiped down her legs, cleaning her up.

'Scott, what if we lose this baby?'

'Then we try again if you want too. But honey, I can't lose you. Not you—not now ...' He kissed her, his lips trembling against hers.

Lisa knocked at the door. 'The doctor in Hwange said to come right away, don't wait. And Boss Kevin isn't at Zebra Pan. Madam Tessa said to drive Madam Ashley to the hospital because Boss Kevin went to South Africa.'

'Dammit!' Scott cursed. 'What is the point of owning half of that stupid aviation company if it's not there when I need it?'

Lisa left the room silently. Renegade sat next to the bed. She put her nose in the air and howled.

'Renegade, stop that!' Scott and Ashley said together.

'All right,' Scott began. 'We need to get you to the clinic, and the chopper is out. So we'll drive.' He went to the bathroom and collected more towels, then removed the soiled towel from between Ashley's legs and replaced it with a fresh one.

'Blood is still coming fast. Let's get you dressed. We go now.' He pushed his hand through his hair as he strode into their closet, where he grabbed the first maternity dress he could find and pulled it over her head. Then he lifted her up and began carrying her towards the workshop where the *bakkies* were parked.

A vehicle started and reversed to the bottom of the stairs. Elliott ran around and opened the back door of Ashley's double-cab-*bakkie* before Scott stepped off the stairs leading down to the driveway.

'Thanks, Elliott,' Scott said as he laid Ashley in the back. Then he ran around the other side and climbed inside with her. He hauled her into his lap. Lisa handed him some towels, and arranged still more on the seat next to them.

Elliott closed the door and went to the driver's seat. He drove like a demon into the Hwange clinic. Knowing that Lisa would have checked in with the doctors, he called on the CB radio, informing the doctor of their progress, answering the questions from the doctor.

'Yes, Madam Ashley is still bleeding.'

'Yes, Boss Scott was with us, but he is holding Madam Ashley.'

'Yes, I am driving as fast as I can.'

Eventually they reached the small clinic. Scott felt as if a lifetime had past on the drive into Hwange. He saw that the doctor had a gurney waiting outside. They transferred Ashley to it quickly and wheeled her inside, all the while the doctor firing questions at Scott as he checked her pulse.

'What time did the bleeding start?' the doctor asked.

'About an hour ago.'

'Your guard did well to get here in that time from Delmonica,' he exclaimed. 'How many towels has she gone through?'

'Six. But I just kept changing them, only the first one was soaked badly, but there was blood on all the others.'

The doctor gave Ashley an injection in her leg and she felt herself growing warm. The world closed around her, Scott's hand clinging onto hers the only certainty.

Slowly Ashley became aware of her surroundings. There was a drip hitched up to a silver stand, slowly releasing some fluid into her. There were flowers next to her bed, and they contained gardenia blooms. She could smell their distinctive perfume. Scott was asleep on her other arm, his forehead pressing into it. She couldn't feel her fingers where he hung onto them tightly in his sleep. The room's small light was dimmed in the ceiling, and the hushed sounds of a hospital broke into her awareness. 'Scott, love ...' she whispered.

Instantly awake, his head shot up. Blood rushed down her arm where the pressure had been released.

'Ashley,' he breathed. 'Thank God!'

Tears shimmered in his eyes, and if she could have moved her arm, she'd have touched his face. Instead, she raised her other arm and reached for him.

He hugged her to him, shaking with emotion.

'Our baby?' Her voice wobbled, dreading the outcome.

'They're still there, amazingly.' He smiled at her and kissed her softly.

'They?'

'We have two.'

'Two? Twins? You sure? How could the doctor have missed that on the check-up? Are you sure? Twins?' she babbled.

'Yah, look, here's a picture.' He showed her a small black and grey ultrasound scan photo that was on her bedside table. 'There, see them? We certainly have two babies.'

'Wow. So what went wrong, what happened that I bled like that?' she asked him, her eyes filling with tears.

'You have a thing called placenta abruption. They said it's "premature separation of the placenta from the site of uterine implantation before delivery of the foetus", to quote them exactly, or as near as. They've given you steroids to help keep the babies in there as long as possible. Apparently, their lungs aren't so strong just yet, but if the steroids don't help within another twenty-four hours, we'll fly you down to Cape Town to the neonatal centre in Groote Schuur hospital to deliver.'

'Oh Scott, why ... how ... what did I do to make this happen?'

'Nothing. It wasn't your fault. The doctor has told me that over and over. There is nothing we could have done different, it simply happens.' He kissed her again. 'I'm so happy you're awake.'

'Me, too. Twins. Oh my ... Scott, two of them.' She was flabbergasted. 'I know there was no ultrasound equipment in the doctor's surgery at Hwange, but heartbeats? Why didn't he hear there were two?'

'I don't know. I think he was so happy we were at last pregnant that he simply missed it. Nice surprise, though. It explains why you are so big at just over five months.'

'I was going into Bulawayo for a six-month scan with the gynaecologist. We would have found out then,' she said.

'I know. Honey, it's not your fault. None of it is.'

'Twins. I still can't believe it. I know I'm a twin, but the chances of it happening ...'

Scott laughed softly. 'I've had a day or two to get used to the idea. Take all the time you need, hopefully they are not going anywhere just yet.'

She looked at her husband properly for the first time since she'd woken up. He looked terrible. He had on a hospital gown and there were dark shadows under his eyes. At least a few days growth of speckled grey showed on his chin. 'You look horrid. How long have I been asleep?'

'Three days. We came by ambulance from Hwange to the private hospital in Bulawayo. You've had a blood transfusion too, but miraculously the babies didn't go into stress. This is the bad part: you'll need to stay here for a while.' He tapered off quietly, as if not wanting to stipulate for how long.

Ashley couldn't help herself. 'I guess we'll worry about the blood transfusion-HIV thing later ...'

'Your sister Peta is flying over but we couldn't wait for her, and you will need more blood than just one person can give you anyway. You might need more for a while.'

'How long is a while? A few more days? A week?' She frowned.

'The end of your pregnancy.'

'You've got to be joking. Scott, tell me you're joking. That's months in bed.'

'I nearly lost you.'

She looked at his serious face and understood that she had been in grave danger, and although Scott was speaking about it lightly, she had almost lost her babies.

'If you're okay, the nurse said to call her if you woke up. God Ashley, you scared me half to death. When I thought I might lose you, and there was nothing I could do to help you ...' he stated simply and honestly to her.

'You are my life too,' she said as she hugged him to her tightly.

A discreet cough from the door broke them apart.

'Mrs Decker, I'm glad to see you are awake. I'm Dr Nolan, your gynaecologist and obstetrician,' the woman said in a very British accent.

'Hi, you can call me Ashley. Thank you for saving my babies.'

'They're not out of the woods yet, but if we can get their mummy right, they'll be just fine.' The doctor smiled as she put her cold stethoscope on Ashley's chest.

'Look, those two machines are baby monitors. We can see their heart rates.' She watched the equipment beside the bed, already hooked up to the babies inside Ashley's uterus. Dr Nolan smiled. 'Man, they're fighters. You're going to have your hands full soon.'

'Will I make it to term? I'm already well into my fifth month, almost six,' Ashley asked.

'We don't know that answer yet. But you and your babies have fought well so far. Has your husband had a chance to speak to you about moving down to Groote Schuur?'

Ashley looked at Scott. He still held her hand but was looking downwards, not meeting her eyes.

'He mentioned it briefly.'

'I think it might be a good option. Think about it seriously. You and the babies would be better off there than staying in Zimbabwe. Here in Bulawayo, we don't have the essential neonatal unit if you need it. Your best bet once you are stable is to fly to South Africa. My vote is on Cape Town. You are lucky, you can afford to do what is best for these two.' She gently patted Ashley's bump. 'Some people can't and must make do with what little we have here.'

'Are you British?' Ashley asked.

'I was. I fell in love with a country cricket player who broke his leg and came to the casualty department when I was doing a rotation in Birmingham. I married him and came home to his family ranch in Africa. We used to live in the Esigodini area.'

'Used to?'

'We were invaded. The war veterans, most of whom were younger than twenty and couldn't have seen a year of fighting, came one night and ran us off. We chose life over possessions. I was an idiot, I thought being a doctor and helping the locals in the area would hold some weight—but it didn't. The invaders were bussed in from another area altogether, and now some Minister of Something-or-other sits in my beautiful thatched house with a fire burning in the middle of the teak lounge room floor, not even in the fireplace.' She sighed heavily, lost in thought. 'It breaks my heart, but Mark won't leave. He says someday he'll get his ranch back through the courts. And I can't leave him, so together we wait for a change to happen. Anyway, enough about me ...' She looked at Ashley.

'That's terrible. I know slowly the white farmers, productive or not, are being driven off their ranches, but—'

'We were one of the first in our area. Luckily, we came away relatively unscathed. Our neighbours were not so lucky. They shot her dead at the gate, then beat him up so badly in front of their kids ... Come on, we have to find something happier to talk about. I don't want your blood pressure to be affected.' She shone a torch into Ashley's eyes.

Scott sat quietly in the chair next to Ashley's bed, holding her hand. He listened to every word exchanged between the women, but said nothing. He knew Mark Nolan. They'd gone to the same school, and had even served time on the board of the Commercial Farmers' Union together. His country was changing fast, and he didn't like the changes heading their way.

Zol and Scott had sat together many evenings talking about it. They hoped that everyone on Delmonica was safe because of the way they had split the ranch into both their names. But Scott wondered if it would hold the invaders at bay for much longer.

Already in the Nyamandhlovu area, twelve white farmers had been invaded. Chucked off their land. The sad fact was that for each white farmer who was displaced, roughly forty black families were tossed aside too. All the workers were usually beaten or threatened, and left the ranch along with the farmer. This was a cruel system, and it was gaining momentum.

The worst thing was that everyone knew that the international community would stand by and do nothing. There were no known oil reserves in Zimbabwe. No rich gains for anyone stepping in and being the humanitarian.

'Now that she's awake, you can have a shower, then you can have some dinner together.' Dr Nolan's voice broke into his concentration.

'Thanks,' he said. At present he was too tired to argue. After three days of sitting by Ashley's bedside wondering if she was going to make it because she'd lost so much blood, he was ready to do almost anything so long as he didn't need to think too hard about it. 'Tell Mark I said hi.'

In the bathroom he took off his clothes and turned on the shower. He couldn't do anything about his beard, except make it clean and fresh to sleep near his beautiful wife. His best friend.

CHAPTER 18

'Congratulation Mr and Mrs Decker, you have a pigeon pair. A healthy boy and girl,' the obstetrician told them. 'And with the Apgar result of seven, I can present your babies to you now,' he said as he placed one on each side of Ashley, inside her arms.

Scott looked at the doctor, a worried expression on his face. 'And Ashley? Any sign of the haemorrhaging?'

'None. She has come through this beautifully. We've still done the hysterectomy we spoke about beforehand. Now that the children are born, the chances of her having a prolapse are greater than ever. And we seriously don't recommend another pregnancy.'

Tears of joy streaming unchecked down Scott's face. For the first time in two months, he allowed his emotions to show, as he wept into Ashley's shoulder with relief.

'I love you, but I agree with the doctors, no more kids,' he said solemnly, into her lips. 'I can't live apart from you and on edge like this again.'

Smiling through her tears, Ashley nodded her head and kissed her husband. The terror was over, the human gestation machine that had been Ashley Decker lying flat on her back on full bed rest for the past two agonising months, had delivered two healthy babies. Now one last procedure, then they could look forward to going home to Zimbabwe, to Delmonica.

After delivering a month early, on 12 May, she knew she'd still need to stay with her babies in hospital for at least another two weeks or perhaps more, depending on their growth and how they fed. But she was happy to stay, and to learn how to look after her precious children. Soon they would leave Groote Schuur hospital in Cape Town and return home to Delmonica. And then, with no one other than Lisa to help her, they would be alone.

She smiled. Women in Africa had been giving birth in the fields for centuries. So she'd had a few complications and had needed a little help, but her children were fighters. They'd proved that already with her difficult pregnancy. There was a new generation of Deckers who she knew would love their land.

'What do you mean Delmonica is on the hit list? What about Zol's rights? I thought we had this covered? Why us?' Ashley fired questions at Scott on the drive home from Victoria Falls airport a month later. Their twins, Brock and Paige, were sleeping snugly in their car seats in the back seat of Ashley's king-cab.

Scott's fingers clenched and flexed on the steering wheel. 'You have been gone just over three months. During that time, there have been rumours. My anti-poaching unit confirmed them about two weeks ago. The war vets have a list of ranches they want, and are claiming. One by one they're crossing them off. Delmonica is moving up on it.'

He chanced a glance at her. His wife had changed in the last months. Her face had stress contours embedded in it, frown lines previously hinted at now grooved into her face. Her hair hung limply around her shoulders, where once it was a shining halo. Her shoulders slumped in a defeated gesture. He'd never seen her like this. His heart ached when he looked at her. He wanted to take away all the harshness she had undergone lately, and smooth it all over, make it all better. But he knew that was impossible. She had been well looked after in hospital and they had been happy to discharge her, giving her the all-clear, both physically and by the psychologist who was doing a follow-up study on how parents coped with multiple births.

But it was more than that. Her shorter hair was dull. She looked stressed, more so than during the poaching trail five years ago, when she hadn't looked like she needed make-up to make her appear healthy. It was as if she had faded in hospital.

He realised that her skin was whiter than he had ever seen it. No longer kissed by the Africa sun. His heart broke for her, knowing how much she loved the outdoors. She looked like an English tourist, without the bright eyes of an anticipated adventure.

Scott dreaded that this time, Africa might have won. Could her time in the city have made her want to leave the bush behind her? Had the bush taken his radiant, vibrant Ashley and killed her spirit for good, or could she bounce back as she had the last time they'd faced a major crisis in their lives?

This time, because of the distance and the necessity to live apart, her in South Africa and him commuting from Zimbabwe, it was as if they had separated and were no longer in sync. She was so quiet. Where was the self-confident woman he'd married?

Her eyes connected with his and he felt her soft hand caress the side of his face.

'Sweetheart, what else have you kept from me while I was in hospital?'

He knew his silence told her there was more. But he couldn't form the words. His throat was clogged up and no sound could escape.

'Tell me. How am I supposed to handle this if you don't let me know what I'm up against?'

Still no words came out of his mouth.

She undid her seatbelt and slid across the seat. She lifted her right leg to accommodate the gear-lever, and snuggled up to him, putting the middle seatbelt on.

'You still have such a thing with seatbelts, even after all this time.' He grinned.

'I guess it's a habit not easily broken.' She laid her head on his shoulder, and he lifted his arm over her head to crush her to him in a hug.

'I love you, Scott. I'm not leaving. But you have to let me in. You have to share things with me. Yes, I was ill and needed a little pampering, but I'm better now. We have two beautiful kids, and I'm worried for you. I need the truth from you more than being wrapped in cotton wool. Let me inside your head and tell me what's going on. What's made your hair turn steel grey in the last month? You have new etchings of stress tattooed on your forehead.' She ran her fingertips over his face, tracing the lines.

'You sure you're not leaving?' he asked, his voice so deep that it almost croaked.

She snuggled deeper into his one-armed embrace, and loudly kissed his cheek. 'Sticking like glue, that extra attachment you simply can't shake or get rid of.'

He saw a small part of her old self shining through. His Amazon princess was still there. A little bruised and battered, but still present. He returned the smile, as a tiny seed of hope settled in his chest.

'Okay. Okay. I have been burning the candle at both ends while you were in hospital. That's why Dale spent so much time with you. My brother knew what was happening. He was giving me space to try to salvage as much as possible for everyone. Between us, Zol and I have managed to strip the ranch of most of the livestock, the game and the safari lodges.'

'Why?'

'So we don't lose everything. We have driven the two cattle trucks, loaded to the max, through the bundu, across the unmarked boarder and into Botswana. Then we drove around the delta and up into Zambia. The border guards there are easier to bribe. My cousin Albert has a safari camp in the Zambezi basin. We stashed everything there. I have left Tobias and his wife Annie in Zambia, and a few of the other workers to watch over the cattle. Our game, what we could capture, had been thrown in with Albert's. We'll sort it another time. At least he has fences to hold it in, but the game stands a better chance of life relocated. If the war vets get it, they'll just shoot it to shit. We have broken every livestock movement law there is.'

'Now what? What happens next?' She caressed his leg with her right hand.

'On each trip, I dreaded that I'd be away when you went into labour. I couldn't tell you what I was doing. The doctors warned me against causing you any unnecessary stress. They feared it might bring on your labour early. The rest is just something we had to do.'

'Okay. I accept that, but what have you done?'

'The last trip, Elliott went along with Zol into Zambia. I knew I couldn't chance another one. Zol and Elliott have just returned, and they're packing another truckload now, as we drive home. This last one is our household possessions. They're packing up our house. Tonight will probably be our last at Delmonica.'

'Why the cloak-and-dagger stuff? I don't understand.'

'The borders between the two countries are open, but the Zimbabwean government have clamped down hard on trucks leaving with goods. No amount of bribing is getting possessions through. It's worse than when they had the sanctions during the eighties, when people left with nothing. So most people trying to relocate, well ... they are migrating the old-fashioned way, through the bush. A huge expanse of unfenced territory has its advantages. But we've encountered a problem. Our trucks are being recognised, and questions are being asked. We're running out of time—fast.'

'I don't know what to say. I knew things were not right, but this has escalated so fast. What are we going to do?' she asked quietly.

One of the twins made a small squeak and she turned to the back to settle the baby. It was Paige. She resettled as soon as Ashley put her hand on her cheek. The tiny baby reached out a small hand and touched her mother, then was silent again.

'You're a natural with them. And to think you were worried you wouldn't cope.' Scott goaded her gently.

'Yeah sure, from the man who has yet to change a dirty nappy.'

She'd been so looking forward to getting home, being a family all in one place, simply being together with Scott again. She could smell his scent in the *bakkie* and was surrounded by it. It made her feel wanted, and cherished, but mostly it was the scent of her best friend. Her lover. Her skin goose bumped with emotion, despite the situation they discussed. It was a sensation that had been seriously lacking from her life in the last three months.

The delivery had been the beginning of a new era, in which Ashley found herself constantly exhausted. She'd been transformed into a human milk machine for the twins. The four weeks she'd stayed with the babies in the 'premmies ward', as the hospital staff liked to call it, were hard. Scott had returned to Zimbabwe, and although Dale, her mother and sister Peta were there constantly, she'd been in need of his time focused on her.

Not her twins.

Her.

She'd missed her husband. When he visited each week, it was only for a night. He was constantly distracted when he was at the hospital, and then he would be gone again. She had begun to wonder if there was someone else in his life, but dismissed the idea as stupid. Scott wasn't like that and she knew it was just her mind, her own doubts and frustration at being kept away from him for so long. Listening to what he had been up to, Ashley was surprised he'd actually managed any time away with her at all.

Kevin's chopper and the three other choppers had all been chartered for the day, but she had assured Scott she was fine to travel the few hours home in the *bakkie*. The twins were nearing feed time again, her breasts hurt with fullness, her back ached and mostly all she wanted was a hot bath and a sleep alongside her man.

They drove over the cattle grid onto their ranch, the sensation bringing her back to the present.

'Nearly home,' she said.

The lights of the homestead eventually came into view. Everything was floodlit. Huge homemade lights on long extension cords stood as bright silhouettes in the dark as they shone their white light at the house.

Delmonica's two cattle trucks were loaded up with furniture. Everything from the house appeared stacked inside. The comfortable rocking chair perched precariously near Elliott, who was up on top tying it on with rope. Zol stood below, tying it down. Both men came over to the *bakkie* to greet them.

'Hello, Madam Ashley,' Elliot greeted her warmly. Gertrude ran down the steps and threw her arms around Ashley. Zol hugged Gertrude, but extended his arms to enclose Ashley, his upbringing and traditions forgotten for once. No barrier between them. She held onto them both.

'I'm home.' She smiled.

'Home is moving, Madam,' Elliott said indignantly. 'They're coming already. Vusi saw a trainload arriving at the Nyamandhlovu station. There are three buses booked for them for the morning. Sipewe radioed from Boss Kevin's. There was a truck full of imported war vets crossing through the reserve, behind Zebra Pan. He said they have settled for the night, and are making fires.'

'Already? I thought we had a few days still. When? Why did they move it up?' Scott asked, mentally kicking himself for not turning on the CB in the *bakkie*. He'd consciously chosen to steal a few precious hours alone with his wife, but now second-guessed himself whether his decision had been worth it.

'I don't know, Scott,' Zol said. 'We got everyone moving. Most of the women and kids from the compound have already left with the anti-poaching units. We'll intercept them later. Kwiella knows the way. I've shown him where to cross into Zambia if he's on foot, so no one will see him. But they'll be going slowly, they are a big group to move undetected. I made sure the units were fully armed, and then some. No one will mess with Delmonica's women or children.' He looked seriously at Gertrude.

'Why are you here, Gertrude? I thought you were staying with the kids in Zambia?' Scott asked.

'You were at the hospital in South Africa. A woman had to be here with the men to help pack up your home,' she said in her defence. 'Anyway, I couldn't leave Zol. My sister, she has our children with her. They are safe in Zambia.'

Ashley reached out a hand and touched Gertrude on the arm in a reassuring manner. She could think of nothing worse than being separated from her children.

Lisa came down the steps. 'Hello, Madam Ashley, where-are-my-babies?' her greeting and question running into each other.

'Lisa, why are you still here?' Scott asked, noting that his well-laid plans had been ignored and changed.

'My Madam. She'll need help. Elliot knows how to protect her, but I know about babies.' And she put her head into the back of the *bakkie* and began *ooing* and *ahhing* at the sight of the twins. Then suddenly everyone was looking at the tiny tots asleep in their car seats, oblivious for a moment of the danger drawing ever closer.

Ashley lay next to Scott on the foam mattress. Their babies in their car seats, Renegade lay next to them, protective of the babies already. 'At least I get to say goodbye to the ranch and see it one more time, and the kids got to sleep in their own home one night.' Scott said, his voice thick with emotion.

'Perhaps one day when the country isn't so mad anymore, we can come home. Fight for our home in court, get Delmonica back,' Ashley said.

'I hope we can. I have never lived anywhere else. Many of our workers have only ever known this as home. It's going to be different heading for Zambia.'

'It's still the same continent. We will just see the stars from a different angle,' Ashley said.

Scott pulled her close to him. 'You smell like heaven. I'm so glad to have you home.'

She put her finger on Scott's lips. 'Sshh.'

'I feel like a fraud, Ash. I want to stand and fight them. Who the hell do they think they are, coming into our home and taking it away from us? But to fight them would mean people I love would die, and I don't believe that any patch of dirt is worth dying for. Not back when my father died fighting a useless war, and certainly not now when I have a beautiful wife and children. We have our lives ahead of us, and I should be fighting to keep it. But instead, I have packed everything up and surrendered.' He let out a huge breath through clenched teeth, his emotions running deep, surfacing now that Ashley was home with him.

She held him tight.

'No Scott, don't think that. It's the right thing to do. You are right. Fighting we would only prolong the battle, we might get rid of this lot, but one day, as you drove out the gate, they would ambush you, kill the kids, hurt me. It's the right thing to simply leave. You are brave and precious. You are taking us all out of harm's way. It takes a real man to make a decision like that.'

'I don't know what I did to have you in my life, but thank you,' he said.

They lay in their bedroom listening to the lack of farming sounds. There were no cattle, no sheep braying in the night as they moved about.

A jackal cried close by and Ashley instinctively moved closer to Scott.

'Come, neither of us are sleeping. Let's move onto the veranda, sit on the steps like we used to and watch for satellites and shooting stars.'

They moved quietly from their room and sat on the cold steps. In the moonlight, they could see a single warthog foraging outside the fence.

'I'm going to miss her,' Ashley said. 'But at least we get to say bye to her.'

'I wish we could have taken her with us. There are so many things I wish we had more time for. Zol said he shot the last five stockhorses before we arrived, he couldn't bear to leave them to the harsh cruelty of the war vets. They are better off dead.'

Tears trickled down Ashley's cheeks and dripped like raindrops onto the cold cement of the stairs.

'He was right to do that. When I first came here, I would have been appalled at that idea, but now I understand it, and it takes a kind man to sacrifice a life to make it better.'

Scott kissed her on the top of her head, and she wrapped her arms around his waist. 'Look, a shooting star …'

'Make a wish,' Ashley said, and closed her eyes.

After a moment, Scott asked, 'What did you wish for?'

'World peace,' she said, and Scott hooted so loudly it echoed across the yard and up the kopjie in the front. The warthog spooked and rushed away into the night, back to its burrow.

'That warthog has the right idea. Run from danger and get to a safe place in your burrow. Then protect your territory from there,' he said.

They sat together watching the stars. As the inky night changed to purple and the night faded and lightness touched the skyline, they rose together for the last time on their ranch and prepared to leave.

At four-fifteen in the morning, the four-vehicle convoy began its crawl out the gates of the homestead compound for the last time. Zol drove the first truck out, and Gertrude and Lisa in Scott's *bakkie* followed next. Scott driving with his family in Ashley's double-cab were third, and lastly Elliott brought up the rear.

Renegade was in the back seat of the *bakkie* with his kids. When Scott had tried to load her in with Elliott, she'd growled at him. When he'd stepped away from her and lifted his hands in the air in a gesture of surrender, she trotted around the *bakkie* and jumped inside, in between the babies, and there she'd stayed, as if guarding them. 'Leave her there, she isn't doing any harm,' Ashley said as she reached in and patted Renegade, content in the knowledge she was accepting the twins so readily.

Ashley couldn't believe they were really leaving Delmonica. She'd come home only to have to spend her last night saying goodbye to her home, to her garden, to everything.

Scott snorted. 'I always wanted to be buried down by the dam under that *umtshwili* tree. That was once my life's ambition.'

Ashley stared at her husband. Her heart wrenched in two for him and how much he was losing by leaving Delmonica.

'But I love you more,' he said suddenly, 'and I won't allow them to hurt you or any member of my family, not over a simple ownership right for some dirt.' He squeezed her hand. He looked out the windscreen, his eyes following the red taillights of the vehicles in front of them.

The CB blared. 'Scott. A second busload has just pulled up at the gate,' Zol, the first in the convoy warned.

Scott lifted his mouthpiece. 'Lock your doors and drive through. Take care, my brother.'

Moments later, gunshots shattered the silence of the night as war erupted around Zol's vehicle.

'Shit!' Scott exclaimed loudly, as he drove into the shower of tracers.

Renegade growled in the back.

A face appeared at Ashley's window.

'Ashley, get down!' Scott screamed.

Even on her way down, Ashley knew the face.

Rodney the albino.

She realised that this was no normal invasion: it was revenge on the Decker family.

They were in trouble.

Renegade barked loudly. The twins began screaming. Rodney broke Ashley's window with the butt of his gun. Standing on the side shelf designed to help people step into the double-cab, he took full advantage of the elevated position and looked into the cab. Ashley was showered in shatterproof glass.

Scott zigzagged the *bakkie* back and forth across the narrow dirt road, trying to dislodge him. Rodney held on and leered at them through the window. Renegade was going ballistic, barking and attempting to get to the intruder. Then Rodney broke the window on the back door. Glass showered over Paige, whose car seat was closest to the door. Renegade launched herself at Rodney out through the window. She latched onto his throat, and together they fell backwards off the moving *bakkie.*

'Renegade!' screamed Ashley.

'Leave her, she'll catch us if she can,' Scott instructed harshly.

The automatic firing continued outside. Scott pressed harder on the accelerator. He'd lost precious ground between the taillights ahead.

'I'm through.' Zol's voice came on the CB. 'I'm out the other side.'

They'd heard nothing yet from Gertrude and Lisa. They were almost out.

He peered at the taillights of their vehicle in front of them, and watched in horror as it launched into the air.

'Shit! No!' Scott cursed.

The vehicle turned over. The lights that should have been horizontal stood vertical. He picked up the radio. 'Elliott, get in here. The ladies are down.'

New gunfire joined in the sporadic shots. A flare was shot into the sky, illuminating the scene in bright green light. Shots were being fired from a new direction. They sounded solid. They were hitting their targets, not firing haphazardly. Scott saw the direction the tracer bullets came from and smiled grimly. One of their anti-poaching units was still close by and had been listening in. Silently, like night cats prowling, they had come to help.

Scott drove as close to the other vehicle as he could. People were rocking it back and forth. He blew on his horn, trying anything to distract the mob's attention away from the two women trapped in the vehicle.

The strong smell of petrol permeated the air.

Heavy tracer bullets firing over the *bakkie* cleared the human pack away. People scattered as they ran for cover. Obviously they had realised there were other armed people around who knew how to shoot straight.

Ashley opened her door and called, 'Gertrude? Lisa?'

Lisa popped her head out the broken window. 'We're coming.'

'Scott, I'm closer. Stay here with the twins, I'll bring them back to our *bakkie*.' She jumped out to rush towards the upturned vehicle.

'Ashley. Don't!' Scott screamed.

But she was already gone and had almost reached the other vehicle. He watched Lisa as she climbed nimbly out of the cab and sat on the doorframe. She put her arm down to reach for Gertrude. Gertrude's shoulder hung limply by her side, and her left leg was broken and useless. Lisa's inhumane strength, driven by pure adrenaline, allowed her to pull Gertrude out and pass her down to where Ashley stood next to the *bakkie*. Lisa jumped down, and together, as more shots covered their movement, she and Ashley dragged Gertrude towards Scott.

He revved the *bakkie* loudly, ready to flee. 'Hurry!' he shouted.

Together they bundled Gertrude onto the floor of the back of the *bakkie*. Lisa climbed in on top of her and Ashley slammed the door shut. But as she reached for the handle to pull herself up into the front seat, a hand grabbed her hair and she was roughly pulled backwards.

She screamed.

Rodney held her. 'I is gonna cut you beetch!' he screeched.

'*Sope, sope, tokoloshe*!' Lisa shrieked.

Truck lights flooded the scene as Elliott caught up with them and Scott could see Rodney holding Ashley from behind.

Trapped.

He flew out of the *bakkie* and bulldozed into them.

Elliott tumbled out of his truck seconds later and was running to help.

The gunfire stopped.

It was as if everyone waited for the outcome between the rancher and the leader of the war veterans. Neither side could shoot, as they risked killing the wrong man.

Scott pulled himself back from another punch and looked for Ashley. She lay still on the ground, where she'd been knocked aside when he'd rushed Rodney. Scott had ploughed into him with a full body slam, and was now pounding him again and again, over and over. Rage, anger and years of pent-up animosity blinded him, and he continued to thrash the albino, his firearm left in its holster at his side, forgotten in his rage.

Elliott rushed to Ashley and picked her up. Rodney, who hadn't put up much of a fight, lay defeated on the ground, an old man curled in a defensive ball, all his energy spent on his last attempt to capture Ashley. Kicking Scott in the butt to get his attention and draw him out of his rage, Elliott demanded, 'Boss! Time to go! Now Boss, we must go! Madam needs you!'

Scott heard the urgency of his friend's warning. He stopped punching Rodney and, turning swiftly, realised Elliott held Ashley. He snatched her from him and headed for the *bakkie* with his kids in it. He saw Lisa was sitting in the driver's seat. Climbing into the front passenger seat, Ashley safely cradled in his arms, he instructed, 'Drive, Lisa. Drive!'

Lisa didn't wait for a second instruction. Scott saw her put the gearbox in 'D', just as Ashley had taught her to do, and floored the accelerator. Within seconds, they had cleared the throng of people who were closing in on them. In the rear-view mirror he saw Elliott jump into his truck, then his lights were in the mirror. He was following close behind, and both vehicles were on the road once more.

The *bakkie* crossed the cattle grid out of the ranch with a loud clatter, and was soon driving up the hill. Scott looked at Lisa as she glanced in the rear-view mirror. She too was driving away from the only home she had ever known, leaving the graves of her parents in the small graveyard on Delmonica. They were all being ripped apart from so much.

But at least they were alive. Memories could always travel with them wherever they went, as long as they were alive to remember.

Rodney, although badly beaten, rose up and staggered around. He steadied himself on his feet, pulled a box of matches from his pocket, lit one, then returned it to the box. The other matches caught almost immediately. He threw the box onto the overturned *bakkie*.

It was quiet for a moment, then the flame caught the spilled petrol and the abandoned vehicle exploded. He was thrown to the ground as flames leaped into the air. Rodney laughed hysterically at the destruction, the sound wicked in the night, its sinister tone drowning out the fury of the flames consuming the *bakkie*.

'*Ek is nee kla maissie*,' he shouted up into the sky. 'I is not fineeshed, girl.'

The war veterans around him, realising that the ranch was now theirs, began to toi toi down the road towards the ranch house.

'*Fook*ing idiots,' muttered Rodney. He got to his feet and buckled over. Examining his leg, he found a bullet hole going through the thigh.

'*Fook*,' he cursed as he tore his shirt to make a tourniquet and bandage. He pulled himself back up and hobbled to the bus. '*Gaan by die huis*,' he instructed the driver, who immediately began to drive towards the homestead.

Rodney sat in the doorway, at the top of the stairs. He watched the road as they passed the youngsters dancing. One could always count on money and wealth being the root of people's downfall. He'd paid each university student one hundred American dollars to attend tonight's takeover. All of it counterfeit. Some tried to clamber back onto the bus, but he kicked savagely at them with his good leg, preventing any entry. Most of the snot-nosed brats hadn't even been born when he'd been fighting for the country. But they had been happy enough to be *toi-toiing* and creating trouble. War veterans, ha! What a laugh.

The only veteran there was him, and perhaps the bus driver. He certainly had no interest in farming the property, all he wanted was to flush out the white bitch. He had seen her, and now she was gone.

When the bus's lights illuminated the house, he smiled. Eventually it stopped outside the security fence gates. Easing out of the bus slowly, like the old man that he was, Rodney didn't cross over the metal strip across the driveway.

He took deep breaths and eventually managed to get himself under control. The metallic taste of blood always did that to him—sent him into a frenzy. His dick wouldn't settle, as he began to hobble towards the house, it bobbed painfully against the coarse fabric of his camo pants. He savoured the sensation.

Slowly, he crossed the line towards *her* house. She'd got away again, but he would find her. He always found those he truly wanted in the end. His mother had taught him well: patience was the key to revenge. No rushing in and spoiling it.

He brought a hanky out of his pocket. He mopped it at his throat and felt skin move. He smoothed it back into place and secured it with the now blood-soaked handkerchief, knotting it at the back. He plucked his shirt from his chest. The large claw marks there were beginning to burn now that his adrenaline level had dropped, more so than his leg. That was a clean shot, but the chest would fester.

'*Fook*ing *hond*.' He limped up the stairs and into the house. He didn't need a light. He'd been studying the house from afar for months.

She hadn't been there. He'd watched and watched for her, but she wasn't present. He'd worried that perhaps she'd returned to Australia. But today, while he executed his plan to destroy her home, he'd seen her. Today, he had new hope to live for.

He always had time to wait for his revenge.

CHAPTER 19

They were on the move again. The second cattle truck was a distance traveller, the 'road train', as Ashley referred to it. The sleeping cabin in the back was small, but Gertrude would at least travel comfortably. They had driven out on the Victoria Falls road, towards Hwange, and stopped.

For Scott, it was hard to see Zol say goodbye to Gertrude, knowing that this separation would cause the two of them still more unwanted stress.

'I put my wife in your care now,' Zol said as he laid his hand on Scott's shoulder. 'She is my life.'

'I know. She is my sister-but-one,' Scott replied. 'Be careful.'

They had waited a week and a day for the all-clear from Gertrude's doctors, giving permission for her to travel with them. Gertrude still needed help but they would manage between them. It was hard watching them part, especially since he and Ashley had only just been reunited after their time being separated.

Scott turned his back on his friend to give him privacy as he said goodbye to Gertrude, then Zol vanished into the bushland. He would see them once he crossed the river into Zambia. Scott knew for certain that Zol's decision was correct. He wouldn't cross at the conventional border post this time, but had chosen to catch up with the farm workers and make sure they got across the river.

Scott walked slowly back to the small convoy of three trucks. Two large cattle trucks and one *bakkie* left. Elliott would drive the first truck and he would drive the other. Ashley would drive the four-wheel drive through some of the roughest bush tracks in Africa, and Lisa would accompany her and watch the children. He grinned at the thought of his wife five years ago and the woman sitting on the rug breastfeeding his son now. There was an inner strength within her that she had once again dipped into, and despite the deep lines of stress that still marked her face, she now looked radiant, like she could take on the world, and he smiled, knowing that if she did, she'd conquer that too.

He'd married a woman in a million.

Zol picked up the anti-poaching unit's spoor. It was not hard to follow a huge group of fifty people, including women and children, through the bush. He knew almost every child in the group from birth. Each little slippery sucker who had sat and watched his wife adoringly as she taught them their ABCs. 'A' for assegai, 'B' for bush, 'C' for Coke. This was his family moving through the sticks, towards the mighty river. He knew his and Gertrude's own children were already safe in Zambia; now it was his job to protect the extended family who had shared his life on the ranch for all those years.

Tobias's old dad, James, as he shuffled along; the old woman who lived up to her name and never had a good thing to say, Miserable. These people were his family, and they had chosen to start a new life along with Scott and Zol, becoming refugees. He needed to be there to protect them. It was his promise to Charlie all those years ago for saving him—that he would always look after the good of the Decker family.

It was simple. Both he and Scott believed these people were worth saving, so he would protect them.

Zol looked at the tracks in the dirt. The grass had already begun to cover the indentations. A week was lot of time to be away from the spoor, but Zol knew he could find the men and their precious voyagers.

He travelled fast, having stripped down to his normal minimum pack requirements before he left the convoy. He took a swig from his water bottle and looked at the sun. He had one hour of sunlight left at most. Already he was near Chizarira Game Reserve's first concession. Here, he had to take care, as the private game rangers also had their own anti-poaching units. He noticed the spoor begin to detour east. It was a good sign. The anti-poaching men had realised where they were, and adjusted their bearings accordingly. He'd taught them well.

The sun slipped behind the trees at his back. He watched his lengthening shadow disappear as the blackness descended into the night. His eyes adjusted to the reduced light, constantly scanning the bush for signs of predators. Lions, leopards or humans.

His nose detected smoke. He grinned. If he was correct, this was the first of the two groups he should find soon. Cautiously, he followed the scent. He switched his radio on. The digital screen time read 19:45, and he adjusted the dimness. The darkness was complete, no moon shining. He clicked twice and waited.

No reply.

He clicked again.

No clicks answered him.

He tried again at 20:00.

Still no reply.

The fire he could smell was not his anti-poaching unit's. He turned in the night and made a large detour to avoid the human contact.

As the sun rose into the sky above the escarpment and shed her warmth on the trees, Zol turned his radio back on and clicked twice. Two clicks returned. After a further half-hour's walk, he strolled towards the camp. He hadn't quite reached it when he was confronted by Kwiella.

'Zol, good to see you,' he said as he clasped Zol's arm, old comrade style.

'Likewise, Kwiella. How are things?'

'We travel too slowly. The old people, they can't walk faster, and we take turns in carrying the weaker ones. Still our time is bad. We'll need to kill for fresh meat at this rate, and that will mean we are poaching on someone's land.'

Nodding, Zol listened intently.

'The children are good. They gather berries, fruits, monkey oranges, even honey as we go, to supplement the rations we all carry. The stronger women have taken some of the older people's rations into their head bundles, and carry more than they should. This is a hard trek, keeping hidden in the bush all the time.'

'How do they manage with their water ration?' Zol asked, almost afraid of the answer.

'We have been lucky and found fresh water troughs twice. Only three men and three children travelled back and forth filling the storage containers. Then we wiped the tracks. The farmers might suspect someone has been there, but it's unlikely, unless they see our spoor further in the bush.'

'You are covering your movements well, even I was having to track carefully to follow.' Zol complimented his guard. 'Any other troubles?'

'No. We have been left alone so far. We have shown the children and women how to blend into the bush. They do it well.'

They walked into the small camp together.

'Zol has come! Zol has come!' greeted some of the children in a singsong fashion. They ran up to him with their small hands outstretched and, as always, he had sweets to give them, his one concession to his lighter travel pack. He rationed out two hard-boiled sweets each for the children in the camp.

After some hot coffee and honey-sweetened *sadza* at the fire, he was ready to move out with the rest of the camp.

He addressed the whole camp together. 'My people,' he said, 'the night we left Delmonica was very sad. As Kwiella has probably already told you, Boss Scott's *bakkie* was lost and Gertrude was hurt. She's been in hospital for the last week, but now she's with Boss Scott in the cattle truck. She wanted to travel with you all to help, but I was being a stubborn old man and wanted her with me. She's broken her leg but she is fine.' He knew Gertrude would forgive him for his white lie. But he needed it to help the group along.

'Madam Ashley and Lisa are looking after her. She wanted to say hello to everyone, and give a lesson to the children while we walked. I promised her instead I would teach all the children to survive this crossing, as that is more important at the moment. My wife was laughing about this. I'll travel for a week with you, then I must leave and meet Scott in Zambia. I'll check the river crossing, and mark the place well for you. Then I'll see you again when you cross. It will be a good day when we are all in Zambia together.'

They all clapped at his words and danced a little. Then they picked up their things and followed Kwiella and Zol out of the camp. Vusi lagged behind, erasing all traces that a group of travellers had camped there for the night. It wouldn't do for the Zimbabwean forces to find the group of travellers planning on border jumping.

Zol surveyed the group. Kwiella carried the old crone, Miserable, and Vusi carried a young child who had woken up coughing badly. The small amount of medicine he had ensured they carried was not adequate for a bad infection but would cure most daily ailments. Marion was showing signs that her baby would be born any day, having dropped low in her stomach. He worried about her being on the move, but knew that for years African women had delivered babies together, each in the community helping the other if needed. There were no midwives and doctors for most deliveries in the bush, and usually they continued with their work or chores afterwards, the baby simply strapped onto the new mum. They were strong.

He thought of the difference in each of Gertrude's four births compared to Ashley's one. He knew the comparison was unfair, but he liked to think his wife the strong Ndebele woman. She had been worth every cow he had paid for her *lobola*.

His radio clicked three times. A sign of danger. He raised his hand in a stop signal to the small band of people walking behind him. Every one of them stopped dead in their tracks, even the children. All fell silent. Kwiella had done a good job with teaching them to follow him.

They listened and heard low rumblings and snapping branches. Jumbo. Directly in their path. The scouts out front had detected them early enough to warn the group not to walk blindly into their midst.

They turned west so they were downwind of the elephant and detoured around them. They would scare away most animals in the bush, but buffalo, rhino and jumbo were the three they had to be extremely careful of and avoid wherever possible.

According to Zol's calculations, they had just crossed the border into the Chizarira Game Reserve. Now they would have to be extra vigilant for traffic coming along the tracks throughout the bush. Not as popular as Hwange or as densely populated with tourist and hunting camps, Chizarira had a reputation as a jewel within Zimbabwe, a last outpost of unspoiled wilderness. Their game guards were as well trained as his, and as protective and passionate about their charges. They had had to be, to stop an influx of poaching on their black rhino population. Slowly, their neighbours, the local Batonka people, were being educated to stop the poaching and enjoy the benefits of the concessions and the game reserve, like the free elephant meat handed to them from the annual legal cull.

The anti-poaching units in the reserve knew Zol and his men. They often ran training exercises together, where Scott organised the two national game reserves swap guards, and ensured that they were adequately trained and knowledgeable of both regions. Zol's men had all been through this course. If they were confronted, the danger wouldn't be that they would be turned in, but that they would be joined by more people fleeing to make a better life.

He inhaled the scents of the bush. It was good to be walking freely after all these years and to have a specific purpose in mind. To be actually going somewhere again—that was something special. He laughed quietly, remembering his last true cross-country trek with Charlie during the war of independence.

'Come on, Zol. Get packed up and let's move out of this godforsaken place,' Charlie had said as he threw the dregs of his coffee into the fire.

'Yes, Boss,' Zol answered obediently. At twenty-five, he'd been with Charlie for ten years, and they were in their second war. Only this one they were not for hire, but fighting for their own country. Zol was riding Elizabeth, or Queen Vic for short—Charlie's first horse—and Charlie had acquired Lady Thatcher. She was a bad-tempered horse, and was named after the Prime Minister of England, who in Charlie's opinion would sell Rhodesia down the drain sooner or later, no matter what they did to try to prevent it.

Lady Thatcher was as hard as brass tits, and as crafty as her namesake when it came to getting things done her way. She'd won the hearts of both men the week before when they'd been ambushed by gooks and she'd shown she had her namesake's balls. She'd performed like the true warhorse she was trained to be, and carried Charlie out of the melee. Zol had been dragged out, literally, by Queen Vic as he held tightly to his stirrup leather after being thrown from his saddle by the claymore that exploded near them. And he loved her for not leaving him behind. But Lady Thatcher didn't even get a graze as she dodged bullets, claymore shrapnel and jumped tripwires invisible to Charlie. She had saved their lives.

'Where we heading now?' Zol asked, as he packed up Charlie's sleeping bag and killed the small fire.

'Northwest. I've had enough war for a while. I heard that just west of here there are diamonds as big as fists lying in the river bends.'

'I heard that too. But there are also guards with rifles and Rottweilers patrolling the area.'

'In South West Africa surely, but not in Angola. That area is too hot with action to have anyone lay claim just yet. With the South African defence force fighting the Angolans in the Caprivi Strip, and the internal strife of the MPLA and UNITA, we dare not head for the Namib Desert. But head north, behind the enemy lines, and we could go make a man's fortune.'

'But what about this war?'

'It'll still be here when we get back.' Charlie laughed. 'Zol, I don't think they will miss one grey scout and his boy for a few months.'

Tightening Lady Thatcher's girth, Zol smiled. He was always grateful to Charlie for saving him, but never more so than when he got these crazy ideas of going walkabout. This was the third detour they'd had in their years together. They had acquired some prime horseflesh on Charlie's ranch, mustangs running wild on the flats of Northern Rhodesia. It had taken time and patience to get them home, but it had been worth every minute.

But it was the diamond fossicking that was going to be Scott and Zol's saving grace now.

Zol smiled at the memory of the desert. He could almost taste the sand and heat as he remembered. But it was not in the desert where they found their riches: it was north, in a country so beautiful and rich with green trees and animals and rivers that defied logic and flowed northwards. Angola. Zol had been there before, but this time he saw it as a man, not a boy. And he saw it as a free man, not a seconded guerrilla terrorist.

Behind the lines the war was worse, and it was the people of the country who were affected the most. They saw suffering and death everywhere. They lost Queen Vic to a landmine explosion that left Zol deaf for weeks afterwards, but they found diamonds on a river bend high up in the Chimbe River.

They worked the bend for four months and then headed home, Lady Thatcher proving she was every bit the survivor as her political namesake, completing the journey with them. Along the way they collected Zahra, a zorse. She was a striped beauty as rugged as her wild ancestors but sterile, as she was a cross between a wild zebra stallion and a horse.

She didn't like Lady Thatcher much, and was fiercely racist towards Charlie, biting him whenever he got close enough, her ears flattening against her head and trying to kick him when he was near her rear end. For Zol, she was the perfect mount. She cost him three large uncut diamonds, but Charlie and Zol figured she was worth it. She'd been trained in the Angolan bush, and was already shy proof. She wouldn't take a saddle, nor a bit, and was totally leg and neck controlled, but he could shoot off her back without her flinching, and her uniqueness helped camouflage their passage through the countryside.

They avoided the guerrillas and the South African defence force the whole journey, and couldn't believe their luck had held. They had enough diamonds to set them up comfortably for life. Instead of heading southeast towards home, they had travelled eastwards, and went via Zambia and Malawi. They found a perfect place to stash some of the rocks in peaceful Malawi 'tree bank' within a national park, then they continued home to Delmonica.

Zol smiled, thinking of his old friend, and now of his grandson.

'He has a boy, Charlie,' he whispered into the bushes. 'And a girl. You would have loved them, Boss. You would be so proud of your son.'

'Zol.' Kwiella's voice interrupted Zol's memories, yanking him back across the chasm of time. 'We are making camp for the night. Marion just had her baby.'

CHAPTER 20

After a week, Zol prepared to leave the group to continue their journey ghosting through the Zimbabwean bush. They had managed to go undetected in the Chizarira district, but had added to their numbers when they passed through the tribal trust land. Their number swelled to sixty. There was no avoiding the trust land, and to only have an extra few was a small blessing.

They rested for three days. No one would notice a sudden influx of black people within this area. Black people came and went from here freely. They sheltered in a small kraal and a handful of the women made a trip into the nearby town on the local bus for new rations as they were beginning to run low. These they separated out between everyone, distributing the weight once again.

On the second morning, the old woman Miserable had not woken from her sleep. They had buried her in the traditional Ndebele style, facing south, and they marked her grave with a large pile of stones. One of the children in the group had put her shoes inside her grave, so she could finish the journey with them. Even though Miserable was a moaner, she was missed, and her death brought home to the group how fragile they all were.

'Tomorrow, we leave here,' Zol told them all at the funeral feast. 'The sangoma said that, under the circumstances, some of the traditional burial ceremonies could be missed out, as he was sure that Miserable's spirit would travel with us. When we reach our new ranch, we can perform the ritual for passing over. I agreed with the sangoma that Miserable would be happy with this, so we must not spend more time here.'

Murmurs of agreement could be heard from all, and the next morning, before the sun rose, the large party was on the move again.

Zol's radio clicked once. He brought it up to his ear.

'We have company,' said Vusi, following as the rear guard and covering their tracks, as always.

'How many? Hostile?' Zol asked.

'They have possessions like they too want to leave. Nineteen.'

'Dammit.' Zol broke with tradition and swore.

He left the group and walked back to where he knew Vusi would be. Sure enough, off in the distance he could see the group of people trying to follow their tracks into the mopani forest: three adults, five teenagers and eleven small children under ten years old. Nineteen all up.

'If we leave them and they are caught by police, they will tell them we are in front of them,' Vusi said.

'I know. But now we are so many people. We are going to have to split into two groups, whether we like it or not. We have got too big and cumbersome to move through the bush undetected.'

Zol began a slow walk towards the small group. When they saw him, they scattered in all directions, trying to hide.

'*Woza. Woza.* Come. We'll not hurt you,' he shouted. 'You can join us ...'

Slowly they crept together again, gathered the meagre belongings they'd dropped in their haste to hide, and advanced towards Zol. On closer inspection, he saw there were no true adults. The oldest couldn't have been more than twenty.

'*Ubabamkhulu,*' a young boy started with the traditional greeting to a grandfather, keeping his eyes downcast in respect. 'I am Lucas. I saw you moving your people this morning and told my sisters and brothers to quickly get up, we are going to leave too.'

'What makes you think we are going anywhere you would want to be?' Zol asked.

'For three days, we have watched. You came into the trust lands as a group, you have armed guards, but the people are not afraid of them. The people, they seem to care for the guards and the guards for the people. They walk freely. This is not a forced march. I think the guards, they are protecting the whole family, moving to a safer place than where you came from in Matabeleland.' He looked Zol in the face, a proud youngster looking at an elder, then he cast his eyes down again in a sign of respect not shown often by youth anymore.

'Why do you have so many family under your care?' Zol asked him.

'Only five are true. The others are family-but-one. They are alone. Most of our parents have died of the thinning disease, the AIDS. It is bad. But we can hunt, and clean houses. And me and Dugewe, we can make old cars go again, we can work and look after our family.'

'You have seen correctly. This is not a forced march, and the guards are private, not government. If we let you join us, you have to listen to them. Will you do this? Will your sisters and brothers obey their every instruction?'

'Yes, sir,' Lucas said, nodding enthusiastically.

Zol smiled. 'If you give us any signs of trouble, we will deal with you in our own way. Is that clear?'

'Yes, sir,' Lucas repeated, a grin on his face as bright as a million-megawatt element that he was not able to stop.

'All right. The food you carry will be shared with everyone and become communal, understood?'

'*Akukho* food.'

No food? Zol stared at him. Each child carried a bundle of sorts, even the smallest girl of about two years old had a mielie-meal sack over her shoulder, but no food?

'Open your packs,' Zol instructed.

Each teenager and child opened their precious bundles. Zol saw only three water containers between them.

He looked at their meagre belongings. A photograph here, a book there and a few clothes. There were cooking pots, a few children's toys, but no food. Zol let out a deep sigh.

Vusi shook his head. 'Zol,' he said quietly, 'they are only kids ...'

'I know. That's what makes it harder and harder to say no to them. Come, we'll still walk for a few hours, until we break for lunch.' Zol opened his pack and handed Lucas four sticks of biltong. 'Share this between you all for breakfast, evenly. We'll manage somehow. Respect our women and children and you'll come to no harm, but if you make trouble, you will be dealt with. Understood?

Lucas nodded. '*Siabonga Zol-dala.*'

Zol laughed at the adding of the *old* onto his name, and ran his hand over his silver hair. 'Don't make me regret this decision.'

'We won't. Thank you,' Lucas said as he cut up the biltong with a small knife he carried, and shared it out fairly. He lifted the youngest little girl wearing a clean but old pink dress back onto his shoulders, and they walked to catch up with the group.

Zol knew he was seeing a trend that had begun years before, and his heart was sore. So many children were now orphans in Africa, first from the wars, but now mostly from the HIV virus that to humans was as bad as the anthrax in cattle. The disease was devastating his people and there was nothing he nor Scott could do to stop it.

At lunch he split the party of soon to be refugees into two smaller groups of forty, Kwiella leading one group, and Vusi heading up the other. They would move in separate directions, one pushing closer to the Zambezi River, the other heading more eastwards, before changing direction and curving northwards to the crossing place. They would join again at the rendezvous point on the bank of the Zambezi River.

He'd kept both new groups separate from the other, and split the staff of Delmonica in two. Each of his two anti-poaching units now guarded one smaller bunch of people. He didn't envisage any immediate problems, and the advantage to the smaller parties far outweighed the negatives. The most important being that it would be easier to cover the tracks of a smaller group, their immediate footprint on the earth would be less visible to the untrained eye, or anyone trying to follow them.

Kwiella drew an item from his pack and handed it to Zol as he was preparing to leave. 'Please, give this to Madam Ashley. Tell her that Renegade rests under Boss Scott's mswiellie tree but her spirit travels with us, protecting us.'

Zol looked at the metal choke chain as it slipped between his fingers, cold in his hand. He shook his head. 'No, you keep this with you. Madam would want you to stay protected. When you get to Zambia, you can give it to her yourself and tell her. Thank you for burying Renegade, I know Madam Ashley will be happy to know that she wasn't left for the hyenas.' Zol handed the chain back to his guard. 'Take care, Kwiella, Vusi. Make me proud,' he said to them in parting, as each disappeared into the bush, covering the tracks of their charges in front of them.

Zol walked northwards alone. He began to put speed into his trek. Now that he knew the staff and children were safe, he needed to make a detour. As much as he wanted to go directly to Scott and Ashley and see what plan they had managed to come up with to transport everyone across the river and smuggle them into Zambia, into their new lives away from Delmonica, the need to visit the tree back in Malawi was greater.

'You were right, Boss Charlie,' he said to the heavens. 'Our rainy day has unfortunately arrived.'

Ashley stared ahead blankly at the Kazungula border post sign, trying hard not to say anything. She rocked Brock in her arms, while Lisa stood next to her with Paige. The twins were fussing in the heat despite being stripped down to their nappies, and the lack of air conditioning in the red brick building meant the heat was stifling. Sweat beaded and ran down between her breasts.

'No. Look, no visa,' the guard said again to Scott, pointing at the passport to show the lack of the necessary visa.

'Fuck.' Scott swore, turning away from the window and walked back towards the trucks.

The three-vehicle convoy had backtracked through Hwange to cross into Botswana, but that had turned out to be their saving grace. As they crossed over the yet unfenced part of the border of cleared trees marking the end of one country and the beginning of another, they'd heard on the CB radios that they were being 'pursued, for questioning' by the police about a lot of counterfeited American money that the war veterans who were now living on Delmonica had attempted to spend.

But they were not out of the woods yet.

They were stuck at the last border post. This seventy-tonne ferry river crossing from Botswana into Zambia was proving the most difficult. They were so close to their destination, and yet so far.

'Elliott, you try,' Scott said, and Ashley watched as Elliott took the three passports and walked into the border post offices.

'At least there is a breeze outside the building,' she said as Brock settled down. Ashley was growing tired of living like a nomad. They had passed through some of the wildest, most desolate places in Africa—wide-open plains that teemed with wildlife—and had seen an untamed Africa people only dreamt still existed. But she was homesick for their ranch in Zimbabwe.

She smiled as she realised that somewhere in the last five years, she'd stopped thinking of Australia as her country, and now thought of Zimbabwe as hers. She was Madam Ashley, a white African.

It wasn't that they had wanted to flee Zimbabwe, that choice had been taken away from them the morning of the ranch invasion, and it still hurt her. The epic motor trek had taken longer than expected, and cost them dearly too. And watching Elliott's face as he returned to their convoy, Ashley knew the price was about to go up. 'Scott, Madam, this guard, he wouldn't let Ashley and the twins out of Botswana. He says because they are on Australian passports, they need a visa to pass.' Elliott paused.

Ashley remembered the proud look on her mother's face when she gave her the passports while she was still in hospital in Cape Town. She had received help from the consulate in Pretoria, and the twins were ready to travel as soon as they were out of neonatal care. Ashley thanked her mother now for her foresight.

Elliott continued. 'But we can get them out if we pay the bribe. I'm going to drive the truck to his house and then return. He wants possessions, then he will stamp the passports.'

Scott shook his head. 'When will this bribery in Africa ever stop? Okay, give them what they want, then we will see you back here.'

While they waited for Elliott's return, Ashley mulled over what Scott had told her about the refugee situation in Botswana. The country was building a fence, for stock control, they claimed. But everyone knew it was to try to keep Zimbabweans on their own side. Botswana could no more cope with the influx of refugees from Zimbabwe any better than they had back in seventies during the war of independence, when people fled for their lives.

After twenty years of black rule, Zimbabwe, once known as the jewel of Africa, was in serious trouble. The land grab was causing famine, chaos and poverty. Millions of people were worse off than they had been under British colonisation, and still the First World communities looked the other way and did nothing. Zimbabweans feared that soon they would face a failed state, but were unable to do anything to prevent its impending doom. The people who stayed continued to make a plan, and did what they had to, to survive.

This was Africa.

But the Decker and Ndhlovu families had chosen to move. Even before the eviction from the ranch, the move had been planned. Zambia was opening its arms to displaced farmers, and they were going to resettle. That was, of course, if they had any possessions left in Elliott's truck.

Ashley had just settled Brock into his car seat when she saw the truck come back around the corner. She jumped down and ran to greet him. 'Elliott, thank goodness you're back. What did they take?'

'Most of your lounge suite, some old garden furniture. Sorry Scott, your prized ride-on lawn mower. But I refused to part with any deep freezes or fridges when the guard's wife pointed to the big freezer in the back. I told the fat woman to load everything back, we would try a different border post, but when she saw me dragging the sofa back to the truck she began wailing, "No *frezza*. No *frezza*. I want *esofas*." So that's all she got. Let's get those passports stamped and get out of here.'

Ashley watched Elliott walk into the red brick building with a defiant spring to his step.

Tired, frustrated, and their vehicles a little lighter, the voyagers' small convoy eventually parked under the trees at the FA Ranch two weeks to the day after beginning their journey from Bulawayo. Fuck-all Ranch in Zambia was not Delmonica, but it was home for a while. There was no going back to Zimbabwe.

Scott's cousin Albert, the hunter and lessee of this particular chunk of dirt, lovingly referred to it as his FA Ranch, and the name had stuck. Situated north of the Sioma Ngwezi National Park, on the banks of the Southern Lueti River, the ranch was now a sanctuary for them—a resting place to regroup and then take their next plan of action.

Albert was a bachelor, but Ashley didn't hold that against him, he just hadn't found the right women yet. Years ago, Scott had told her that Albert still held a torch for Rowena, a girl they had grown up with who had died tragically in their teens, but Ashley hoped one day someone would come along to take her place.

Before Albert moved to Zambia, he had been a commercial farmer. He'd grown vegetables, and also invested heavily in the safari business. He was a motivated farmer and an accurate hunter. She liked to think he was also Scott's friend.

Albert had been allocated the land a year ago by the Zambian government, after the Zimbabwean government had taken the ranch that had been in his family for three generations. He hadn't been as fortunate as Scott, and had not known that he was about to lose everything. He'd walked away with only the clothes on his back.

Nothing else.

The Zambian government had leased the FA Ranch to him, thankfully on his reputation, and not worried about his lack of farming implements. Despite that lack, he'd already managed to erect his major game fence, plough three fields where fresh vegetables grew, and build dams to irrigate his small operation. As yet, he hadn't built a house, but lived in a tent.

Granted, it was a smart, modern two-room one, but still, it was only a tent. Apparently, his hunting clients 'loved roughing it' with him. So he'd been more focused on getting his game secured and his crops in than his personal comforts. Slowly, his staff were beginning to trickle in from Zimbabwe and find him. Despite not being able to employ them for a wage yet, they were settling in, living off the land, and working for a new home beside him.

Gertrude's kids had been running about excited to see their mum, and had now rushed off to show Uncle Elliott their campsite. The adults were left alone with the twins.

'Scott, go show Ashley the site, we'll watch your babies,' Gertrude said.

'Thanks. We'll take you up on that.' Scott gently took Ashley's hand and led her to the *bakkie*. He was content to steal a moment or two alone with his wife.

He closed her door and went to the driver's side. Starting the engine again, they headed out, back into the bush.

'Honey, it'll be all right. We have each other, Paige and Brock are safe, and we didn't lose a life in the invasion. We'll hear from Zol soon about what happened to Renegade. Who knows, maybe she's travelling with them.' He reached over and pulled her against him, to sit in the middle. She grinned at him and didn't bother putting on her seatbelt.

'There's no house, Scott. Nothing. We're going to have to build everything from scratch.'

'Al's place doesn't look flash, that's true. But I would never expect you to share your home area with hunting clients either. We plan on setting up away from him. We are nearly there. I want your opinion on this great spot Zol and I found to make our temporary home.'

'So, where's this place?' she asked, sniffing slightly.

'Patience, Mrs Decker.' Even after being married for five years, he still loved hearing those words. That she had chosen to marry him.

They drove slowly for about a quarter of an hour along a badly overgrown dirt track, the trees scratching the paint on the *bakkie* as it passed, the sound grating on Ashley's nerves like fingernails scraped down a blackboard. Scott stopped as they broke into a clearing. 'Here. Right here.'

They were on the edge of an escarpment and below she could see a murky brown river meandering slowly across the land. A green belt of trees followed the water, making it appear almost snakelike in movement. A cool breeze rose up from below and there were large trees around them.

'This will be home once we set up our own camp, until we can sort out land for ourselves. My cousin Albert dreamed of making a safari camp right here.' Scott got out and walked a little towards the edge.

Ashley followed, and when he held out his hand, she took it like a drowning person reaching for a lifeline.

Scott pulled her close and hugged her tightly.

'I need a tissue, Scott. Do you have one on you?'

'No, I'm all out. Use my sleeve if you need to.'

'I hate Africa,' she cried. 'I hate the unlawfulness, the unfairness. I hate that they can take our home and we can't do a thing about it. I hate it! I hate it!' She wiped her running nose on her sleeve. 'And we don't even have a goddamn tissue!'

At last, after everything that had happened over the past months, Ashley broke down. Tears streamed down her face and shudders rocked her body. She had been pushed past her level of endurance and needed the release.

Scott stroked her back and kissed the top of her head. He held her body against his, comforting her, while she wept. Eventually her sobs turned to hiccups and he tilted her face up towards his. He brought his lips down in a gentle melding to hers. 'Hello, beautiful,' he said against them as he kissed her.

She hiccupped.

He smiled and returned his mouth to hers. Slowly, her body contoured into his and stopped shaking with fury. For a moment it relaxed, and then it ignited with raw need.

'The doctor did give you the all-clear before we left Cape Town, didn't he?' Scott managed to check with his wife. He was on fire. They hadn't been able to make love to each other since the day Ashley had been rushed to hospital. Their last night at home had been about goodbyes, about letting go, and they hadn't had a chance to celebrate their reunion, being back together after months apart.

Even on the trip through Botswana, they had been surrounded by the others all the time, sleeping in tents along the way and not able to steal a moment alone. Then there were the twins, constantly needing care.

She reached up and dragged his head to hers again; her hands rough in his hair. 'You betcha,' she murmured against his mouth.

'Hello, my wildcat,' he barely spoke above a whisper into her open mouth and then sealed his lips to her as he pushed his hands up under her dress.

They moved to their 'holiday camp', as Ashley referred to it, the same night. Albert helped them set up a fire pit and brought over his spare generator, on loan until they could unpack their own. He strung lights in the trees, and by nightfall they had a homely-looking camp.

They took a few days to unpack their trucks and sort out their small camp, making a thornbush boma around them, digging toilets, setting up a water line and pump into the river, and a tap. Ensuring that the cattle they had previously moved into the area were still healthy. They also attempted, unsuccessfully, to get Tobias to move his camp in with theirs.

After a full week of being in their new home, they celebrated the milestone with a big bonfire.

'Zol!' Gertrude squealed, as he materialised out of the bush just as they all sat down to dinner. She started to hobble towards him, but he quickly covered the distance between them and picked her up. Silently they clung to each other for a few minutes, then he put her back down on the chair near the table.

'Good to see you,' Scott said to his friend, as he gathered another fold-up chair, and opened it at the table.

Ashley smiled at him. 'Hi ya, Zol.'

Just then his kids swamped him, and as he fell on the ground beneath the four wriggling bodies, tears of joy ran down his face.

CHAPTER 21

Much later that night, Zol and Gertrude's kids went off to bed, despite the huge excitement level of having both their mother and father back, and Ashley managed to put her twins down to sleep in their tent, ensuring the baby monitor was switched on and she would hear the slightest squeak they made. The twins were sleeping through most nights, but tonight they had taken a while to go down, as if they too understood the excitement of having Zol come into the camp.

It was only then, when things had quietened down, that the adults had the opportunity to talk without interruption.

Zol brought out a sketchbook from his small backpack. 'Take a look,' he said, pushing the book towards Ashley.

He had sketched the escarpment perfectly from memory. It was obvious that he'd spent many private hours working on the plan. Each small rondavel drawn was neatly decorated in different ethnic designs and had an initial outside the front door. And each had breathing space between itself and the neighbour nearest it. Two of the larger buildings had an 'S'.

'Why two S's?'

'Scott's home,' he pointed to the smaller of the two, 'and school,' he pointed to the larger one.

'This looks great,' Scott said. The plan was meticulous in detail. Zol had placed everything similar to the set-up they had finished building at Delmonica the year before for their safari camp. It was just as they'd discussed, but Zol had taken the time to fill in more details on the plan—extras, like where they were putting in the generator house before the power-lines pushed through.

'Londamela,' Zol said as he spread his hands wide.

Ashley grinned. 'What a lovely name. What does it mean?'

His face looked almost sad when he said, 'Sort of "sleep here". A friend once had a safari business with that name, but his partner outgrew it and went on to bigger business along the way, but I liked the older family set-up better.' He seemed to zone out, as if thinking of another time.

'What are the buildings made of?' Ashley enquired.

Zol shook his head as if physically snapping back to the present. 'There's a lot of stone around, and many trees. We can bring in cement.'

'What about when we leave? How long do we live here? If we make a permanent camp, it'll cost money and then more money again, when we have our own place.' Ashley spoke her thoughts in quick succession, her mind working overtime.

Scott leaned in and ran a finger along her forehead, attempting to straighten the deep frown there, and she smacked his hand away as one would a mosquito.

'Albert won't mind,' Scott said. 'He's a single man, so building things doesn't happen as fast as he would like. He's previously spoken to Zol and I about all this, and is happy to contribute towards it, too. And we have sold a lot of the cattle, as the lions here would have thought they were easy food.' His voice was that of a man accepting his fate, and making the best of it.

'Oh Scott, your stud herd—'

'It can be rebuilt when we get our own ranch,' he interrupted her. 'I kept the base stock. But right now, our first priority is to make a home for us. Start on a home for all those families coming soon across that damn river. The happy wanderers should be here within the week, so, if we manage to have the cement here by then, everyone can help build, and the structures will go up a hell of a lot faster with so many hands.' He looked at Zol for confirmation.

'Two weeks. They're travelling slower than I expected, and there are more of them. Others keep joining along the way. But there have been big rains up river, and there's more coming. They're going to need help getting across.'

Scott nodded. 'Extend that by a week then. How long before we need to get to the river to help them?'

'Probably good to be there early, just in case,' Zol said.

Lisa filled everyone's coffee cups again and put out a fresh tin of rusks, the hard biscuits freshly baked. She sat down next to Elliott. 'You comfortable there, Gertrude?'

'Perhaps the leg could use another cushion under it,' Gertrude conceded, and Zol hopped to it to make his wife comfortable.

'What are you actually saying, Zol?' Ashley asked, once he'd finished fussing over Gertrude. 'Please tell me I'm reading your conversation wrong. Our staff are all coming so far and then they won't be able to get across the river? Which river are you all talking about anyway?' She still found she had gaps in her information from her time spent in the hospital and then on the isolated trek, often with only the twins for company as Lisa would often sit with Elliott too.

'The mighty Zambezi, Madam,' Elliott said.

'Oh my God!' Ashley put her hands over her mouth, then removed them to talk again. 'What have we asked these people to do?'

'No, we didn't ask them at all. They chose to come,' Elliott told her. 'In Zimbabwe there'll be no jobs for them now that the Decker family has gone. No jobs. No food. The government will hurt the families more. If they get here, they have Boss Scott and you, and they have Zol and Gertrude. They chose to do this, Madam. Even you couldn't have made one of them stay behind. If you had left them, they would have heard where you settled, and they would come and find you anyway. At least now, with the guards, they are safer on their journey.'

She looked at the men seated around the table, then at Gertrude, as she always did when there was a serious discussion going on. Gertrude was silent. 'Gertrude? Is this true?' She needed to know Gertrude's answer, not just some macho crap that the men were so good at handing out.

'It's true. They'll make it. They travel with both the anti-poaching units, without Zol now, but there are still twelve honourable armed men. No harm will come to our people.'

Ashley rubbed her forehead with her fingertips. 'How do we explain them to the Zambians when they get here?'

'We don't,' Zol answered. 'They simply work on the new camp, and when we leave to our new ranch, they move too. Everyone sticks together. There aren't too many locals left in the areas that they "lease" to the Zimbabwe ranchers. They were deserted during the war and have never returned. So there is not a big danger from the local population demanding jobs that we can't provide. And, if we are unlucky enough to go into an area where there is a resident chief, then we will deal with it then.'

'But—' Ashley started.

'The Zambian and Mozambican governments have established a resettlement program with the displaced farmers,' Scott said. 'They are leasing out land on a ninety-nine-year agreement scheme. The white farmers from Zimbabwe are resettling a country once torn apart by war. Zimbabwe's loss is their gain. We put in an application. We won't own our land to begin with, but we can buy it soon enough, once we start turning a profit again. We know a few of the farmers who are here, and they have gone through this already. Started again, with less than we have, and are now farming successfully. The government doesn't care who you have on your work force, as long as you help feed their population.'

'What about later? What about voting? Pensions? Citizenship?' she asked, now fairly agitated with herself that she hadn't thought of all this before.

'Give it a few years and we'll all be given citizenship, blanket style. It's Africa. The benchmark moves daily and you can suffocate under the red tape, but eventually everything works out, somehow.' Scott hugged her to him, and she gazed up at the contours of his face. Blanket amnesty in one country, and blanket citizenship in another. Ashley shook her head.

'Okay. How much money do we need to build this camp? How much have we got left?' she asked.

Scott smiled quickly. 'Enough for now.'

'Enough,' said Zol at the same time.

'Hey, my doting African males, business partners. Remember me? I'm not suddenly suffering the "the little wife syndrome" because I had the twins ... Details please?' Ashley said, her voice dripping with sarcasm.

Zol lifted his hands in a gesture that said Scott should take over all the talking and he settled back into his chair. He'd never got comfortable with having a woman know the state of their finances. In his world, the man made the money, he ensured there was enough money to keep his wife, and he spent that money wisely to ensure his wife didn't need to worry. Scott and Ashley's way of sharing financial information was alien to one of his traditional characteristics, and he just couldn't change. No matter how much Gertrude encouraged him to.

'Sorry. I guess I fell into that old habit again too easily,' Scott admitted, and squeezed Ashley's hand.

She smiled. 'I don't need exact facts and figures now, but I do need to know where the closest city is. Should I think about going back into engineering consulting?' Ashley said, conscious of Zol's views on an open book financial arrangement between them.

'Livingstone is hours away on a bad road. You don't want to even think about that possibility. There are other options, but for now we'll manage,' he said. 'We have lodged money with the Zambian government for a land claim, and showed proof of farming implements, so we are already on the list for priority reallocation of land, and there is a little more in our South African accounts. I also moved forex into a Zambian account while you were in Cape Town, but we need to go to the bank and put your signature on the account too. At the moment it has just Zol and I as signatories, but your name is there. Like I said, we'll manage. Besides, if it gets too bad and we are desperate, we can sell our half of Kevin's aviation business to him. He would love to own the whole thing.'

'No. If it gets to that stage, we'll find another way ...' Ashley protested. She knew how much Kevin and Scott liked being business partners, and how profitable their business was. It would be throwing money away if they contemplated selling their half of that business for a short-term fix. She'd discussed all their finances with Scott before they got married. And when it became time to sell her share of her Australian engineering business to Bronwyn, Scott had been involved in the negotiation. Ashley's savings had been pooled into Delmonica's account years before, ploughed into the ranch as working capital, and used to enlarge the size of Delmonica when another ranch next door had come up for sale early in their married years.

What was his was hers.

Once they were alone, Scott and Ashley would hash over the figures together.

'Madam Ashley, we have enough money for everything now and when we move to our own ranch,' Zol said.

Scott looked at Zol, who winked, and Scott smiled.

Ashley smiled too. She tapped Zol's plan with the pen and changed the topic. 'So, about this river crossing that our staff are going to attempt. We don't own a single boat. How many boats does Albert have?'

'Four,' Elliott said. 'A houseboat, a fishing boat with a cabin and two that are more rubber ducks than boats. All have good working engines, but that's not the problem. We have to get them down to the Zambezi. That's the hard part.'

'How did he get them here?' Ashley asked, her interest as an engineer piqued.

'The big two have their own trailers, and the other two probably came on the roof of his *bakkie*. They sit on pallets so that the mice don't eat the rubber. But there is no good road down to the crossing place,' Zol said. 'It's better than it used to be, and there's a new track I found, but it is rough, really rough.'

'Okay, let me think.' She took Zol's notepad. 'I hope you gave me a study in my rondavel,' she said, glancing at the plan, then turned over the page. 'I wish, Scott, that you had thought to discuss these plans with me earlier. I could have planned more.'

'Healing time, remember?' He nudged her gently and smiled.

Smiling back, she returned her attention to the notepad and began her mind mapping on the clean page. 'Our end result, the safe arrival of the rest of the staff,' she wrote. She put in the four boats and the expected flooding river. 'Can they cross somewhere else?'

'No, that's the safest place. I have a map.' Zol stood up and grabbed a dog-eared map from his backpack.

'See, here?' He pointed. 'The river. This is where they'll cross. Here they won't be bothered by the police, nor anyone else, for that matter. It's where the steep walls of the gorge end. Occasionally there is a safari outfit that canoes past, but if they cross early in the morning or late at night, they won't be seen. But in the rain, this bend here, it'll be bad.' He pointed to the green area around the river. 'These are reed beds, nothing here but crocodiles, hippos and nesting birds. During the dry, the big game comes here for food and water. But in the wet, the reeds will pull anything down. This is the biggest danger. If we use a boat other than an inflatable duck, the motor from the boat could get bogged in the reeds. We'll need to put both the ducks in here, along this dirt road from Undaundato, then bundu bash into the valley along that track I marked, and launch here. No reeds here.' He showed her another section.

She stared at the map. What he was proposing seemed impossible to her, but she knew Zol and the way he thought details through, and any plan he proposed would be manageable.

'But the police from both countries have patrols here.' Zol pointed to where they would launch. 'They have tried to stop many refugees already. This has always been where people cross, even during the independence war. Many people know this is the part of the river where it flattens out, and the current is not so strong, and you can see the crocodiles coming. But on the Zambian side there could still be a few landmines leftover from the wars. We can't take the big trucks down there, only *bakkies* and lighter vehicles. The mines should be deep and if we sweep in front first, we'll be okay.'

Ashley looked at the map, her mind ticking into engineer mode, unconsciously tapping the pencil on the table in a rap-rap rhythm as she bounced it up and down.

Scott put his hand over hers. 'Sleep on it,' he said quietly.

She sighed heavily. 'Okay.' She closed the notepad with a snap sound and handed it back to Zol.

In the last few years, as with all the construction they had done, theirs had become a four-way partnership. Extending the school, building and designing the safari camp on Delmonica, Ashley was the practical side of the process. She was the one who made it all work out. Scott had the ideas, Zol visualised them on paper, Gertrude put in her five cents' worth if she thought it helped, but often wouldn't comment, it wasn't her way, and Ashley made things work. This was the team that had made their ranch successful. Once again, they would build, and build again when necessary. That was just how life was.

Scott yawned. 'Time to chuck in the towel for the night. Thank you for getting here Zol, and everyone else, for working on the plan tonight, despite the fact we were supposed to be celebrating ...'

Ashley grinned at him.

Lisa and Elliott stood up, took all their cups to the washstand, made sure no food was lying around that a wild animal could be attracted to, and left to go to bed. Zol walked slowly alongside Gertrude, bearing her weight and making it easier for her to get to their tent.

Scott and Ashley retired to theirs. Zol arriving that night was a bonus to the one week celebration of being at the FA Ranch. Everything now seemed possible. Another move loomed over the horizon, but as Ashley had learned from experience, one simply lived one day at a time in Africa.

After checking on the twins, Ashley climbed into their bed and pressed her back against Scott's warm body. His fingers immediately began stroking her shoulder, causing her skin to goosebump with emotion.

'Listen,' he said.

She lay still and concentrated. The night was alive with sounds of distant animals: the familiar sonar pings of a bat, the mournful howl of the black-backed jackal in the distance, a distinctive voice of a spotted eagle owl, and the grunts of tsessebe hiding in the darkness of the night bush. The hideous screams of a spotted hyena horde were audible, fighting over a kill. But nearer, more threatening and distinctive, they heard a distinctive cough, almost a grunt but not quite.

'Leopard,' he told her. 'Don't go out of the tent tonight.'

'Oh Scott, I think I've learned that one by now, don't you?' She laughed and dug her elbow into his ribs.

Dawn broke, brilliant in jewelled colours of pink and blue hues scattering across the new sky. Ashley fed the twins and carried them outside. Signs of night visitors greeted her. Leopard spoor crossed over by hyena stared at her from just beyond her tent. In the bright sunrise she knew the creatures of the darkness were gone, disappearing in the light of day. She laughed as she read the morning news on the ground as a city girl would read the newspaper.

Scott and Zol were nowhere in sight. She lugged the twins to the dining table, amazed that her two children could be getting so heavy, so fast. Elliott had coffee brewing. He peered into the carrycots. 'I'll watch them for you.'

'Thanks.' She went to the 'ladies', threw water on her face in the wash tent, and was ready to face the new day.

'Any cereal left?' she asked when she sat down at the table, peeking in at her babies, checking they were still asleep.

Gertrude looked up. 'None. Lisa mixed bread last night that should be nearly ready.'

'Yum, hot bread for breakfast.' She stretched her back, arching it like a cat would. 'Elliott,' she said, putting her arms behind her head and stretching more. 'Did you ever imagine your life different from what you are living?'

'I'm happy to still be living,' he said as he turned and went to the fire to get the bread. He had never disclosed much information on his life to her, even when she'd asked him directly.

Ashley contemplated his answer as she ate the bread put in front of her, dripping with sweet fig jam made by Lisa in the kitchen at Delmonica. Tears welled in her eyes. They had lost a lot. She'd learned so much in her five years in Africa, and now her newest priority would be the safe arrival of their staff to their new home.

Looking after everyone was second nature to Scott and Zol, but to her, it still felt unreal that she would share responsibility for all the displaced people's welfare. She mopped the last of the jam from her plate, picked up Zol's map and spread it out over the table. There was work to do.

Lisa sat next to her—something that under normal circumstances would never have happened. Lisa and Elliott were staff, they were brought up not to share their bosses' table. But boundaries had been crossed and decisions made that affected everyone. Accordingly, everyone had changed and boundaries had shifted.

Everyone except Zol. Because of his white hair, he was considered an old man and was forgiven for keeping his traditions. Change didn't come easily to most old men. To Ashley, Zol appeared timeless. He hadn't aged in the years since she came to Africa, but seemed suspended in time. His presence glued everyone around him together.

As if conjured by magic, Zol and Scott broke the cover of the trees.

'Breakfast,' Scott declared, waving at them with the leg of some type of venison slung over his shoulders.

Lisa jumped up and met him at the second camp table in the kitchen area, where he easily flipped the carcass onto its surface. Ashley looked away from the butchering that was needed on the buck. She knew that once it was skinned, gutted and deboned where necessary, Lisa would start cutting steaks from the rump, but she still didn't have the stomach to watch. She'd lost much of her city constitution, but seeing an animal be butchered and being okay with all the blood was a skill she'd yet to develop. Soon the delicious smell of chargrilled steak filled the air.

Albert arrived in time for breakfast.

'Typical bachelor,' Ashley mumbled good-heartedly. 'They can smell the food the moment it's cooked.'

But Albert surprised her. He had no hunting clients with him, and he'd brought along a few supplies from his fridges.

'Thought you guys might need some of these by now,' he said, smiling and thanking Lisa as she placed a cup of coffee in front of him. She took the eggs and fresh vegetables from him with glee.

They all sat around the table and tucked into eggs and steak with hot bread, washed down with coffee.

'When do we start building?' Albert asked.

'You got any cement?' Scott looked at his cousin.

'Ten or so bags. It's in the flat trailer.'

'What flatbed trailer?' Ashley enquired excitedly, almost as if she'd caught a huge fish on a tiny line.

'I have two trailers under the trees at the back—'

'How big? What suspension do they have on them?' She shot the questions at him like a volley from a semiautomatic weapon.

'Ashley, slow down. We'll take a look after breakfast,' Scott said, laughing.

'I can see why you stay married to her, other than her looks, cuz,' Albert said.

Scott looked at Ashley and winked. She grinned at him. 'Well, sun's up and it's time to get going,' Scott said. 'Thanks to the chef as always.' The breakfast party broke up, with a murmuring of thanks to Lisa and Elliott.

Gertrude called out to Ashley and Scott. 'I can watch the twins this morning if you're going to look at those trailers. The kids and I love having them around us.'

'Thanks, Gertrude,' Ashley said, passing her Paige. 'I fed them an hour ago, so that gives me about three hours. Half-hour round trip travel time, two and a half hours to check out everything stashed at Albert's ranch. You sure you're up to it?'

'I'm fine. I put up with mine jumping on the mummy trampoline all the time. Besides, your babies are not work yet, they're still too young. Anyway, rather you than me poking my nose in Albert's things.'

Ashley laughed at her. It wasn't often that the sparkling personality beneath Gertrude's quiet exterior was visible, but today it was shining brightly.

'I'll watch out for man-eating lion-sized rats, shall I?' she said, laughing at the joke of her being a foreigner and supposedly not knowing what they would find in the bachelor's belongings.

'You bet you!' Gertrude took Paige willingly. Her eldest daughter Florence, now five, took Brock eagerly.

'I'll be careful, Uncle Scott,' she said. Already manners were being drummed into her, but the break with tradition in calling him Uncle rather than Boss was a huge one for Zol's family.

He patted her hair. It was in neat plaits, tightly bound to her head and decorated with beads. Gertrude kept her children proud of their heritage and traditions.

Elliott, Zol, Scott and Ashley piled into the double cab. Zol still got in the bin section, despite the fact there was plenty of room in the cabin. Ashley had long stopped asking him to join her. Elliott hopped on the back with Zol. He grinned at Ashley. It was still a point of debate between them, even after all this time.

Albert's stash proved to be a goldmine, and was more readily accessible than their own implements, which were stored securely under tarpaulins and sitting on wooden pallets to keep them off the ground. Ashley made a list of two trailers, a converted four-wheel drive game-catching vehicle complete with a rocket launcher for nets, and tools. He had the normal grinding machines, drills and even a small lathe. And everything was simply sitting under a makeshift shelter under trees, with fertiliser bags covering the equipment motors to keep the rain out.

'Your cousin should get this stuff into a workshop,' she told Scott.

'I think now that we are building him a home and a safari camp, that will become his next priority. Remember that he moved here with nothing, already he has performed a miracle just getting up a decent fence,' he replied, swatting her bum as he passed her. 'Perhaps when we are finished the camp, we can help him build the workshop area too, although for that he'll need to pay for all the materials.'

She saw no man-eating rats, but there was a huge python. She was happy it was a python and not a cobra that had made its home within the shelter.

Elliott moved the snake away for Ashley. Although she now tolerated snakes, she still wouldn't touch one.

'She'll come back, Madam Ashley. She keeps the rats away,' Elliott told her as they watched the snake slither out of their sight.

'As long as it's when we are finished here.'

They dragged out the equipment and supplies Ashley said she needed. At a drink break, Scott asked the big question.

'What's your plan?'

'One boat, we only need the largest of the ducks. The flexible duck—it could be our saving grace. It already has two motors, and we can take one spare. If we take the flatbed trailer and change the suspension by cutting into the—'

'Ashley, too many details. Get to the point,' Scott interrupted her.

'Okay. We modify the trailer. Take two *bakkies*, ours and the game catcher, and one trailer. We leave the cattle trucks somewhere on the main road area, with someone to watch them while we are away from them. Then we take the lighter vehicles down into the valley. With the mods on the trailer, it should make it down the gulley and across. Ideally, we need to get there before the next rains start. The duck will carry eight at a time across the river. If we get there and the water is too swollen, we use plan B. The rocket launcher should take the rope across, and we can feed a steel cable next. The guards on that side can tie it down. Then we take the boat and use it as a ferry, and we won't have a fuel problem.'

'Sounds feasible. What about getting it all back?'

'People first in the two vehicles, and those who can walk out do. We hide the duck and come back once everyone's safely on the main road, winch it back onto the trailer and drive it out with only one vehicle.'

Scott looked at Ashley, her face flushed with exertion as she rummaged in Albert's belongings. She smiled at him and his heart melted. He still couldn't believe he was so lucky that she'd married him and stayed on in Africa. She'd made his life so much better. She'd enhanced it. She deserved more than the life Africa had dealt out to her.

He'd had wealth in Zimbabwe that most people only dreamed about, and had lost it. He'd lost it. While other white farmers were squirreling money out of the country, he'd believed in his country and kept most of his wealth in his land. Sure, a few hundred thousand was in the bank, but the real value was in his soil. He'd improved his infrastructure, bought more land around Delmonica, and grown his ranch.

Now it was gone.

He acknowledged that hindsight was a brilliant thing to have. He should have put more away, kept an account in South Africa and offshore as a rainy day fund. Kevin had insisted, three years earlier, that Safari Aerospace move its base into Botswana. That decision had been their lifesaver. He'd started as Kevin's silent financial backer all those years ago, but it had been Kevin who had looked after their investment with his foresight. Before, it had always been Kevin that was the footloose and fancy-free bush pilot, and Scott the sound business partner. Boy, how things had changed over the years. How they had both matured.

Yet despite having to move money and assets from county to country, Scott couldn't leave Africa. It was in his blood. One day, when the government in Zimbabwe changed, he could try and get his ranch back for their children. He understood how much Ashley had given up in leaving her homeland and adopting his, because he knew that although everyone told him it was safer and better for his children, he couldn't imagine a life anywhere but in Africa.

There were values there that First World countries wouldn't understand. And there was Zol, and all the workers from his ranch. He could never desert them; they were his responsibility. They were his family. No overseas country was going to take them all in, and there was no way he could afford to keep them all together in another place other than Africa. But moving south into South Africa wasn't an option. They had their own problems. The people had begun a war on the white farmers, and were killing them there too.

But here in Zambia, they would be all right. Things would be tight until Zol could offload Charlie's diamonds. He felt bad for not telling Ashley about them, but he would not take a chance that she might freak out and call them blood diamonds and not want to use any of the money they would generate. He worried that with her First World Australian upbringing, she would not accept that they were uncut free ranging diamonds, not conflict diamonds that people had died retrieving and were used to fund wars. He just wasn't in the right frame of mind to explain how his father and Zol had picked them up all those years before, and had them stored away, safe for a rainy day. One day he would, just not today.

He would never sell Kevin out of their company. That was part of the future too, expanding to wherever their ranch was allocated. It was going to be better to ride out the tough time, sell the stones and trickle the money through as if he was taking the profits from the aviation company to slowly re-establish everything else.

This was Africa and there was always a plan. He still had his family, his wife and two beautiful babies. Others who had lost their land had not been half as lucky.

'Look what we found,' Zol called excitedly, breaking into Scott's deep thoughts. 'We can do the first two buildings elevated on decking.'

'That's great,' Ashley said, running her hand lovingly over the plank of wood.

Zol and Ashley continued looking through Albert's accumulated stash under the tarpaulins by the trees while Elliott and Scott loaded cement onto the trailer, along with a load of flooring. As he helped load more planks, Scott silently acknowledged that he would never understand the affinity that his two best friends in the world shared for building things. He simply wanted things to run well.

They thrived on building them.

He was sure if left on their own, Zol and Ashley would build a city, simply to test out different materials and construction theories.

CHAPTER 22

Construction work started the next day. Elliott and Zol drove the tractor to the camp with the front loader attachment, and they began selectively clearing and levelling the land. Scott and Ashley returned to Albert's camp and work on modifying the trailer became their main focus. Lisa accompanied them to watch over the twins.

Gertrude had suggested they start solids to supplement the twins' feeds, as having two babies was taking a lot out of Ashley. With the absence of a midwife, and relying upon Gertrude's previous experience, Scott and Ashley agreed. But it was Lisa who got the job of trying to get the twins to eat a thin mielie-meal porridge for lunch. As they had no baby formula, they decided that the staple food of Africa would do.

The feed went well. There was mess all over Lisa and down the twins' fronts but they had managed to swallow the fine porridge through their bottles as Lisa had enlarged the holes in the teats to accommodate the textured food. The twins were growing fast, and at almost two months old were strong kids, just smaller than one would expect at that age. They held their heads steadier and they had developed control over their tiny bodies. Already Brock was batting at the mobile above his crib while Paige sucked on two of her fingers. When Ashley looked at them, it was hard to believe they had been four weeks premature, they looked like miniature pictures of health.

'You know what, Scott,' Ashley said as she gazed at her children. 'Before we know it, we'll be unpacking those highchairs you bought a few months ago.'

'They will be here somewhere, I can look for them,' he replied.

In the afternoon, while Ashley welded the trailer, Scott hunted through their possessions for the baby paraphernalia they needed. He found the camera, with extra spools of film, and spent the rest of the afternoon taking photos of his children and wife. He realised that other than the first shots of the babies in hospital, and those Alice, as proud granny, had taken with her polaroid camera, they had no photographs of the twins. Survival had got in the way of sentimentality.

For nearly the whole week, they kept up the driving pace. Zol, Elliott and Albert, with Zol's elder children underfoot, erected pilings to hold the flooring, and then the flooring. Soon a huge wooden structure began to take shape. They had started on the school building first. It would serve as the main meeting place for everyone, a dry place if the wet season came early, and an area where everyone could congregate.

They cut down trees and dragged them with the tractor and the big hay trailer back to the camp and used them to make roof trusses. Eventually, half a building stood ready, waiting for more timber to be purchased. Zol ensured they only took trees from a decent distance away as the shade from the closer trees was a necessity in the midday heat for anyone. Albert's ranch would benefit from the new infrastructure too.

'Kind of a safari camp in lieu of rent and lodging for as long as we need,' Scott had said. Ashley thought rent might have been an easier option.

'One thing worries me,' she said as they stared at the amount of work still to achieve. 'We came via Botswana, then on the ferry to Zambia. The drive then took us northwest, until we got here. Why must the others cross over where you say? That section, at the bottom of the gorge of Lake Kariba—why there? It's a long trek from this side of the Siona Ngwezi National Park to collect them and bring them here.'

'Sweetheart, that's the only place we have a remote chance of getting to them to help them cross. A single man, or even a couple, they can cross over undetected in other places, but that group was close on eighty people when Zol left them. He split them up to travel in two separate groups, but they have a great danger of being detected by the authorities. There are simply too many people. Zol ensured they were safe before he left them. By now they should be within spitting distance of Mana pools. Already they travel west along the flood plains.' Scott put his arms around her. 'We'll get them all here safely. You worry about getting the trailer ready to go bundu bashing. I'll worry about getting them across and back up the escarpment.'

'The trailer is nearly done. One more day, and it'll be ready to carry the duck.'

They had climbed the wooden steps up onto the deck of the schoolroom, where the makeshift kitchen and lounge area now stood. Scott passed Ashley a diet soda. She flopped down into one of their ex-formal lounge recliners. 'It's heaven to have at least one comfy leather chair.'

'Yeah, the only one left from the whole lounge suite. Enjoy it,' he told her as he sat in a less luxurious fabric one that had previously been in the volunteers' quarters.

'I will,' she answered saucily, flicking up the footrest.

'You could join me.'

Scott needed no second invitation. He was in her chair and hauling her onto his lap in a nanosecond.

'Cheeky sod,' she whispered into his lips as she kissed him.

Elliott, Zol and Albert arrived just then.

'Stop that, you two. Anyone would think you wanted more of those babies hanging around.' Albert pulled a face at them, then turned to go to the fridge.

'No more kids for us. The nursery's closed but the playground's open,' Scott said.

Ashley squeezed his hand, remembering the reason for her hysterectomy, but dismissing it quickly. Besides, they had two beautiful babies. Even if something happened to them, her children were irreplaceable. She didn't want more. Neither did Scott.

'Livingstone is two days' drive away in the cattle trucks, the roads are not flash,' Scott said. 'Once the trailer is finished, we should get going. Pass through Livingstone and give them our order for the wood and more roof trusses and cement. Then we continue on the main road towards Lusaka. We head off towards Kariba, then onto the smaller tributaries—'

Albert interrupted. 'You know there is now a road down from Chongwe to the Kafue River. It doesn't show on the older maps, but it's there. The canoe safari companies use it as backup for their river treks. There's also another that heads east into the Lower Zambezi National Park.'

'Do you have a map showing it?' Zol asked.

'In my tent. I'll bring it next time I drop by.'

'Great. That's going to make our lives a lot easier in the road department,' Zol commented. 'I wish I'd known about this newer road, it might have made my trek here easier too.'

One day later, as the sun dipped in a fiery copper ball below the horizon, the group sat eating dinner together. Ashley hugged Scott around the shoulders, breathing in his scent. He had to leave soon to retrieve the staff, and she would miss him. Deeply. The baby monitor, her constant companion at night once the twins were settled for the night, was thankfully silent, giving them a chance to talk.

'I'm done, we finished the modifications today. Everything's complete,' she said. 'I changed the steel cable for the crossing to rope, as the weight of the cable was too heavy to transport and too bulky. I also found four plastic washing baskets full of nylon rope in the front hatch of that cruise craft of Albert's that he wants to take to Kariba one day. I spliced the ropes together. Elliott and I have measured it out, and marked it with a green tag, every twenty metres. The coloured tag changes in the last fifty metres to purple, every ten metres. The red markers are the last ten metres, marked out one metre at a time. You have five hundred and fifty-three metres of rope. That's all.'

'Okay. Then we should leave at dawn,' Zol said.

'You are coming with us, Al? If possible, I need you to drive the smaller of the two trucks,' Scott said.

'Why, where will Elliott be?' Albert asked.

'He and Tobias will stay with Ashley and the women to protect them, should the need arise. I hate the idea that I need to leave them behind at all, but knowing they are in safe hands makes it tolerable,' Scott said.

'You know, the protection detail shouldn't be necessary. FA Ranch is the middle of nowhere, who would come here? I often left it with no one here, and never had any problems. Guess now I have five resident workers, they can come help too. They're all Zimbabwean, we can trust them.'

'The extra manpower would be great. But it's not negotiable that Elliott and Tobias stay. Besides, now that my ranch has been unloaded into yours, there's plenty of property to steal. The bush talks, and even the empty bush has eyes. Tobias is here with his family; he has two sons old enough to sleep near your tent. Tobias will keep an eye on what's left of my cattle, and his wife can continue her work on their small kraal. I've armed both of them, and Ashley, Gertrude and Lisa.'

'Scott, this is Zambia, not Zimbabwe. We don't have too much trouble here. Well, not in this part. I hear there is trouble brewing in more populated parts, where chieftains are demanding the white farmers give more tributes—'

'Do you remember when I married Ashley?' Scott interrupted his cousin. 'The trial of the poaching ring that brought down the President's Guard? It created political chaos at the time. One of the poachers, the albino Rodney, he was let out of jail in a mass amnesty a few months ago. The morning we left Delmonica, he had a lynch mob waiting for us. I don't think he's given up on revenge for bringing them in. Despite everything that happened, Renegade's attack, being shot in the leg, and the beating I gave him, he made it out from the ranch. My guards went back in, looking for his body later in the day, and they saw him take the bus away from Delmonica. He's alive, and it's only a matter of time before he finds us. He'll go for Ashley again. He appears to have an unnatural obsession with her. My hope is that he hasn't healed enough yet to trek through the bush to get here, before we are back to full strength with all guard units surrounding her.'

'Geez, man. I didn't know any of this.'

'No worries,' Scott stated.

'You sounded like your Aussie wife for a second there ...'

Zol hitched the winch on the front of the *bakkie* to the chassis on the game capture vehicle. It was the second time in three hours since they had left two men with the cattle trucks on the main road and started down the road into the gorge that one of their vehicles had got bogged. This time, it was the lighter game capture vehicle, buried down to its axles. Tempers were beginning to fray.

Zol signalled to Scott who was now in the driver's seat of the bogged vehicle and returned to the *bakkie*. He switched on the engine and left it in neutral. Slowly, the winch tightened up, groaned and complained loudly, but it began to pull Scott clear of the bog. Zol slipped the *bakkie* into reverse and, keeping the tension even, backed up, making sure both capture vehicle and trailer came through the sodden path.

As he'd predicted, it had been raining heavily since the day they left FA Ranch. They could see the Zambezi in front of them, and were in radio contact with the units in Zimbabwe on the other side of the river.

'Base one, come in,' the CB called to him.

'Base one, talk.' He instructed into the mouthpiece as he stopped the *bakkie* and the cable loosened.

'We're at the river. The rain has lifted the level a little, but it looks good.'

'Affirmative,' he answered, as Scott popped his head in the window to listen.

Scott smiled. 'We should be there in an hour.'

Zol nodded in agreement, and spoke into his CB. 'One hour. Keep covered.'

'Affirmative. Will buzz when we have visual of you. Out.'

Zol looked at the CB. He knew Vusi had now switched his radio off to conserve battery power. They had an hour, and then they would begin the last stage of leaving their home and country. The workers from their ranch were about to become voluntary refugees.

'... If we don't bog again,' Zol said.

One and a half hours later, they had reached the river. The mighty Zambezi had slowed considerably after its rush down the gorge from the Kariba dam. Here, on the flood plain, it spread out like a lazy snake, and it had deposited a beach of sand on the outside of the S-bend on the Zambian bank. The water slugged past the beach in ripples, its dirt saturation point at a maximum, as it lazily swept past them on its journey eastwards.

Through high-powered binoculars they looked for signs of life on the opposite bank, but couldn't see any.

Zol's radio clicked.

'Where are you?' Kwiella asked.

'At the river's edge. We have no visual. Send out some smoke,' Zol instructed.

They gave a few minutes for the anti-poaching unit to get the fire going and then smoking, but they still couldn't see it, not with the naked eye nor binoculars.

'No visual,' Zol confirmed again. 'We can't see you.'

'We must be lower downstream than we should be. There were hunters in the area yesterday, and a canoeing safari.'

'All right, we'll come look for you. Over.'

Zol turned and spoke to Albert and his men. 'Unload the boat, we need to cruise to find them.'

While Albert and three of his men unloaded the boat, Zol and Scott prepared to launch into the river. They already had full tanks of petrol and a spare jerry can strapped to the duck. They loaded their hunting rifles. The last thing they wanted was to lose the duck to an overly aggressive hippo.

'Ready,' Zol said.

'Let's go.' Scott put on his polarised sunglasses.

Together, the friends clambered into the duck and fired up both engines.

'I love you, Ashley,' Scott said into the wind, and Zol smiled broadly, thankful that Ashley could fix anything and everything she put her hands on. The engines on Albert's duck had been working but in bad repair—the reason Albert had picked up the boat for a bargain price. Ashley had worked her miracles on them, coaxing life into the poorly maintained mechanical monsters. Albert and his staff pushed them off, away from the bank.

Zol sat at the front of the duck as they sped downstream, his feet braced against the rubber, and his bottom pressed hard into the wooden bench seat that he and Ashley had fixed inside. Scott drove the vessel, looking carefully into the water for submerged obstacles. Twice he avoided tree stumps and hidden sandbars. Racing the sun, they had to find the group of refugees and learn the crossing path before dark. They were running out of time, the whole group had to cross during the night and be far away from the river by morning, so they would not be detected by a police or army patrol.

Within half an hour, Zol spotted the small column of smoke that rose up from the opposite bank and then vanished. Not even a minute later, it reappeared and vanished again. 'Bingo.'

Scott swung the duck towards the Zimbabwean side of the river and headed for the green trees. Kwiella stood on the bank, a lone figure on lookout. But when he focused on them, he waved enthusiastically.

Only after they had landed the rubber duck on the bank, and Kwiella gave a low continuous guineafowl call, did the staff began coming out of the trees.

'There are more than eighty people here,' Zol said as he looked at the crowd.

'We picked up a few more stragglers, and there was a family waiting when we got to the crossing place. They were scared to try and cross on their home-made raft because the crocodiles are so big.'

'Not quite the set-up we had envisaged, but let's start loading. We take everyone,' Scott said. 'The first load will have three anti-poaching guards, three children and one woman. When we return, we'll take the women and children. Once we are down to forty people left, the next three guards will cross. The men will come only when all the women and children are across safely. The last to leave here will be Vusi's team. They will move behind you and do a total sweep clean. On this side, no one must see our crossing points.' He pushed the boat out into deeper water in preparation for loading the weight.

Kwiella separated the guards and children and the one old woman to travel across. Nobody argued. Everyone had total faith in Scott and Zol, and those who were new to the group and didn't know them knew the guards well, and didn't try to disrupt the organised proceedings. They were simply grateful to be taken care of.

Scott radioed Albert.

'Is it possible to move the *bakkies* downstream about five kilometres?' he asked.

'I'll send a scout,' Albert replied.

A long while later, Scott's radio buzzed.

'Negative, can't pass. About two and a half k's down there are problems. Over.'

'Move as far down as you can, and wait. We are on our way. Over and out,' Scott said into the CB.

They avoided the various islands in the river, and then they were across. The river was wider downstream, the flood plain flattening out, but the waters were fast-flowing through the channels between the small islands.

After unloading the first group, Zol returned alone in the duck to collect the next batch of children. By the time he returned, they had lost the natural light and the inky black night sky covered them in darkness. On the front of the duck, he had a piccaninny of about eight years old, who proudly shone the torch to guide the way, highlighting any debris in the water and keeping a lookout for hippos.

Unfortunately, they'd had to make on-the-spot decisions, and the rope-ferry idea that Ashley had concocted for economising on fuel and having the safety line across the river was useless. With the change in crossing place, they didn't have a clear access across a single expanse of water. Scott was forced to divert from the plan to get everyone across.

His solution was simple: they had no choice. They had to power the duck both ways. Scott calculated that, between the silent battery motor that Ashley had installed as a backup, and the two petrol ones, they should have enough fuel to complete the whole crossing before morning, but they would have to siphon petrol out of the *bakkies* to achieve this. At least they knew that they would have sufficient fuel for the crossing, but now they might need to get more petrol from the drum being carried in the cattle truck parked away on the road, before they could make it out. And if they were lucky, and there were no border patrols sneaking through the animal tracks, they had enough time, provided no canoe safari passed them on the river.

After a few trips, Scott took over from Zol. They kept the piccaninny in his place. He was light and doing a fantastic job of spotting the hippos in the dark.

When they reached the Zambian side once more, Albert put a cup of coffee into Scott's hands. 'How are you doing, cuz?'

'Good. Still worried that we are going to find ourselves at daybreak with people on the Zimbabwe side, and this rain isn't letting up. We can't be caught ferrying people across. The canoe safaris start early in the morning and we cannot afford to have them photograph us in the act.'

'The water is rising slowly, but it's rising,' Albert said.

'As long as they don't open those floodgates 'til we're done, I'll be a happy man.'

'How many trips left?'

'Probably another six or seven. An hour tops.'

'You had better step it up. Each trip is taking you fifteen minutes on the water, twenty with loading and unloading. We should get a helping hand from nature with the light situation from about four o'clock.'

'I know. At least the women and kids are done. It's just men over that side now. In a way it's harder, they have more problems with the water than the kids had,' Scott said.

Zol moved up next to him, also drinking a steaming coffee. 'Time to move again,' he said quietly. 'I'll come back over with you on this trip and help clean up on that side with the unit, then return on the last trip with them.'

'Good idea,' Scott said as he drained the last of the coffee and handed the cup back to Albert. 'Make sure you have plenty for the men in the next few crossings, with lots of sugar. Some of them will need it.'

CHAPTER 23

The copper sun was threatening to rise over the horizon. Lazily it shed light upwards, splashing the dawn sky with radiant earthly hues of rustic colour.

'Enough,' Zol shouted to Vusi, as he loaded one more person and their belongings into the rubber duck. Zol climbed out and spoke to Scott. 'Only one crossing left after this, just what's left of the unit on this side. I'll finish sweeping the area clean. Go, take this load.'

'Okay,' Scott replied, as he edged the rubber duck out into the deeper water and started the petrol engines, the electric motor long since flat and useless returned to the *bakkie* to lessen the weight load. Now he relied totally on the petrol engines and the spare jerry can of petrol, syphoned from the game capture vehicle.

It was still raining; the rain was dripping from his all-weather hood down his face, obscuring his vision. The exhausted piccaninny's place at the helm of the dingy had been taken up by Kwiella's son Adam. At fifteen years old, he was coping with the responsibility thrust upon him. Scott looked at him; he'd grown into a man during the last year. Scott knew Kwiella was proud of his firstborn son.

Scott smiled at him. The rain ran into Scott's mouth, and his smile turned into a grin. Adam grinned back, then turned his head into the onslaught of water falling from the sky and began peering into the dappled light, his focus just below the surface of water, looking for darker shadows.

Scott heard the noise first. He switched the petrol engines off to listen properly. The men on the boat all nodded: they had heard it too. Quickly, Scott restarted the engines. He didn't need more time to listen. He knew all too well what the hollow sound was: a solid body of water coming downstream from the gorge.

Sometime during the night, Kariba had opened its floodgates.

The duck and its passengers were more than threequarters across the river. They could see the headlights of the truck retreating up the riverbank on the Zambian side, the landing party all too aware of the danger.

'Everyone, find a place to hold on tight, and wedge your feet in, too. We are about to get bumpy,' Scott instructed.

He saw the whites in Adam's eyes flare brightly in terror. Like most of the men in the duck, he couldn't swim. The boat rocked as men found places to secure themselves.

'Boss, look!' Adam shouted.

Scott glanced to his right and saw the small wall of water released from the first floodgate, riding over the top of the river like a wave. Brown foam flicked into the air in front of it. He turned the duck sharply to ensure they met it head on.

Wham!

The duck collided with the wall of water, then lifted over and settled down again on the new level. The men on the boat cheered.

But the terror was not over. Twice more Scott turned the duck to nose over solid walls of water riding over the top of the river.

The Zambian bank was within spitting distance. They could see the *bakkies* and make out the people moving around on the bank. With the water rising higher all the time, Albert had moved the vehicles and trailer back about five metres above the water line. The trees were already showing signs of submerging under the onslaught of water, the original meeting site under water.

Instead of chaos around the retreating vehicles, there was organisation. The anti-poaching guards who had already crossed the river were shouting orders to the refugees, and they were responding.

'Boss!' Adam's frantic voice broke into Scott's thoughts.

Almost on instinct, Scott turned them upstream again, into the force of the oncoming water. But a huge tree was heading directly towards them, followed by the mother-of-all walls of water. Kariba had obviously opened two gates in quick succession, or both together.

The wall was at least a half a metre high.

'Shit,' he cursed.

Revving the engine to its maximum, he turned them left and broadside to the wall, in an attempt to avoid the tree. The wall lifted up the tree, and both water and tree slammed into the side of the duck. Scott saw Adam fall into the water as he felt excruciating pain in his stomach. He saw sky, and felt air beneath his butt. Then the world was upside down. He couldn't see anything but brown muddy water. He felt water invade his lungs and he kicked his legs furiously to get himself upright and head up to the light.

Scott broke the surface with a huge intake of breath. The water, cold and dark, swirled around him. He looked around frantically for the duck but couldn't see it. He searched the bank for the lights of the *bakkies* and saw them. With immense relief, he struck out towards them. He was grateful that the *bakkies* served as a lighthouse, ensuring he was swimming in the right direction. They didn't look too far upstream, but the current was strong and was carrying him further away from them every second.

He stretched his legs downwards and felt ground. The water was fast, but it was shallower than he expected, owing to the topography of the crossing place. He was lucky with being thrown from the duck here. Slowly, he half-walked, half-swam towards the bank, keeping his head above the water and touching the ground whenever he could to help himself. Eventually, the water became even shallower, and he could walk out.

He looked around, but couldn't see anyone near him. Cold and dripping, he looked at the Zambezi River. 'Bitch!' he shouted. 'You bloody Snake God, give me back my men.'

He tried to run up the riverbank towards where he'd last glimpsed the headlights but pain ripped through his stomach. Taking a deep breath, he scanned the water for any of his men. To his left he saw Adam lying face down, half in the water. Adrenaline pumped through his body. He held his hand to his stomach and his own pain eased as he rushed to him.

'Adam! Adam!'

He turned him over. There was no breath coming from the teenager. Scott dragged him out of the water completely and laid him on his back. He thumped Adam's chest hard with his fists together in a hammerlike fashion. Once. Then he turned his hands, interlocking his fingers, and pushed hard on Adam's chest performing compressions. Adam gurgled.

Quickly Scott rolled him onto his side as Adam began to vomit.

'Thank you, God,' Scott acknowledged, his head thrown upwards to the heavens that continued to pelt rain down on them.

'Come on, Adam.' Scott lifted him up once he'd finished emptying the Zambezi from his stomach. He helped the young man walk along the bank with him.

'We need to find the rest of the men.'

Torchlight flashed in front of them, dull and distant in the blanket of rain. At least the twinkling artificial lights were still visible.

'Scott ...' the distant call echoed.

Together Scott and Adam continued their journey towards the voices. As they rounded a bend in the river, they saw Kwiella running towards them. 'Boss Scott! He's alive!' he shouted into his CB radio. 'And Adam.'

Kwiella hugged Adam. He rocked him in his arms, side to side, as tears ran down his face in rejoicing that his son was alive.

'Kwiella, have you seen the duck?' Scott asked.

'It went downriver.'

'I need your radio.'

Immediately Kwiella handed the CB over to his boss.

'Albert, come in,' Scott called.

'Shit, it is good to hear your voice.' Albert's reply came back loudly.

'The duck went downstream. Who's followed it?'

'Four of your anti-poaching unit. I've kept my guys here to protect our tribe, but there was no keeping your team, especially not Kwiella. He was running before the duck began its descent.'

Just then, the other three men from the anti-poaching unit jogged out of the bush. 'Albert, send someone for Adam. The unit just got here, so we can't be too far from you.'

'Okay.'

The unit were each shaking Adam's hand for having survived the mighty *Nyaminyami* in the river and still being alive. They looked to Scott, now off the radio.

'Boss,' they acknowledged with a small nod, but their faces showed they were glad to see him.

'It's good to see you all. But we have ten other passengers to find, so move out,' Scott instructed, and the three guards silently left and melted back into the bush, jogging as best they could down the soggy riverbank.

'There's someone coming for Adam,' Scott told Kwiella. 'I need you with your men.'

'I know, Boss, I'm going, after ...' Kwiella looked at his boss. This man had led these men into and out of some of the worst poaching situations. He had the ultimate respect for Scott. '... after I check your stomach, Boss.' Kwiella stood his ground, choosing to challenge his Boss whom he saw was wounded.

Scott looked down. Only when he saw the dark red stain on his white t-shirt inside his torn jacket did he remember the pain and that he was hurt. He jerked his jacket and shirt up together.

Kwiella rushed across the small distance between them and placed both his hands on Scott's stomach. 'That tree got you good, Boss,' he said. 'You are not running upstream today because you need to get your guts back inside you.'

'You kidding?'

'No. Your clothes must have kept them in, but now you have lifted it, they are pushing out. Lie down so they don't drop out on the ground, and bend your knees, that makes the muscles in your stomach relax a bit.'

Kwiella reached for his small first-aid kit in the pack on his back. Like Zol, he would have considered himself naked without it. Stretched to the limit during the journey to the river, the kit was seriously depleted, but it still held a single pressure pad and a triangular bandage. He went to the river and washed the loose sand off his hands, then opened the kit. He poured some of the water from his bottle onto the field dressing.

'Zol always said, for the guts it must be wet,' he told Scott. 'I must not push them back, but if they are covered right, you can go for a little bit before you go to hospital. We must stop more coming out.'

Kwiella stuck the pad carefully over the small protrusion of intestines and onto the tear, and tied the triangular bandage around Scott's stomach, knotting it tightly.

'Adam, stay with Boss Scott. Don't let him walk anywhere now. Soon he'll feel his stomach. He needs Zol to stitch him up.'

'But Zol is still in Zimbabwe, Father,' Adam said.

Kwiella nodded at Adam. 'He will come for Boss Scott, my son. He will cross that river. Boss Scott needs him now.'

Kwiella turned away, knowing that Adam would listen to him.

'Ten, Kwiella. Bring back ten men,' Scott instructed as he handed back the CB radio.

'Yes Boss,' Kwiella said. Then he touched his son's shoulder, and turned away and began a slow jog to catch up to the rest of his team.

Two hours later, the sun had touched the horizon in the east and the birds in the valley began to call their morning greetings. The fish eagles cried as they searched for their breakfast, and the Egyptian geese's constant chatter between the large flock nearby had begun. Albert gawked at Scott's abdomen and cursed. 'Holy shit, we can't stitch this up. You need a doctor and a hospital. Now.'

As he lay on the tailgate of the *bakkie*, Scott tried to focus on his cousin. 'You have to do it, Al. It'll take up the rest of today to walk out of here with everyone and get to the trucks tonight. Then we still have to drive to Lusaka for a doctor. Just stitch it.'

'I don't think it's that easy,' Albert hesitated, as his CB shouted out into the quiet morning.

'Scott, come in.'

Zol's clear voice gave Albert an excuse to break off the confrontation. He passed the radio to Scott.

'I'm here.'

'Good, we are ready to move out. Area clean.'

'Zol. There has been a problem. The duck is gone. Adam and I are out, but we are searching for the others.'

'At least *Nyaminyami* didn't want you, my friend. Injuries?'

'Adam's fine, now that the water is out of him. I've a slash in my stomach and my guts were hanging out a bit. Kwiella put a wet dressing on it, but Albert is refusing to stitch it.'

'Good, the gut is too tricky. How much is hanging out?'

'A handful.'

'Not good, Scott. I have seen men die from intestines coming out of the body. Have you got cell phone coverage? Otherwise use the sat-phone. Call

Kevin to collect you in a chopper. Albert, don't stitch that,' his voice shouted louder for Albert to hear clearly.

'Hang on, I'll check,' Scott said. He began to sit up but a wave of nausea passed over him and he broke out in a cold sweat. 'Shit,' he cursed, and collapsed back onto the hard *bakkie* floor. The adrenaline that had so recently flooded his body had dispersed and he was starting to feel pain. Real pain. Sweat dripped from his nose, and he fought the urge to curl up into a ball.

'I'm already looking in the glove box. Stay where you are, Scott,' Albert called. Moments later he said, 'Thank God, we have a signal on the cell.'

He scrolled down Scott's contact list and stopped on Kevin's number. Despite being only five-thirty in the morning, Kevin picked up after four rings.

'Scott. Always good to hear from you, even so early in the morning. What's up?'

'It's Albert. Scott needs help. He needs a hospital.'

'Coordinates?'

'Hang on.' Albert reached for the GPS and gave them to Kevin before hanging up. 'He's on his way,' he called to Scott.

Scott raised his arm in acknowledgement that he had heard Albert, and the small motion of his arm hurt him in the gut. Pain waved black before his eyes, and he blinked rapidly to try to diffuse it. He could hear Albert talking to someone, but his shivering was getting worse. One of the staff's wives came over to him and covered him with a *kaross*. She put her cool hand on his hot forehead. It felt wonderful. He couldn't fight anymore. Slowly he let the intense and savage pain in his stomach claim his consciousness, and he floated into a painless abyss.

Scott woke to the sound of raised voices.

'You found how many?' Albert was shouting into his CB.

'Five dead, four alive, still looking for one.' Kwiella's voice, distorted by crackle, came back over the radio.

'Okay, got that. Over.' Albert walked around the *bakkie* and peeked in at Scott. 'Hang in there, we'll soon be moving to an easier access place for Kevin to fly in.'

'What's Kev's ETA?' Scott asked.

'Depends. He was flying to Harare then taking one of the helicopters. He'll refuel at Mana Pools. He said he'll get clearance from Harare to use one of your jets to fly you to Johannesburg.'

'Did the men find the duck?'

'Yes, with four men hanging for their lives on it.'

'That wasn't supposed to happen.'

'No shit, Sherlock. Even if it were daylight with no rain, you would have battled to see the size of that tree in the foam. It was fucking massive. You're lucky you got off so easily. I thought you were a goner for sure.'

Scott let out a huge breath, slowly. It hurt to move. He closed his eyes and blacked out again.

Zol heard the distinctive throb of an inbound helicopter. He and his men stepped out into the clearing and quickly lit a small fire with green leaves, creating a big smoke cloud. The chopper flew low, barely skimming the tree-tops as it traced the fat swollen river heading west.

'Albert, are you in contact with Kevin?' Zol spoke into his CB.

'Yes.'

'Ask him to pick us up en route. Tell him to look for the wood smoke.'

A long silence followed. Zol swore loudly and his anti-poaching unit waited with him as the chopper closed in on them. The rain had eased for a moment. Instead of pelting down in sheets as it had been, it now pitter-pattered softly, preparing for its next deluge.

Zol watched Kevin fly in low over the Zambezi. He could make out his distinctive profile. The helicopter was almost directly over them, before it dropped quickly into the small clearing.

But instead of landing, it hovered just above the ground. Kevin beckoned to Zol and he ran, crouched over, while his unit waited behind on the beach. He opened the forward door and clambered in next to Kev, who was signalling with his hand to put the headphones on.

'Put two men in the back, one in the front and the other two will have to hang onto the skids,' Kevin instructed him.

'Thanks,' he said, then he removed the headphones and ran back to his team. Zol signalled to two of them to get in the back of the chopper, then he told James to get in the front.

'Vusi, my old friend, it's you and I on the outside, just like the old days.' Zol knew that out of all the anti-poaching guards, he and Vusi probably had the most experience in flying on helicopters. He was semi comfortable to be on the outside of the aircraft and he was sure Vusi would be, too.

Vusi smiled as he sat on the skids and wrapped his legs around the uprights and hung on. Both the men knew it was useless to try to stand on the skids like they had during the bush war because Kevin's sleek commercial chopper had the luxury of doors. Each gave a thumbs up to Kevin when they were ready. The chopper didn't lift back into the air. Instead, it did a running launch up the small beach before it broke right and over the river, as if feeling overloaded. Sluggish. Zol held his breath as they passed over the wide expanse of water. In the daylight they could see the height of the floodwaters and the debris that it brought with it. He tightened his hold on the skid; he didn't want to fall. He might only get found in Mozambique, when the water spewed into the ocean, it was rushing so fast.

When they neared the Zambian side, Kevin dipped lower and as they arrived at the landing zone, he flared the helicopter. Zol and Vusi knew they had to jump, or risk being crushed on landing. Both men dropped down and rolled away on impact. Zol ran for the *bakkie* he could see at the edge of the clearing. The chopper landed, and when the engine stopped, the blades came to a standstill and the men climbed out.

The world seemed silent.

'Scott,' Zol greeted him as he went directly to the back.

'Zol. Take the staff home, make sure they are safe—' Scott began.

'Naturally. And I'll get Madam Ashley to you, wherever you are.'

'Thank you.'

'Load him in, Zol,' Kevin called.

Zol was no stranger to pain, but when he looked at Scott's ashen face, he understood it was one of a man barely holding on. He knew that there was nothing he could do to help his friend with the pain he was about to inflict on him. He cut a piece of webbing from his pack and placed it between Scott's teeth. 'Bite down, my friend. I have to lift you.'

Zol motioned Albert to help him, and together they lifted Scott between them, one arm under his bent knees, the other under his shoulder, and wrapped around his chest. Zol felt Scott pass out, his weight becoming leaden.

Kevin flew fast over the treetops. He'd abandoned his plans to return to Harare when he knew the seriousness of the situation, and chosen instead to head for the new hospital in Lusaka. He rechecked the fuel gauge. There was enough, they would make it. It felt strange flying without his coms and the snug-fitting earphones over his ears, but if Scott woke and said anything, this way he would hear.

He leant over and checked Scott's pulse. It beat steadily.

'Scott, talk to me. Try to come back,' he said. 'I'll get you there in time; they can fix you up in no time. Come on, partner ...'

But there was no reply.

'Dammit Scott,' he swore loudly. 'What am I supposed to tell Ashley? That I couldn't fly fast enough and you died on me?'

'Not dead yet,' Scott said through clenched teeth.

'Thank God!' Kevin said.

'Kev,' Scott said, and took a breath. 'If I don't make it, tell her I love her.'

'You'll make it. Lusaka is only another twenty minutes away, you just hang in there.'

'Sure,' Scott said, and slipped back into a world that blocked out the pain.

Kevin pushed his chopper for more speed.

CHAPTER 24

Rodney lit a match and laid it in the small pile of grass stacked against the tent. As always, he'd waited patiently and planned his revenge.

The white bitch wouldn't be his this afternoon, but soon.

Once, he'd thought of her as an angel, but ever since she'd helped put him in jail, he hated her with the same passion he'd felt for his German boss in South West Africa.

His penis twitched at the thought. A slight rising. He adjusted his combat pants around it and massaged his balls softly.

He didn't get hard often anymore, not like he used to when he was younger. But thinking of her made his body respond. Now he looked forward to his new memories.

His revenge on her.

Payback for the healing scabs around his throat from her dog, and the slight limp he still had from the bullet taken in his leg. Payback from his years confined inside those walls.

Jail life still haunted him. Its shadow clung to every fibre of his body. Its stench itched his skin and the walls crushed the air out his lungs. He was lucky, he'd had blood and release in the jail, spilt by him, not taken from him.

He blew on the small flames licking at the outside of the tent.

A crooked smile on his face, he moved to the next pile of dry grass.

His penis rose higher as he set that alight. Holding the match too long, it burned his finger and thumb. The fine line between pain and pleasure crossed over for a second, then it was gone. He giggled quietly in his delight, almost like a young girl, as one old hand clutched his hard long penis through his pants.

'Stupid *fook*ing *kaffir*,' he muttered as he thought of the past two days. Watching the ranch had been easy. With so much natural bush around, covering his tracks, making new ones and laying false paths had been fun. He'd enjoyed himself.

He grinned that Zol had not remained behind when the men left. He was a more worthy adversary. But his young scout was not that far behind in skills. Zol had trained him well. He was cunning like a hyena, but not as brave as a leopard.

Rodney had everything ready. Tonight was his night. Tonight he would escalate his revenge attacks on the white bitch who haunted his dreams.

Tonight began now.

He lit five piles of grass, and each one was soon licking up the side of the synthetic fabric of the tent. There was nothing of great value in the tent anyway. The white pig who lived there had travelled away earlier in the week. He deserved to lose it.

The fire reflected in his eyes, and he almost howled in anticipation. Soon, he would finish what he had started back in Zimbabwe. Zol should have known that borders meant as little to Rodney as they did to him. They were men of Africa. Africa belonged to them. No fence or white man's boundary line could stop their migrations.

He chuckled as he thought of Zol. Of all the stupid things to do, he'd left only one guard with the white bitch. Him and Scott must be off doing something interesting, and Rodney wondered what it was.

He rubbed his cock slowly as he thought of her. His white witch.

Once before he had felt hair like hers, but it wasn't as soft. When he'd held her hair that first day when they ambushed the anti-poaching unit, he'd known he had to have her. She was a major bonus, not expected, and better than any Christmas present. Her life that day had become intertwined with his, but he still had to own her. Make her his.

Almost subconsciously, he felt the hair bracelet on his wrist. He'd kept the handful of hair from the struggle through her window. A thick clump had wrapped around his hand, and he had put it in his breast pocket, close to his heart, before he went to her house. That had kept him going through the bush after her, once he knew which direction she was heading. His trek across countries had ensured the bracelet now looked black and dull, but he only needed to wash it with soap to see his most prized possession.

Her hair.

It was the same colour as his. Almost. But where his was dull, hard and wiry, hers was soft, long and shiny. He had the beautiful hair plaited around his wrist, and bound together with elephant hide. He lifted it to his nose and sniffed. It no longer smelled of her, but had taken on his scent. Soon, she would too ...

No one could keep a secret in Africa. The bush always talked. He'd watched the trucks remove their possessions from Delmonica for weeks before the invasion. Finding out that they were heading into Zambia and exactly where had been easy. Scott had a cousin who was also a displaced farmer, and he had land from the Zambian government. Rodney knew this was where they would start again.

White people were strange like that—they always relied on family. Following their path, after he had recovered sufficiently from his beating from Scott, had been easy. The war veterans had taken one of his family's farms a year ago, and that cousin had taken up the Zambian government's land redistribution program. He knew Scott had moved his cattle and game across the bush before his attack on their ranch. The white witch was living on the banks of the Southern Lueti River. Checking that his assumption was correct with eyewitnesses along the way had been fun. He sighed at the memory of one in particular. Before he slit her throat, the fat greedy wife of the customs worker on the Botswana–Zambia boarder at Kazungula had a lot to say. A superb *fook* ...

CHAPTER 25

Ashley sat quietly with Paige on her lap. Gently rocking her daughter backwards and forwards on her knees, she sang quietly to her and smiled as little Paige reached out with a chubby fist and attempted to pull on her mother's hair that tickled her face. Taking first watch just after the sun had set and before the new moon in the sky had a chance to cast any light on the world, Ashley, engrossed with Paige, did not notice that the stillness, now so much part of camp life, was shifting.

She swotted the pesky mosquito that insisted on humming around her head and looked over Paige into the night. In the distance, an orange glow came from Albert's tented area. She stared at it for a few seconds, until suddenly it dawned on her what she was seeing.

'Fire! Albert's camp!' she screamed out.

Gertrude sprung up like a lithe cat, despite her recent injuries, and looked outward. 'No!' She began waking the children. 'Florence, sweetheart, we have to fight a fire. Come on, get the girls together and stay close.' She kissed her daughters' heads.

The acrid smell of smoke began to permeate the camp, blowing downwind from the fire. The cattle kraaled nearby milled around, baying softly, not yet alarmed but alerted to the danger lurking on the horizon.

Ashley had her twins in their carrycots within seconds. Although Paige was awake, she was not fussing, and Brock slept on, oblivious of the chaos around him.

'Water! Sacks!' Ashley instructed. The teenage boys ran to switch on the generator that pumped water up from the river and into the camp. Ashley secured her kids in the back seat of the *bakkie,* then moved it out the rough kraal and to the pump. The boys had two empty 44- gallon drums waiting, and they quickly lifted them into the back. The water rushed into them, spilling over into the back, the smell of molasses strong in the night air as the barrels flushed clean. Gertrude came running with a few empty feed sacks they had in the storeroom at the back of the school building, and everyone piled in or onto the *bakkie.*

'Is everyone armed?' Ashley asked, as she patted her 9mm snuggled against her body under her blouse. As they all called out their replies, Ashley smiled gently. 'Thank you for the lessons, Scott,' she said quietly. The larger gun no longer felt like an alien or cold metal object, but an extension of herself.

They raced towards the blaze.

Hours later, the fire was out at last. The small group collapsed on the tail-gate of the *bakkie,* totally exhausted. The twins were sleeping in the cab, as were Gertrude's youngest two. The adults were black with soot and smelled of burnt plastic. There was no comforting smell of wood smoke, only the metallic odour of burnt plastic and man-made materials.

Albert's camp was gone.

So too were his stores under the tree.

A good number of their farm implements taken from Zimbabwe had been saved, but most of Ashley and Scott's personal possessions were burned. The fire had destroyed everything, including whatever protection Albert didn't have on his ammunition pile, stashed only God knew where.

At one stage, shots had begun firing into the night and everyone hit the ground for cover, thinking they were under attack, but it hadn't been so. The heat of the fire had simply made the bullets discharge. When they were sure no more ammo was going to explode on them, they carried on with their efforts to drag items away from the hungry fire. It hadn't spread up into the trees, other than the three large ones within the immediate camp area. Thankfully, Elliott had known where the chain-saws were stored. He had accessed them quickly and given one to Lisa, and together they had attempted to stop the firestorm before it got out of hand.

When the flames were only in the tops of the trees, he and Lisa had been able to cut them down. The first had crashed into the second, almost destroying the younger tree on its way. The last tree had taken both of them cutting at it before it fell, and it would have crushed Lisa on the way down if it hadn't been for Elliott's quick reflexes and a violent push to get her out the way.

Eventually the fire had been contained, but at a heavy price. Lisa lay on the ground near the *bakkie*, her eyes were closed but she was awake. Quietly waiting, regaining her strength. The shotgun lay next to her.

Tears streamed down Ashley's face. She wiped her nose on the top of her sleeveless blouse. It was already sweat stained and filthy from the fire. She didn't care. She had no energy left to reach into the *bakkie* and get a toilet roll to use instead.

Nothing was going to change Ashley's mind now that it was made up. Elliott had confirmed their camp had been rummaged through, and the single set of footprints left behind near the schoolroom didn't belong to anyone on the ranch. He was convinced they belonged to the albino, although the man walked a little differently, as if his leg hurt. It had changed his footprint, but only a little.

Ashley decided they were not staying another moment. Without all the anti-poaching units and Zol and Scott, they were vulnerable. A soft, easy target. Despite the fact they could arm themselves to the max, with so few of them they wouldn't get much sleep taking turns on night watch. Without a cell phone and the CB radio to Scott and Zol totally out of range, they couldn't even call the police for help. For the second time in a month, they were evacuating a ranch. Only this time, they were leaving everything behind, except for a small suitcase of clothes.

They could return when Scott and Zol came home, which shouldn't be long—a day or two at most. Until then, they needed to find some sort of motel in Livingstone. There, they would be safe.

'Right, Tobias. Let the cattle out of their pen so they can take their chances with the lions and leopards. Everyone gather clothes for a few days. We are leaving,' she instructed.

'Madam Ashley, let me stay,' Tobias said. 'The cattle are my responsibility. I must stay behind, that is our way. Since Boss Charlie's days, I have been with the cattle.'

'I ...' She looked at Elliott. He was slowly shaking his head, his hand at his waist, in a stop position, indicating to her not to argue. She cleared her throat.

'Thank you.' She looked the older man directly in the eyes. 'But you must promise me you'll stay close to the camp and not attempt to be a hero. No going after this trespasser and thief. Just look after the cattle, and if it's a cow's life or yours, I would rather see every animal dead than you. Do you understand?'

'Yes, Madam.' Tobias nodded.

'I have to accept that for now.' She knew that life had to carry on. The cattle needed to be tended to, watered and protected. Tobias was armed, so that was all she could do for him for the moment.

'We need to leave as soon as possible. Meet back here in five minutes,' she instructed. 'No one else stays ...' Seeing Elliott nod silently at her, she broke off her sentence and strode away to gather clothes for herself and the twins.

The sun was rising as they set off in the *bakkie*. Lisa and Elliott stood at the roll bar on the back, guns ready. Gertrude, Florence and Marie, her two oldest daughters, sat on a mattress in the back, with pillows and blankets around them to cushion the bumpy road. The two smallest girls were inside the cab with Ashley and the twins. No woman was being left behind for the albino to get his hands on. Annie and her older sons, Isaac and Philemon, were also in the back, safe. The teenage boys had wanted to stay with their father, but Tobias had told them to protect their mother in the big city for him, and help Elliott watch over Madam Ashley.

Both sons stood proudly when their father asked that, and Ashley smiled at them. Isaac, who was only about fifteen, had filled the *bakkie*'s tank from the cans of petrol that had escaped the fire. He'd made sure they had two spare jerry cans full, and put them in the back. Ashley didn't remember being so responsible at his age.

Now the small party was on the move again, on the road, heading for the nearest motel. Just where that was Ashley didn't know, but when they got to the main road and the sun came up, they would find some people and ask.

Zol fought the steering wheel for control as the tarmac beneath the truck disintegrated. The road into Livingstone was a mess, with the potholes in the bitumen filled with water from yesterday's rain. They had become unfathomable depths and certain death-traps for the weary driver of any vehicle.

But the cattle truck was handling most of them with ease, if he steered around the worst of it. They were on their last twelve-hour stretch for home, and he could almost smell the closing of the distance. Through his open side window, he could hear the cicadas. In Zambia they were eaten as *nyenje,* or *chenje* in the east, but to him, they sung in the wrong season. In Zimbabwe, they emerged later and their arrival signalled the beginning of the wet season and the lead-up to Christmas. That's why they had their nickname, Christmas beetles. But in Zambia, they began to emerge during the dry heat of August. They had begun their shrill monotonous sound too early. He would have to adjust his thinking for the new country. He wound up his window to block out the noise and watched the road carefully.

The drive until the main section of Livingstone had gone well, with little difficulty. Vusi drove the capture vehicle behind him, with Albert's vehicle coming up the rear, the dead bodies from the disastrous final crossing wrapped in blankets and covered over in the back of his *bakkie*. The last stretch from Livingstone to FA Ranch was going to be the hardest part as they would hit it at nightfall, and the abundant game on the road would be an added hazard. He rolled his head on his neck.

Soon, everyone could rest. Until the next move, when the land they had applied to the Zambian government for came through. When Scott completed the applications, he had stipulated his preference that he and Zol were next door to each other and near a game reserve, so they could continue their anti-poaching training business. It would take time to grow in Zambia, but it would happen.

Once they were settled, he would travel into Namibia to exchange some of their 'rainy day fund' that he had already retrieved on his journey and stashed safely on FA Ranch. But he would only do that once they knew where they were going, and leave Scott and the anti-poaching units to watch over Gertrude and Ashley. Once Scott was better, that was.

He had seen men with their stomachs on the wrong side of their bodies before, many years ago. And many had survived. As long as there were no other complications, the doctors could stitch it all back. But if the intestines were damaged, that was a problem. He silently preyed to his ancestors, wherever in Africa they were, that Scott would be all right.

He had seen so many people cross over. He remembered when he'd lost Charlie. For a time, he thought that his own heart would break, and he too would join him. But life had carried on. *Inkosana* Scott had tugged at Zol's heart, needing a man close by who understood his love of the land. Needing a friend.

Zol had stayed and he had watched over Boss Charlie's young child. And over the years as he matured, Scott had become his brother-but-one.

Ashley sat with Gertrude and Lisa in the garden outside the hotel. Elliott sat with his back against the jacaranda tree, his rifle next to him, a sign that the ladies and the children were under his protection and not to be approached by anyone. His presence was the only indication that life was not tranquil in the manicured garden of the hotel.

The small patch of grass under the tree was cool. Ashley's twins slept peacefully under mosquito nets in their prams, oblivious to the tension that settled heavily on the small group of people under the purple canopy. Gertrude's children played a game of hopscotch nearby, etched deeply into the dry sand with a stick, a brown pod used for keeping the spare place during the game.

Ashley had tried Scott and Albert's phones multiple times, with no answer. They were obviously all out of cellular cover, and she suspected they had the sat-phone switched off as that didn't ring either. It was nearing teatime, and she decided to try again. Dialling Scott's number on the hotel's portable handset she had requested from the reception desk, she put the phone to her ear and listened.

The phone rang twice then Zol's voice came over the wireless connection loud and clear. 'Hello.'

'Zol!' she said.

'Madam Ashley, give me a moment to pull off the road.'

She could hear as he pulled to the side of the road and let out the exhaust breaks.

'I can talk now,' he said.

'Scott there?' she asked.

'He's not with me. There was an accident—'

'Is he okay? What type of accident?'

Gertrude looked at her, a frown creasing her copper skin.

'A bad one. I am thinking you might want to start driving to the airport at Livingstone,' Zol replied.

'I'm already here.' She gave him the name of the hotel they were staying at. 'We had some trouble of our own.'

'I'm only about half an hour away. I will meet you there.'

'Zol! Wait, where is Scott?'

'I will explain as soon as I get there,' Zol said, and hung up.

Ashley ran into her room, threw everything into her case and slammed the top shut. The sound of the zip was loud in the quiet room. 'Scott,' she whispered, 'please be okay.' She lifted the case onto its wheels and dragged it out the door. With Lisa's help, she buckled the twins into their car seats. Elliott jumped into the passenger seat next to her, and Lisa squashed in between the twins. Gertrude and her girls were already seated in the bin at the back and the boys were waiting too, standing up holding onto the roll bar. They drove to the hotel's gate to wait for the convoy.

Their immediate problems she could deal and fix. Scott was the unknown factor. The one she wanted desperately to control but couldn't.

Finally, the cattle truck rambled slowly past, filled with people. It stopped a small way from the gate, and Zol jumped out and closed the distance between them.

'Zol!' both Ashley and Gertrude called.

Reaching them, Zol hugged his wife to him and nodded to her. 'Madam Ashley.' He kissed the top of Gertrude's head and let her go. Turning, he reached for Ashley. Totally against his traditions, he hugged her to him, as an old man would comfort a young child.

'What happened? Where's Scott?'

'Scott is with Kevin in his chopper, going to hospital. He is very bad. And we lost some crossing the river, Madam.'

Ashley's knees gave out under her and Zol held her tight to prevent her falling. He wouldn't let her sit in a heap on the dusty ground of the street.

She tried hard to control the emotions that threatened to spill over and choke her. 'Where did Kevin take him?' she asked, her voice heavy.

'Lusaka. But his stomach, it was pulled out.'

A chorus of joyous screams behind them signalled that Zol's girls had stopped playing in the back and spotted their father.

'Stand, Madam Ashley. You have to stand,' he said.

She forced her body to respond and take her weight. There was so much more said in Zol's command, and she was instantly alert.

The girls threw themselves into Zol's embrace, giving Ashley a few minutes to compose herself, to find her courage again and think on what Zol had said. The workers had got out of the cattle truck and as they gathered around, their hushed whispers penetrated Ashley's head.

She straightened her back.

Albert walked through the group and hugged her.

'Ashley, you all right?'

'Yes. No. It's Scott ...' she said, but knew that it was more for her own sake that she spoke the words. Albert and everyone else had been there. She took a deep breath. 'Let's deal with one thing at a time.'

She motioned Zol to walk a little away from the group, and Albert walked with her, his arm supporting hers. When she was sure the group wouldn't hear them, she asked, 'Zol, what are the burial arrangements for those who died?'

'First, we get them all home to FA Ranch, then we bury them. To take them to a hospital here would bring the authorities,' Zol said in a hushed tone.

'I agree.' Albert said. He realised she didn't need as much support and released his grip on her. 'Usually I would say no way, but I'm happy to have a small graveyard on FA Ranch. It's where these people were told they were going, so it's right that they rest there and not in some Zambian city cemetery, where their families can't visit easily.'

Ashley looked at the two men. Both had valid points. 'Fair enough. Have you had any contact with Kev since you separated?'

'No.' Albert pulled his cell phone from his pocket and held it high checking for a signal. No messages bleeped through. 'The reception improves as we leave the town, perhaps you can give Kev a call when you're on the road to the airport?'

'Good idea. Albert, there isn't good news on FA Ranch either. The albino attacked us, and he's burnt your tent. You'll need to pick up a new one, or move into the safari compound with us.'

'Shit!' Albert said. 'That's why you're here and not waiting at home?'

'Yep. But now everyone's reunited, the guards will take care of him when we get back. There'll be more people keeping watch for that bastard, it'll be easier.'

'As long as you're all unharmed?' Zol said.

'No harm done to us. We've just been living it up in the city for a night.' She tried to lighten the mood, but it fell flat. She swallowed the croak that threatened to bubble up her throat. 'Let's head for a better reception area, I want to know what's going on with Scott.'

She turned her back on the men and walked back to her *bakkie*. Her arms felt icy and leaden. She could hardly breathe as a huge weight pressed into her chest. Action. She needed to do something. And any action was better than nothing at all. She pulled on her seatbelt and began to drive to the outskirts of town, looking for a better reception patch.

Zol took comfort from Gertrude sitting in the cattle truck with him, his girls crammed into the front with them. He was not surprised at the efficiency with which Ashley had organised the hotel checkout and got everyone moving again. She was still the wildcat who had stepped off Kevin's plane five years ago. He remembered Ashley's first moments in Africa, at Zebra Pan airstrip, and other important moments in her time with the family. And it was then that he realised that not only was she one of them, part of the extended Decker–Ndhlovu family, but she was a true African.

She wasn't running away. She had organised her people, putting their welfare first.

Even now, when the stones on the *Morabaraba* were against Madam Ashley, she continuing to move the pieces, to somehow complete the puzzle. She was sticking by them. He smiled. Zol knew she would sort out everything, and if, God forbid, Scott didn't make it, she'd be there always.

Fighting for them all.

It was a good day when Ashley had stepped into Scott's life, and they would see through the troubles of late, and good times would come again. They had to.

He looked across at Gertrude. The girls were reading books and playing with string. He winked at his wife.

'Welcome home,' she said.

'Lusaka ground control, this is CHN062, air charter. Requesting emergency clearance into Zambian airspace, and permission to route direct to Lusaka hospital for urgent medical assistance. Estimated time still en route, half an hour.' Kevin spoke into his sat-phone.

'State the nature of your emergency?'

'I've a man needing immediate medical assistance. His stomach has been ripped open in a white-water rafting accident.'

'You are cleared for Zambian airspace, and there will be a medical team waiting at the hospital for you. What's the patient's status?'

'He's unconscious.'

'I'll relay that information. Make sure you come into the airport and file your flight plans when you are finished.'

'Roger that, and thank you for the assistance.' Kevin sighed with relief.

Scott hadn't regained consciousness again. 'Hold on, my friend,' Kevin said to him, even though he knew Scott couldn't hear him.

Twenty-three minutes later, Kevin landed his chopper on the hospital's helipad, in the centre of Lusaka. True to his word, the air controller had the medical team waiting, and Scott was rushed away from him on a trolley.

Kevin quickly moved his chopper away from the main pad and tied it down. Thank God for small mercies. The hospital had been planned recently, and the modern architect had understood African needs.

Striding into the emergency room, Kevin shivered at the coolness of the air-conditioned building. The sickly sweet smell of antiseptic wafted around him.

Scott was better off in Lusaka than in Zimbabwe's Harare hospital. Lusaka had international doctors employed at their hospital. The government was trying hard and succeeding at rebuilding their shattered country, while

Zimbabwe was struggling with few professionals, and more were leaving all the time as the country slid deeper into poverty.

A trauma nurse took Kevin through to a smaller waiting room.

'Your friend's in theatre,' she said. 'You can wait here for news. I will be at the desk if you need anything else.'

After twenty minutes, she returned.

'Excuse me,' she said as Kevin bounded to his feet, eager for news. 'Scott Decker is still in theatre, there have been complications.'

'Complications?'

'His stomach has perforated. That means that not only were his intestines coming out of his body, but they are broken inside. All the stomach acids have gone into his body. They are trying to clean it all out. His own body is poisoning him.'

Kevin sank down heavily onto the chair. Scott was in more trouble than he'd thought. His best friend could die, and he didn't have any way he could contact Ashley to help to get her here. He looked at his cell phone. He didn't have Ashley's number but he knew Zol or Albert had Scott's phone.

He looked at the theatre doors. A sign advised that all cell phones had to be switched off, so he walked outside, trawling through the phone's menu for the last number that called. He dialled it.

'Hello.' An African voice answered, but he would know that voice anywhere.

'Zol!'

'Kevin. How's Scott?'

'Not good. Listen, I need to get hold of Ashley. Are you almost home?'

'No, I'm driving out of Livingstone. She's in her *bakkie* behind me. Just wait a moment, I will stop and give her the phone.'

Kevin could hear the exhaust brakes of the cattle truck being released, and Zol running on loose gravel, then the drone of Zol's voice in the background.

'Kevin. Hi. How's Scott?' Ashley said, her words almost running together.

'Ashley ... he's bad. Real bad. I'm in Lusaka General. I'm coming to fetch you.'

'H –' Nothing else came through the phone's receiver and he heard her swallow. 'How bad?' He heard her hiccup.

'He's still in theatre. His stomach was perforated.'

'Holy shit!'

'Ashley, I need to refuel and file flight plans. Can you get to Livingstone airport and I'll collect you there?'

'How long do I have to find the airport?'

'Two and a half hours, tops.'

'I'll be there. Kevin, tell him to wait for me.'

Ashley, Zol, Lisa and the twins made their way to the airport in Ashley's *bakkie*, leaving Elliott with Gertrude to drive the cattle truck to FA Ranch. They watched as Kevin touched down and cut his engines. He waited for the blades to slow almost to a stop before opening his door and tumbling out onto the concrete. Just one look at Kevin's face and the droop in his shoulders and Ashley suspected they were too late.

Kevin enveloped her in his embrace. 'Come on, we need to hurry.'

Strapped into the helicopter, Ashley thought back to another time when she had been so filled with hope and passion when flying with Kevin in his old plane. The nice plush helicopter was a far cry from his plane, but she had enjoyed that first journey a helluva lot more than this mercy dash. The trees and rivers beneath them blurred in a swirl of colour as they raced above, but she couldn't make out a single landmark. This whole land was so unfamiliar to her.

Kevin constantly checked in with the hospital on his sat-phone. They assured him that Scott was still listed as critical, which meant that he was still alive. Scott could fight critical, but he couldn't fight dead.

Finally, they touched down on the hospital's helipad. Ashley, with Zol close behind, ran into the main building. Lisa was unloading the pram and the twins. Kevin had to move his chopper, and would follow them when he could.

Ashley went to the main desk.

'I'm Ashley Decker, my husband Scott was flown in for emergency surgery?'

'We have been expecting you. Your husband is in room 212. The orderly will show you the way.'

The orderly was around Ashley's height and dressed in starched whites. He smiled hesitantly then gestured for them to follow him, and she thanked the office clerk as she left, striding after the young man. They walked down a few corridors and he pushed open a door that led to the intensive care unit.

The nurse helped her into a surgical gown and booties, a hair cover and gloves. Zol was similarly attired. Finally, they were shown to Scott's room.

Zol held the door and Ashley walked into the room.

Through the mask that covered her nose, she could smell the strong antiseptic wash. The machines attached to Scott made noises foreign to her ears. She went to the bed and reached for his hand that didn't have a drip attached.

'I'm here, Scott,' she said. 'Zol's here, too.'

The ashen-faced man on the bed didn't move except for the rise and fall of his chest, which she knew the machine was making as it helped him breath.

'You must be Mrs Decker. I'm Dr McKenzie. I'm glad you are here. Please take a seat.' The doctor spoke as he walked into the room, and motioned to the chair next to the bed. Zol immediately lifted the chair and put it behind her legs, and she sat down. He remained behind her, his hand resting reassuringly on her shoulder.

'Your husband is still critical. There are complications. He has suffered what we refer to as a penetrating abdominal trauma. However, one or more of his intra-abdominal organs have also been injured. His small intestines were perforated, so we had to perform a colostomy. Basically, we've removed part of his small intestine, and then closed his rectum and attached his intestine to a bag. When the time comes, we can reverse this and he will have normal bowel function again. This perforation has poisoned his whole abdominal cavity. We attempted to clean it as best as we could, but his body was going into shock. He also had a shattered kidney, which we were not able to save. His liver is also damaged and we can already see signs of sepsis. Infection. We have him on strong anti-inflammatory and antibiotic drugs to try and help him.'

'Will he make it?' she asked.

'Too soon to say. But it will be calming for him to have you here.'

'Thank you. Is there anything else we can do to help him?'

'If you believe there is a God, you can pray,' he said.

She looked at him. This man of medicine was telling her to pray. Scott's life was in serious danger.

Suddenly, a machine next to the bed began to beep, and the doctor rushed to Scott's side. She could see that even in the short space of time that the doctor had been speaking to her, Scott's pallor had changed.

'Stay over there,' he said sternly, pointing to the back of the room. 'We are going to need space to manoeuvre.'

Three nurses rushed in. The doctor began barking out orders and carts of equipment were wheeled in. All the time, Zol held her shoulders, keeping her in the back of the room while the machines beeped and the doctor's stern voice created organisation out of what looked like chaos. The hum of the ventilator as it squished in and out continued.

After what seemed like an eternity, the ventilator went quiet, the beeping stopped and an unnatural silence fell over the room. Dr McKenzie turned to her, and removed his gloves. 'I'm sorry, Mrs Decker ...'

'No!' she shouted. 'No, it's not fair! Tell me he's not dead. Tell me—'

'He's gone. You can sit with him for a while if you want to.'

'Noooo ...' The high-pitched wail somehow forced its way out of her throat.

She knew she was only standing because Zol held her up, she could feel his heat searing her cold body, as he stroked her hair, her back, and up and down her arms. The arctic was warmer than her, and there was no fire on earth that would make her feel again.

Her love was gone.

Her best friend.

She was alone. How could he leave her here without him?

She turned to look at Zol. The big man was stooped and giant tears rolled freely down his face, his shoulders shook but no sound came from his body.

'Oh God, Zol,' she said as she put her arms around him.

'I'm so sorry, Madam Ashley,' he said.

'Me too, Zol. Me too.' She stood with her arms around him, and his around her, lost in her grief. Huge sobs racked her body and she gulped for air.

Her Scott was dead.

This was not supposed to happen.

Her head felt light and she couldn't breathe. The pain in her chest increased and eventually she gasped a breath, but it burned her lungs. Her heart shattered into a broken mess and she sobbed.

'Not my Scott.'

Ashley walked to the bed, bent over and hugged her husband.

Kevin ran into the room, took one look at the scene in front of him and sank to his knees. 'No!' he cried.

For a long time, the three friends grieved in the room. Finally, Ashley let Scott go and smoothed his cheek. The nurses had put plaster on his eyes to keep them closed. She wanted to rip it off so that he could open them and see the world, tell him to wake up.

But she knew it was useless.

Zol went over to Kevin and squeezed his shoulder. Kevin got up, wiping his eyes on the back of his sleeve.

'Thank you, Kevin,' Zol said, and extended his hand. 'For getting us here. He waited for us, then he crossed over.'

She watched as the two most important men in her husband's life shook hands. His best friend and mentor of the bush, and his business partner of the sky, united in their grief, and both of equal importance to the man they held so dear. She looked down at her trembling hands. The sunlight from the window refracted sparkles through the diamonds on her rings and the rainbows danced across the ceiling. Africa had given her great happiness, and then cruelly snatched it away.

At that moment she hated the continent more than anything else in the world, and the anger burned low within her body at the injustice done to her small family.

CHAPTER 26

Three weeks after Scott's funeral, Albert collected two official letters addressed care of FA Ranch when he was on a grocery run. The first was addressed to Zol. It denied him land lease in the reappropriation program, on the grounds he was black, and there were lots of black farmers in Zambia without land who would be given land before a black Zimbabwean.

The second letter was addressed to Scott.

Ashley ripped it open. It granted Scott Decker the ranch Singita, in the north of Zambia, adjacent to Sumbu National Park.

Ashley broke down and cried. Great big sobs of relief and sadness emanated from her body. What one country was tossing aside, its neighbour was eagerly collecting and putting to work to help their economy: the white farmers. This was what Scott had wanted; this was his dream. To continue caring for his family.

Taking her twins and returning to Australia had fleetingly crossed her mind, then the lives of all the people around her made her think twice. As devastated as she was at the loss of Scott and his support, their support was also now missing. Scott had provided for so many people and they had all counted on him. She couldn't turn her back on them in their time of need. Besides, this was her home now. She needed to bury her sorrow and pain far down inside herself and lock it up for now, because life had to go on. For her twins' sake, for her own sake and for every worker in her care.

'Madam, that is a good name for a ranch,' Zol said. 'In Shangaan it means "place of miracles".'

'Well, fat bloody miracle it is, when Scott isn't alive to see it,' she sobbed. 'At least we have land just as you and Scott planned. It doesn't matter that there's only one ranch.'

Zol took her letter and re-read it. 'The lease agreement, it's in Scott's name. Let's hope the government still grants it to you, as his widow.' He touched his hand to her shoulder. 'Madam Ashley, I was Scott's brother-but-one. I know he would be happy to get that land and move everyone there. Rebuild. He never turned his back on anything. He would want you to go sign the document, get legal custody, make a new home. For you. For all of us, together. The Decker and the Ndhlovu families, always together.'

She looked into his black eyes, the white looking yellow and shot through with red lines of age, and she smiled. Sniffing, she returned the ancient gesture to his opposite shoulder.

'Years ago, I might have run away, believing that I couldn't look after everyone, but not now. I can and I will provide for us all. We'll rebuild. I'm not sure just how, but we'll do it. I just wish Scott was here to share it with us.'

'He's always alive, Madam, in here,' he touched his heart, and reached towards her, his big hand gently hovering above her heart, 'and in here.'

More tears ran down her face, and she smiled. 'Thank you, my friend.'

'You're welcome,' he replied, and walked away.

The following morning, Zol sat down next to Ashley in the dining room. 'Madam Ashley,' he began, 'the threat from the albino is still around, although we have seen nothing of him since we all got here to guard you. There are other threats now with Boss Scott dead. You and me, we will go hunting for rations, with Albert and Elliott, but it must be you who shoots the kudu.' He waited for her to react.

Ashley's eyebrows rose, then a deep furrow of worry curved in between her eyes.

'Remember when Scott tested you with your Land Rover? Once again, you need to prove you are strong. Prove you can do everything. Some of the men who came across the border with the workers, they don't know you. They believed in Scott, but you must now make them believe they have a strong madam. A madam who's not afraid in Africa. A madam who will always be in Africa and not run away, back to her country across the sea. A strong leader who they can follow.'

'That's ... ridiculous,' Ashley said.

'Unfortunately, it's not. We can't have any of them look to me as the new Boss; it would put you in big danger. You are the white Madam, they must look to you, respect you. If they don't respect you, you are better off taking your twins and leaving Africa. It is the way. So when we go to Singita, only those who are loyal to you will follow from this place. They need to believe you are in control. The others, the ones who don't believe in you, they'll stay with Albert, here. They will say they are tired of travelling, but really it will be because they don't trust that you are strong enough to stay in Africa on the land and provide a new home for them and their families.'

'So after all this time, how am I meant to prove this to them? Why can't they just accept me?'

'You are white. You still speak with an Australian accent. They don't know you. Even the people who do, they are waiting for you because they are unsure if you are staying or going. If they will always have the home they were promised. But one way is for you to prove you are strong. Another is that I leave you for a while. Let them see that you are in charge, not me, not Elliott and not Albert. But I can't do that. You are a Decker and my place is with you, always.'

'Let me get this straight, Zol. I need to make sure the new people who joined my workers, on a trip that we provided protection, and food for, understand I'm their boss?' Ashley said, her voice rising slightly at the absurdity of the request.

Gertrude sat down next to Zol. 'She isn't taking this well, is she?'

Zol shook his head. 'Singita will run just like Delmonica. We will run it as one big identity, just as Scott and I planned, back when we put in the papers, when you were in Cape Town.'

'Except there we had enough money to do everything we needed. Now, I can't see how we're going to function again,' Ashley said.

Gertrude looked at Zol, then back at Ashley. 'It's time you were told. Scott and Zol didn't tell you because you were having problems in your pregnancy and they were worried about the extra stress. Zol went to fetch something when he was moving people across the countryside. Something that belonged to Boss Charlie and Zol. These things will secure all our futures. But until we are settled down at our new ranch, he can't leave to change it over into cash.'

'Gertrude, I have no idea what you're talking about,' Ashley said.

'That's all right, it's old Decker–Ndhlovu history. But once Zol knows the workers' loyalty to you is unquestioned, he will travel away from us. And when he comes home, you will have enough money to make Singita as beautiful as Delmonica. But to do that, you must ensure the workers follow you as the head of the ranch. Or we will have no workers, just people who will steal anything they can, take everything they can, and we will not prosper. You need to gain their trust and loyalty. It is the only way. They all know about the albino attacks here, and they know that you left the ranch. To some this will be seen as weakness. You have to understand that we will always be with you, but to others who are simple people, you need to be seen as the leader of all of us. The chief.'

Ashley put her head into her arms at the table, and blew great breaths to stop herself crying. She knew deep down in her heart a challenge like this was bound to happen, and that she would need to rise to it and prove to the workers that she could provide for them. But everything was just so hard at the moment.

She must kill an animal to be recognised as 'the Boss'.

She detested killing.

What more could go wrong?

Elliott drove the hunting *bakkie* slowly down the worn game path, towards the river. Ashley stood on the back, next to Zol. Seated in the tray were six of their workers, the women sat quietly while the men talked in hushed tones together. Kwiella and Vusi from the anti-poaching unit, and a few of the older children who had made the journey to Zambia. A big enough crowd to ensure that the word spread that it was Ashley who made the kill, not Zol.

They had been hunting for two hours, looking for a trophy bull they could kill. A hushed silence clung to the vehicle. Everyone was waiting.

'There,' Zol said, pointing to a small clump of trees to Ashley's right. 'At one o'clock.'

'I see him,' she said.

The kudu that stood eating from the trees was magnificent, his horns completing a double twist before pointing skywards. An old bull, his mane dark, the white marking on his face distinctive. His ears tatty, damaged from years lived in the teak forests.

Ashley had always valued life. All life. On Delmonica, when meat rations were needed, it was Scott and Zol who sorted it out. They would either kill an ox or they would go hunting. Together they would kill a kudu or two, or go 'bunny bashing', where they would shine a hunting torch and stun the spring hare, then run up to it with a club and kill it with one smack to the head. They would collect enough of the vermin for rations that way to ensure no one was hungry on their ranch.

But Ashley had chosen preservation of life—looking after the water pump project in Hwange, fixing everything that was broken and ensuring any new settlements they made would work properly, that they had power, running water, sufficient sewerage pits. This had become her niche on the ranch. Although she had shot things at Delmonica, she had never actively gone hunting with the sole purpose to kill an animal.

She lifted Scott's .303 rifle to her shoulder. As she looked down the butt of the varnished wood and into the telescopic sight, she knew that one of her biggest decisions in life was about to take place. To put those crosshairs on the forehead of the kudu and bring it crashing down was not just about her, it was about the lives of her children too.

In Africa, if a woman was weak, she was treated as a sub-citizen.

But if a woman could show her strength, she and her family were treated with respect usually given only to a male.

She needed to gain that respect.

Despite going against her Australian upbringing and beliefs, she acknowledged that she had been in Africa long enough to have adopted many of their ways, habits and rituals.

She chose to protect herself and her kids.

She squeezed the trigger slowly, letting the rifle jump back into her shoulder as the bullet thundered down the barrel and cleanly ended the kudu's life.

. . .

Although the men and women who hung onto the hunting vehicle cheered and raced towards the dead beast, she saw no glory in the kill. This had been a means to an end—a guarantee of her family's safety.

A simple show of force that she could handle a weapon as well as any man, and would do everything in her power, including taking a life, to keep her little family together and safe.

She was their white Madam, Ashley Decker.

Ashley couldn't contain her smile as she left the stuffy air of the Land Rights office behind her. Zol and Elliott waited outside, next to the *bakkie*. She stood at the top of the steps to the building and shouted at the top of her voice, 'We got it! It's ours!' and ran down to hug Zol and then Elliott, all three joining hands and jumping with joy as they celebrated.

The small hold-up while the Zambia officials changed the papers from Scott's name into hers had been worth the wait. Now she had the signed papers in her pocket and there was no denying it: Ashley Decker was the Madam, and had just secured them all a new home.

She knew that shooting and killing the kudu had been worth the challenge, ensuring both her and her children's safety with the workers. Showing she could provide rations for her workers had been the first step, now having their ranch given to them was the second.

She danced on the spot again. Elliott linked his arm in hers and spun her around while Zol clapped and stamped his feet as if gumboot dancing.

Eventually she climbed into the driver's seat and started her *bakkie*. Elliott sat next to her in the passenger seat. She heard the loud click of Zol's seatbelt in the back seat as he strapped himself in. The door closed firmly.

'Thank you, Zol,' Ashley said.

'Times are changing, Madam Ashley,' he said. 'Perhaps it's time I tried sitting inside with you. We can carry on our celebrating with a drink too, if you could stop at the Spar.'

Ashley laughed. It felt good.

She knew her third biggest challenge was going to take place when they left FA Ranch and headed to Singita. She wondered just how many of her workers would cross Zambia again to continue to make another new life with the Decker family, and how many would stay with Albert, not prepared to entrust their lives to their new madam.

And the shadow of the deranged albino weighed heavily on her mind.

But for today, she would celebrate.

CHAPTER 27

The silence of Singita was deafening. The absence of wildlife had been one of the first things they noticed on their arrival at their new home. The quietness.

No birds chirped.

No cicadas sang their constant tune of the wild.

No eagles sored overhead.

A landscape that was holding its breath for the return of the creatures that should have inhabited it.

Ashley looked around at the deep green bush. The tall trees. Lush and dark, they held a promise. Just like the gentle hills that surrounded them. The *kopjes* held boulders that reminded her of the Matobo in Zimbabwe, giant rocks balanced upon another. But the beauty of the place did not diminish the fact that they had been granted this ranch because of their expertise in anti-poaching, and poaching had clearly taken its toll. The wild game had moved away, migrated to a safer area.

There had been nothing on the land: no fence, no house. It took them two days simply to get their vehicles along the old dirt track into the ranch, with the *bakkies* in front, then the cattle trucks, followed by the trailers. Tractors, front loaders and grading equipment were strapped securely to the trailers.

She smiled at Albert. He was helping her with the mammoth move to Singita. He'd rescheduled clients so that he could be with her. Support her.

Leaving his ranch in the care of his workers, and travelling north with her household and all her workers.

Not one of those who crossed the Zambezi remained behind except the dead.

They would have to return to FA Ranch for more of their possessions, but for now, they could make do. Albert had been with Ashley and Zol in Kevin's chopper weeks before when they had flown over Singita and assessed the situation from the air and then landed for a ground inspection.

'Put everything over there,' she instructed, and pointed to an area that Zol had suggested they base the new camp on. They were remaining around the original home site on Singita, but planned to keep it as wild as they could.

She remembered, after the fly-in visit to her ranch, how they had made a list of all the equipment they thought necessary and essential to be within the first convoy, and had packed accordingly. After a much-needed stop in Lusaka to buy in a few new items she'd had to order, they had carried on their slow journey north.

Singita would have to be totally rebuilt, but it would be therapeutic and significant, representing the slow rebuilding of their shattered lives. In a way, it was a fitting journey's end for the weary travellers.

The land and its people could recover together.

There had been few local Taabwe people in the area to protest her bringing in her motley group of illegal workers, just as Scott had predicted, so one hurdle was passed without too much fuss. She'd learned that they were also referred to as Sila, or Shilas in Zambia, when they crossed over the lake. Their tribe name meant 'to be tied up', from the days when their tribe was besieged by slavers. Ashley knew they would soon come to her looking for work, trying to avoid the urban rat-race and stay in the bush areas. But that was another problem for another day.

Ashley stood on the back flap of her *bakkie*, Zol and Gertrude next to her, as was Elliott. Her workers gathered around.

'We are home,' she said. 'Singita is where we put down our roots again, and we make this our home. No more travelling.'

The workers responded with a loud cheer.

'We have a lot of work ahead of us. You all know what teams you have been split up into so that you can complete your different tasks, like toilet digging, making fires to heat water to bathe. Some ladies will help Lisa with the kitchen fires and cooking, and by tonight, we'll have a boma around us and the animals, just in case there are still predators out there. The anti-poaching guards already have their schedules as to their night watch, and soon they will begin their massive jobs of walking our fence line and snare clearing.'

She saw many of her workers nodding, listening intently to what she had to say. She grinned. 'But tonight, after all this is done, we'll have a celebration, a welcome home party. A big communal bonfire and a dance, because we have finished our travelling. But before we all start our settling in, I wanted to say thank you to everyone for believing in us, the Decker's and the Ndhlovu's, as a family, for making the trip from Zimbabwe, for crossing the Zambezi, and for helping to complete the camp site at Boss Albert's quickly so that we could come home to Singita once we knew we had land for a new home.'

She listened to the cheering and watched the *toi-toiing* before the workers broke up into their designated groups and began the tasks assigned to them. She jumped nimbly from the *bakkie*. Lisa passed her Paige, who was now fussing from the noise.

'You have your team already set up, Lisa. Make sure you have enough food for tonight's feast. I don't think it'll go on long, we're all tired from travelling, but I for one am looking forward to sorting out our new home.'

Lisa smiled. 'Thank you, Madam Ashley, for being our madam.'

'Oh, Lisa,' Ashley said as her eyes filled with tears, the emotion raw. 'Thank you, too. I couldn't do this without everyone who supports me.'

The two women parted ways as Lisa went to sort out the meals for the night and Ashley to check on the progress of the tasks assigned. Paige was soon asleep, wound tightly in a towel on her back, as Ashley carried her daughter African style.

Within two days, Ashley had the first of their diesel water pumps fitted to the abandoned borehole and working. Fresh, sweet water gushed up from the ground and filled the rusted water tank that had new silicone patches to plug the holes. Ashley hoped the twenty-year warranty promise on the silicone container would hold true, or at least until she could afford to buy a new tank. There was money, but she didn't want to waste it, and Gertrude and Zol were still being secretive about the money coming in. Ashley wondered what was so African about its origins that they kept her in the dark. At that moment she knew that no matter what it was, so long as it wasn't drug or arms running, she would just be happy knowing that the money was there.

She looked at the tank again. They had been lucky. Only a single spray of bullets arcing upwards had penetrated it. Other tanks, found further away from the burnt-out homestead had many more, and one had been blown totally apart, as if someone had put a hand grenade inside it. The twisted metal base remained half concreted into the footings but was lethally sharp and savage looking. Ironically, a small nest of mice had made a home inside one of the pieces, a safe haven from large predators, serving as a savage reminder that all was not as tranquil as it seemed in the new land.

The war that had raged in the area might have ended years before, but the regrowth and recovery took time.

Miraculously, the shaft, sunk deep into the earth so many years ago, and the iron rods that had once pumped the water attached to the remnants of a windmill, were undamaged. Ashley found she didn't need to rebore, once she had retrieved them. Setting up the pump and getting the water was the first of many important steps in their new life.

The children had frolicked in the fresh water, bathed and celebrated together with the adults. The small miracle that they had fresh water near their camp and no longer needed to haul buckets of water from the nearby debris-filled dam to the fire for boiling was a relief felt by all. Now they only needed to boil water if they wished to bathe, while they waited for the donkey boiler to be built and underground pipes laid.

Zol had drawn a rough layout of the ranch, including the old homestead area, and they had decided to base their new camp just a little east of the wreckage. So far it had proved a wise choice, utilising the resources that were already on hand. They would be able to use the old home site later.

Once the water was flowing from the pump, they removed the tree trunks that formed a natural barrier in the broken dam wall and drained it. Using the tractors and physical manpower, they'd waded into the mud to rescue the fish and placed them in feeding troughs as they cleared the debris from the dam. Finally, they'd dug it deeper and painstakingly repaired the wall with the homemade gabion's holding stones, piling the sand back up and reconstructing a new and sturdy dam wall.

She had diverted the water from the pump through irrigation lines into the dam, and released the fish. So far, they had only a small amount of water in the dam, just enough to keep the fish going until it could fill naturally.

It was hard to believe how much they had accomplished in a week. There had been a few storms, and there was a good stream of water making its way into the renovated dam. Their timing couldn't have been more perfect if they'd planned it.

Perhaps Singita really was a place of miracles.

Ashley smelled breakfast. She looked at her diary, two months had passed since they arrived at Singita. Brock and Paige were already seven months old. She'd heard Lisa come in earlier and remove them from their cots, change them and take them to the kitchen for a bottle and to be fed. The fact they could now sit helped Lisa and Ashley, and their highchairs were in full use. Although they still loved to throw food around, more of it went inside their little mouths than on the floor.

Her stomach grumbled. Abandoning her paperwork, she walked slowly towards where the food was being served at the communal kitchen on the edge of the huge boma. From day one, it had housed the cattle they'd trucked in as far as they dared on the derelict road, then walked them slowly the rest of the way. Initially they had been let out to graze and brought back into the safety of the camp at night. Now a new kraal had been made for the cattle further away from the living quarters, where the big emerald-bottomed flies and busy dung beetles were welcome to the constant piles of cow poo, and the loud noise of the cattle was removed from their night's listening. The boma had been swept clean and was now treated as part of the communal space attached to the kitchen.

The kitchen had since become the meeting place of the whole camp each mealtime, then at night, they entertained each other and the children put on plays, practised during their school hours with Gertrude. The anti-poaching units gathered here for briefings before and after their patrols to exchange information, and it was the place where Ashley sat for hours, watching her twins as they gazed at and started to play alongside those children orphaned by the crossing that had ultimately taken her husband too.

The festive air around the breakfast table was always wonderful, and

Ashley now knew each face, name and history of everyone within her small tribe. Her family.

'Hello, Madam.' Vicky, one of those orphaned, called to her, as she ate her breakfast, dished up by Lisa. They had named the different houses, and the children had spent time making them carved wooden signs for the front doors. Vicky lived in Lallapanzi—'come sleep here' was a good name for the extended family that Lisa and Elliott had made. Four orphaned girls of varying ages—Sheila being the eldest, Helen and Mary, then Vicky, the youngest—and two small boys, neither of whom were school age yet.

They had been lucky there were not more. The adolescent Philippi was taken in too, and under the wing of Lallapanzi, after his mother had died of the thinning disease within a month of joining them at Singita. Ashley grimaced. AIDS was already taking its ugly toll on her workers.

Lisa waved at Ashley, who sat down at the end of one makeshift table and homemade bench, to join in the simple mealie-meal porridge breakfast. Lisa dished some onto a plate for Ashley, and added a large dollop of butter on the top. She walked over to where Ashley sat.

'Eat up, Madam. You are looking too much like a foreign woman and not like us Africans.' She laughed as she made a well-rounded figure with her hands.

'Thanks, Lisa,' Ashley said.

'I heard shots last night,' Lisa said. 'The anti-poaching unit say anything to you this morning?'

Elliott said, 'Not yet.'

Ashley reached for her plate. 'Zol will be taking their debrief today, when he gets back, but yesterday the amount of snares brought in was a new record.'

'So I heard. Incredible that there is so much poaching and yet supposedly so few people in the area. Something is not right,' Gertrude said.

'Perhaps. Perhaps not. Some were so old they had rusted through. What is unsettling is the newer ones. I worry about the origin of the poachers. Are they coming across Lake Tanganyika and moving freely around this area? Or are they locals from Zambia and poaching has become a way of life to them?' She took a sip from her hot chocolate. 'When are you and Elliott going to get married? Have you set a date? You need to give those orphans something to celebrate. Their adoptive parents getting married would be a big deal, you know.'

Elliott looked down but smiled.

Lisa smiled broadly. 'Soon. Elliott and Zol are worried about the albino spoiling the wedding. They said it's too quiet. It makes no difference to our orphan clan if we are married or not. Nothing will change, we'll still be one big family. To us it will just be a big feast, and a party.'

'We can't live in fear of him and let him rule our lives. Life's too short, you know that. You need to grab life in both hands and hold on to the precious time you have. Losing Scott taught me that.'

'You were lucky that you found him. He loved you, and just look at those children he gave you. You must be happy for them.'

Ashley looked to where the children congregated. Brock was on Sheila's lap being bounced on his chubby legs. He seemed to love the feel of his own weight and wanted to stand a lot more these days. Paige lay on a blanket, still content to bat at the mobile above her and make happy noises while holding onto anything she could. The live doll of the children's area.

'Oh Lisa, I am happy with my life and my beautiful children. But I do miss him. It's like a part of me is waiting for him to return, part of me is still missing. Logic reminds me I still have his ashes in a small wooden box in my house, but it is not the same as having him here in the flesh.' Tears pricked her eyes, and the dull throbbing headache that had lately become the norm drummed a soft beat at the base of her neck.

'About dates. You nearly ready to put the Boss under a tree? Let him rest?' Lisa asked. 'He needs to cross over.'

'I will, soon.' Ashley rolled her head around, rubbing her stiff neck with her fingers and massaging her tight muscles.

'You still got that headache?' Gertrude asked.

'Loud and proud.'

'I'm not surprised with the stress we are living under. What I wouldn't do for a massage.'

'Now that's a great idea. When we open the safari lodge we'll have a day spa included in the package. Many lodges are doing that now, as part of the pamper package deal,' Ashley said.

'Work, you're always thinking work,' Gertrude said.

'No it's not work, it's next year's groceries.'

Ashley noticed Tobias walking purposefully towards her. The cattleman had his head bowed low and didn't look happy, but he was definitely coming in her direction. It was as if something had sucked the life from his step, and Ashley suspected it wasn't the heat.

'Tobias, come, have a cold drink with us. Tell me what's wrong, *Madala?*'

'Madam Ashley,' Tobias acknowledged her as he nodded.

The old traditions did not stop easily in these people, thought Ashley, who had got used to their customs. She nodded back.

'There's a poacher here. Bring your gun, Madam. Someone hurt the cattle. Last night they were in the kraal and were safe, no lions came, nothing. So today we herded them back out, but then my youngest son, Philemon, he came running to me. He says the one big red bull is hurt. Someone *umsiko* the back legs so he can't walk away, then they cut his throat.'

Elliott sprang up immediately. 'I'll look at it,' he said. 'Check your weapon is ready.'

Ashley patted the holster on her hip. 'I'm armed.'

'Zol is out with the anti-poaching group on the far side of the ranch. I'll radio him, then meet you here in a moment.' Elliott walked towards the *bakkie* and the mobile radio.

'I don't like this, not with the guards so far away on patrol,' Ashley said. 'Gertrude, Lisa, come. Let's get you armed with the elephant gun, or better yet, that automatic shotgun of Scott's while we're out checking the kraal. I don't want anyone sneaking into this camp like we had at FA Ranch,' she said, already retreating towards her home.

Ashley went inside and unlocked the gun safe, which had been one of the things she'd instinctively placed in her bedroom area, just as it had been in Delmonica. Reaching inside the metal monstrosity of a safe, she took out the trusty .303 and looked at the .458 Ruger, which everyone referred to as 'the elephant gun'. She'd seen firsthand that this rifle could bring down an elephant in full charge. She remembered her initial sighting of the slaughtered elephant when she'd first came to Africa, and Scott had showed her this rifle and told her what it could do.

She grabbed a handful of extra bullets and shoved them into her pocket. The magazine held three thick stubby rounds, but Ashley wished it housed more. Then she stopped. She put both the ammunition and the gun back. This was a man, not an elephant. She slung the .303 over her shoulder and reached in for the shotgun. Outlawed in some countries, the automatic shotgun was more a weapon used by mobsters during shoot-ups rather than a farmer in Zimbabwe–Zambia, she reminded herself silently. But this shotgun could stop most things, though perhaps not a raging elephant. It was a lethal but not accurate weapon. She pocketed a box of birdshot from the ammo shelf, relocked the safe and turned to re-join the others.

'Here, take this,' she said to Gertrude, holding out the .303 to her. Gertrude was sitting in a chair with Brock on her lap and Florence held Paige. It was obvious that they understood the gravity of the danger lurking in close proximity. She handed Lisa the shotgun and the box of ammo. Lisa immediately slipped the seven shells into place.

Ashley put her hand on the 9mm on her hip. 'Okay, I'm armed and have spare ammo. Gertrude, here are your spares.'

Gertrude smiled. 'Ashley, did you really think Zol wouldn't arm me?' She flashed a 9mm of her own, hidden under her loose-fitting shirt. 'But if anything comes near the perimeter of the camp, I can now drop it through this scope without moving out my chair,' she said as she ran her hand up and down the .303's barrel. She turned to the children gathered around. 'Girls, keep close to us. I've explained what to do if you see anyone. Scream loudly.'

Ashley looked at the children. They were so young to be exposed to this type of danger. She hoped that it would all be okay, whoever it was, but her stomach churned at the thought of confronting the albino. She turned and walked away to investigate further with Elliott and Zol.

The sky was streaked with pink and gold, the sun disappearing, when Zol, Elliott and Ashley called out from the trees. 'It's us! Don't shoot, Lisa.' Ashley understood that they were silhouetted against the trees behind them, and it would be difficult for the people in the camp to identify them.

Ashley sat down at the dining table, where the women were seated. She reached out her hand and ran it over Paige's baby cheek and then Brock's, who were being fed in their highchairs by Lisa and Vicky. Gertrude had control of her four girls. Elliott sat down next to Lisa and Zol sat with Gertrude.

'What did you find?' Gertrude asked.

'There was a trespasser, but he didn't want any meat. He didn't take anything except the heart from the bull. We followed the spoor to the reserve, but we lost him. We left Kwiella's team searching for him.'

Ashley looked at Elliott. His worried expression had grown worse. He wasn't managing to hide his emotions from the women, and Ashley knew what was about to come out. It had been all they could discuss since leaving the camp that morning.

'Spit it out, Elliott. What else?' Lisa asked.

He looked at her. 'Lisa, how come you always know when I don't tell you everything?'

'Call it women's intuition, maybe because I love you. Now, what else?'

But it was Zol who answered. 'The way that the best bull was picked, and the slashed tendons on his legs and only his heart taken, it's a signature calling card from the albino.'

Having Zol tell them brought the reality of the situation home to everyone. Ashley felt the blood drain from her face. She sunk into a heap, and cradled her head in her arms on the table. Gertrude reached over and patted her back.

'You okay?'

'Exhausted.' She paused as she lifted her head. 'I've asked Tobias to bring his family and the cattle back into the camp tonight. We can't protect everyone spread out over two areas. We are a team of anti-poaching guards down already, they're too far away to come back tonight. We just sent Kwiella's group to follow a spoor that might find him, but they will take time to do that. So we are down to one set of anti-poaching guards, and us.'

'We have discussed the situation already while walking home,' Zol said. 'The right decision has been made to gather together closely because, if it is the albino, he'll be more angry than last time. Especially since we escaped Zimbabwe, then left FA Ranch instead of staying the night, so he's had to find us again. That albino, he's unpredictable and I'm not sure what he'll do.'

The cattle were worth thousands but so was the new camp: the beginnings of the homestead and all their furniture and the farm implements, the tractors, the harvesters and ploughs, everything that had been replaced by insurance when fire ravaged them on FA Ranch. They were all just material possessions, but the animals, they could be made to suffer, even worse than the one bull had already. The albino had a track record to be afraid of and Ashley wasn't taking any chances now they suspected that he was around.

'We need to move the cattle back into this boma,' Elliott said. 'We have the generator and we can floodlight the area if there's trouble.'

Lisa said quietly, 'Tobias is old, but he fought during the wars, and his wife Annie. We can give them weapons. And perhaps easy ones for his eldest sons? They will not leave those cattle. Tobias has seen that herd grow from nothing to its prime in Zimbabwe, and he hopes to see it back to that standard again. You can bring those cattle in, but Tobias will stay with them during the night now that they are threatened.'

'There are a few more rifles in the safe. We can arm everyone who came from Delmonica. But not the newer staff, I still don't know them well enough.'

Elliott and Zol nodded.

'Drink, eat, you will need this to get you through the night,' Lisa said as she placed a mug of hot coffee and a plate of stew with mealie-meal porridge in front of each of them.

They ate in silence, contemplating the night ahead.

Ashley watched as Elliott left the camp to help herd the cattle. He carried three extra rifles. The makeshift boma for the cattle was ready, and the floodlights illuminated the area much like a stadium in the middle of the bush. The generators hummed softly. They hadn't had to make a too secure fence for the cattle as they were used to being handled on a daily basis, and although the Brahman had a reputation for being violent and unreasonable, Scott had always claimed that those were only the feral ones.

The sky had turned an inky blue before they heard the first sign that the cattle were on the move, their low bellows at being disturbed echoing loudly on the crisp night air. They trudged into the camp and were soon kraaled together safely, milling around in aimless circles and mooing softly as a few sat and chewed their cuds and others began to settle for the night.

Tobias's wife, Annie, sat on the corner of the boma, at the point allocated to her to guard. She ran her hand along the barrel of the .458 Ruger that had been issued to her.

Ashley's stomach flipped. The grotesque picture of someone who looked like a granny having to arm herself against danger brought bile to her throat.

Despite the fact that Elliott sat not three paces away from her, she was scared. 'Scott,' she whispered into the darkness, needing him now more than ever. The kidnapping, the day she gave birth to the twins, Scott's death; never had she felt this utter terror. She was responsible for all the people on her ranch. The albino was here, and from past experience, she knew that anyone who got in his way would be collateral damage. The danger had followed her here because she had stood up in court and her testimony had sent him to prison. Zol had a history with him too, but their animosity didn't match the all-out obsession the albino had shown towards her. She double-checked her 9mm was at her hip, and she silently unclipped the strap on the top of the holster.

Her brow struck in a permanent frown, she looked at her sleeping babies in their carrycots next to where she sat, on her allocated corner on the other side of the camp from Annie. 'I'll die rather than have him touch either of you,' she said quietly to them.

He was not getting his hands on her kids.

Ashley looked over to where she knew Gertrude sat at the opposite corner of the kitchen building. She didn't have another adult with her, and it worried Ashley that Zol had had to go out into the night, leaving his family behind. But he was the best tracker they had, a man of the bush and a worthy adversary for the albino. Besides, she couldn't have kept Zol in the boundaries of the camp if she'd tried. He was unstoppable, and determined to get the albino.

Florence was still awake. She had heard her talking to her mum a few moments before, but she could imagine the other three asleep in camp-out style, on mats on the floor. Ashley wondered if it would have been better to keep the kids closer together. 'Don't second-guess yourself now, Ash,' she reprimanded herself.

Zol and the one full unit of anti-poaching guards were out there in the black night patrolling, looking for the albino, ensuring that he didn't get into the camp. To any of the women. Or the children. Or her.

Time ticked by. Second by second. Each one feeling like an eternity.

The star formations in the sky changed over their watch on the dark African plains, sliding westward. Nothing stirred around the small party on the ranch.

The seconds ticked by into hours.

. . .

Dawn broke, brilliant in pastel shades of promise, and the cattle began their restless stamping of feet, bellowing, and generally wanting to be set free.

Ashley strode across to the breakfast table. Lisa had the coffee ready, and was handing out steaming cups to all the adults and to Tobias's oldest son Philemon. Zol returned from yet another perimeter check as the dawn light enabled him to inspect the boma and the surrounding areas. There were no signs anyone had been near them during the night. Kwiella had checked in from the fence line of the reserve, and there had been no movement there either.

The patrols had seen nothing.

'It's like he wants us to be scared, to know he's coming, but not know when,' Zol said to Ashley.

Elliott nodded his agreement.

Lisa yawned loudly, putting her hand in front of her face. 'I remember, as a little girl, I was more scared of his reputation and what he could do than anything else,' she said. 'It's the uncertainly that kills you, as much as his deeds.'

Ashley frowned.

Annie had finished her coffee and rusks. 'Come on, life goes on. These cattle need to go to water and then graze for the day.' The older women didn't look any worse for having a bad night's sleep.

'You should try to keep them as close together as you can,' Elliott instructed the two herd boys. 'Keep your rifles, and if something goes wrong, fire two shots straight into the air in quick succession and we will come looking for you. Got it?'

They both nodded and solemnly went about their task, whistling to the cattle.

'You have good kids there, Annie,' Ashley said.

'Yes, but when they marry, will they stay obedient and respectful like that? Not likely.' She shook her head as she walked to help her sons with the cattle, the Ruger slung over her shoulder as if it weighed nothing.

CHAPTER 28

The next two days and nights passed without incident. The camp reeked of cattle dung once more. Ashley and Zol were beginning to wonder if the bull had been killed for strong *muti* and not by the albino.

None of the women went anywhere alone. Always in pairs. The children didn't leave the confines of the homestead camp.

Suspended in their own lives, they waited for their silent assailant.

They slept in shifts and, better organised than the first night, they sat in pairs. Gertrude and Ashley were together, and their kids slept between them. Elliott stayed with her, as always.

Early before the light of the fourth day had begun to show itself in the sky, Ashley heard a grunting sound. It was almost lion-like, but there was something odd about it. Looking at Elliott, she saw he was already alert, his hand ready on his rifle.

Ashley threw a small stone at Gertrude, who woke with a jolt but didn't make a sound. Ashley pointed to her ears.

Gertrude listened. 'Lion?' she mouthed.

Ashley shook her head. The sound was similar to a lion, but not quite the same. It was almost throaty, like the animal had something broken in its throat. Not one hundred per cent right.

The cattle were shifting restlessly, but it was too early for them to be waking. Something was out there in the dark, spooking the Brahmans.

Ashley took her 9mm out of the holster and slid the safety catch off. She saw Gertrude lift her rifle and sweep over the camp with her telescopic site. Elliott was on his feet performing a similar action.

Ashley had learned that although the scopes were not made for night vision, one could always see better through them than with the naked eye, even in the dark. She lifted the radio and tapped it three times.

Zol was out there, and so was Sipho's team, on sentry duty. They tapped back to tell the ladies they acknowledged their distress call. Ashley silently thanked Scott and Zol for saving so much of their equipment from Delmonica. She relied heavily on the radios on the new ranch.

The cattle began to mill around, backing away from one part of the temporary fence in the darkest part of the camp. Ashley heard a small, almost inaudible bump from the area of the kitchen building where Tobias and Annie were standing guard. She strained her eyes to see what was happening, but she could make nothing out. Elliott flicked the generator switch and the floodlights blinked on, illuminating the kraal in the middle of the camp. Extra lights had been found during the last few days to enhance those already placed around the camp. It was not quite daylight strength, but close. Their major weakness was the amount of extension wire needed to run the light in series together. The exposed cords were easily detectable, but then they hadn't designed their new home compound as a fortress, just as a safari camp. Large outdoor sports-style lighting was a foreign invasion into their plans for peace and tranquillity.

The cattle, now totally confused, glared directly into the lights and complained as if being branded by a hot iron. They crushed towards the building, no longer uneasy but with blind fear causing them to panic. The excruciating sound of an animal bellowing in pain cut the night.

'There,' Elliott said as he spotted the yellow-haired intruder trying to push his way through the cattle towards them. Towards Ashley.

'He's in the cattle,' he shouted into his radio.

Pop. One light was shot out. Rodney obviously had a high calibre accurate rifle.

Clink, tinkle. Another light out.

One line faded, then another, randomly shutting off the lights. Obviously, someone had tampered with them.

Another one failed.

'Shit,' Ashley swore, as the one closest to their building dimmed down to a dull yellow and then vanished. The darkness seemed blacker than before.

She was night blind.

Elliott carried an older FN rifle along with a 9mm, but he couldn't shoot at the intruder who dodged between the cattle, crouching low, because he could hurt the cattle by mistake. He pulled his knife out of his belt, ready to defend Ashley.

The cattle broke through their temporary barrier in their frenzied scampering and funnelled out of the kraal, bellowing to each other. Spooked beyond reasonable behaviour, they stampeded into the night.

Ashley and Gertrude had the six children between them, and sat facing outwards. They were in darkness. All lights in their direction had blown. Gertrude threw a blanket over the kids.

Florence woke up. 'Mummy,' she called.

'Sshh ... hush, be quiet and hide under there,' Gertrude whispered back to her.

Ashley squinted in the darkness. She could see nothing now the cattle were thinning out.

Elliott called softly to them. 'Madam Ashley, Gertrude, you all right?'

'Elliott, where is he?' Ashley whispered back.

'He was in with the cattle. I don't know where he is now,' Elliott said. 'We stay here, it's a good defensive position.'

They sat, almost frozen to the spot, waiting. With their eyes again accustomed to the dark, they searched for any sign of movement. The cattle had all filed out into the night and only the unsettled dust remained, silently drifting back down to the dry earth from where it had been disturbed.

Ashley wondered briefly how many of their cattle would fall prey to night hunters, but then brought her mind sharply back to their present predicament. The people in the camp were more important than the livestock.

Nothing moved in the camp. Ashley, Gertrude and Elliott remained vigilant, adrenaline keeping their bodies primed for action.

A few minutes ticked past.

Zol, with Sipho's team right behind him, rushed into the camp. Zol waved to Ashley and signalled that he was doing a sweep of the camp. His team split up quickly and disappeared.

Elliott stayed with her.

Ashley could make out Lisa sitting at her post with the shotgun and could see she was waving to her. She waved back. Then she looked to where Tobias and Annie were stationed. They were not there.

Dread flooded Ashley. Where were they?

Already it was light enough to see further than before, the natural light growing in strength as the dawn lit the sky in her splendour. Ashley stood up.

'Gertrude, you see Tobias and Annie?'

'No, hang on,' Gertrude said. Standing too, she looked across the compound. 'I don't see them.'

'Annie, Tobias,' Ashley called.

Gertrude bellowed, 'Tooooobbbiiiiiaaaaassss, Aaaaaannnnniiiiiee-eeeeee.'

Silence.

Zol spoke on the radio. 'I've found them. The albino got to them.'

'I'll stay with the kids,' Gertrude said. 'Go!'

Ashley and Elliott rushed over, their weapons drawn and ready. But guns were of no use. Annie and Tobias were obviously dead. Annie's throat had been cut and Tobias was lying on top of her, as though trying to protect her even in death. A hunting knife buried to the handle and into his heart protruded from his back. Their rifles had been taken.

Ashley stared at the couple, tears running down her cheeks.

'Damn him to hell,' Zol cursed.

'What about the boys?' Ashley asked, looking at Elliott, his fatigue showing on his face.

'They broke their cover and ran after the cattle into the night.'

'Sipho, you and Dumalong, find them,' Zol instructed. 'James, stay with Elliott and guard the women and children. The rest of the team, with me.' Shifting his rifle to sit comfortably at his hip, he began following the tracks leading away from the corpses.

Half an hour, Sipho radioed Ashley. 'The boys are safe, they are with the cattle now. They'll put them into their outer kraal after they've had water. There are a few missing and we are helping look for those, but the main body of the herd is intact.'

'Thank you for letting me know,' she said. 'Stay with the boys, make sure they are safe.'

'Yes, Madam,' Sipho said.

Ashley sat down next to Annie. 'This is my fault,' she said quietly.

Elliott looked at her. 'Madam Ashley, it's not your fault. You did everything to keep your people safe.'

'If I were not here, he wouldn't have come to Singita,' she said.

'If you weren't here, he still would have attacked, only we wouldn't have had a hope in protecting anyone against him. This albino, he is the nightmare that legends are made from. He has haunted Zol forever. Many good men have gone after him, and all have failed. You have done everything you can to help protect your people. They know that. Tobias and Annie, they believed that you were worth making a new home with, and even after so many years, picking up weapons again for. Their deaths are not your fault. They are the albino's.'

'We have armed him,' Ashley said quietly, her voice thick with emotion. 'He needed weapons and I opened the safe and handed them to him on a silver platter. Look at these two old people, how can I have given them rifles?' She used both her hands to point to the couple. 'Now they are dead.' Anger began bubbling through her voice, and she began to shake.

'Madam, these two people were an active couple in the resistance against communist invasion during the war of independence. Tobias is decorated many times by the Rhodesian army with medals, and Annie, she was one of his soldiers. He called her his "floppy". They were fighters; you made them proud to die as soldiers, and not herders of someone else's cattle. You gave these two people a death with dignity, never think otherwise.' Elliott shook his head. 'The attack appears to have been only to get weapons.'

Ashley stared at the dead couple. In a perverse way it was so romantic that Tobias had thrown himself onto his wife to try to protect her.

'Mum.' Florence called at a volume that surprised even Ashley. She turned, and Florence was near them, having crossed the camp to where they all stood. 'Mum, can we come out from under the blanket now please?'

'Yes,' Gertrude called back to her, 'but stay together and go back to the building, stay inside.'

And it was as if a child calling out pulled everyone back to their respective duties. Lisa got the fire going again and made coffee. Gertrude and Ashley attended to their children.

Elliott, with help from a few of the farm helpers, got the old couple cleaned up and ready for burial, so that when their sons came home, they wouldn't see the violence of their deaths, just that their parents were taken from them.

He put plasters over their eyes to keep them closed, and bound their chins up with bandages. He tried to stitch Annie's throat closed, so that in the after world, before her crossing over, she'd still be able to breathe. Then he washed them, removing as much of the splatter as possible, and wrapped them in their own *karosses*. Then he laid them out in their traditional burial position.

He did not eat breakfast, and it was nearly lunchtime when he'd finished getting them ready for burial. He covered them with wild palm fronds from down near the river, as there were no banana leaves around to keep the bodies cool in the African heat. He walked out of the makeshift mortuary and continued slowly out of camp, towards the cattle kraal. It was time to inform the boys about their parents. Isaac, as the oldest son, would be called upon to perform the burial rights, but Philemon could take over some of those responsibilities if they wanted to share them.

Ashley's heart broke and an involuntary sob escaped from her throat as she watched Elliott leave. She sighed deeply and thanked God that it hadn't been her. Who would look after her children if something happened to her? Her children would have been sent to Australia, to a foreign country to them, to live with her sister. Someone they didn't even know. Having them taken away from Africa didn't sit comfortably. Scott would have wanted them to grow up in Africa, just like he had. Yes, compared to Australia it was a whole different upbringing, but it was one she wanted for her kids. One she had chosen to stay and fight for.

Tears filled her eyes but she blinked them away. One thing she had learned in Africa, it was no use breaking down about things. The only way to make them better was to fix whatever you could control yourself, and accept the rest. Annie and Tobias's deaths were unfixable.

She would always hold herself responsible for their deaths, and she prayed that they would forgive her as they rested in peace together. The only thing she could do was to ensure that their children were fully educated, given chances in life and treated fairly. She had to focus on what she could fix, and that was making sure no one else died out here.

'Gertrude, I don't want to have to ask the government to step in. We're going to have to handle the albino ourselves,' Ashley said as they sat together quietly, waiting for the boys to come in from the cattle.

'Do you believe Singita is worth fighting for?' Gertrude asked.

'I thought Delmonica was, but Scott always said that you can't fight a corrupt government.' She paused. She didn't want the albino to win; she didn't want to be driven out again. This was their home. The government had made it clear that they would back up her as a white farmer, with force if necessary. They needed the commercial crop growers, and the income the safari companies brought in helped the country. The Zambian government were not idiots. They had seen what had happened with Zimbabwe's redistribution of land in the snatch and grab program, and were doing everything they could to try to prevent it happening in their own country. 'But here, the Zambian government is behind us with support. And yes, Singita is more than worth fighting for.'

Gertrude nodded.

'Perhaps we could contact them and ask them to lend us an army guard to help our units?' But even as she said it, Ashley realised how impossible it was to involve the authorities. When the troops arrived, they would find a ranch filled with illegal immigrants.

Gertrude shook her head. 'We all have to die sometime,' she said. And then she looked at Ashley. 'But I think we can kill him first.'

Ashley grunted. As did Lisa.

They were interrupted as movement caught their eyes. The boys walking either side of Elliott had just appeared in the camp. The women fell silent, as they watched Elliott lead them to the makeshift mortuary. Too soon they could hear the boys' hollow sobs, as their world was torn apart.

'Food, the boys need food,' Lisa said as she busied herself getting yet another meal together.

As they all sat at the table, Elliott broached the subject of the burial ground.

'We need to dig the holes for Tobias and Annie,' he said quietly, speaking respectfully of the dead. 'Have you any idea if they had a favourite place on this new ranch?' he asked Isaac.

'My mother said once that she knew she would die on this ranch. This was going to be her final home. She wanted to be buried on the small hill by the lake, so she could look out over the water and the whole plain below,' Isaac answered, and Philemon nodded his agreement with his brother.

'Well then, we need to find her a resting place where she can sit with your father, and they can do just that,' Elliott said, and he drank the last of his coffee.

He checked that James was guarding Ashley and the women, then he set out in the *bakkie* with the boys. They came back soon, and Isaac started the tractor and collected the digger section, his younger brother riding shotgun on the mudguard above the huge wheel. They had obviously found a resting place. Elliott drove away again, alone in the *bakkie.*

The women made a collection of wildflowers and leaves to place on the graves while Ashley constructed a double coffin from their building materials. Lastly, she fashioned a single wooden cross and with a soldering iron burned in: *Tobias and Annie, together, in love for all eternity.*

When the men returned, they had a shower outside and then loaded the bodies into their coffin on the back of the *bakkie.* Lisa put the flowers inside the coffin so that they could always smell the bushlands. Ashley closed the box but didn't nail it down completely, as she was worried about its weight. A double coffin had been a romantic idea, but it wasn't a practical size. It sat on the iron seats moulded in the back, so it was unsteady.

They climbed onto the *bakkie,* Ashley driving, with Paige and Brock in their car seats, and Gertrude and her youngest two in the front cab as well. Lisa and the older of Gertrude's girls went in the back with Elliott and the orphaned boys, sitting around the coffin awkwardly, trying hard to show respect and not sit on top of it. Lisa and Elliott's family of orphans had climbed in too. Another three *bakkies* followed behind, their backs packed with workers. Most of them had done the overland trek through the Zimbabwean bush, but there was one or two who had joined the ranch since. Everyone was mourning the loss of the old couple.

Slowly, Ashley drove to the gravesite on a small crest looking out over the plains below. Vusi's unit was standing guard, the six anti-poaching guards sweating under the strong sunshine, but standing proudly in tribute to the older couple. They must have run all day to get back to the ranch in time for the funeral. Eight workers helped the boys to manoeuvre the coffin.

Ashley nailed the coffin closed and they lowered it into the grave with ropes, with Annie and Tobias's bodies facing the lake, so they could look at the water and the vast landscape. The group said simple prayers for them. Without a minister or a sangoma it was difficult, and everyone looked to Ashley to lead the service in English. They sang the first verse of Psalm 23, as that was all that most of them knew, and then they sung Nkosi sikelela Africa.

When it was over, Isaac and Philemon climbed onto the tractor and used the digger to fill in the grave. When they had all finished piling rocks on top, Ashley placed the cross on the grave.

'Thank you, Madam, it's nice. Thank you.' Philemon said, and after a while he walked back to the tractor to sit on the wheel arch. Together the boys began their journey home to the camp.

'If they stick together, they'll be okay,' Elliott said.

Ashley nodded. 'I know, but it's still so hard to watch them go through the hurt.'

'Come on, the roast should be almost done, and at least we can give them a good funeral feast,' Lisa said as she turned and walked back to the *bakkie*.

The others followed as the funeral procession made its way back to the homestead.

Vusi's unit melted back into the bush. They had a perimeter to patrol.

Zol and the rest of Sipho's unit were still chasing shadows of the albino.

Lisa cooked a traditional burial feast that night and, despite the worry of another attack, they had their feast, minus the traditional beer—they needed everyone to have their wits about them. The cattle had been brought back into the makeshift kraal, and the lights that could be fixed had been repaired.

In addition to checking everyone's rifles, Elliott had sharpened Isaac and Philemon's hunting knives on his oilstone and made sure they were razor sharp. Then he took one of his own from his belt and handed it to Lisa.

'This was my first knife. Don't lose it,' he told her.

'Well it's not a ring, but I will accept it as it's a whole lot more practical,' she said, and she hugged him.

Ashley was so tired she wanted to drop where they sat sorting out their roster. Gertrude offered to take first watch, and Ashley was eternally grateful. She could grab a little sleep. Although it was years ago, power naps had got her through university and they could get her through this.

They changed their set-up within the camp. Ashley had called the whole ranch together to discuss their plan.

No longer would they stay in smaller groups, but they would all be together. Having more people together on watch would hopefully make it harder for the albino to hurt anyone.

They put all the children in the boma building in the middle of the homestead, and all the adults slept around them, with teams of people taking turns on watch. Three four-hour watches during the night, starting at six and ending at six.

As morning dawned, everyone sighed, their relief evident. There had been no disturbance during the night.

'It's not good,' Elliott said. 'He's waiting for us to split up and make it easier for him again.'

The silence of those around him confirmed their agreement.

Shortly after breakfast, Zol and Sipho's unit returned empty-handed. The albino had vanished into the thick African bush.

CHAPTER 29

Three months had passed since Tobias and Annie's funeral and things were slowly returning to normal, with only a few changes made as a result of the albino's attack. The cattle had been returned to their kraal outside the homestead area and Isaac and Philemon had taken over their father's job, helped by four extra men so the cattle could be guarded around the clock. Electric lights had been installed in the kraal, and they had their own generator to create the electrical current that now ran through the fence that kept them in and predators out. The electrical lines were buried deep within the earth so that they couldn't be tampered with.

Zol had trained and formed another anti-poaching unit, headed by Robert, one of the older guards from Kwiella's unit. They were still green, but they worked well together. Now there was always a unit patrolling the homestead area.

Paige wouldn't settle. She niggled and cried, and rubbed at her sore gums with her tiny hands. She kept waking Brock, just as he began to nod off for his afternoon sleep. The slight breeze blew through Ashley's half-constructed house, lightly settling dust on the unplastered walls and rough wooden fixtures. Without the breeze, the heat could have melted light bulbs. Brock lay in his cot, covered by a mosquito net and almost asleep. Paige was on Ashley's hip.

'Teething is always hard, seems like you have a fever, darling,' Ashley said as she gently brushed her hand down her daughter's flushed cheek. She went out and sat on the concrete step, Paige snuggled into her.

Gertrude came and sat down next to Ashley. 'Her fever back?'

'Yes, and I've given her paediatric Panado already, but it hasn't come down.'

Gertrude nodded. 'Give it time, sometimes teething is difficult. I remember Florence when she was this age. She had a permanent runny nose, foul stomach, bad appetite, but once those big teeth broke through the gums, she was smiling again. And look at her, still smiling.'

Ashley smiled. 'I hope I'm as relaxed as you when they get older. She's beautiful, your Florence. Such a placid child—'

'With a hidden temper like her father, believe me,' Gertrude added.

'I bet.'

'Brock asleep?'

'Yes, thank goodness. I brought her out as she keeps waking him.'

'You look beat. Why don't I take her, and you can have a rest with Brock? I know you were up till all hours with Elliott and the other men, working on that game fence. You think it was deliberate?'

'I do. Can't think of any animal that can use bolt cutters, can you?'

The women laughed together. Gertrude said, 'How many did they think crossed into the national park?'

'A group of about ten. It's strange that they suddenly came this way, and not simply over the water, like they have been doing. Makes me think it isn't a normal poaching party, that's why I wanted the fence repair completed last night. A show of strength to them that we were aware of their movements, and we won't tolerate their poaching within the reserve area anymore.'

'I hope they don't cut it again, on their way out.'

'Don't hold your breath that they get out. Kwiella's unit followed their spoor. The Zambian government is as strict as the Zimbabwean used to be on poaching.'

Sheila, one of the older teenagers who was part of Lisa's and Elliott's Lallapanzi family, walked past.

'Hi, Madam Ashley,' she called out. 'Gertrude.' She gave a little wave.

'Hey, Sheila,' the women said together.

'Is Paige asleep, or can I take her for a walk?' Sheila asked. On cue, Paige lifted her head, rubbed her face and cried.

'Awake,' Ashley said. 'And it might do her good to have a walk around the camp. Thanks.' Ashley looked at Gertrude. 'Well, this way you and I can put our feet up, eat that small tin of chocolates I've been saving for a rainy day, and rest for half an hour.'

'Hang on Sheila, I'll just get the pram for you,' Ashley said as she went inside the house. She could hear Gertrude talking to Sheila outside. The girl had only her grandmother left from her family, and the old lady had seen their chance at a better life when she spotted the Delmonica migration through the bush outside her small home. Unfortunately, she had died of old age soon after reaching FA Ranch, and had never seen Singita. But her dream for her grandchild was attained. Sheila was nearly sixteen, and in a normal rural environment would have been married and producing offspring by now, but being part of the Decker–Ndhlovu family had changed her traditional future.

Ashley wheeled the pram out and buckled Paige in.

'Keep near the camp,' she said, and kissed Paige goodbye on her forehead.

'I always do, Madam. See you now-now.'

Ashley watched Sheila walk away happily chattering to Paige, then she went back into the house and fetched the promised chocolates. She and Gertrude sat on the step eating the sweet treats one by one, putting a few aside for Lisa. They talked about nothing and everything, just enjoying each other's company without the children biting at their heels.

The sun waned in the sky and the camp came awake after the afternoon siesta. Men called to each other as construction on one of the buildings continued. A hammer sounded bluntly on wood, and the diesel engine clicked on in the water-pump shed. The sounds of a working ranch were sweet music to Ashley's ears.

Brock woke up, as active and lively as always, calling 'Mum-mum' from his cot. Ashley knew it wasn't a true formation of words just yet, but it sounded more like 'Mum' every day. She took him into the boma to be with the other children, putting him down with the toddlers. Brock held onto her hand, and she watched him standing. He slipped his grip to only holding onto her little finger, then he let go and stood alone. More and more, he was gaining confidence. At just on a year old, she knew his first step was close. She glanced around for Sheila with Paige, but didn't see her.

Gertrude arrived with her four.

'Have you seen Sheila?' Ashley asked.

'No, not since she took Paige for her walk.'

Ashley knew she was frowning, and no amount of tape between her eyes could erase the wrinkles already imprinted there. 'Can you watch Brock?'

'Sure. Florence honey, come and take little Brock,' Gertrude said.

'Thanks,' Ashley said, already moving away.

She searched the camp. At the construction site, she asked the workers. 'Have you seen Sheila? She had Paige in her stroller, they went for a walk.'

'Yes, Madam,' Peter said. He was a toothless old man, apparently a Taabwe local, who had appeared out of the bushes one morning, seeking work in exchange for a meal. It was nearly two months later and he was still there, settled into their camp as if he'd always been part of their family. And he was proving to be a good investment.

His knowledge of the local flora and fauna, specifically the trees, and the weather patterns, had been a great help, not only to the ranch but also to the anti-poaching guards. He knew the layout of the national park, and when Zol and Elliott had spoken with him, he'd told them he'd been one of the rangers but they'd retired him when he got too old.

Their loss was Ashley's gain. Old age was not a disability in her eyes; it was a library of knowledge to be tapped and passed onto the next generation.

'She went down to the dam. A flock of flamingos had come in to rest on their migration path,' he said.

'Thanks,' Ashley said as she changed direction, heading towards the dam, her heart pounding in her ears. Although they had scaled back their intense vigilance after months of no sightings of the albino, they were still conscious he was out there.

Waiting.

A restless feeling came over Ashley.

Sheila frequently went to the dam with Ashley's children, and often she took Gertrude's kids along too. But something didn't feel right. Sheila knew that siesta would be finished, and the children normally congregated in the boma after that for a story from Gertrude. Everyone loved 'story time' with Gertrude, and Sheila was always back by then.

The communal childcare centre, as Ashley loved to call it, was fantastic, with the older children watching over the younger, and always a woman or two present, sparing the time to help out. Although there was much to be done to make their new home habitable, and the women worked as hard as the men, the children's care took priority.

'Elliott,' she called, making her voice loud.

He answered from a distance, within some construction. 'Coming, Madam.'

'I'm heading for the dam area,' she yelled back.

'I'll be there,' he shouted to her, his voice less muffled. She strode off in the direction of the dam, knowing he wouldn't be far behind her.

Her mind focused above the long grass looking for Sheila walking with the stroller, she almost fell over her body lying in the path. Sheila's eyes stared blankly up at the sky, her face almost serene in its death mask. Her throat cut, before she could call out.

'Elliott! Oh God! Elliott! Elliott! Zol! Elliott!' she screamed.

Instantly the adrenaline surged through her body, creating superhuman strength and stamina. Her hand already pulling out her 9mm from its holster as she looked around wildly for the albino. She dropped next to Sheila and checked her pulse. Nothing. 'Elliott, he's killed Sheila!' she screamed again. Then, she looked into the stroller lying on its side. It was empty.

'He's taken Paige! He's got Paige!'

Everything took on a slow motion quality as she saw both Zol and Elliott sprint towards her, their rifles at their hips. Behind them, the workers from the construction site, armed with hammers, bricks, anything they could grab, rushed towards her. Then both Zol and Elliott were there, and Elliott was kneeling down beside his dead adopted daughter. He held her to him and, as Lisa pushed through the commotion, her high-pitched scream penetrated Ashley's surreal detachment from the scene around her.

She sprung into action.

'Elliott. I'm so sorry about Sheila, but he's got Paige. She could still be alive ...'

Elliott stood up. Ashley could see the moment his heart was buried deep inside his body and his soldier's training was all that made him stand up.

Zol took charge. 'Robert, stay here with Sheila. Everyone else, move back to the camp for now. Stay in a lockdown formation. The unit will patrol inside the camp, protecting you. I need to find his spoor, to follow him.'

Immediately the workers did as Zol asked, and in a hushed silence they left the site. Lisa and Gertrude remained, as did Peter. The old Zambian began searching in concentric circles around the group, looking for the spoor to follow.

'Where are the units, Zol?' Ashley asked.

'Too far away to help. I sent two into the reserve to follow the poachers, and the third unit is up north a little. Only Robert's new unit is nearby doing home patrols.'

'Contact them all. Pull them home. Tell them to get here!'

'I can do that,' Lisa said as she held the dead girl in her arms. 'I can contact them.'

'No. I'll do that,' Gertrude said. 'You stay here with Sheila. You take your time saying your goodbyes.'

'Thanks,' Lisa said, tears running down her face.

Elliott nodded. 'They'll still take a while to get here, but it will be worth having them.'

'He's gone there,' Peter said. 'The *tokoloshe* is carrying the baby in his arms.'

'You know the albino?' Ashley asked Peter, shocked that he would know exactly who they suspected had kidnapped her child. 'But you weren't here when he attacked last time.'

'He's an old enemy to Zambia too, Madam. Many animals and people disappear when he's around,' Peter said. 'He walks now like an old man, but I know his footprints in the sand like my own.'

'Gertrude, please look after Brock. I'm going with Zol and Peter to get Paige,' Ashley said.

'And me,' Elliott said, standing up again.

'You sure? You don't need time here?' Ashley asked.

'No, I can't do anything more here. I must protect you, but I will also avenge my daughter's murder.' Elliott started trotting towards the trees where Peter waited.

'Here.' Gertrude passed Ashley her own 9mm. 'Just so you have two—in case.'

But as she put her hand out to take the weapon, Vicky appeared, running with Ashley's semi-automatic shotgun held out in front of her.

'Vicky,' Ashley said. 'What are you doing?'

'Going to shoot the man who killed my sister.'

Ashley looked at the child. Already she had seen and experienced so much in the world. She had gone to Ashley's house and got into the gun safe, somehow knowing where Ashley hid the key, and helped herself to the shotgun.

'Did you bring the bullets too?' Ashley asked, almost afraid the answer would be no.

Vicky put her hand in her pocket and pulled out seven bullets.

'But I don't know how to load it,' she admitted.

Ashley shook her head. At least the child hadn't done that. Taking the shotgun from her, she loaded it quickly and slung it over her shoulder. She bent down to Vicky's level.

'You can't come with me, but I promise we'll get the *tokoloshe*. And thank you for bringing my shotgun to me.'

Lisa put her hands on Vicky's shoulders and drew her to her side.

'Thanks for the thought,' Ashley said to Gertrude, 'but it looks like I have two already. You keep it and protect all the children from him.' She straightened up.

'Get him, Ashley.' Lisa smiled weakly and hugged Vicky close to her.

'I intend to,' Ashley said, already running to catch up with Zol, Elliott and the surprisingly agile Peter.

Ashley didn't even know she was breathing. The hot volcanic lava that pumped through her body propelled her forward. She felt nothing but a dull ache where her heart should have been.

The albino had her little girl.

CHAPTER 30

Rodney stopped and listened. Not only did he have a good lead, he had the advantage over his prey. He knew exactly where he was heading as he'd spent the last few weeks ensuring his traps were set and ready for her. This time there would be no mistake. The white bitch would belong to him.

After months of planning. He knew it.

He looked at the pathetic child in his arms. The only reason it remained alive was that it wore pink. He had the bitch's female pup.

He heard his pursuers change direction; they had caught up quickly.

'Zol, yous still good,' he whispered into the darkness, 'but did yous teech yous pup good enouff? Yous not find Rodney this past munff. Whot ebout tonite?'

Rodney ducked as he passed by two large trees, their shade making the darkness smear to almost velvet. Many animals had sheltered here, eaten the grass and hidden from the cruel copper sun. He pulled the small pillow he'd carried from the pram from between the child and his body, and dropped it onto the bare dirt. He passed unhindered under his first trap. His penis bobbed, fully erect in his pants as he pressed silently on, towards the river. The beautiful pain swam black before his eyes.

CHAPTER 31

Ashley lengthened her stride, almost pushing into Zol's back. There was no space in the thick bush to run next to him. She couldn't hear Elliott behind her; he moved as silently as a savannah cat. Day had turned to night and still they ran on.

Zol held his hand up in a stop motion and instantly she responded. It had been many years since she'd had her first survival lesson with Scott and Zol, but some things were never forgotten. The urgency and will for survival was still strongly imprinted on her brain.

They listened and heard a movement off to their right, something brushed against a bush. They changed direction and headed downhill, towards the river.

Suddenly Zol froze. Ashley almost ran into him this time. Stopping again so soon was not what she wanted to do. Her Paige was out there, and she wanted her back. She could taste the metallic salty blood she wished to draw from the son-of-a-bitch who'd taken her daughter. She glared angrily at Zol's back. He looked at the dark patch under the trees. Recognising the danger lurking in the night, he hesitated.

'Come on, Zol. He's getting away,' she moaned at him, desperate to get moving.

'Madam, look in the darkness. What do you see?' Peter hissed from behind her.

Ashley looked. Although her eyes were totally used to the low light of the new moon, she could see nothing.

Just blacker darkness, if that were possible.

'Nothing, I see blackness,' she said in irritation.

'Yes, that's right. Why would he bring us to this place? There's a trap here. Look carefully, we cannot pass under these trees.'

Ashley stared into the darkness again. 'Can we get any closer?'

Together they all shuffled their feet forward a small way, but Zol put his hand up and pointed.

Ashley saw the pillow.

Anticipating her reaction, Elliott grabbed onto her shirt from behind. 'A trap, Madam. A trap. Come, we can go around, back up to where we came in,' he said.

Ashley knew both Zol and Elliott were right and that she should trust them and obey their every instruction, but instinct made her want to snatch up the pillow and hold it tight. It was Paige's, and she knew her daughter's baby scent would still cling to the fabric.

Elliott tugged her backwards. Reluctantly, she backed up. 'I'm getting that pillow in the daylight, understood?' she said a little loudly, and Elliott hushed her as he let her go. She followed him around in a circle, away from the traitorous trees, Peter following silently behind.

They crept slowly through the bush, trying not to make a sound. Zol, Ashley, Elliott and Peter could hear the albino now, his laboured breathing giving him away in the unnatural silence of the night. It was a welcome sound. The psycho-maniac had set two other traps, which they passed safely.

Ashley looked at Zol in front of her. His clothes were dripping with sweat. On his face, she knew there would be deep groves channelled into his forehead at the intense concentration required in searching for the next trap. She knew he was anticipating the albino's next move. Second-guessing him. Ashley probed her mind for any other survival pointers gleaned from Scott and Zol. Those bush and fighting skills had never been as important to her than at this moment. Paige's life depended on them.

'Jump!' Peter shouted suddenly.

She jumped as high as she could, instantly obeying him. A blast of shot passed underneath her and Elliott, but struck Peter in the foot. In shouting to her, he'd delayed his reaction by a fraction of a second. He fell to the ground.

'Shit! Madam, did he get you?' Elliott asked.

'Ashley!' Zol called out.

'I'm-fine,' she said, her words running into each other, she spoke so fast.

They heard Peter curse.

'Peter-he-got-Peter,' Ashley babbled.

'How bad are you?' Elliott asked.

'A few holes,' Peter said as he inspected his feet, still in his boots.

'Take your boots off. Perhaps we can try wrapping them or something,' Ashley said.

'No,' Zol instructed.

'No,' Peter said at the same time. 'If I do that we'll get nowhere tonight.' He stood up and slowly tested each foot. She saw him bite down on his lip but he didn't cry out again.

'Come, we must carry on,' he said, 'we need to save the baby.' And although he was a little slower when he hobbled forward, he motioned for Zol to once again take the lead.

Ashley's eyes strained in the darkness as she followed Zol on a non-existent path through the bush.

They came to the riverbank. And the last trap was well concealed. As they stood on the bank, the ground beneath them gave way, and together they tumbled downwards.

Ashley knew the moment she lost the shotgun in the fall, when it was jarred out her hands. When she staggered to stand up, unhurt, the albino had Scott's .458 Ruger pointed at her chest. She'd have recognised it anywhere. When she last saw it in Annie's possession, the wooden butt had gleamed from beeswax polish, love and attention, now it was dull, as if rubbed over with mud.

He held it like an assault rifle, balanced on his hip.

She looked around wildly for any of the men. She saw Peter had not gotten away so easily. His legs were trapped beneath a large tree trunk. The trap had been simple and effective. Hollowed out from the soft riverbank and covered with a cloth and stick latticework laid with sand to make it look like solid ground. When they'd stepped onto the trap, it broke beneath them and they'd tumbled downward. At the same time, three large logs released from under a camouflage tarpaulin had rolled into the hole.

It was a deadly trap. A trap that one man could possibly make and conceal in a few days. Rodney must have had months. He'd outfoxed all the trackers in the anti-poaching units by not fleeing, but staying right near their camp. He had been there all along.

Waiting and watching.

She looked around frantically for Elliott and Zol. She saw Peter sit up, at the same moment the albino shot him. He was thrown backwards with a strong jolt, and slammed into the riverbank. He lay there, unmoving.

'No!' she screamed into the night. She went to run towards him but the albino shot into the ground at her feet. She lifted both hands in the air.

'*Nee*, don't go by the dood man, wommens,' Rodney said as he reloaded the gun from the magazine. Two shots used. She knew there was still one left, and possibly one more shot in the weapon. Scott's voice, imprinted on her memory, whispered in her ear, 'A good professional hunter will only have three bullets, Ashley, only three. Make each one count or the elephant will crush you like a flea. Remember that. Sloppy hunters travel with one up the spout, four bullets, but the chance of a gun jamming on you are greater.'

She stood still, knowing the damage this rifle could do. She'd been an unwilling witness when foreign hunting clients had paid thousands to bring down a trophy bull elephant, the money so vital to the wild animals' welfare, the sacrifice of the ancient bull worth every cent.

She stared at the albino.

'Where's Paige?' she asked him, her voice steady, not betraying any of her tortured emotions.

'Woo?' he sneered at her.

'My baby. Where's my baby?' she shouted at him.

'By the *boom*,' he answered and nodded his head in the direction of a large fallen tree further down the riverbank.

Ashley couldn't hear Paige. Her heartbeat increased and the hairs on her neck stood up.

'Is she dead?' she asked, scared of the answer.

'*Nee*, not yet.'

Relief flooded through her. Her baby was alive. But a thought niggled in the back of her head, Scott's words so many years ago haunted her: *There are worse things in Africa than death.*

White-hot anger bubbled up again from deep inside her. Her stomach burnt as acid churned. She knew that no matter what happened tonight, if she wasn't dead the albino would be, even if she had to rip him apart piece of skin by piece of skin. 'What do you want? Why are you doing this?'

'*Fook* the wit bitch who's puts me in prison,' he said slowly. 'Thems walls, they's kill me inside.' He put his free hand on his heart. 'Me, I is a *tokoloshe*. You made thems policeman close me in prisons.'

Ashley shook her head. 'You're a poacher and a murderer. You should have been hanged, not just put in prison!'

'*Ja*. I is, but I's like woomens, not men. I like blood and *fook* woomens.'

Ashley felt ill at the thought. She looked around wildly. In the rubble, she could see the magazine of the shotgun sticking up slightly. It was close to Peter's left hand. An ache in her heart leaked through the emotional jigsaw as she focused on the still and lifeless body of the old man.

She had her 9mm strapped to her, and the albino didn't appear to have noticed it. But her 9mm versus the elephant gun? She'd lose badly.

Her ears strained as she heard a small cry from the direction where he'd pointed out Paige was, and like a massive electric shock of 42,000 volts, she was re-energised and ready to fight this man who had caused her family so much pain.

She slowly began to lower her hands.

'*Nee*. No. Up. Up.' He motioned with the barrel of the gun.

She raised them again.

'Goes there.' He nodded to a large tree. She could make out ropes around the base of the tree. If she was tied up she knew she'd be a dead woman. And her daughter, too.

She had to play him along. She had to defeat him.

Where were Zol and Elliott? Did they also fall into the trap or had they somehow evaded it? Were they dead and covered under the rubble? Or would they be able to help her? She shivered as pure fear rippled over her skin.

Slowly, she walked towards the tree. He obviously wanted her alive for her torture—that was part of his sick, perverse way. He'd proved it years before, when she'd been his captive. She looked around for anything she could use to cause a distraction, but she saw nothing. Her 9mm hummed silently on her hip, still concealed.

She reached the tree and turned around to find him close behind her, as if trying to smell the air after she'd passed. 'I want to see my child,' she said. 'I want to see Paige is alive.' As long as she kept him talking, she had time.

To think. To stay alive. To formulate a plan.

'*Nee*.'

'Yes, I want to see my baby!' This time she screamed at him.

He sneered. 'After I's ties yous up by the *boom*.'

'No. Now. I want to hold her, and see that she's alive,' she said in a normal voice, trying hard to control what she sounded like, to break through the albino's hatred and have a chance to escape.

'*Nee*.'

Perhaps a more authoritative voice might help persuade him? Raising her voice, she repeated her needs. 'I want to hold her and see that she's alive. She's my baby.'

He sneered again but didn't refuse her. She smiled inwardly. She'd found the kink in his character she could use against him. He seemed to like it the more she shouted and screamed, as if he preferred to be the dominant male over a weak woman. She needed to make him think she was not in control.

She screamed louder. 'Let me see Paige. Give Paige to me!' Her throat hurt from the strain but she could see the pulse in the veins in his neck increase. He was getting excited, and she hoped his mind wouldn't be focused. She waited, ready to take advantage of his slightest mistake.

'I's ties yous up first,' he said.

'No. I want to hold Paige. I can't do that if I'm tied up.' Her voice was getting husky from the volume she was using to converse with this madman.

He rocked his pelvis forward suggestively and rested the Ruger on one hip. His free hand slipped to his pants and she watched with disgust as he unzipped his fly and his penis jumped out from its barrier.

Oh-my-God! Oh-my-God! she thought, keeping a lid on the terror tremble that threatened to pass through her.

She was like a stunned animal. Mesmerised. All she had to do was look away and the spell would be broken, but she couldn't, her body had frozen. Last time she'd done nothing, when she was six years old.

But she wasn't that child anymore, and so much had happened in her life since then. She was stronger. Scott had helped save her when Rodney kidnapped her, but now there was no one and it was going to be all up to her.

Paige's life depended on her.

'Yous not gonna likes this,' Rodney said.

His words snapped the spell.

She didn't need anyone to save her. She was strong enough to save Paige and herself. Oh yes, there was a way out.

It was so obvious. How had she taken so long to see it?

She almost smiled. His anger wasn't making him lose control. He enjoyed the theatrics of a woman in pain. She couldn't create an opening that she could take advantage of using anger, but she could use his lust to make him falter. That was his weakness.

She switched tactics.

'Okay, you win,' she said, her voice as calm as the Dead Sea. 'I'll even suck for you, but only after I see Paige's all right.' Silently she prayed to any God out there under the African sky that, by playing up to him, she'd be able to get the better of him. Get to her gun before any more damage was done.

He looked at her, stunned at first, then the lopsided sneer reappeared.

'Truly,' she said, noticing that already he was hesitant, not as sure as he had been just moments ago. 'After I see my baby, I'll do things to you that any whore would blush at,' she continued the ruse. 'I'm good in bed. Really good. I can do things to you ...'

Almost panting, he wiped the back of his hand across his mouth. Then he pointed the gun towards the direction where she'd heard Paige earlier.

She walked along the riverbank in front of the gun that was now tipped towards the ground. He was beginning to let down his guard.

She lowered her arms.

He didn't seem to notice.

Ashley walked a little further, to the fallen log. Paige was tied to a small tree and gagged with a cotton hanky. She bent down to touch Paige's face, and with her other hand unclipped her 9mm.

The metal was warm in her hand as she slowly cocked the weapon against her body, quietening the sound. Once again, she put a hand on her daughter's cheek. The touch of Paige's skin seared her heart. She looked deeply into Paige's blue eyes. Ashley glanced heavenwards in a thank you gesture, then forced a smile to reassure Paige. She was talking gibberish to Paige. Again and again, she spoke baby talk to her. Her daughter, oblivious of the danger and not understanding her restraints, niggled and complained now that she could hear her mother's voice and see her.

'Enough talk talk talk wif the bratt. Times for me *fook* now,' Rodney said behind her.

White anger boiled within Ashley.

This man deserved to die.

Slowly she stood up, still with her back to him, and turned around quickly and fired. He didn't realise that she'd pulled the trigger. Her first shot ripped into his stomach at less than five paces away.

She heard the distinctive sound of a 9mm firing join hers. She saw the albino turn his head, looking for the second shooter, when a shot from the opposite direction clipped him in the shoulder moments before the Ruger exploded, scattering the sand near her feet.

Ashley felt as if the world had stopped spinning on its axis and she was not on it but outside, observing. Watching.

Rodney dropped to his knees in front of her, the gun's barrel dipping into the sand, a startled expression in his eyes. From far away, she heard Zol and Elliott shoot again. The albino fell backwards, his legs splaying out on the incline of the riverbank.

Zol ran towards her. As he reached her, he pushed her behind him, so that he stood between her and the albino. He kicked the Ruger away from Rodney and lifted it by the butt, but the albino opened his eyes and moved his left hand towards his hip.

Zol righted the Ruger and fired it at point-blank range. An empty click sounded as he attempted to reload it.

The albino didn't move. There wasn't much left of his upper body. Ashley could see sand where part of his chest cavity had been.

She lost it. She pushed past Zol and kicked Rodney with all the hatred and pent-up energy that had smouldered inside her since their first meeting.

'That's for cutting me, that's for Jabu and Alan.' She kicked again. 'That one's for Sheila, and this one is for Paige because you dared to take her from me!' She used her whole body for leverage and slammed her boot into his stomach. 'Because of you, I lost Scott!' She booted him again. 'I hope you rot in hell!'

Zol pulled her away from the body and held onto her. 'Madam. Ashley,' he said sharply, bringing her back to reality.

Ashley turned and ran to her daughter. Speaking calmly to Paige, she undid the gag around her mouth and untied her. Holding the screaming child to her breast, the tears began to trickle down her face then changed to a torrent as she sobbed uncontrollably. 'It's okay, Paige. Mummy's got you,' she soothed, patting her baby's hair with an unsteady hand.

Realisation that she'd shot someone settled over her, chilling her to the core. She retched violently into the sand.

'It will pass. Witnessing your first kill is always the hardest,' Zol said as he walked to her and patted her on the back.

He passed her a hanky and she wiped her mouth. 'Thanks. Oh my God, Zol. I'm no better than he was. I shot him. He's dead, and yet I still want more revenge on him, want to make him suffer more!'

'You are not a killer. It's not who you are, it's not in your nature. But it's African justice. You need to push that feeling deep inside you now, and never let it surface again. I protected Scott so that he never had to do what you have just done. I'm so sorry I couldn't protect you enough. But know that you didn't kill him. Your shot was to his stomach, it was me who ended it.'

'Oh no, Zol. I still shot him. It's not your fault, it was my decision. I came after the albino. I wanted him dead. But there is a big difference in wanting and reality. I'm just not sure I want to ever cross that line again.'

'Good. It is better if you are not responsible for taking other's lives,' he said. 'Come, we still have work to do here, and a long walk home.'

'Zol, where's Elliott?' She began to walk towards where she thought Elliott's shots had come from. 'Elliott?' she called. She knew he wasn't dead, she'd heard his shots ring out, joining hers. She had seen where they'd entered the albino's shoulder, disarming him. That was the reason why his shot had missed her. Elliott had been a fraction of a second faster than her to shoot, and he had saved her life.

'Elliott, where are you?'

'He's the other way,' Zol said.

Realisation hit her. It was Zol's shots that had saved her. Zol had been quicker to fire than she had.

'Thank you,' she said.

He nodded. 'Come, we need to get Elliott.'

They began to climb up the riverbank in the opposite direction. She saw Elliott lying on the ground, his head back on the grass, his body relaxed.

'You okay?'

'I'm all right. You're all right, and Paige, she isn't hurt. Sorry, Madam. Zol and I, we couldn't shoot him earlier, we had to know where he'd hidden Paige. We split up so that we both had clear shots of him. Zol's shot was the best, but I got him too. He wouldn't have got you. I promise, we'd have shot him before he hurt you again.'

'He's dead now. Thank you, Elliott.' She lay down next to him, adjusting Paige on her front to lie with her and patting her nappy softly as her child still niggled, and looked up at the stars.

Zol lay down on the other side of her. Tears leaked out from the corners of his eyes. 'It's over,' he said quietly. 'He can't take another Decker from me.'

Ashley reached across and held Zol's hand. She brought it up to her lips and kissed the back. 'Thank you, for always being here for us. I wouldn't be here if it wasn't for your support, protection and love.'

Zol smiled. 'We can go home now, but first I want you to know why that kill belonged to me. Many, many years before you were even born, it was a younger albino who took me from my true family. He took me into a terrorist camp when I was just a kid, and he taught me things no child should ever know. It was him who broke every bone in my feet and my hands. Charlie always said one day I would get even with him, but I needed to be patient. Become a man first, mature. But even before I could do that, he caused Charlie's death. After I had taken Charlie home I wanted to go back and search for him, once I had kept my promise to Scott. But Scott needed me, he was just a boy, and he was alone. Many years passed and the albino wasn't part of our lives, but then the poaching started and he came back. He was the cause of Scott's death. This kill belonged to me. It took me too long to collect that prize.'

Elliott stood up and held his hand out to Zol. Zol clasped his arm and rose to his feet. Their hands still gripping the other's wrist, Elliott shook Zol's hand. 'Thank you, *Madala*,' he said.

'Oh my God, Peter! We forgot Peter,' Ashley said.

They went to where she knew Peter lay. Looking down at the old man, she had to be sure he was dead before they walked back to Singita. Bending down, she put her hand on his neck. There was a pulse.

'He's alive,' she said, dropping to her knees next to him. She looked at him clinically. He was breathing, but it was shallow. His left arm was amputated below the elbow. The albino's shot had missed his torso. His heart was intact. Her eyes carried on along his body. His legs were still trapped.

Paige clung to her front like a little monkey to its mother, terrified of being separated. Ashley tapped her on the back. 'Paige, I need to help Peter. I'm putting you on my back. Can you hold on there, please?'

She helped Paige shift around onto her back. Then she took off her belt and placed it around the top of Peter's arm. Tightening it, she cut a new hole and pinched the belt closed as a tourniquet.

'Paige, I need to take my shirt off,' she said, as she shrugged out of her cotton top. Paige immediately clung to her, wrapping her arms around Ashley neck. Ashley had to rearrange her little hands so that she could breathe. She ripped up her shirt to make a poultice for the wound and a bandage to tie it on with.

Elliott and Zol had been checking the tree. 'We could move it, the bulk of the weight is not on Peter.'

Working together, they heaved the tree off him. Then Zol and Elliott grabbed him under his arms and dragged him away from the unstable area of the landslide. Ashley crouched down next to Peter and felt his head. It was warm, not hot. Fever hadn't set in.

Zol knelt on the other side. 'He has lost a lot of blood.'

Ashley nodded. 'The main artery seems to have been closed by the bullet, though. If it was still open he would be dead by now.'

'Lucky. We need to get him stable,' Elliott said.

They made a simple triangular patient transport with saplings as thick as a man's arm they found along the riverbank and used their shirts and belts to support Peter. Elliott and Zol took the weight of the front on their shoulders, with Ashley coming up the rear where it dragged on the ground, watching for any sign from the old man that he was in more pain. Ashley's plain white bra was stained with dirt and sweat, and she walked with one arm behind her back, holding onto Paige. The little girl clung to her mother's back, her arms wrapped around Ashley's neck. No one would pry her off for a while, of that Ashley was sure.

They began their slow journey back towards Singita, and the transport they would need to get Peter to a hospital.

The moon was high in the sky providing natural light, but hours had passed since they began their trek home, fatigue was beginning to show as they slowed their pace, and forced the last few metres upwards dragging the makeshift travois, a promised rest at the top. They had barely broken from the embankment when they saw lights of a *bakkie* in the distance. A strong hunting lamp swept the bush, and a second one duplicated the sweep on the other. Ashley stepped into the edge of the beam, and it turned, illuminating them fully, a trained eye behind the lamp catching the movement and rechecking. She sheltered her eyes in the glare. It could be no one else except their anti-poaching units. She waved. The driver continued their slow journey towards them, but didn't dim the light.

Gertrude jumped from the back of the still-moving vehicle and flung herself at Ashley and Zol, drawing them closer together. 'You're okay! You're okay! The guards arrived home after the SOS call, I don't know how they got here so fast. Then we heard the gunfire. We were all coming after him. We thought he got you.' Tears poured down her face, and she hugged them both again. This emotional display was unusual from her friend, and Ashley hugged her back. Gertrude reached over her shoulder and stroked Paige. 'Hi ya, Poppet.'

The second anti-poaching unit slipped off the *bakkie*. They lifted Peter into the back and Mistake passed his medical kit to Zol. Together they began to administer first aid, and Ashley could hear them talking in low tones. Elliott stood nearby, talking with them.

A hyena's call sent shivers down Ashley's back. It was close by. She could almost imagine its jaws already bloodied with what was left of the albino.

Nature takes care of its garbage, she thought. A fitting end to the cruel monster who had destroyed so much she held dear. She blinked and shook her head, attempting to rid herself of the gruesome image.

'Mistake, take two of your unit with Miss Ashley and help her get to the hospital,' Zol instructed. 'The other three, stay here.' The *bakkie*'s driver got out, called to a different duty.

'Zol?' Ashley asked.

'Clean up. Have Mistake with you all the time at the hospital. He's good with the local dialect,' Zol said, and he squeezed Gertrude's hand in parting.

Ashley understood exactly what was going on. Even though killing the albino had been self-defence, the unit would remove all traces of her involvement in the incident and no one except those present would ever know the truth about what had happened tonight. No evidence to ever say who shot him, and how many times. The police would be called for Sheila's murder, but would never find her killer. While they were at the ranch, the unit would provide the albino's body as a poacher they had shot dead, but no court case would come about, no charges would be pressed.

African justice was complete.

Gertrude got in the front with Ashley, who still held Paige close to her.

'She's too young to remember any of this, she'll forget,' Gertrude said.

Ashley nodded. She had faced her nightmare tonight, and she had beaten the psychopathic *tokoloshe* and won. But she worried about the price she'd have to pay for her victory.

Forever she would have the image of Rodney's body riddled with bullets etched in her mind, a photograph imprinted into her soul, tainting it with evil.

CHAPTER 32

Ashley stood on the veranda of her newly finished home and watched the sun rising on the horizon, painting pink pastels across the morning sky. It was the six-month anniversary of moving to Singita, and one glorious mostly stress-free month since the death of the albino. Her house was a stone and cement-built safari dwelling, complemented by a thatched roof, and she loved it. Almost unconsciously, she looked towards the next bungalow. Gertrude and Zol's home matched hers, an exact replica, placed further way and into the trees. The roof was completed and the Ndhlovus had moved in.

One day, they would build other homes further away from the main populated area, where they would have more privacy. Zol's plan was to build their homesteads on the bank of the dam, where they could see the game coming to drink in the sun-kissed waters and hear the ducks as they flew in and settled on the water. With wide verandas to keep the homes cool, and decking to blend with the environment. Her present home would join the ranks of tourist lodgings, but until that day, it would do just fine. Eventually, this temporary compound would become a tourist camp and the staff would get new housing on the opposite side of the tourist camp, allowing them better family lives in individual houses, unlike the large-scale shared rooms they had to make do with now.

They had worked hard. Further along, another twelve homes were finished, and still more were in various stages of construction. To the left was the large three-quarter covered boma.

Paige started fussing, her new teeth again worrying her. One had broken through the gum yesterday, and Ashley expected the other one to peek out any time soon. She lifted her daughter up and went to sit on the rocking chair on the stoop. Amazingly, the chair had survived the night they fled Zimbabwe, and the fire at FA Ranch. It had a deep black gash where a vehicle part had exploded onto it but not ignited, branding the chair and serving as a constant reminder that they were lucky. They had escaped with their lives, and that was more important than any possession in the world.

She nursed Paige on her breast. Soon, she'd give up breastfeeding altogether. The twins were already so active, and at thirteen months old it was more of a comfort for them than a necessity. She turned her head at a small rustling noise, and there, sitting on the step, was Zol.

'Oh my God, Zol,' she said. 'You scared me!'

'Sorry, Madam,' he said smiling, but he didn't look at her while she was feeding. Some traditions never changed.

Paige sat up and looked around, wide-eyed at the goings-on. 'I'll just put her down,' Ashley said as she rearranged her shirt and lifted Paige. She walked into the coolness of the house and put Paige in her cot. Winding up the mobile, she watched as Paige lay contented on her back, grabbing at the shadows that spun over her as the tune from *Dr Zhivago* tinkled into the room.

Ashley went to the kitchen and got a Coke for Zol and a diet Coke for herself from the fridge. 'Cheers!' She clinked her can with Zol's.

'I have something for you. They were also Charlie's, but I don't think he would mind if we used them now. His rainy day fund,' Zol said, digging in the pack he carried with him.

'What is it?' Ashley said, looking at the three small dirty bags casually tossed onto the kitchen table.

'Diamonds.'

'What?' Ashley's voice was raised a little, not believing what she heard.

'They were stashed in Malawi. I collected them even before Scott's accident, and have kept them hidden since.' He grabbed a kitchen cloth from the shelf behind him and spread it flat on the table, then he opened the first bag and spilled the contents onto it.

'Those look like chunks of stone, or cut glass,' Ashley said.

'No, I promise they not just any stones. Uncut diamonds. Charlie and I found them when we travelled together many years ago. These are our future now. The Ndhlovu and the Decker families.'

Ashley stared at the stones. 'Don't you need a licence to deal in uncut stones?'

'Licences can be bought, just like everything else in Africa.' He passed her one stone. 'The black market for diamonds is lucrative, despite De Beers' stronghold, or the "diamond cartel" as they are jokingly referred to, trying to close the back door.'

She lifted the stone in her palm. It was heavy, and probably just smaller than the size of a large marble.

'In your hand, you hold the electric fences that will keep our game here.' He picked up a smaller one and placed it in her other hand. 'In that hand you hold your new home, completely fitted out with any luxury you want, away from the tourist camp.'

Emotion choked up her throat and she croaked out, 'Thank you, Zol.'

'It only took a little time to collect them, my friend. The fun days of collecting the stones themselves passed too fast. But keeping some for a rainy day was Charlie's idea. Now I can purchase Con Amore, the ranch next door, and you can purchase Singita from the government and we can make this place better and better.' His whole face shone, as if memories of his adventure long ago had rekindled a love for life, a lust for adventure and a thirst for living. Ashley could see the happiness radiating from him.

'How many bags of these diamonds do you have?' she asked, realising they were talking a substantial amount of money.

'Enough for our needs,' Zol said. 'And some still stashed away for another rainy day, if it's ever needed. Charlie and I, we spent a lot of time picking up these rocks instead of fighting a war and getting killed. He always said that you needed a plan, just in case things went wrong. Hiding these diamonds and not using them right away, that was his plan, to ensure that his family was always all right. My share of the diamonds was there too, for my family. But they are no longer Charlies' or mine; they are ours. The Deckers' and the Ndhlovus'.'

Ashley stared at the stones on the table. 'This was the plan that you wouldn't tell me about?'

'Yes. We worried that you would think of them as blood diamonds, and because of your upbringing you would not want any part of what they can achieve. But I have learnt that I was wrong. I was old-fashioned in my thinking, and that is why I have brought them to you now. It is time.'

She smiled at him. 'They are not blood diamonds. No one died so that you could profit from them?'

'No. Charlie and I had many good days collecting these.' His forehead creased and he looked sad. 'I'm getting old, Ashley, my time here is shorter than I'd like. My days are less than a young man's. The albino, I wish now that things had been different, that Charlie and I had killed him years ago. But I can't live in the past, what is done now is done. You must never think that Scott would have wanted the outcome any different. You are more than a simple Madam.' He placed his hand on her shoulder. 'Anyone who thinks you are weak, they will find out that you are African. You are Mother Africa. And no one will mess again with anything or anyone that is under your care.'

Ashley smiled at Zol. 'I wish it didn't have to end the way it, did but I'm glad he's dead.'

'Good,' he said, dropping his hand to his side. 'You are safe now, and everything is running smoothly. Elliott and I need to go away for a while. I have to show him where the 'tree bank' is, so he will come with me to learn a few of our family secrets—the diamond stash, and other things. I will teach Brock when he's older, but just in case, if I have crossed over, Elliott will teach him. Pass on the secrets to his children and mine too.'

'Six years and you are still surprising me, Zol. There were always secrets between Scott and you, which Gertrude and I can only dream about. But thank you for this one. Thank you for this.' She bounced the diamond on her palm. 'Please, tell me there is enough for Gertrude to start another school?'

Zol laughed as he tossed a fourth bag onto the table, as if it was already all planned out in his mind.

CHAPTER 33

2003

Zol sat on his veranda and watched his children play some hopping game with Scott's twins. Lisa, her stomach heavy with her pregnancy, sat nearby. He smiled as three-year-old Brock organised the small group of kids. He was like his father had been at that age. It was hard to not call out, '*Inkosana* Scott,' to Brock as he had so many years ago when Charlie introduced him to his first-born son.

He looked over to the school, and could see Gertrude at her big black-board, writing neatly for the school-aged children all gathered there. He grinned. He knew he'd found a treasure all those years before. His Gertrude had a heart bigger than Lake Tanganyika. And he loved her more than the dirt beneath his feet.

Africa ran in his blood. But Gertrude held his heart within her hands, and if he ever had to choose, she'd win the argument. Africa would lose.

He saw Ashley walk into the workshop, her new group of volunteers close on her heals, attentive to her every word. And Elliott, right by her side, always with her. Her shadow, her brother-but-one.

He thought of the new arrivals that morning. Hillary had unfolded himself from the small plane Kevin had brought in and Ashley had started laughing. Zol had been with her the day before, when she'd spent hours making sure the quarters were set up for both female and male volunteers, and now she had four males. No woman. It was karma, with a sense of humour.

His eyes followed their own leisurely path to the big tree, under which Ashley had at last laid Scott's ashes to rest just that morning, together with Renegade's chain. They had all stood together under the tree at dawn, listening to the fish eagle call, the crickets' incessant chirp, and the forest doves' love symphony.

The small white picket fence she had erected around the base of the tree was oddly at peace with its surroundings of the African bush. A marriage of the ancient—the ethnic and the colonial.

Zol watched the huge elephant slowly walk to the fence and stop, as if waiting for something. The bull had the biggest tusks Zol had seen for many years, an ancient survivor in a land torn apart by violence. Scott stood against the tree. He wore his khaki pants and a crisp white shirt.

His feet crossed at his ankles were in his *veldskoene*, and his hair looked neat, as if he'd just combed it.

Zol looked at Scott and blinked. It was then he realised what he was seeing. Scott was smiling as he reached out his hand in a farewell gesture. Zol lifted his hand and saluted his friend, tears pooling in his eyes and running down his face.

His eyes remained fixed on Scott as he walked through the picket fence and climbed up into the giant, curled ivory tusks of the elephant. The image blurred in a shimmering light, as if a heat mirage had once been there, and both jumbo and Scott were gone. His journey had come to its end.

Scott was at peace, and had at last crossed over.

Zol smiled. 'Goodbye, my brother.'

GLOSSARY

Akukho - Zulu: No
Ant Bear - Common name for an Aardvark
Assegai - A traditional spear, used for fighting
Bakkie - South African word for a pickup truck, a ute in Australian
Baleka -Zulu: Run fast/sprint
Bantu - Black ethnic workers who speak an African language
Biltong - A kind of dried meat
Boer - The Afrikaans and Dutch word for farmer
Boma - An area surrounded by a fence used to keep animals enclosed, also can refer to an area used for outdoor meals and parties
Boomslang - (*Dispholidus typus*) a venomous snake
Bundu - Slang for the bush
Bundu-bashing - Taking a vehicle through the bush and making a new trail
Bushbaby - Galagos, bushbabies or nagapies (Afrikaans: meaning night ape). With large eyes, long tales and nocturnal behaviour, these primates are delightful
Catty - Also called a slingshot – or a catapult
Chimanimani Mountains - Forming a natural eastern border between Zimbabwe and Mozambique, this mountain range is distinguished by large peaks, the highest reaching to 2440 m and stretching for some 50 km

Chinhoyi Caves - (Originally name Sinoia Caves) are limestone caves located in the Makonde District, Zimbabwe, they have amazingly clear blue deep water in this cave system

Cicada - A large insect (*Hemiptera*, suborder *Auchenorrhyncha*) with large transparent wings, and big bug eyes. The ones found in Zimbabwe and Bulawayo vary, but I refer to the black/grey ones that are roughly 2.5cm long and make a beautiful 'song'. They are also eaten as a food

Coloured - A mixed blood, a black and a white persons' offspring

Comrade - Left over from communist times, a comrade usually fought in the war with you—but in Zimbabwe it is used as a term of friendship. To be a comrade, means that you are in the same circle

Dagga - Marijuana

Deka - Safari Area State-owned land that is protected and utilised, with a conservation strategy, ensuring that significant financial earnings revert to the rural communities in that area for their benefit

Dete - Town in Matabeleland North, Zimbabwe

Doppies - Afrikaans: shells from spent bullets

Duck - An inflatable boat usually with a hard bottom and inflatable surrounds, with a motor at the back. E.g. make: Zodiac - *Ek is nee kla maissie.* Afrikaans: I am not finished with you girl (Phonetic spelling used, correct Afrikaans spelling is *meisie*)

Ek sal jou moer, jy is een dood kaffir - Afrikaans: I shall kill you – you are a dead *kaffir*

Esigodini - (Originally known as Essexvale) is a village in 43 km south from Bulawayo

Esofas - A couch or sofa, is a piece of furniture that seats two or more people

Fok - Afrikaans: Fuck

Frezza - A freezer

Gaan by die huis - Afrikaans: Go to the house

Gabions - Baskets of wire that are filled with stone to reinforce structures like dams and used to stop erosion. Can be made in different sizes depending on the application you need to use it for

Gook - Used in Zimbabwe during the War of Independence against anyone who was on the opposing side – a terrorist is referred to as a gook

Hond - Afrikaans: Dog

Ikhaya - Home, hut made with mud and thatched roof. Pronounce: ee-kai-a

Inkosana - Ndebele/Zulu: The chief's (boss's son) As long as the chief is alive, he will continue to be called inkosana, no matter how old he is. Only when the chief dies will he be called *inkosi.*
Isipho - Zulu: a gift
Isipho Rodney - Most Zulus have a Zulu name and then an easily pronounceable English name that they are known by to the wider community
Ja - Afrikaans: Yes
Ja Oom, ek verstaan - Afrikaans: Yes Uncle, I understand
Kaffir - The word *kaffir* has now evolved into an offensive term for a black person. But it was previously a neutral term for black southern African people. Also was used in the term of a non-believer—referring to the black people not being of Christian upbringing
Kalimbas - The thumb piano is an African musical instrument, usually with a wooden back board, with different lengths of metal are attached. To play it, hold it in both hands, and using your thumbs to play a tune on the iron 'keys'
Kan - Afrikaans: can
Kaross - Blanket made from animal skins
Keghla - Zulu: Wise old man – grandfather figure
Knopkierie - An African club. These are typically made from wood with large knob (wood knot) at one end and a long stick protruding from that. They can be used for fighting (smashing someone's head) or throwing at animals during hunting. Ideal size to also be used as a walking stick
Koeksister - Plated deep fried doughnut, dipped in a sugary syrup when hot to absorb the liquid. An Afrikaans sweet 'cookie' from the Dutch decedents but could be adapted from the Malay heritage too
Kop - Afrikaans: Head
Kopje - Afrikaans: Also known as *koppie* or *kopjie*. A small hill rising up from the African veld
Kraal - Afrikaans but used commonly in South African English, is an area where animals are kept, usually found inside and African village/settlement, and is usually circular with barricades to keep the stock inside. Can also refer to an African cluster of huts together
Lobola - An African tradition of an arranged payment between a groom and the bride's family in exchange for their daughter. Can be paid as cattle or cash, and the higher the *lobola,* the greater value the bride is held in the groom's eyes. This payment is the groom's way of thanking the parents for

raising a good daughter. It is still applicable to many South Africa traditional weddings

Landy - Short for Land Rover

Madala - Zulu: Old man

Marula - *Sclerocarya birrea.* A medium sized tree, mainly found in the woodlands of Southern Africa. Now popularised for its fruits being used in the liqueur Amarula. When ripe, the fruits have a light yellow skin, with white flesh. Many animals love this fruit to eat, but it does ferment. Even the seeds/nut inside is eaten by rodents once the flesh of the fruit has gone

Melktert - Meaning 'milk tart' with an Afrikaans influence, contains boiled milk, egg and flour, like a thick custard tart, only with less milk. Usually dusted with cinnamon on the top of the yellow filling in the tart

Meneer - Afrikaans: Mister (Mr.)

Middle mannetjie - The dirt bump in the middle of the two tyre tracks in the road

Mielie-meal - Maze ground up and used as a flour. The staple food of many African people

Moenie fok nie - Afrikaans: Don't fuck no. (In Afrikaans there is a double negative used.)

Mopane worms - *Gonimbrasia belina* is the species of moth, whose large edible caterpillars are referred to as mopane worms

Mopani - The mopane or mopani (*Colophospermum mopane*) tree grows into South Africa, Zimbabwe, Mozambique, Botswana, Zambia, Namibia, Angola and Malawi

Morabaraba - (Southern Sotho: 'mill' or 'go around in a circle'). Twelve Men's Morris is a two-player board game. Commonly known in South Africa by its Xhosa name *umlubulubu*

Mossies - The Cape Sparrow or Mossie (*Passer melanurus*) is a medium-sized sparrow at 14–16 centimetres. They are mostly coloured brown and grey, and the male has some black and white markings

MPLA - Popular Movement for the Liberation of Angola

Muti - Traditional medicine in Southern Africa, coming from Zulu origin. It is used in South Africa as a slang word for medicine in general

My wena - Zulu: translates roughly to Oh goodness

Mzilikazi - Meaning 'The Great Road'. He was the Zulu who split from King

Shaka, moved north and founded the Matabele kingdom (Mthwakazi), Matabeleland, Zimbabwe
Ndebele - The Ndebele are an ethnic group in Zimbabwe, descendants from Mzilikazi
Nee - Afrikaans: No
Nightjar - The Swamp Nightjar (*Caprimulgus natalensis*) is a species of nightjar in the Caprimulgidae family. A nocturnal bird
Nyamandhlovu - Nyamandhlovu is a village in Matabeleland, northwest of Bulawayo. Ndebele: meat of the elephant
Nyaminyami - (Zambezi River God) is a legendary creature. It is described as a creature with a snake's torso and the head of a fish, with fangs. The local Tonga people believe that the spirits of *Nyaminyami* and his wife residing in the Kariba Gorge and are God and Goddess of the underworld
Nyenje or chenje - Refers to edible cicadas in the Eastern province of Zambia. The large cicadas are de-winged, fried on a hot pan until they are crunchy, and salted. They are served with the nshima staple meal
Op die plaas - Afrikaans saying for Life on the farm
Panado - Paracetamol medication used for headaches and fever
Piccaninny - A small black child. At one time the word may have been used as a term of affection, but it is now considered derogatory. In this story this word is used with affection!
Plaas - Afrikaans: Farm
Putzi fly - *Cordylobia anthropophaga,* the mango fly, tumbu fly, tumba fly, putzi fly or skin maggot fly is a species of blowfly. The larvae, known as Cayor worms, penetrate the skin and lie in the subcutaneous tissue, causing the formation of large bumps as they grow. (Yes, the maggot sits under your skin!) On reaching full growth, the larvae break free from the skin and fall to the ground
Quelias - A small finch/weaver bird native to Africa. Often referred to as 'feathered locusts', they can form nomadic super-colonies of up to 30 million birds, feeding on grains
Riempies - Ropes made with animal hides
Rondavel - A westernised version of the African-style hut. Round hut with a pitched thatch roof
Samp - Dried corn kernels, with the coasting around the kernel removed

during the pounding and stamping process, it is maize broken down, but not ground finely like mielie meal or mielie rice. Quite chunky pieces
Sangoma - Traditional healers, practitioners of traditional African medicine. Often still holding onto the Sharman aspect of mixing witchcraft with herbal medicines
Seuntjie - Afrikaans: Small son. Youngest son
Shaya insimbi - Zulu: hit the iron
Siabonga Zol-dala - Ndebele: Thank you Old Man Zol
Snuff - Product made from ground or pulverised tobacco leaves. It is generally snorted or 'snuffed' through the nose
Sope - Shona: something magical, inhabited by powerful and bad spirits. Albinos are called '*sope*' in Zimbabwe
Spoor - Afrikaans: tracks – usually left by animals
Steenbok - The steenbok (*Raphicerus campestris*) or steinbuck or steenbok, is a common small antelope of southern and eastern Africa
Sadza - *Sadza* is the staple food in Zimbabwe of the African people. It is a thick maize meal porridge
Suid Afrikaanes - Afrikaans: South African, but pronounced badly by this character – so this is not a spelling error, it's how the author wants it pronounced.
Tanganyika - Formally the Republic of Tanganyika, now known as United Republic of Tanzania
Teak Forests - Zambezi Teak Forests area (Baikiaea plurijuga)
The thinnings disease - In Africa, HIV is commonly referred to as *the thinnings disease.* One of the symptoms of full blown AIDS. People who lose lots of weight suddenly more often than not have HIV. If you have the thinnings disease it is assumed that you will be dead soon as there is not a lot of intervention by the government with drugs
Toi-toi - A dance of the African nations, usually a joyous dance—but can also be used at rallies and places where a statement is being made and can erupt into violence
Tokoloshe - A really bad spirit. A *tokoloshe* can resemble a zombie, or a poltergeist, or a gremlin, any demon like thing. A *tokoloshe* in this book refers to something evil
Tombe - Ndebele: teenage girl or 'little woman'. Pronounced tom-bee

Tosholotsho - Tsholotsho (formerly known as Tjolotjo) is a village 65km north-west of Nyamandhlovu and 98km north-west of Bulawayo
Tsessebe - The common tsessebe or sassaby (*Damaliscus lunatus*) is a shy medium size antelope found in Southern Africa. Tsessebe can run at a maximum of 80 km/hr
Ubabamkhulu - Zulu: Grandfather
Ubani gamalaku - Zulu: What is your name?
Umsiko - Zulu: Cut /slashed (also can say *umsiga* further north)
Umtshwili - Leadwood tree (*Combretum imberbe Wawra*) grows up to 20 metres tall, it has a single thick trunk, with distinctive bark
Umuthi - Zulu: *Muti*
UNITA - Union for the Total Independence of Angola
Veld - Veld, or veldt, is a generic term defining wide open grass or low scrub rural spaces of Southern Africa
Veldskoene - Afrikaans: Bush shoes. These are suede ankle leather boots, usually worn without socks
Vlei - Afrikaans: (pronounced 'flay') 'shallow minor lake', mostly of a seasonal or intermittent nature
Wag-'n-bietjie - Wag-'n-bietjiebos – The Buffalo-Thorn Tree (*Ziziphus Mucronata*). Any of several plants having sharp, often hooked thorns. Literal Afrikaans translation is wait-a-minute
Woza - Zulu: Come
Yebo - Zulu: Yes

Please note that bastardised Afrikaans is used in this book intentionally to indicate Rodney's restricted ability with the spoken language.

ACKNOWLEDGMENTS

A book might be written by a single person, but its journey is helped along by many others. Thank you to everyone who has helped my book in any way at all. Forgive me if I leave you out in name, but know that in my heart I'm grateful for your part in bringing this book to fruition.

THE WRITING WORLD

Firstly to my long suffering critique partner, Gayle Ash. Thank you for sticking with me.

Robyn Grady who was so instrumental in helping me focus on my writing rather than a hundred other distractions. I'm forever in your debt. Also for your labour of love in reading this book in its entirety before I sent it to Mira, for your help, comments and guidance. Thank you.

To Amy Andrews and Rachel Bailey who are always there to support me and keep pushing me along. Even when they are on their own deadlines. Thank you.

To RWA Australia, for seeing potential in this story and putting me into the five day intensive program in 2010 (5DI) with this book and being mentored by Fiona Brand. It was an amazing week, and although it took a few more years, know that it got there in the end ...

To my beta readers and red pen warriors who correct my spelling, grammar and generally bad English along the way before anyone else sees it —thank you Mariette Bailey, Caren Wilde, Bernice Wilde and Sam Eeles.

To the Bribie Island writers group who, despite mostly writing poetry, listened to parts of this many years ago, and have continued to support me.

To the Toowong writers group (Inkies), thank you for your support and friendship over the years and for your input.

The amazing Haylee Nash/Kerans who insisted on reading this story despite me telling her she would never publish it ... Thank you for buying my book and believing in my story.

MY INDEPENDENT TEAM

Creative Space – Madeline Ash, who went above and beyond as a final proofreader. Thank you.
Cover created by: Mecha

PERSONAL THANKS

Aunty Val Caldwell, whose bookshelf of Harlequin romance novels allowed me to pick one up when I was fourteen or fifteen years old and enter a new world. One that I wanted to be a part of. And for allowing me to continue to raid her books throughout high school.

Aunty Marie Louise Cole, who noticed that I didn't read and encouraged me to try different genres and once she realised I was reading romances, introducing me to the library, saturating my spare time with words.

Helicopter pilot Gary Fonternel, for his help and expertise in his field. Any mistakes made in this area are my own.

To my Aunty Gay Wilde, the inspiration behind my story of a strong Zimbabwean farmer's wife. To zooggoos, nana-naps and rift valley fever shots in the butt!

I love you lots like jelly tots!

To Elliott, look after Khulu like always, stay by his side. Continue to be my Uncle Ceddie's Brother-But-One. We are getting into our prime years now you and I, but in my heart, we are always young, and running after horses together.

To my sons Kyle and Barry. Thank you for putting up with burnt dinners, late school pick-ups and my continued absentmindedness while I lived in my alternate universe.

To all Zimbabweans who stayed and to all the displaced Zimbabweans spread across the world: May you find a place to always call home and forever let Africa's rhythm beat strong inside your heart.

PERSECUTION OF PEOPLE WITH ALBINISM

THE HISTORY

Africa has a problem with persecution of people with albinism. A white baby born to black parents was an unexplained phenomenon. There is a dark traditional belief that their body parts hold magical powers. This superstition has been fuelled by propaganda from sangomas and others who profit from the use of these body parts in use in rituals, *muti* and potions that claim that their magic will bring prosperity to the users. Their body parts are also used in *muti*-murder. Where a sangoma curses someone to die and their belief in this tradition is so strong, that the recipient of the curse actually dies. Because of this, people with albinism have traditionally been persecuted, killed, and dismembered.

Steeped in ancient traditions, people with albinism have been banished and killed because they are presumed to be cursed, and because they bring bad luck. Even in death they are not safe, as they are dug up, and their grave desecrated.

NOTE FROM THE AUTHOR

I condemn the treatment of albinos in Africa.

My character Rodney is FICTIONAL.

I based Rodney on treats of 'the *sope*', from stories told to me by my nanny when I grew up in Zimbabwe during the War of Independence. If there really was a terrorist who was an albino who operated in the Nyamandhlovu area, I have no knowledge of him. But just the mention of the *tokoloshe* were enough to keep me in line many years ago, and the aura and mystery around the albino race has remained with me—however, Rodney's character exists simply in my imagination and has no relevance to anyone alive or dead or to any modern day albino.

T.M. Clark

Shadows Over Africa

CHILD OF AFRICA

A thrilling novel of a courageous fight to save the children of Africa

T.M. CLARK

PROLOGUE

FINDERS KEEPERS

Binga Area, Zimbabwe, 1996.

The elephant baby lay on its side, its trunk limp in the dry dirt.

'Do you think it's dead?' Joss asked, approaching slowly.

Bongani put his hand on the elephant's shoulder. 'No, it is breathing, but might be sick, as it is unusual for a baby to be separated from the herd—'

'What can we do to help it?'

Bongani shook his head. 'The kindest thing to do would be to shoot it, put it out of its misery.'

Joss ran his hand over the legs of the baby elephant. 'I can't find any hot spots and there doesn't seem to be anything broken. I think it's just tired, and hungry. We can take it home with us.'

'Your mother will not like this—'

'Mum will adopt any animal, you know that! Perhaps if we give it some water?' Joss said. He took his bottle from the webbing he carried across his shoulder. The regulation army-issue flask was too long for him and sat on his thigh not his hip, but at ten years old, he didn't care. Water was water, and when you were out tracking and hunting all day, you needed to carry your own. He poured some in his hand and then put the tip of the baby elephant's trunk into his palm. The elephant was still for a second, then it moved its trunk as it smelt the water.

'It wants it,' Joss said as he pulled Bongani's hands forward. 'Cup your hands and I'll pour the water into them—'

The elephant curled its trunk to drink from Bongani's hands, and put the water in its mouth.

'At least it is old enough to have control of its trunk,' Bongani said. 'A good sign.'

'How do you know?'

'Many years ago, before I came to work for your family, I was with the Parks Board. It was a long time ago.'

'Why did you leave there?' Joss asked, putting more water into Bongani's cupped hands.

'The bush war came. I met your father during that time, and I came to work for him instead, before you were even born.' Bongani paused. 'We could get into lots of trouble from the Parks Board for having a baby elephant. They will want to know where we got it, and how we came to have it at the lodge.'

'Mum will sort that out. Let's try to get it back on its feet.'

'Do not rush it. Give it some more water first. Slowly, in case it gets a tummy ache. It will get up when it is ready, if it can. It needs some relief from the heat. We must make a shelter for it, and then, when it is cooler, we can encourage it to walk.'

They collected dead wood from the forest floor and broke branches off the trees in the mopani forest. Slowly the lean-to took shape around the young elephant, protecting the animal from the harsh African sun.

They sat with the baby for over an hour as it drank all the water from both their bottles.

'If it is to live, it must get up. It must walk to the road,' Bongani said. 'We cannot bring a vehicle in here; the bush is too thick.'

'It'll walk,' Joss said as he returned with a handful of leaves from an acacia tree.

The baby attempted to eat the leaves, taking them from his hand and putting them into its little mouth, but it didn't seem to like them much. For a while it just lay in the shade. Joss sat next to it, stroking its cheek, waiting for the elephant to feel better as the sun began to lower.

'We need to get it moving soon,' Bongani said. 'Is it a boy or girl?'

'Hang on,' Joss said as he bent over and looked underneath the elephant. 'She's definitely a girl.'

'Good. She should not be as moody as a male to look after, and perhaps when she is older, she will come back with her babies to visit, not come back in musth and break the fences, destroying our crops.'

'Come, Ndhlovy,' Joss said, 'you have to get up, you have to come home with us. If we leave you here, the leopards or the hyenas will get you, because your mum is not here and you are all alone.'

The elephant put her trunk into his hand. The tiny hairs on it prickled but he didn't mind. He continued to talk softly to her: 'Bongani and I need to get home; my mum will shout at us if we don't get back before it's dark. It's her one rule when we go hunting: be home before the sun sets. So you need to stand up and walk to the road, then Bongani will get the tractor and you can ride home on the trailer. But first you must get yourself to the road. It's not far.'

Bongani said, 'You are naming her Ndhlovy?'

'Yes. Then you can't leave her behind; she's my pet, she has a name.'

Bongani shook his head. 'We need to leave now. Perhaps if we walk away she might follow us, like the calves do.'

Joss got up and dusted the dirt off his trousers. 'Come on, Ndhlovy.'

The baby lay still, but her amber eyes followed him.

Joss walked further away. He looked back over his shoulder. Ndhlovy had sat up and was watching them leave. 'Come on, ellie, time to go home,' he said a bit more sternly.

The baby elephant staggered to her feet, her little ears flapping. She wriggled her trunk, thrashing it in an uncertain manner, a little unsteady as she balanced her weight.

Bongani smiled.

'Home is this way,' Joss said. 'Come on ...'

The baby elephant walked after them.

Bongani nodded. 'This is good.'

'Keep coming, Ndhlovy,' encouraged Joss.

The baby elephant walked with purpose until she caught up with Joss, then she placed her trunk in his hand, and settled just behind him. Every now and again she bumped him, as if trying to reassure herself he was there.

'That's it, Ndhlovy,' said Joss, 'you just keep walking.'

'You keep heading homeward with the elephant. I will fetch the tractor and trailer and the men from the village to help us load her. Keep sharp now.'

'Okay,' Joss said just as Ndhlovy bumped him a bit harder and he almost lost his balance.

Bongani smiled. 'You keep moving to the road and then home, understood?'

'Yes. We'll be coming.'

'Watch for leopard; we are in their country and they might think you are easy prey. Swap weapons with me. I know the .303 is heavier than your .22, but you might need to use it.'

Joss nodded and switched rifles.

Bongani watched him adjust to the extra weight. 'The ammo belt will not fit around your hips – put it across your chest.'

'This is heavy. Can't I just take a few rounds and put them in my pocket?'

'No. You need to be fully armed out here. If a leopard comes, or something worse ...'

Joss adjusted the heavy rifle and ammo belt onto his shoulders.

'I'm reminding you again, shoot or be killed,' Bongani instructed.

'I got it, Bongani. It's not like I haven't ever been alone in the bush before—'

'But you have not been alone in the bush as much as I have. You are still young. There is so much still to teach you.'

'I'll watch for leopards and hyenas and anything else that can eat me and Ndhlovy while you're gone. I promise, cross my heart,' Joss said as he crossed his whole chest with his free hand.

Bongani nodded as he increased his stride. 'You are a true African, *inkosana* Joss. In your heart. You want to save the babies of this land, not kill them. I am happy to tell your mother about the baby, and have her get mad at me, because you have chosen to nurture this Ndhlovy. Today you have proved you are a child of Africa. I will see you now-now.' He waved as he walked away.

Joss watched as Bongani adjusted the strap of his .22 rifle, which hung from his shoulder tight on his back, then he started to jog back towards the village. He didn't look back.

The sun hovered low above the tree line, a huge ball of orange. Joss watched as their shadows danced along, already three times longer than he and the elephant were in real life. He headed steadily southeast, towards the lodge and safety, with Ndhlovy close behind, her baby feet imprinting like giant saucers over his tracks as she walked. All the while he kept up a conversation with the elephant, explaining how they needed to walk through the village before they could reach their lodge on the bank of Lake Kariba, and about the noise that the others would make when they arrived to help. A coolness descended as the sun sank lower into the horizon.

He heard the sound of whistling, then a donkey bray, and men singing in harmony, before he saw Bongani. He was driving the cart that belonged to his father's village: three donkeys pulled the converted back of an old *bakkie.* Six men stood in the cart, holding tight to the cabin guard.

Joss smiled. Ndhlovy would be able to save her strength. The cart would not be as fast as the tractor, but it would scare the little elephant a lot less. He moved off the road into the bushes so that there was room for the donkeys to turn. The elephant pulled away from him as the donkeys drew near, but he rubbed her ears and encouraged her to be brave.

'Bring it to the back. The donkeys do not seem spooked by it,' Bongani said.

Joss walked towards the cart. The elephant followed, even though its ears flapped at the unfamiliar animals and the new men. Bongani had unloaded the cattle ramp and Joss started to walk up it, still holding the little ellie's trunk.

But Ndhlovy didn't follow.

'Come on, baby. Up you come,' he said.

The elephant looked around, her ears flapping, the white of her eyes clearly visible.

'Trust me,' Joss pleaded.

The men went to move behind the elephant, as if herding cattle.

The elephant turned towards the threat, ears flapping, her little trunk high in the air.

'Stand back!' Bongani shouted.

The men retreated from the threat of the elephant charging them.

Joss came back down the ramp and stood in front of Ndhlovy.

Bongani said, 'Slowly-slowly. Wait for Joss to get her to start up the ramp.

Joss, get her to move around again. We are about to lose all the light. As it is we only have one torch to shine the way for the donkeys.'

'Come on, beautiful, come with me,' Joss said as he took her trunk in his hand once again and patted it. 'Come on, turn around, that's it. Just walk with me, that's it.'

The baby elephant slowly plodded up the slope, sticking close to Joss, as if all the bluster she had shown in her mock charge had sapped her energy.

Joss walked to the front of the trailer. 'Okay. You can close up and climb inside. Ndhlovy's real scared.'

One by one, the men climbed up and into the cart. Holding out their arms, they touched the elephant, and braced themselves against the edge of the trailer to help cushion the ride.

The moon had risen and the bright stars watched from the inky heavens by the time they had driven through the village and down to Yingwe River Lodge. When they arrived, Ndhlovy backed herself off the trailer without incident and walked into the stables behind Joss. She showed no bravado, just stayed close to him, as if he were now her lifeline.

The ridgebacks arrived before Joss's mum. Ringo, Paul and John came into the stable, their hackles up, but George remained close at his mistress's side.

'Enough. Outside,' Joss instructed and pointed. The dogs immediately went outside. His mum made her entrance within moments of her dogs being banished and although they danced at the gate, they stayed out of the stable.

'So what have you brought home this time, Joss Brennan?' she asked.

'An orphan elephant. Bongani thinks her herd left her behind, or they got separated somehow ... she was on the border of Chete. She's weak—'

Leslie Brennan walked further into the stable and knelt in the straw. 'Hello, young one,' she said quietly and reached her hand out to the little elephant, who was now lying in the thick straw that Bongani had had the groom prepare.

The dogs whined.

'Stay outside,' she instructed. They lay down quietly near the door. 'Does she have any injuries?'

'No, Mum. Not that I could find. She's just weak and tired,' Joss said, still holding Ndhlovy's trunk.

'She needs some nourishment and something to drink. Mossman, go warm up some calf formula. Let's see if she will take a bottle. I know nothing about baby ellies but I can call around and find out who does.' She pulled her hair back with her hands and held it there, before letting it go. When it fell forward again, she tucked her long fringe behind her ear. 'Bongani, make sure there's someone guarding this little one all night. Armed, in case the leopards decide she's an easy dinner. Get a few of the horse blankets in here to keep her warm too.' She stroked the elephant's trunk as men ran to do as she'd instructed. 'Have you given her a name yet?'

Joss nodded. 'Ndhlovy.'

'It's a nice name. So, let's get her on her feet and better. Then we will find out what ZimParks want us to do.'

'Thanks, Mum,' Joss said. He knew that his mum would always allow him to keep the strays he brought in. The Egyptian geese babies she'd helped raise until they flew away with the migrating birds were regulars at the small dam they had for water at the safari lodge, nesting and raising their own goslings, bringing them to the house to introduce them, and then returning to their wild life, a tiny part of their hearts always with their human family.

Or the tortoises that were kept in a large brick pen by the house. Each had been brought in with an injury – one was missing a leg completely. His mother had sprayed the wound with gentian violet and it had healed over. Although the tortoise would never win a race, it was alive and happy. Joss had wild birds mixed in with his racing pigeons too, those that could never be returned to the wild because of some injury or another. But not nearly as many as his mother had treated and nursed back to health before setting them free again. From birds to baby duikers, now to an elephant, his mum would raise any animal and claim that it belonged to her child, even though her son was at boarding school most of the year.

His father, on the other hand, was always reminding them that the safari lodge was established as a gateway to Lake Kariba, that it wasn't a zoo, and the animals could only stay until they were well enough, then they had to leave. It was survival of the fittest in the real world, and because he'd once been a head ranger in the Chizarira, Joss knew that he understood all about animals, but he just didn't seem to want to take care of them like Joss and his mum did.

Joss chewed his lip, not sure how his father would react to the elephant baby. He remembered that last year a rogue elephant had come from the park and destroyed the village's vegetable patch and flattened their moringa tree seedlings. It had uprooted trees on its way to their village and had even torn a roof from one of the *ikhaya*s. When they had attempted to drive it back into the Chete Safari Area by beating feed tins and hitting metal plough disks, the jumbo had become aggressive and mauled one of the villagers.

His dad had got permission from ZimParks to shoot it.

Joss had thought that perhaps it was just a hungry animal and if they left it alone, it might have walked back into the safari area, then into the national park itself. He didn't think it was a pest until they frightened it.

Joss didn't want his ellie to land up like that – shot and in someone's cooking pot.

What his father would say when he got home was going to be interesting, but first, they had to make sure the baby lived. He would worry about his dad's reaction later.

Mossman returned with a bottle of warm milk, and Joss watched while his mum teased the baby into taking the teat into her mouth. But Ndhlovy refused to drink from it.

'You try, Joss. She seems to already trust you.' Leslie gave him the bottle.

'Come on, Ndhlovy, you need the milk, you need to drink it.' He dribbled a little like his mother had on the elephant's lips tucked up underneath her trunk, and the little trunk made room for the bottle, arching and resting on Joss's arm as she attempted to suck on the teat with her lips.

'That's it,' Leslie said, 'come on, baby.'

Ndhlovy latched on to the teat and began to drink.

'Perfect. Step one accomplished,' Leslie said. 'If she takes milk, we can get her stronger.'

'How often do you think she will need a bottle?' Joss asked.

'Probably every few hours, although she doesn't seem to be a newborn; she's already well over a metre tall. Let's start at two hours, because she's weak and in need of hydration. Mossman, add extra calf supplement in the next feed, double mix.'

Mossman nodded.

'Right. Let me get on the phone to Rodger, see what tips he has. Don't get your hopes up, Joss. She could still die.'

Joss shook his head. 'We can't let that happen, Mum.'

Leslie put her arms around his shoulders as he fed the baby elephant. 'We'll try everything we can. Perhaps if we can just get her well again, you and Bongani can take her back into the reserve, and find her a herd to live with. I don't know if she will be adopted back smelling of humans, but it's worth a try. I don't know how long an elephant baby stays with its mum, but I know it's a long time. I remember watching a documentary where a herd adopted a calf when its mother died ... we can only try.'

Joss said, 'Will you make sure Dad doesn't shoot it when he gets home from Durban?'

'I'll talk to him about it, but you know his view on orphaned animals.'

'I don't understand why he hates animals so much.'

She let go of Joss and straightened up, arching her back to stretch it. 'Oh, Joss, he doesn't hate animals, he just doesn't see them as pets. Remember, he was a ranger, and he is a hunter. At the end of the day, he worries that he needs to put food on everyone's plates. Make a decent living. Lots of people rely on him for their wages too. The boys here at the lodge need to be paid so their families can buy food and attend school. The villagers need their cut from the lodge so that they can eat and survive. It's not just you who needs your dad's income to be educated and healthy.'

'It's just one elephant, Mum,' Joss said. 'One little elephant.'

'That will grow huge. Now, we don't need to make any decisions tonight. Let's just get her better, make sure she survives. Then we'll deal with the rest. How does that sound?'

'Can I stay here with my ellie tonight?'

'Sure. I'll bring you some dinner and a sleeping bag, and I'll leave Ringo behind. He can sleep inside the stable with you. That way if a leopard even puts its nose into the area, he'll wake you and Bongani up.'

'Thanks, Mum,' Joss said as Ndhlovy finished the milk in the bottle.

'I'll see you just now,' she said as she kissed his forehead. Once outside she said, 'Ringo, inside, sit. Stay with Joss.'

The dog leapt to his feet and walked into the stable. Still not sure of the elephant, he approached with caution, but Joss called him to his side.

'Come on, Ringo. Meet Ndhlovy.'

As the dog sniffed the elephant, his tail began to wag. He settled in next to the pachyderm, licking her every now and again in a reassuring way.

Ndhlovy didn't seem to mind the ridgeback next to her, and touched him with her trunk.

'Well, look at that,' Leslie said. 'Anyone would think those two were long-time friends.'

Joss smiled. 'You know what, Mum, when I'm old like you, and I'm a Royal British Marine, I can save as many people and animals as I like, and I won't need anyone to watch over me at night, not Ringo nor Bongani.'

'True, but then you'll be an adult, and you will be looking after everything you save, down to every last detail, like all the phone calls, getting all the right food, having enough money to enable you to do that saving, and dealing with all the authorities and their different points of view – and don't forget the local community; they want their say too. It's never a simple rescue, Joss, there are always more things in the background that need to be sorted out that as a kid you don't need to worry about. Enjoy your time with Ndhlovy while you have her. Hopefully she'll be able to go back into the Chizarira soon and live her own life too. Don't rush this time away, my son, it's not as great as it looks to be on this side of the fence, being that adult responsible for others.'

CHAPTER 1
DREAMERS

Kajaki Hydroelectric Scheme, Afghanistan, 2008

The four kilometre-long convoy snaked into the Kajaki Hydroelectric Plant. Joss Brennan watched the turbines arriving at the dam wall through his binoculars and wanted to dance around, even though he was just one of five thousand troops who had played their part in protecting Turbine T2. But celebrations would have to wait.

Seven sections of turbine, each weighing between twenty and thirty tons, had been transported the final one hundred and eighty kilometres from Kandahar air base, through the Helmand Valley and the desert and finally up to Kajaki Lake. Some optimist had painted holy slogans and an Afghan flag on the containers to try to dig deep into the patriotism the locals had for their country – T2 belonged to the people. It seemed to have worked, because the heavy convoy had arrived at its destination. The people of Afghanistan would soon have two working turbines, creating power and bringing them electricity.

Chinook helicopters flew overhead, loud as they passed low, sweeping the area.

Ten days of hell were almost over.

The eighty-ton crane was the next piece of equipment to come to a halt. As important as the segments themselves, it would help the engineers lift the parts off the trucks. Each minute the sections sat around was a minute longer that the troops had to protect them from the Taliban.

Joss adjusted his binoculars and looked further up the hill, following the line carefully, looking for anything out of place in the rugged terrain. The word in the barracks was that almost two hundred insurgents had been cleared on the route through and around the dam. He hoped that was true and they were unable to return, but there were always those who, like snakes, slipped through the cracks to come back to bite their butts another day.

He scanned the compound in a grid pattern, making sure no one would threaten this precious cargo, not after the epic mission they had just accomplished. This was his job, the sniper, the tracker, the spotter in his company. Who knew that watching the animals in Africa all those years ago would be such good practice for hunting the enemy when he became a British Marine Commando? Who would have known that the hours spent with his father and Bongani in the bush, learning the skills of a hunter, would help him be the ultimate marine?

Joss went over the grid a second time. 'Check two o'clock on the ridge. Shadow protruding beyond the wall,' he said into his mic. 'Definitely something moving in the compound.' But in the next moment, the shadow had gone, and all that remained was the edge of the wall.

'Affirmative. Suspect unfriendlies,' Mitch's Australian twang answered.

'Don't jump to conclusions, might be the locals. Eleventh troop mobilise. Sweep compound,' Lieutenant Colonel Johnathan Tait-Markham – Tank to his friends – ordered over the coms.

After a quick glance at the convoy still rolling in, Joss packed his binoculars. Mitch put his hand out to help him up.

'Crack on, we have a compound to clear,' came Tank's voice.

Joss bent and ran with Mitch just a few steps behind. The stones at their feet slid loosely until their boots gripped the baked surface beneath.

They reached the compound and were soon hot-footing it along the mud wall. Joss remembered this village well – they had previously cleared an IED from exactly where he walked now. They'd returned a few times since the initial clearing, but that didn't mean that there were no more IEDs. Insurgents could creep in at any time and rearm a place.

'Affix bayonets. Two break left, two break right,' Tank instructed.

Joss saw Mitch and Tank break left. He rounded the corner of the same hole they had blasted in the mud wall a few weeks back, Cricket, one of his fellow marines, with him. He heard the wasp sounds as bullets flew close to his head. He hit the dirt and rolled for cover.

'Contact. Contact,' Tank shouted into the mic.

Crawling after Cricket, Joss slipped into a room. They swept it quickly.

'Clear,' Cricket said.

'Wait,' Joss said as he saw a carpet hanging on the wall move. He indicated with his head towards it. Outside he could hear the shallow *pop-pop* sound of the insurgents' AKs and the deeper sounds of their own rifles.

'Joss, where are you?' Tank called. 'We need a sniper.'

'Clearing this—'

He got no further as the carpet came to life. Someone was screaming, and the whole thing came down, exposing an insurgent with his gun raised.

Cricket and Joss shot him down in a hail of bullets.

Joss approached the body. He kicked the AK-47 away, and looked at the man.

Correction.

Boy.

Joss knelt down and checked for a pulse, but there was none. He was relieved and sad.

No more than fourteen, the boy had only the wispy beginning of a moustache. His black turban still clung tightly to his head. He looked too young to be carrying a weapon and trying to kill them. He should still be in school.

This was someone's son. Someone's child who might not have wanted to be a soldier.

Or worse, this could have been a child who chose this path, thinking it was his shortcut to glory in the afterlife.

Joss swallowed. It was survival – if they hadn't shot him, they would be the ones lying on the floor. 'Dead,' he told Cricket, and together they moved out of the room, to help the rest of the troop.

The stone chips pitted Joss's face, flicked up by bullets that were unnervingly accurate and close. One whistled past his ear. Joss adjusted his scope. 'Bogie at three o'clock.'

He squeezed the trigger.

The man's head jerked back. Joss slid the bolt of his rifle, ejecting the shell and loading another.

'Three o'clock,' he said as he shot the next man who was keeping his troop pinned down.

Again he reloaded.

Taking a breath, he looked for the third insurgent he'd seen. He had gone to ground.

'Lost visual,' he informed Mitch.

Mitch looked through his binoculars, scanning the small hill on the other side of the village. 'Four o'clock, blue/black turban. Behind a wall – must be a ledge beneath it that he's using.'

Joss adjusted his weapon and took aim at the designated place, even though he could see nothing there. The turban rose as the man wearing it peered over the ledge to check where his enemy had got to. Calmly, Joss fired, and the man dropped out of sight.

'Hit?' Mitch asked.

'Affirmative,' Joss said as he reloaded.

Mitch nodded. 'Bad angle, I couldn't be sure from here.'

The firing had stopped. The silence that followed any fight was always deafening. The wait for the next shot terrifying in case it came right for you.

'Any more?' Mitch asked.

Joss took a deep breath and swept his scope over the side of the hill. A single goat nibbled at non-existent grass. 'Wait ... look left of the goat.'

Mitch focused on the goat, then left. 'Bogie,' he affirmed. 'He has a rocket launcher.'

They saw the tip of the man's head, his arms outstretched to launch the deadly missile at them or at the precious convoy of trucks.

Joss took him down. The sound of the single shot was loud in the silence that had descended.

The goat bleated and tried to run away, but it seemed tethered to the insurgent. Panicked, it bleated some more.

'Continue to clear area,' Tank shouted over the coms and the men came out from where they had taken cover to sweep the village.

'If we let that goat go, it'll lead us to where they came from,' Joss said. 'Find their base.'

'Negative,' Tank replied. 'It's getting late; we pass that on to the American troops to follow up. I'm in contact with HQ, and they have a command passing us in ten minutes. Check fire. Friendlies approaching from behind.'

Joss watched as the American marines chatted to Tank on their way through. He pointed to the goat, and their leader nodded. Then they were off, along with the goat, over the small hill and out for their night patrol.

Joss's company gathered and headed towards their temporary barracks, spirits high, adrenaline levels beginning to lower. Joss grinned. This was what he had been born to do – to wear his green beret and serve the greater good, just like his grandfather. To help people who were unable to stand up to tyranny. Fight for freedom and justice when those around couldn't.

Tonight he would pen another letter to Courtney, like he always did when something significant took place, then he would watch it burn, as was regulation. He would rewrite it when he got back to England, after he was out of the desert, a more sanitised version. An emotionless version that would never depict the true horrors they experienced out here, or the simple joys of just waking up, knowing that you had achieved something amazing.

It didn't matter that Courtney didn't write back often; he just wanted her to know he was okay out here in the world beyond Africa. He kept the letters he'd received from her in England, and any that he received while on the front line he would read, commit to memory, then burn so that the enemy would not get their hands on them.

Letters to his best friend, and phone calls to Bongani, his lodge manager, were his only connection to his home in Zimbabwe now that his parents were gone.

ALSO BY T.M. CLARK

ADULT BOOKS

Shadows Over Africa series

- Child of Africa
- Cry of the Firebird
- My Brother-But-One
- Nature of the Lion
- Shooting Butterflies
- Song of the Starlings
- Tears of the Cheetah
- The Avoidable Orphan

COMING SOON

- Daughter of Africa

PICTURE BOOKS

- Slowly! Slowly!
- Quickly! Quickly!

Printed in Dunstable, United Kingdom